This is book II of the Legends of Evorath series of stories. This series takes place sixty years after the Evorath trilogy and is part of the Legacy of Evorath universe of books.

Read free stories online and keep up with future releases.

www.evorath.com

Please see the end of this novel for an appendices section, which provides a reference for Evorath, a map, and presents additional information within the world.

Author's Note

If you're reading this, I assume you enjoyed the story found in book 1, *The Shadows of Erathal*. Before you dive into this text, I want to say once again "thank you" for picking up the second novel in the Legends of Evorath series. I hope it enhances your appreciation for Evorath's rich history.

Aside from the prologue, this story takes place in the aftermath of the Battle of Paxvilla, which you read about in *The Shadows of Erathal*. Like the other novels in this series, the prologue includes an event from earlier in Evorath history, one that has a profound impact on this story, as well as the other Legends of Evorath.

A reminder, that while I make efforts to ensure this story can be shared in a family friendly fashion, there is no skirting around the dark nature of some historical events. Graphic descriptions are limited, but some scenes may be upsetting. In other words, this story is not for the faint of heart.

Concerning the research involved in preparing this novelized account, core details were constructed using the firsthand accounts of those characters described herein. Where major historical figures did not journal or otherwise make notes of these events, other historical accounts are considered as well.

In some instances, I looked at archeological records and third-party historical accounts available from the time. All of these are tied into the direct accounts I could find, and the story is presented in the 3rd person limited perspective. That is, each chapter considers one or more historical figures and communicates the events from their perspectives.

I hope you will forgive any creative liberties taken in the capturing of this story. I assure you, the integrity of Evorath's history is near and dear to my heart. In those instances when precise details were limited, I did my best to ensure the story stayed true to the period these events occurred in.

Remember as you read that even as sophisticated as our methods may be today, these actual events occurred nearly nine centuries ago. So, I pray you'll overlook any minor historical inaccuracies and enjoy the core of the story.

While the events may include strife and conflict, this is a tale of love, loss, companionship, community, and most important, of hope. As we look back on these events, try to imagine yourself living in these more primitive times.

Sit back, grab your favorite beverage of choice, and enjoy learning about Evorath's history in this exciting novel.

Peace and Blessings,

Joseph P. Macolino

Scribe of Evorath's History

Continent of Erathal
Runeturk Mountains
Sister Island
Marftaport
Jyrimoore
Paxvilla
Dumner
Felite Confederacy
Castle Felite
Abandoned Camp
Ornithorn's Camp
Felite Outpost
Erathal City
Lizock City
Lake Asgarath
Lake Elaje
Hajeona
Lizock Town
Hidden Castle
Mantz Plains

I seek you Evorath as I lay down for rest

That I may be worthy and always blessed

And should I hear a bump in the night

I pray that I'll remain in your light.

Safe from the hájje and all nighttime horror

Please my dear Goddess, let me see tomorrow.

- Ancient Elvish Bedtime Prayer

PROLOGUE

Lake Algarath
6 Pertga, 1088 MT

A northern breeze blew over the lake, the faint memories of winter giving way to the first blossoms of spring. Valkyrie, queen of the hájje, stood at the eastern bank of the lake, hands resting on her pregnant belly as she stared into the depths. This was not how a queen was meant to live.

She considered the sun reflected in the lake. At its halfway point in the sky, the afternoon air was delightful. But if this past week had proven anything, it was that her minions were incapable of handling this work themselves. So rather than enjoying this beautiful afternoon from the comfort of her courtyard, she was stuck supervising the search.

"My queen!" Verandas trudged up from the lakeside, wiping his hands on the sides of his pants as he approached. He had a peculiar smile on his face.

"That smile better bring good news with it," Valkyrie spat. "Or it's liable to be your last."

Verandas nodded. "You were right to have us come out here. Malum has just came back up -he found the sword!"

Valkyrie smirked, her fingers tingling with anticipation.

"And why do you not have it with you?" she asked with a stern tone.

"I'm sorry your majesty," he offered a slight bow. "It's just that Malum has also found His body. It seems the creatures of the lake have left it relatively untouched, so he is wondering if he should descend to retrieve it."

Valkyrie pursed her lips as she considered. A watery grave was hardly fit for a god.

"Yes, have him retrieve our Master," she ordered after a few seconds of reflection.

"Urgo!" Verandas did an about face, scaling back down the rocky terrain to approach the lake below.

Stepping as close as she could without having to descend the terrain, she glanced down. She could just see Malum at the edge of the lake, his leathery crimson flesh still dripping wet. And just beside him, planted in the loose dirt beside the river, was Yezurkstal's sword.

Extending her left hand, she called for the blade. The moonstone in the pummel vibrated with arcane energy, the green adamantium blade glowing as she called out to it. In that moment, she felt a chill run down her spine and the wind picked up, shifting south. She felt a strange connection with the sword, her hands tingling with dark energy.

Before she realized what she was doing, she willed the blade to her hands. It cut through the air, spinning end over end before planting perfectly in her left palm. Wrapping her fingertips around the handle, she felt a surge of dark energy.

And then came the jolt as the power enveloped her, her eyes jerking skyward as memories filled her head.

There were symbols and runes, all of which suddenly made sense to her. Visions of Yezurkstal, his work forging the blade. Then a flash of red, her Creator pouring his own essence into this sword. And that was only the beginning.

She wasn't sure how long she was in the trance, but as the vision faded and she opened her eyes, she stumbled back.

"My queen!" Verandas dashed over, offering a hand.

Regaining balance on her own, Valkyrie shook her head. More time had passed than she had realized. With both hands clasped around the sword, she glanced around at her surroundings.

"Our Lord continues to provide," she whispered.

"My queen?"

"Have Malum retrieve the body," she replied with a grin. She held out the blade in front of her, inspecting it from top to bottom. The moonstone still emitted a faint glow, and the queen could feel a massive amount of arcane energy from within.

"He already has," Verandas motioned down to the lake.

Valkyrie stepped forward, squinting towards Malum. Her heart nearly jumped from her chest as she spotted the body of her husband and Lord lying prostrate beside the demon.

Leaping from the outcropping, she grabbed the sword with both hands, holding the blade towards the ground beneath. She channeled magic from the moonstone, the black energy circling around her body like a shroud and slowing her descent. She landed softly beside Malum and Yezurkstal.

She looked with disgust at the soggy ground, shuffling her boots to shake off some of the mud. Sneering at her futile efforts, she examined Yezurkstal's body.

He appeared to be in one piece, his skin mysteriously smooth despite being submerged for more than a week. An arrow was planted in his left eye, the fletching partially disintegrated from its time under water. But what made her flinch was the look of his chest, broken and crumbled in from some tremendous outside force.

Those savages had utterly desecrated her husband.

Malum bowed low, extending his left hand out and flourishing his right behind him. He held this pose as he gave homage.

"I present Lord Yezurkstal to her Highness." His voice was raspy and discordant. Valkyrie considered him, the loyal and submissive demon with one broken horn, a body shaped like an apple, and wings that didn't even work for flying. He really was the perfect little servant.

"Thank you Malum," breathed Valkyrie with an air of condescension. "You and Verandas will transport Him. And take care with His body -this is not some husk of a demon corpse; this is your Lord Yezurkstal."

Still in his bowed position, Malum nodded. "As you wish my queen."

Smiling from ear-to-ear, the queen of the hájje was ready to embrace her destiny.

CHAPTER I

Somewhere in the Runeturk Mountains
23 Julla, 1149 MT

Growing up fighting with twenty-seven brothers, sisters, and cousins, Castora was no stranger to pain. She had earned many scars over the decades, fighting tooth and nail to win her place as a general over the hájje army. And yet, none of that conditioning prepared her for this.

She jerked awake, the stabbing pain in her side screaming for her to lay back down as she remembered her surroundings. A black kettle sat on the crackling embers just a few meters away, steam rising from it. The cave walls glowed with candlelight, mismatched sconces holding them up with others scattered about in candelabras on the floor. Glancing up, she marveled once again at the glimmering crystals decorating the ceiling, the faint sound of trickling water suggesting there was a nearby spring.

Hand clutching her left side, she glanced down at the stab injury. The area was still discolored, black, yellow, and red around the uneven stitches. It throbbed as she prodded around, touching the exposed areas of her stomach and hip to see how bad the damage was.

It was better than yesterday. Or had she been here two days already? The whole thing was still a bit of a blur. She remembered tumbling down the cave and -wait.

Where was the gnome?

She jerked around, scanning the cave for any signs of her rescuer. That thought might have hurt more than the injury itself, but she knew it was true.

The gnome had saved her life.

Ignoring the pain behind her eyes and the soreness in her neck and back, she groaned and stood up to full height. Wiping some of the dust off her black pants, she glanced down at the slash on her right arm. Somehow, the barghest's claws had been sharp enough to cut through her gauntlets, leaving three gashes running diagonally across her forearm. Looking at them now, messily stitched up, her recent memories crystallized.

She sighed, considering the rest of her surroundings. Whatever was cooking smelled good, hints of onion tickling her nostrils as she walked towards it. The cavern itself was massive, with ceilings stretching up higher than Castora cared to guess. And despite the mismatched lighting, it appeared to be a formal space of some kind.

At least, she guessed as much by the apparent alter elevated to the north. Though she couldn't discern the path to it yet, she found the alter itself alluring, which was odd. Visually, it was unassuming. It looked like someone had haphazardly carved out the stone, leaving two uneven columns around a level piece of granite.

Even stranger than the unimpressive construction of the altar was the piece it seemed to be displaying. It looked like an ancient pyxis from this distance, the small cylinder begging to be picked up. From this distance, she guessed it was made of bronze, a greenish patina covering the surface. Why would someone put it on an altar and leave it to rust?

Then she remembered how she had tumbled down here in the first place. That must have been the source of magic she felt. Perhaps if she could reach it, she could do a better job of patching herself up and get out of this dank cavern.

"Ah, look who's still in the land of the living," came a gruff voice from behind.

Castora startled, yelping as she twisted around. Her eyes scanned the empty air before she remembered to look down.

No more than a meter tall from the bottom of his boots to the top of his head, the grey-bearded gnome looked up at Castora with a wide grin. His brimless, pointed green hat matched his tunic; his dirty brown pants matched his shoddy leather boots. And in his hands, he held the smallest crossbow the hájje general had ever seen.

With the signature ebony skin of his people, the old gnome stood as still as a statue, blinking as he awaited her response.

"Do you have no manners?" Castora scowled. "Sneaking around like a dirty rat." She shook her head, wincing as she battled a bout of dizziness.

"You probably turned around too fast," the gnome replied with a shrug. He stepped over to the kettle, placing the crossbow down at its side and stirring the contents with the black ladle. Castora lifted her right hand, wagging her index finger to demur, but the gnome cut her off.

"It's my own recipe," he said nodding towards the pot. "Carrots, potatoes, onions, rabbit, and my own special mix of spices. I imagine by now you're famished."

Castora stood with her mouth agape, slowly lowering her hand as the gnome spoke.

There was something about his demeanor and the calming tone of his voice that relaxed her. And though there was a voice in her head telling her to kill him, she took another route. One that surprised even her.

"Thank you," she muttered, looking down at her boots and shuffling her feet nervously.

"Ha! I knew that was in there somewhere," the gnome looked up at her with a smile. "With the way you were cursing and screaming yesterday, I thought I might have to dig deeper to find it, but there it is."

"There what is?" Castora crossed her arms, glaring down at the bumptious gnome.

"Aand it's gone."

The gnome shrugged, turning around, and walking further into the cave to the east. Castora narrowed her eyes and tapped her foot, waiting for the gnome to turn back around and continue the thought. But as he slipped out of sight behind some mineral formations, she was left to ponder.

After a few moments contemplating the gnome's audacity, the hájje flared her nostrils and followed him.

"You're not a typical gnome, are you?" She balled her fists and stomped east.

Plodding around the mineral formations, she scanned the area for the gnome. At first, she just spotted the tip of his green hat, which was sticking out of a hole a few meters away. Drawing near, she slowed her approach and peaked down with curiosity.

There was a small hole carved into one of the rocks, with a wooden storage chest built into it. The gnome was fiddling with something in the hole, but Castora couldn't tell what.

"Are you deaf, old rat?" Castora scowled.

The gnome turned and looked up at her, placing his left hand over his mouth and tapping his index finger against his nose. His eyes looked like they were staring right through Castora.

"Most gnomes would say I'm quite ordinary. Perhaps boringly so. But you," he said pointing towards Castora. "You aren't the typical hájje, are you?"

"Hmph." Castora straightened her back, holding her head up proudly and crossing her arms over her chest. "Of course not. I am Castora, daughter of Yezurkstal and General of the Hájje Royal Knights."

Lowering his hands to his hips, the gnome leaned over, as if looking behind the hájje general.

"Well, I don't see any army with you now. In fact," he paused, pointing at Castora again. "You appear to be an uninvited guest in my cave."

"Your cave?" Castora tilted her head. "I'd heard you were a primitive and uncivilized sort, but I expected you'd have a hovel of some sort to live in at least."

The gnome chuckled, shaking his head. "And you were complaining of my manners. I take it your royal highness doesn't have many friends?"

Castora fumed, her nostrils flaring as she glared daggers at the gnome. She considered strangling him, but a soft voice held her at bay.

"I am one of the most skilled warriors in Evorath. There are thousands of hájje who would live and die by my word."

The gnome sighed, nodding along as Castora spoke.

"I don't know why I'm even bothering with you," the hájje stammered, sucking in a deep breath.

"As I thought," replied the gnome. He turned back to his chest, tinkering around with items unseen. "Ah, there it is."

Just as Castora was about to scream, the gnome tossed the item her way. Instinctively grabbing for it, she winced as her side flared in pain. Opening her palm, she recognized the item as a small, silver hairpin. The hairpin was expertly carved, adorned with Evorath's tree of life.

"What is this for?"

"To hold your hair up. You're calling me primitive, and you don't know what a hairpin is?"

"What? Of course, I know what a hairpin is! Why do you think I'd want a worthless trinket from you?"

The gnome shrugged. "If you like your hair looking like a rat's nest, I suppose you don't need it. Ah, I know!" the gnome bent back over, reaching into the chest. "Here we are!"

He pulled out a mirror. It looked huge in his hands, but as before he flung the mirror up. This time, Castora was prepared, catching the mirror in her right hand.

Like the hairpin, it was more intricate than she expected. The silver handle was engraved with flowers, the reflective mirror in the center surrounded by a thin border that looked like carved wood.

She gasped as she looked at her reflection. There in the mirror, staring back at her, was a demonic visage. Her skin looked blotchy, swatches of black and red covering her normally flawless pale features. The eyes that looked back at her were not her own -they were red and fiery. And her hair really did look like a rat's nest, twisted and knotted in all different directions.

"What sort of trick is this?" she pulled the mirror away, flipping it around and inspecting it more closely.

"What do you see?" the gnome smirked, his hands resting on his hips as he looked up at the hájje.

"Some sort of hideous demon!" Castora stammered.

"Sounds right to me. Or are you telling me you're not a hideous demon?"

Castora felt like she might burst. She dropped the mirror, lunged for the gnome, and grasped him by the arms, pinning him against the wall.

"How dare you, you little foul blooded rodent!"

The gnome smiled, his eyes wide and carefree. And as Castora balled her right fist and clenched her jaw, she could feel her anger boiling over. But looking into his mythril blue eyes, that soft voice from earlier grew louder. She didn't want to kill this gnome.

She loosened her jaw, lowered the gnome to the floor, and stepped back. As she looked down at her trembling hands, she recalled a question the elf had asked before stabbing her. What did motivate her to kill?

"And there is it. Mercy can do amazing things for a person. But why show it to a foul blooded rodent?" The gnome remained stoic, like a patient teacher trying to explain a new concept to his student.

Castora stood dumbfounded, her mind racing for answers.

"Why don't you take this mirror back?" The gnome retrieved the mirror, holding it for Castora to take. Without thinking, she accepted, gazing again upon her reflection.

For a moment, she caught a glimpse of her face. Black eyes, flowing black hair, thick red lips, and a smooth pale face. She smiled, proud to see her own beautiful face. But as the smile formed, the image distorted, her skin turning red and irritated, her hair splitting apart and knotting together.

Frowning at the change, she looked down to the gnome, her eyes pleading for an answer.

"It's an interesting mirror, isn't it?" The gnome inquired. "You see, it shows your heart. When you showed mercy, it saw the real you, the beautiful, loving, kind hájje that you can be. But if I were to guess, that image turned sour, no?"

"I look like I ate a bad fish and rolled around in the mud afterwards," Castora touched around her face, making sure it felt smooth and blemish-free.

"I assure you, your skin is just as alabaster as ever," said the gnome. "But the mirror sees a lifetime of prejudice, hatred, and misplaced pride. Your heart can shed all that faster than you might think, but you must want it."

"And why should I want it?" questioned Castora holding her arms out. She glanced back at the mirror, considering the ugly reflection one more time before dropping it again on the cave floor.

"My heart works fine the way it is," Castora's voice rose in pitch. "I don't know why I'm still here anyway. You tended to my injuries, so I'll spare your life. But you should be grateful to even stand in my presence!"

Her skin burned with rage; her mind overwhelmed by a terrifying thought: what if the gnome was right?

If hájje were truly as superior as Castora had always believed, how had Paxvilla put up such a resistance? How would primitive, uncivilized creatures be able to unite and fight back against them. And why did she keep thinking of that elf and his beautiful hazel eyes?

Castora groaned, stomping away from the gnome and his odd box of trinkets.

"How do I get out of this cave?" she yelled and pulled on her hair with her left hand.

"I can show you out if you wish," the gnome's voice remained unperturbed, free of any signs of stress.

"Would you stop doing that!" she spun around, ignoring the stabbing pain in her side and stomping her right foot. Shaking her hands to make an exaggerated choking motion, she realized she still held the silver hairpin.

"And take this!"

She spiked the pin against the cavern floor, heaving as she looked down at the gnome. It felt as if steam might escape from her ears, her face flaming with rage.

Finally, the gnome lost his composure, but only for a moment. His eyes widened, his mouth twitching as he ran to pick up the hairpin. Inspecting it closely, he looked up at Castora with a smile.

"If you wish to refuse my friendship, that's one thing. I'll gladly show you the door. But this hairpin," he held it up, glaring into Castora's eyes as he did. "This hairpin was my wife's. Even you cannot be so callous to fail and recognize the importance of that."

As before, the gnome maintained a patient and calm tone, speaking slowly and deliberately. But his eyes told a story of their own, the deep blue clouded over with grief and despair. For the first time in her life, Castora felt what she could only describe as pity. And it was followed up by a healthy dose of remorse.

She felt nauseous, the room spinning around her as she staggered to a cave wall. Her chest felt tight, her breathing heavy as she considered the look in the gnome's eyes.

It couldn't be. That look wasn't some primitive loyalty or childish affection. She could feel the gnome's pain.

"You loved her, didn't you?" Castora asked, her voice shaking as she fought back tears.

"As much as any gnome could love another. And even after all these decades, I keep her favorite hairpin as a reminder of the gnome I can be."

Castora fell to her knees and heaved. She could hear the gnome's footsteps echoing on the cave walls as he approached.

"There, there," he reached out and patted her on the shoulder. "It's never too late to change the path you are on. And if you've changed your mind about leaving, I'd love to sit down and chat over a hot bowl of stew."

Looking into the gnome's eyes, Castora struggled to hold back tears. Her lips quivered as she took a deep breath, slowly exhaling as she shifted her position to sit against the cave wall.

"Why do you want to be friends with me?" she asked, struggling to keep her voice steady.

"If you'll forgive my impertinence, I sort of just assumed you don't have any friends. And since I'm all alone here, I thought it was a winning treaty for us both."

Castora huffed, brushing some rogue hair away from her eyes as she considered the gnome's words. If this gnome could feel so deeply for a wife he lost decades before, what else didn't she know about gnomes. Or for that matter, what else had she been taught about Evorath's other creations that was wrong.

"Well," Castora said after about a minute of contemplation. "I can't be friends with someone if I don't know their name."

The gnome smiled ear-to-ear, his eyes glistening as he held out the hairpin again.

"My name is Zodim. And I'd like you to have this hairpin as a token of my friendship."

Hesitating for only a moment, Castora reached out and accepted the hairpin from Zodim's little fingers. With an involuntary smile on her face, the dark elf parted her hair to the left, pushing the small pin into place.

"How does it look?" she asked the gnome.

"See for yourself!" He hopped around, scooping up the mirror and offering it to her.

She glanced down, her usual reflection greeting her. In fact, as she looked at the silver pin in her hair, she looked better than she had ever before.

"Why don't you hold onto the mirror too? With a bit of practice, I bet you could keep your reflection looking that good all the time," suggested Zodim.

"Thank you," replied Castora with a nod.

"I should be thanking you!" exclaimed Zodim spinning around and walking towards the kettle. "I don't get many visitors here, so this stew will be extra special."

"What does the taste of the stew have to do with the presence of a visitor?" Castora asked, eyebrows raised as she approached the gnome.

Zodim grabbed a couple clay bowls, smiling up at Castora as he spooned stew into the first one. After filling the bowl, he placed a spoon in it and offered it up to Castora. She accepted the bowl, stirring it with the spoon and taking a deep breath.

The fragrant smells filled her nostrils, the steam releasing tension from her neck and shoulders. Her stomach growled as she thought of taking her first bite, but she could tell that it was still a bit too hot. So, she waited, watching as Zodim filled his bowl halfway and sloshed the ingredients around.

"I know it's a small bowl," said Zodim as he regarded Castora. "You're welcome to another if you'd like."

Castora nodded, carefully scratching her arm around the claw marks. "Thank you. I know this seems a silly question, but" she paused looking down and shifting her stance, "how long have I been here?"

Zodim chuckled, lifting a spoonful of stew and tipping the spoon over to splash it back into the bowl.

"It's still too hot. I'd give it another minute. And mentally or physically? Because mentally, I don't think you arrived until this evening when I returned. Physically, you stumbled in here two days ago."

Castora nodded, stirring her stew, and considering.

"Well, I should say it properly then. Thank you for helping me. And I'm sorry for any trouble I gave you."

The gnome lit up like a morning sunrise, his eyes shining bright as he smiled.

"You surprise me," he said after holding her gaze for a few moments. "And I forgive you. We are all Evorath's children after all. It wouldn't have been right to leave you injured as you were. I'm quite sure you wouldn't have survived the first night."

Though certain Zodim was right, Castora had to repress her initial angry response. Regardless, he had saved her life, and she was grateful for that, even if a lifetime of prejudice made it difficult to admit.

"What do you mean by 'Evorath's children'?" she questioned. "As far as I've seen, Evorath abandoned her children after she created this miserable world."

Zodim walked over and leaned against the wall, balancing his stew in one hand, and slowly bending down to sit on the floor. Taking a spoonful, he closed his eyes and after he finished swallowing, he released an exaggerated exhale.

"Try the stew and tell me what you just said again."

Castora narrowed her eyes, lifting the bowl closer to her mouth and taking a spoonful. She hovered the spoon over the bowl, looking at Zodim a moment longer before taking a bite.

Perhaps it wasn't such a miserable world.

CHAPTER II

Castora laughed, clutching her side as the injury flared.

"But it didn't stop there either!" Zodim held up his left index finger and shook his head. "You see, Sora was determined. And when my Sora had it in her mind to do something, you better damn well believe she would do it."

He clapped at the word 'damn' for emphasis, a large smile on his face as he continued motioning along with his words. "So, wouldn't you know it? Sora dove into the river, fished out the now ruined cake, and knelt as she offered it to the priestess. I don't know how she kept a straight face, but with perfect composure she held up the disgusting lump and said simply 'It's a bit wet'."

Zodim laughed, slapping his thigh, and shaking his head. Through fits of laughter, he continued. "No one could stop laughing after that!"

Castora covered her face and shook her head, giggling as she imagined it. But then her own childhood memories crept in, cutting her laughter short. It must have shown, for Zodim frowned looking up at her.

"What's wrong?" he asked.

"Oh, nothing," Castora shook her head, forcing a smile. "That's really funny."

"Come now young lady. I've shared enough stories to fill a collection of books. Let's hear what's on your mind."

Castora shook her head and held her right palm out.

"No, you've been telling such cheerful tales. I don't want to dampen the atmosphere."

"Nonsense. I'd say you owe me a good story, even if it isn't cheerful." Zodim stood up, walking over to the stream, and dipping his cup in. "And I've found sharing those unpleasant stories is the best way to let them go." Taking a gulp of the fresh water, he walked over and plopped back down cross-legged, looking up at Castora.

The dark elf sighed, taking a sip of her water. She didn't want to share anything, but that quiet voice in her mind was growing louder. Perhaps the gnome was right.

"You see," she paused, leaning to the left. "Your story just." She shook her head, standing up and beginning to pace.

"Hájje aren't so forgiving as gnomes seem to be. Even for simple disobedience, a brand is commonplace back home. I received my fair share of them growing up." She reached back, gently massaging the base of her skull.

"Which is funny to hear me say, because I was taught, sorry to say, that gnomes are basically like rabid dogs. Uncivilized, unsanitary, and illiterate; three things you've already shown me to be untrue. But you see, I was always taught growing up that hájje were superior to all other creatures of Evorath. And we showed that superiority by behaving in superior ways."

"Funny enough, those 'superior ways' showed up in rituals much like the one you described with your wife and the priestess. And the story you told of your wife and the priestess just reminds me of one such memory."

Castora paused, closing her eyes, and taking a deep breath. She started pacing faster, walking over to the spring before turning around and walking back past Zodim. Recalling the vivid images of the day, she continued.

"See, as part of the royal family I was expected to maintain the family line. Part of that is the Jullari."

Zodim chuckled, immediately holding up his left hand and frowning.

"Sorry," he uttered. "It's just funny to hear a people claiming to be so superior to everyone else stealing an outdated elvish tradition and using it. I'm familiar enough with Jullari. The Erathal Republic also still observes that absurd tradition."

Ceasing her pacing, she regarded the gnome. She thought perhaps it shouldn't have come as a surprise, but it still did. Since leading the attack on Paxvilla, Castora was beginning to doubt whether anything she was taught was truthful.

"Well, in hájje tradition, the Jullari starts at age fifteen," Castora resumed pacing. "And in that year, there were only thirteen of us to participate; six boys and seven girls. With my twin brother being one of the six boys, I knew the odds were against me. And unlike the other girls, I didn't have the benefit of a mother to help me.

"Despite that, I worked my hardest to prepare for the coming out party on the first night. I had gotten a traditional dress from my cousin who had gone through the ceremony the year prior. But I'm afraid while most of the girls my age spent time learning skills like sewing, I focused more on combat."

"As you can imagine, re-fitting the dress was difficult enough, and it took me until the day before the event to finish. But to make matters worse, some of my cousins decided the morning of the event it would be fun to sneak into my room and pour green dye on my dress.

"I spent the entire afternoon trying to fix it. And by Frogatha's hair I managed to pull it off. But with all my attention on the dress, I forgot about my slippers, which had also been hit by some of the dye. I did my best to cover it up, but after the preliminary start of the event, it came time to present ourselves to the Queen."

Castora could recall the disappointment on her Queen's face that night. The color in her cheeks, the anger in her eyes, and even the tone of her voice all haunted her as she paced faster and faster through the cave.

"When Queen Valkyrie noticed the green dye on my slippers, she was furious. I'm not sure which was worse, the public humiliation that evening or the flogging that came later that night. But long story short, my lack of decorum disqualified me from starting that year. And as a result, I am the only daughter of Yezurkstal to not be wed to another child of Yezurkstal."

She clutched at the stab wound in her side, leaning against the wall, and recalling the shame she felt. Now as she spoke about it to Zodim, considering the stories he had shared, it suddenly felt less significant. Why should she care about a ritual stolen from elves? Of course, that soft voice reminded her why it still bothered her so.

"I sense that's not the whole story," said Zodim. Castora looked down at the gnome, his eyebrows raised as he peered into her soul.

"I don't know," Castora muttered, looking down at her boots. "Let me ask you something. You mentioned that Erathal observes Jullari. And I know you had a wife of your own. Do all the people of Evorath observe marriage traditions?"

Zodim shrugged. "I don't really know about all the people of Evorath. But I know many have similar traditions."

"I see," replied Castora, considering what to say. Her instinct told her to lie, to cut the conversation short. Perhaps she could make the excuse that she was tired. After all, she had just met this gnome. Even if he saved her life, that hadn't earned him intimate details about that life.

Or did it? That soft voice kept creeping back, encouraging her to share.

But she wasn't ready.

"I think that's really all to the story that I feel up to sharing now," she declared, looking sternly down at the gnome.

"As you wish," Zodim bowed his head and held up both his hands, palms out. "Just remember, a burden shared is a load lightened."

"Hmph. I think my father would disagree with you. He'd always tell me the opposite. 'Keep your fears to yourself or your enemies will learn to exploit them'. He would say it differently every time, but that was always the sentiment."

Zodim narrowed his eyes, placing his cup on the floor and staring at Castora with his mouth agape. His face went two shades lighter, his eyes trembling as he stood up.

"What do you mean he would 'tell' you that?" The gnome's voice was uncharacteristically timid.

The dark elf tilted her head, squinting down at the gnome.

"Well, my twin brother and I were *privileged* to spend more time with my father than most of our cousins. Since my mother died, he wou-"

"What do you mean 'spend more time' with him?" Zodim's shouted, his entire body shaking. "Your father was killed…six decades ago now!"

"Ha! My father is undying. No one is powerful enough to kill him, and if even they were, he'd come back. Do most people believe he's dead?"

Zodim looked a thousand kilometers away. He leaned back against the wall, slinking into a seated position. With a loud sigh, he closed his eyes for a moment before looking back at Castora. His eyes were pleading as he met her gaze.

"How could that be?" the gnome whispered, his words just barely audible to Castora.

She considered the gnome's reaction, thinking about all the times her father would discuss the dangers outside Hájjeona. And the story of how her father had bravely repelled an evil army marching on the fortress and killing so many of their people, including Castora's mother. Was that all a lie?

Castora felt a surge of emotions. Unsure whether it was her own revelation or Zodim's shock, she screamed, throwing her cup against the cave wall and pulling on her hair.

"Is the entire hájje legacy built on lies?"

She stomped, huffed, heaved, and circled around the cave in frustration. Her mind was moving so fast she couldn't keep the thoughts straight. Lessons on the barbarity of all non-hájje, how centaur would hunt and eat dark elves, how satyr would get so drunk that they'd burn down entire villages as part of their profane celebrations. How the Kingdom of Erathal had decimated the hájje because of their lighter skin.

Yezurkstal was painted as the savior of her kind, a holy avenger keeping them safe from the vicious chaos of the outside world. But the stories Zodim shared of love, compassion, and fellowship with his fellow gnomes. Maybe that was it! He hadn't really talked about the other people of Evorath -perhaps gnomes were the only ally the hájje could rely on. But why was Zodim so clearly terrified of her father?

With a groan, Castora stepped back over to Zodim, slinking down next to him.

"I'm sorry about the cup," she muttered after a moment.

"It's just a cup," he uttered back. "But discovering a whole lifetime of lies; that's something worth discussing."

The dark elf rubbed the bridge of her nose, breathing in deep and contemplating. She always preferred the direct approach in battle, so perhaps it would be best to keep digging until she understood the extent of the lies.

"All the stories you've shared make it clear that gnomes are not the feral, uncivilized creatures I was taught to think you were. So, it makes me wonder if all the people of Evorath are more civilized than I was taught. And now I can't help but feel that perhaps it is my father who is the monster."

She felt nauseous as she said this, her instincts telling her she deserved a flogging for such blasphemy. But that quiet voice grew even stronger, reassuring her of the truth.

"I think it's time I shared the most important story of my life," said Zodim. He bent over, grunting as he pulled himself up to his feet.

"I'm getting old," he muttered, shaking his head. "Anyways, I guess there's really no good place to begin." He looked up, tapping his left index finger on his nose.

"It was almost exactly sixty-two years ago. Sora, as I'm sure you already figured out, was always fascinated by caverns and the geological wonders they held. So, she and I joined an expedition and ventured to the eastern formations of these mountains to do some prospecting and see what treasures we could find."

Zodim brought his hands together, hovering his steepled fingers before his face and closing his eyes.

"There were about two dozen of us in that expedition. And I still remember the smell of the mountain air that morning. The spring breeze blew in from the east, bringing hints of lilac and sweet elderberry."

The gnome stuttered in some air, releasing a loud sigh.

"I remember that smell so clearly because while the rest of the expedition continued ahead, I decided to take a break. My wife even asked if she should wait with me."

Zodim sniffled, rubbing his eyes.

"But I told her 'no'. I assured her I'd only be a few minutes. I never imagined how much life can change in such a short time."

Zodim took in a gasp of air, his voice cracking as he continued.

"But you need to savor each moment; I know that now. Because as I sat sitting on the ridge, taking in the gorgeous view, and smelling the sweet spring scents, the rest of the expedition. My wife!"

He burst into tears, burying his face in his hands. Somehow, Castora already knew what happened next.

"The screams that came from that cave," Zodim spoke between tears. "I had never heard such cries of desperation and fear. And when -when I arrived at the entrance. I -oh Evorath!"

He rubbed his face, wiping away tears as he looked up into Castora's eyes.

"That's when I saw your father. A gnome…ripped in half, held in either of his hands. A dozen more, at least, lay dead at his feet," he sucked in more air, heaving between words. "And my wife. Sora was so brave."

Castora knelt, placing her hand on Zodim's left shoulder and holding his gaze.

"No," Zodim stepped back, swiping her hand away. "You have to know it all," he cried.

"I just stood there and watched. My legs were too heavy to even lift, the horrid sights of the massacre still so clear in my mind." He curved his fingers to a point, tapping his forehead to emphasize his words.

"But Sora charged him with nothing but a pickaxe. I watched, as my wife was murdered -and then I ran. I couldn't stop myself." His voice cracked.

"I ran!" He shouted. "Like a coward. Like the mindless beast your father would have you believe I am! So, in my case, perhaps your father was right."

Zodim was shaking as he fell to the ground, hands over his face sobbing. For the second time in her life, Castora felt pity.

"No." she said softly. "If your story convinces me of anything, it's how wrong he was. And, how wrong I've been."

It felt like a great weight was lifted from her as she said those words. Her entire body tingled with the admission. And though she wasn't sure how, she knew what she had to do.

She stretched her neck and cracked her knuckles. Standing at full height, she looked down at the gnome.

"I'm not sure how, but I know what must happen next. I'm going to kill my father."

CHAPTER III

Runeturk Mountains
25 Julla, 1149 MT

Castora moaned, her side searing as she pulled herself over the next ledge. She looked over the horizon, taking in the scenic mountain view.

There was nothing but rocky terrain for as far as she could see. Glancing back east, she could no longer even tell where they had started the journey, the rocky cliff-faces all blending. The taller peaks to the north looked enormous, even from this high mountain plateau. And facing south, she saw the steep slope of the mountain and the green tops of the trees below, but she couldn't even guess how far away they must be.

But what was most concerning was the treacherous path to the east. Facing steep rockfaces and rugged terrain, she was really starting to wish she took healing magic more seriously. Her side ached and her arm itched.

"Are you sure this is the easiest path?" she called ahead to Zodim.

The gnome popped his head up from behind some rocks, grinning as he held up his left index finger.

"Ah, but I didn't say this was the easiest path. I said it was the safest. Between the dwarves and gnomes, we have cave systems running through this mountain that could get us to our destination faster and easier."

"And why aren't we taking one of those paths?" the hájje scratched the back of her head.

"With the story I shared of meeting your father, how do you think most dwarves or gnomes would react to seeing a hájje travelling in their tunnels? We may not be the savage beasts you were taught we were, but I don't see you being received with open arms either."

Castora closed her eyes, rubbing the bridge of her nose as she inhaled. "I suppose we should keep moving then."

And so, they did. They climbed, crawled, and walked for hours, the sun moving higher into the sky. With each kilometer they traveled, the dark elf felt weaker and weaker. The bag on her back grew heavier, and she was constantly wiping sweat from her eyes. Ascending to the top of another peak, she cried out in frustration.

"Please tell me we don't have to go any higher! I feel like my stitches are about to burst open."

Zodim, who had reached the peak a couple minutes before her, turned around and smiled. He loosened the straps on his pack, placing it on the ground.

"I reckon you're not used to the air this high." The gnome reached into his bag, pulling out a waterskin and tossing it to the dark elf. "Have a drink."

Reacting instinctually, Castora held up her arms and caught the waterskin. She offered a slight nod before tipping her head back and gulping down some water. Her side was burning, the area around the stab hot to the touch.

Wincing as she felt around it, she lowered the waterskin and inspected the wound. It was bruised and inflamed; the skin red all around the stitches.

"Are you sure this is healing?" Castora asked.

Zodim was looking over the southwest ledge, surveying the area ahead. He didn't respond immediately, walking back over and pulling out another waterskin. Taking a swig as he walked over to Castora, he squinted and looked at the wound in her side.

"I'm sure we want to get to our destination before this infection gets much worse. But, I had you bring that chest for a reason. I was hoping we wouldn't need it, but let's see."

The dark elf looked down at him in astonishment as Zodim pulled his chest out of the bag. An infection? Why was he being so nonchalant about an infection? She felt hot, her temper boiling to the surface. But as she opened her mouth to berate the gnome, she found herself distracted by what he was doing.

Pulling out item after item, the gnome was creating a pile of junk on the top of the mountain. There were platters, shoes, rope, clothes, and knickknacks of all varieties. But most perplexing of all was watching Zodim pull out a full-length, steel bastard sword.

"How much can that chest hold?" she stood dumbfounded as Zodim continued to rifle through.

"Did you think the pyxis was the only magical item I had?" the gnome asked without looking away from his search. "This one is bigger on the inside."

"What does that even mean?" Castora shrugged, scratching the back of her head.

"Ah, there it is." He pulled out a small glass bottle, filled with a clear liquid. Pulling the cork out, he held it close to his face, fanning the air away from his nose and scowling as he took a whiff.

"Yep, that's the stuff. It'll burn like dragon's fire, but it should help clear out the wound. You want me to pour it on, or would you rather do it yourself?"

With a frown, the hájje bent over and grabbed the bottle. Even from half a meter away, she could smell the overwhelming stench of alcohol. Frowning, she closed her eyes and clenched her jaws, pouring the liquid over her stab wound.

She seethed in pain, clenching her fists as the liquid washed over her wound. It felt like her skin was burning off, but as she emptied the bottle, the sensation quickly subsided, the immense burn diminishing in only seconds to an almost refreshing heat.

Dropping the bottle, Castora ran her hands up along her face and pulled back her hair.

"That's a perfectly good bottle!" Zodim dove and caught the glass just before it struck the ground.

"It's just an empty little bottle. What is the purpose of all this stuff you are storing in that chest?"

"Mind your own business," replied the gnome. "If the chest can fit it, why would I get rid of it?"

Castora sighed, shaking her head, and strolling to the western ledge. There was still nothing in sight but treacherous mountain paths and rocky terrain in the valley below. But aside from a steep immediate decline, it did appear the terrain had a more gradual slope at least. From this vantage point, it even looked like they might be moving into some wooded hills if they continued the same western trajectory.

"You're right to be relieved," said Zodim walking up beside the dark elf. He pointed down towards the forested area.

"We're heading that way. But I'll warn you now, after the main descent to the forest, we'll have to ascend a hill." He moved his hand up, pointing towards the base of the next mountain peak. "Old Medicus has burrowed out a fine little home at the top of that hill. Or at least it was fine last time I visited."

Pulling back his hand, he gave his beard a slight tug and held his hand over his face, tapping his left index finger on his nose, gaze drifting up as he did.

"How long ago was that?" asked Castora, arching her eyebrows.

"Evorath knows," quipped Zodim. "Some decades ago I suppose. I'm sure he's still there."

"So that chest of yours," Castora glanced back at the pile of junk. "Did you make that as well? Why don't I sense the same magic I do from the pyxis?"

"I suspect because the pyxis is a much more powerful container. And the magic you sense is what makes it so whatever goes in doesn't escape."

"As for the storage chest," Zodim continued, looking past Castora. "I built that for Sora as a gift for our century anniversary. Whereas the pyxis is its own pocket dimension, the chest just sends items through the ether to another location."

"Wait," Castora scratched the back of her head, scrunching her face in thought. "Where is the other end of the chest? That seems an easy way to lose things."

Zodim shrugged. "You seem to think I have too much anyways."

He turned around and walked back over to the pile of junk. He started tossing the items back into the chest, setting aside the rope and a couple of small metallic objects.

As he continued loading up the chest, Castora walked over and reached into her pack. Pulling out the hard leather pouch, she grabbed a handful of jyrberries. After inspecting the small red berries, she glanced back at Zodim.

"You sure these are edible?" she asked.

The old gnome shrugged. "Edible, yes. Just remember, the darker the color, the tarter the berry."

She scrunched her face, pursing her lips as she considered her options. But knowing this was the only food she could eat without preparation, there really wasn't much of an option. So, she tilted her head back and dropped a couple berries in her mouth, closing her eyes as she chewed.

The berries themselves were soft, similar in texture to a blueberry. But the flavor was something entirely different. With only a slight hint of sweetness, she scowled as she chewed through the berries and swallowed. And yet, as the flavor lingered on her tongue, it left a sweet aftertaste. She imagined if she ate a lemon followed by a drop of honey it would taste about the same.

Though a far cry from the usual food she'd bring on a hike, it would have to do. Without another thought, she threw the rest of the handful into her mouth and chewed. Her eyes shut tight as the tart flavor filled her mouth, she reached in and grabbed another handful.

"I guess that's a seal of approval?" Zodim asked.

The gnome extended his hand. Castora offered the pouch, allowing him to take it.

The duo stood there for the next few minutes, eating the berries, and looking down on the amazing view. And as with many experiences over the past few days, she found herself looking at the world a bit differently. This mountain was no longer just an obstacle to climb.

This view was breathtaking.

"Well," started Zodim after a few minutes of silence. "I think it's time we get started on the descent. But fortunately for us, this part should be easier than the climb!"

He replaced the berry pouch in Castora's bag and walked over to the rope. Pulling one of the metallic items from his pocket, he held it up over his head and spun it around. Taking the hint, Castora looked over the object. It looked like a nail with a coin for its head, an unfamiliar rune carved into the top.

"I'm not sure what I'm looking at," the dark elf scratched behind her head.

With a smile, the gnome held up his right index finger and sat down on the ground. He took the small hammer from the belt at his side and hammered the strange nail into the rock. To Castora's surprise, it just took a couple strikes with the hammer for the nail to stick.

"Now, watch this," Zodim said pulling the other metallic object from his pocket. This one looked like a gold coin with the center cut out, more unknown runes carved around the border.

"Return!" He exclaimed. As the second syllable left his mouth, the nail shot up from the ground and landed securely in the hole of the gold coin. Castora blinked a couple of times, the utility of the device not fully registering.

"Oh!" she clapped her hands together as she realized. "Will that little anchor really support our weight though?"

"This one little anchor could support 1,000 kilos, at least! And if my eyes are right, this rope will allow us to descend all the way to that landing." He stepped back to the edge, pointing down to a small outcropping about fifty meters below.

"With any luck," he continued, "we'll be able to get all the way down using these."

Castora nodded, crouching down, and placing the chest and pouch back in her bag.

"Then let's keep moving."

CHAPTER IV

Runeturk Mountains
26 Julla, 1149 MT

"That just seems so ineffectual. So, they don't have a citizen registry of any kind?" Castora swatted a gnat buzzing past her face.

She glanced at Zodim to her left. Though he had shown himself well-equipped for mountain travel, navigating the overgrowth of this forest was proving to be a greater challenge. His small stature left him vanishing into some of the taller grass, while overturned trees and small boulders were proving to cause a continual delay.

Castora secretly enjoyed the slower pace though. She wouldn't say so, but the stab wound in her side was a constant source of pain, a yellow puss starting to form over the stitches. Combined with the occasional chills she was feeling, she worried the infection was getting worse.

"It's really not so strange," replied Zodim with his eyes trained ahead. "I know the dwarves, elves, and lizock maintain a rigid hierarchy -sounds like your people do as well. But for many species, that structure has proven to do more harm than good. Take the centaurs for instance. The history books say they had a huge empire in Erathal. But over time, that empire fractured into small villages."

Zodim coughed, pushing through some overgrowth.

"And here's the interesting thing," continued Zodim. "After your father's initial campaign six decades ago, all the centaur reunited in Dumner. But they didn't try to build bigger or stronger. Instead, the news is that Dumner's chieftain gave up most of his power. Like Marftaport, they are now calling themselves a 'free settlement'. Every centaur is his own master."

Castora shook her head as she stepped over a rotting log.

"But how is that possible? Without someone to rule them, how do they not all kill one another? They must have a lot of disease and starvation affecting their people if they don't take care of them."

Zodim chuckled. "That must be a convenient paradigm."

"What do you mean?" Castora asked defensively.

"You believe rulers are necessary for a functioning society. And you happen to be one of those would-be rulers. Maybe you're right. Maybe your people need a ruler. But did you ever stop to consider what harm it could cause if you're wrong?"

"Well, I," she paused, considering her jumble of thoughts. The constant headache wasn't helping anything. And this thicker brush was getting on her nerves.

"This stupid overgrowth! How are you managing it? I'm struggling and I'm almost twice your height!"

Zodim ducked under a downed log, crawling beneath the warped branch, and standing up on the other side. He dusted himself off and continued forward with a grin.

"Changing the subject on me?" he asked.

"I just can't stand all this overgrowth!" Castora growled in frustration, swatting aside some vines.

"And as you wish this overgrowth was all orderly and neat, you want all people on Evorath to be the same?"

"Yes, exactly!" Castora exclaimed. "Order is what ensures a species can thrive. I mean look at this forest! No one maintains it and it becomes a tangle of vines and rotted old logs. It's absolute chaos!"

"And what's wrong with a little chaos?" The gnome stopped in his tracks, eyebrows raised as he motioned towards a gnarled oak tree.

Squinting at the tree, Castora followed Zodim's gaze and looked up towards the canopy of branches above. The branches reached out in all directions, gnarled, and tangled around one another. Moss was growing upon some of the branches, vibrant green leaves swaying in the wind.

"Just take it in," said Zodim. "Those beautiful branches snaking around and forming a work of art. All without any interference from a living creature."

It was beautiful. In fact, as she stood and admired the branches, she felt a touch of nostalgia. She had a flash of a memory from childhood when she was…perhaps nine years old? Yes, nine sounded right. And she used to admire trees like this, sitting under their shade and simply enjoying the beauty of the world around her.

When did that change? She wondered.

Shaking her head, she continued west.

"It's aesthetically pleasing, yes. But sentient life isn't about aesthetics. People need to be ruled -they crave it!"

"And who taught you that?" questioned Zodim.

"Pfft!" Castora walked through a spider web, pulling at her hair to remove the remnants. "Doesn't history show that?" she retorted.

"History? Somewhere in that chest in your bag there's a collection of history books. Some written by elves, some by dwarves, some by felite authors, a couple by lizock, and even one by a satyr historian. You know what I've found in those texts?"

"What?" Castora shook out her hands, grimacing as she ducked under another web.

"Aside from the Demon Wars, all the conflicts recorded in history were started by rulers who shared your belief. That is, the belief that the world needed more order."

"The Demon Wars?" Castora scrunched her face, glancing down at the gnome. "Is that what you call it when the people of Evorath revolted against and banished the demons from this world?"

Zodim laughed, shaking his head as he climbed over a thick log. Castora stepped over the log and waited as the elderly gnome made it to the other side.

"You may want to consider the possibility that the feral and lawless nature of non-hájje is not the only lie you were taught growing up. Did your father teach you demons were the victims?"

The dark elf stopped in her tracks, scratching the back of her head as she considered. Could it really all be a lie?

"I don't know. I have too much of a headache to think about this. Can we talk abou-"

"Shh!" Zodim held his left index finger over his lips. "Did you hear that?" he whispered.

Castora looked around, rubbing her temples as she listened. She smelled the various odors of the woods, decomposing wood, and damp earth. She saw the trees blowing gently in the breeze. But it wasn't until she closed her eyes that she heard a faint noise she couldn't place.

Keeping her eyes open, she leaned to the left. It was voices, coming from the foliage to the south. And they were growing louder.

Pivoting, the hájje looked around for a good spot to hide.

Fortunately, this part of the woods was full of large trees, including an Erath just ahead towards the mountains. It was at least ten meters wide.

"Come on," Castora grabbed Zodim's arm and dragged him behind the tree. She winced but fought through the stabbing pain in her side. Taking a position behind the Erath, she crouched down and looked around.

"I may be old, but I'm capable of moving myself," whispered Zodim, brushing himself off.

"Next time I'll just leave you to get eaten then."

"To get eaten?"

Zodim held his arms out with palms up. His eyes narrowed, and lips tight as if suggesting Castora had made an unbelievable claim.

But as the voices grew closer, they both refocused their attention to the south. In addition to the voices, she could just barely make out what sounded like a horse and wagon. Too curious to stay put, Castora crept around towards the left edge of the tree, peering out to watch as the voices became audible.

"You think this will be the last shipment?" the first voice spoke. It was deep and throaty, the subtle accent suggesting it belonged to a dwarf.

"I reckon it could be," came the second. This voice was smoother, but still deep and dwarven in its inflection. "It really just depends on if they found another vein."

"I suppose that's true," replied the first. "But from what I've heard, Keldor's other prospectors haven't had a lick of luck - they haven't even found new veins of mythril. If Jyrimoore is out of adamantium, it may make that alloy he's been working on that much more important."

"I reckon you're right," said the second. "It's dangerous out there, especially with the return of the hájje. I hear the Hunter's and Mage's Guild are working together to come up with more defensive measures around town."

"I'm not sure we should even be traveling like this. What if we ran into a hájje out here?" the first asked.

The pair was drawing closer, and as Castora peeked her head out, she caught a glimpse of them through the foliage.

The dwarves pushed through some overgrowth into the clearing. They led a donkey behind them, which was hauling a large wagon. Of the two dwarves, Castora assumed the shorter one was the first to speak. He was only about twenty centimeters taller than Zodim by the looks of it and had a long white beard and wrinkled skin. The other dwarf, who was at least ten centimeters taller than his elder, had a smoother complexion along with a shorter, brown beard.

In addition to the wagon their donkey was pulling, both dwarves had matching leather packs on their backs and various tools about their belts. And neither seemed too imaginative in their fashion style, wearing matching brown boots, leather pants, and simple tunics and vests.

"If we run into any hájje, I'll get a chance to show you how good I've gotten with this pickaxe." The younger one tapped the pickaxe on his right side.

The older dwarf laughed, a boisterous bellow.

"More likely you'd soil your britches and run all the way back home."

"Hey! That ain't nice." Objected the younger dwarf. "I bet you'd just stand there scared while they killed us both."

Snap.

Castora jerked her head around and glared at Zodim. The old gnome held both hands over his mouth, his face flushed as he looked down at the broken stick beneath his feet.

"Is someone there?" asked the older dwarf.

With eyes wide, the hájje shook her head. She stared daggers at Zodim, but realized in an instant it was pointless.

Zodim stepped out from behind the tree, holding his hands up above his head as he approached.

"Sorry to startle you my friends," he called ahead.

Both the dwarves jumped at his appearance, the younger one fumbling with his pickaxe before dropping it on the ground.

"Pull yourself together son!" shouted the older dwarf. He huffed out a breath of air and shook his head. "What's the idea jumping out on us like that?"

"Again, I apologize." Zodim walked forward, slowly lowering his hands to his side. "My name is Zodim. Are you two coming from Marftaport?"

The younger dwarf stood back up, securing his pickaxe at his side. Seeing him look towards the Erath tree, Castora pulled her head back, making sure she remained out of sight. She felt dizzy as she did, her headache ramping up to a heavy throb. Closing her eyes and rubbing her temples, she tried to listen as best she could.

"We're from Marftaport, yes," replied the older dwarf cautiously. "What's it to you?"

"I thought as much. For why it matters to me, are you familiar with an old gnome named Medicus?"

"The old hermit to the east?" the older dwarf inquired. "Calls himself a 'doctor', whatever that is meant to mean."

"Yes, that's the fellow!" exclaimed Zodim.

"What of it?" asked the younger dwarf, his tone harsh.

"Well, I'm bringing a travel companion that way and we're just hoping to make it safely. She is injured, you see. So, I'm just hoping as followers of Evorath that you'll let us continue on our way unmolested."

"By Kelgen's beard, you've nothing to fear from us." The old dwarf's voice rose in pitch. "We're just heading to Jyrimoore to pick up some ore. And despite his enthusiasm, I assure you my traveling partner here is harmless."

"Very good!" exclaimed Zodim. "I knew you looked like peaceful folk. Castora, I think it's safe for us to be on our way. These two won't cause you any harm."

Wouldn't they? Castora wondered. But with a throbbing headache and a bout of nausea overcoming her, she wasn't quite sure about anything. So, she stumbled out from behind the tree, clutching her side as she crept towards Zodim and the dwarves.

"What in the?" The younger dwarf drew his pickaxe, this time without fumbling it.

Zodim held up his hands again, stepping between Castora and the dwarves.

"Now let's remember, no one means anyone here any harm. We'll just," Zodim glanced back at Castora, arching his eyebrows as he looked her over. "Are you feeling alright Castora?" he lowered his hands.

"I reckon not," interjected the older dwarf. "Even for a hájje, you look a bit pale sweetheart."

Castora scowled, but she found it difficult to think or speak clearly. She held up her right hand as if to object, but her vision blurred.

Her legs felt like jelly, the world spinning around her. And as she tumbled to the forest floor, she found herself thinking just one thing.

Please don't let me die like this.

CHAPTER V

Medicus's Burrow
27 Julla, 1149 MT

What is this sensation? Castora wondered.

The white light was blinding. She recoiled, covering her eyes. But then she realized something else.

The pain was gone.

Looking towards the stab wound, she peeked through the cracks in her eyelids. Her flesh was completely restored. She opened her eyes wide, the light softening as she looked at her arm next -the claw marks were gone.

But where was she?

As she pondered this question, she only just realized she was upright. But she wasn't standing. No, she was floating through a void, darkness closing in around her. Except for the white light in the distance.

The light moved towards her. She opened her mouth to speak, but no sound came out. In fact, there was no sound or smell as far as she could tell.

Am I dead? She asked herself.

"No." came an unexpected response from the light. That single syllable filled her with energy, her body tingling with anticipation. The voice was soft and motherly, but somehow also powerful and terrifying.

Eyes fixed on the light, Castora watched it move closer. The light flashed outward, causing the dark elf to shield her eyes. But as she lowered her arm, she saw the light coalescing into a female form. It was difficult to look at directly.

Castora opened her mouth to ask, "who are you?" but no words came out.

"You know who I am." The voice echoed in her mind, filling her with warmth and assurance.

What is this place? Thought Castora.

"It is a dream. And I visit to assure you of the path you're on. Help the gnome with his quest, and you will find fulfillment in your own."

The form drew closer, the white light growing brighter. Castora held on as long as she could, shielding her eyes with her hands. The light was too bright.

She closed her eyes and felt a warm embrace.

And for the first time in her life, she felt free.

Castora jerked up from the bed. She sniffed the air, the smell of lavender mixed with burning wax filling her nostrils. A light ringing in her ears brought about a pinch of pain in her head, the remnants of a headache.

With the dream still fresh in her mind, she lifted her injured arm to find it wrapped in a white cloth. She looked down at her side, considering the aching stab wound. She was alive.

She let out a breath she didn't realize she was holding and turned to take in her surroundings. The bed was small, her feet hanging over the edge as she sat up. But it was plush, perhaps even more comfortable than the luxurious beds she was accustomed to.

Considering the room itself, she felt cramped. She winced and stood up, rubbing around her wound as she sized things up. The room was no more than two meters long and three meters wide. And as she raised her hands overhead, she was able to touch the sloped stone ceiling.

She looked around at the rest of the room. She considered the round doorway, which she'd have to duck to pass through. And she took a moment to observe the painting on the left wall, a cavern landscape. There was a small end table to the right of the bed, two candles left burning. Both were at least half burned through by the looks of it, the wax melting over onto the table. Considering the plethora of colored rings staining the wood, it looked like a typical occurrence.

Confident that she was in no immediate danger, she regarded her wound yet again. It was freshly cleaned, the skin still a soft red for a couple centimeters around the wound. From the looks of it, the stitches had been replaced, these ones appearing cleaner and more uniform than before. And as she poked around the area, she felt only a light pressure.

Castora rubbed her eyes, running her hand down her face as she sighed. She wondered: was the dream real. Or was it just an illusion brought on by the infection?

And the soft voice in her head answered: yes. It wasn't just a simple dream. It had to be real.

Still trying to process why the goddess Evorath would deign to visit her in such a way, she sat back down at the foot of the bed. She held her hands in front of her face, looking at the lines in her palms and the callouses on her fingers.

These hands had been conditioned with decades of martial training. She had used them to punish her subordinates and to crush her enemies. And just a few days ago, she had used them to slaughter countless foes. Or had they really been her foes?

As she reflected on the dream, her hands began to tremble. She had been the villain.

Finally able to accept this, she broke down and wept. She cradled her face, sobbing as she recalled the faces of some of her most recent victims. The looks on their faces as they drew their final breath would haunt her for the rest of her life.

Knock. Knock. Knock.

A rapping on the door drew her attention. She let out a long exhale, hastily wiping the tears from her eyes.

"Come in," she uttered with a sniffle.

The door creaked open, and Zodim stepped inside. Offering a faint smile, he glanced around the room before stepping inside and shutting the door behind him.

"I'm glad to see you are awake." He met Castora's gaze, looking into her eyes. She looked away at first, wiping away some final tears before turning back to meet his gaze.

"How did I get here?" Castora sniffled, wiping the bridge of her nose.

"I had to carry you the rest of the way," Zodim replied with a shrug.

Castora leaned back, narrowing her eyes and tilting her head just slightly to the right.

"How did you?"

"I'm just kidding," the gnome replied with a chuckle. "Those two dwarves were kind enough to help. We loaded you in their wagon and brought you here. You've been out of it for nearly a full day."

Castora blinked, trying to piece everything together.

"Where exactly is here?" she asked after a moment.

"Medicus's Borrow, of course! I told you he'd fix you up, and I reckon by the look of your wounds that you shouldn't have to worry about an infection anymore."

"I thought those dwarves might kill me," she glanced up at the ceiling, scratching the back of her head.

"Ah, but you see," Zodim held up his left index finger. "Most people are generally kind. Those dwarves had an easy choice: leave you to die or help you live. And despite their fear, they made the same choice most of us would make."

"I'm still not sure most people would make that choice," replied Castora. She swept some stray hairs away from her face and stood up.

"Are you hungry?" the gnome asked, motioning towards the door.

She considered the question. Though she didn't really feel hungry, she figured it had been more than a day since she last ate.

"I think I could eat something light. I'm hoping there's a bit more room outside that door though."

Zodim smirked, pulling open the door and motioning for her to step through. "After you, princess."

Castora pouted, shaking her head as she walked through the doorway.

She was pleasantly surprised as she walked into this next room, gazing up at the large ceiling with exposed wood beams. Aside from the height of the room, the area was clearly larger as well, but as she looked around, Castora still felt a touch of claustrophobia. The room was bursting with clutter. So much so that the hájje felt too overwhelmed to even process what all of it was.

There were crates, barrels, tables, chairs, more candelabras than any one person should ever need -and that was just what she saw immediately to her right. As she scooted through the clutter, she spotted another gnome standing before a wood-burning stove at the center of the room.

He was a few centimeters taller than Zodim, and a few centimeters thinner around the waist. His skin was weathered and wrinkled, and a full shade lighter than Zodim's. He wore an unusual white coat and matching pointed hat. And his nose poked out like the beak of a goose.

But what was lacking on his person was most peculiar to Castora. His face was clean shaven, no sign of facial hair. And by the lack of visible hair atop his head, it seemed he was completely bald. As the dark elf looked down at the gnome's feet, which were far too hairy and large for a creature of his size, she immediately looked away.

This shift in focus made her aware of another unusual mystery. She had ignored the faint clicking and hissing, but looking to the left of the room, she found herself in awe of the source. There along the wall, past some more piles of clutter, there was a cleared area along with a long worktable.

Beyond this table, the wall was lined with copper tubing and large steel canisters. There were various other machines placed along the wall, as well as some large glass containers with liquids of various color shades. At the far end of the strange contraption, a clear liquid was left dripping from a final pipe into a large, round-bottomed flask.

If Zodim hadn't already convinced her, it would be easy to recognize now that gnomes were much less feral than she had been taught growing up. As for the purpose of this strange machine, she couldn't even begin to fathom.

"Ah, I am delighted to see you've awoken," said the gnome with a low bow, confirming Castora's suspicion as he removed his hat and revealed his shiny, round head. Standing back at full height, he replaced the hat on his head and motioned towards a kettle on the stove.

"Would milady care for a cup of tea?" he asked.

Castora glanced over at Zodim, who had stepped just to her right. Seeing his smiling face reassured her, and she turned back to the other gnome, forcing a smile of her own.

"I would, thank you," she said as softly as she could manage. "Am I to take it that you are Medicus?"

"Ah, if you would milady. It's Doctor Medicus, or just Doctor if you must shorten it."

Again, the gnome took her by surprise as he smiled a toothy grin, revealing the most extraordinarily white teeth she had ever seen. She grinned and nodded in response, pulling her head away and blinking a few times.

"I will remember that, Doctor Medicus."

"Ah, there it is. And it sounds much better when you say it, wouldn't you say so Zodim, old chap?" The Doctor held his head high.

Zodim looked up at Castora, catching her gaze as he shrugged. "If you say so."

"I do! And you know what else I say," Medicus grabbed a thick towel, using it to protect his left hand as he grabbed the kettle. "We should all enjoy this beautiful morning outside. Let's see." He stood for a moment, pivoting left and right.

"Umm, here we go." He stepped over to a round table less than a meter away, brushing off the contents and depositing the kettle and towel. "Lady Castora, would you grab those cups over there?" he pointed behind the dark elf.

"And Master Zodim, if you would take the kettle?"

Castora turned around, looking at the three different tables around where Medicus pointed. One of them was tall enough to be used by hájje or other full-height species. Two of them were gnome-sized and had various cups strewn about. But the one on the left looked to have the perfect teacups.

Like most gnome implements, they seemed rather small for what she was used to. But as she inspected a stack of four tan ceramic cups, she couldn't help but admire the craftsmanship. They appeared nearly identical in their dimensions, with leafing etched around the rim of each cup.

Taking the cups, she spun around and followed Zodim towards the front door. She turned sideways, cinching her way through the narrow walkway. Perhaps they weren't feral, but Castora couldn't help but wonder if all gnomes weren't disorganized hoarders.

But as she stepped through the round door and took a breath of the morning spring air, she felt the tension leave her shoulders. She paused just outside the doorway, looking out upon the rolling green hills and down to the forest below. Sunlight was just trickling through the peaks of the mountains to the northeast, the cool morning air refreshing on her skin.

Sniffing lavender in the air, she looked to the east and beheld a great field of it. Continuing to take in her surroundings, she noticed fields sown with all manner of different herbs and flowers. She had to pause as she moved her gaze back west, just barely catching a glimpse of some gnomes working in the fields - they were only visible due to their signature hats.

Stepping away from the door, she looked back to consider the house itself. It was unlike any structure she had seen before, the dome structure built right onto the hillside.

From the looks of it, the location was chosen due to the massive stone jutting up from the site. The massive rock was lodged into the top of the hill, tilted out at a forty-five-degree angle (or thereabouts). It appeared someone had dug out much of the ground beneath this rock and built-up framing to ensure it remained stable. With thick walls for dirt on the sides and raw tree trunks supporting the front.

Aside from the rounded doorway, there were round windows to either side. Of course, both windows were blocked with junk on the inside, which seemed to defeat their purpose.

Zodim made his way to the east of the structure. As Castora ascended the hill to follow him, she caught sight of the outdoor seating Medicus had alluded to. Like much of the structure and contents inside, it appeared the table and chairs were built for gnomes.

The chairs were simply large chunks of tree, cut into short cylinders. The table appeared to be crafted from some thicker logs, cut in two and stacked up next to one another. Despite their raw appearance, the tabletop itself looked to be perfectly smooth. In total, it offered seating for twelve.

Zodim placed the kettle down in the center of the table, smirking at Castora as she climbed to the top. Arriving at the table, she separated the cups and spread them around the kettle.

"Is something amusing?" she asked.

"I'm just wondering what it must be like for you. How does this compare to what you grew up with? And, what about the stories you were taught. Is the world outside Hájjeona as bad as you imagined?"

The dark elf gazed north towards the Jyrimoore mountains, breathing in the gorgeous view. Her hair whispered in the wind, a cool westerly breeze blowing through. She hadn't even realized the wide smile forming on her face as she considered the questions.

"From where I'm standing now," she replied looking down at Zodim. "The world is much more beautiful than I could have imagined. Though, when it comes to the gnomes, I've yet to see how much fruit the tree bares."

Zodim chuckled.

"Why don't you go back and see if Medicus needs a hand with the breakfast?" He glanced up and started pouring the tea into the first cup.

"Hmph," Castora brushed her bangs away from her eyes and started back down the hill. Even with her slow descent, she felt a dull pain in her stab wound. And it faded away quickly as she made it back down to the doorway of the burrow.

As she approached, a soft knock from inside the door stopped her a few meters away. The next moment, Medicus burst through the doorway with a large round platter held overhead. He looked unsteady, wobbling as he stomped outside and swaying in the breeze. Castora let out a gasp, rushing over and grabbing hold of the tray. She lifted it up, holding it in her right hand.

"I can take that for you," she said. The savory smells wafted into her nose. She licked her lips in anticipation, the combination of pork, eggs, and herbs causing her stomach to rumble. Perhaps she was hungrier than she thought.

"Thank you!" exclaimed Medicus with a smile. "I think it'll just be the three of us, so let's dig in!"

He looked like a rabbit running from a fox, bounding recklessly up the hillside. Considering the tray of food, Castora took her time.

She still felt a bit weak, and after all the climbing and hiking from the previous days, her legs burned as she ascended. But after reaching the table, she placed the platter down next to the teacups and regarded the food, which was neatly organized on three different plates.

"Should we?" she started, but Medicus grabbed his plate and plopped down in a middle chair. Zodim, who was on the other side of the table, also reached out and grabbed a plate and utensils. "I guess so," she finished.

"Please, have a seat," Medicus motioned for the stump next to his own.

Castora took the remaining plate from the platter. Placing the last knife and fork on her plate, she moved the platter to the side and sat down. She hesitated for a moment and then grabbed one of the filled teacups.

"Wonderful!" exclaimed Medicus. "Zodim, if you would start off our prayer please."

Zodim nodded and bowed his head.

"May this meal nourish us and may our hearts look ever towards your glory. Please Evorath, extend your blessings on us today and every day."

"Yes!" Medicus slapped the table. "And thank you for this unexpected reunion with a dear old friend and this introduction to a new one."

Castora picked up her utensils, ready to dig in. Medicus cleared his throat obnoxiously, giving her pause. Both he and Zodim were looking at her expectantly. She looked between the two, put her utensils down, and bowed her head.

"And thank you for my return to health?" she bit her top lips, looking between the gnomes for approval.

Both returned a wide smile and picked up their utensils.

"Amen!" they said in unison.

"Amen," the hájje whispered. She felt a tingling in the back of her head. Waiting a few moments before starting on her plate, she watched Zodim take his first bite of the eggs and then picked up her knife and fork, listening as she cut away at the thick cut.

"How is your side feeling?" Medicus mumbled, his mouth full of food.

"It's the best I've felt since being stabbed. And my arm isn't really bothering me either." She glanced at the white bandage around her arm. Come to think of it, she realized it hadn't really itched her at all this morning.

"Excellent!" Medicus coughed, spraying small specs of food into the air. Castora bit her tongue, closing her eyes and breathing deliberately. She was grateful that this gnome had helped patch her up, but that didn't stop her from some fleeting thoughts of violence.

With a quick look at both gnomes, Castora skewered a bit of egg and pork, taking her first bite of the food. Her eyes shot open wide as she chewed, the aromatic flavor of the pork unlike any she had eaten before. It was tender and juicy, and the soft and fluffy eggs were cooked to perfection. She felt like it was her first time eating pork and eggs.

"You like it?" Medicus asked, leaning in a bit too close.

"Yes, thank you," Castora leaned away, holding her hand over her mouth as she chewed.

"I have to admit Doc," Zodim held out his fork, a piece of pork hanging off the end. "This is the best breakfast I've had in a while. You always knew how to cook!"

Medicus sat back in his chair and shrugged.

"I hope you'll stick around long enough to have it again tomorrow. Which reminds me," he said stuffing his face with another fork full of food. "You never finished telling me where you are headed after this."

Castora stopped with her fork just centimeters from her mouth and glared at Zodim. She wasn't sure if she could handle eating too many more meals with such a messy eater. And she hoped her expression conveyed that uncertainty.

"I'm not so sure if we'll stay the night," said Zodim after he finished chewing. "I was thinking I'd show Castora around the grounds after breakfast, and we'd discuss from there."

"You'll show her around?" Medicus burped. "I wouldn't have it!" he skewered another lump of food, stuffing it in his mouth before continuing. "I'll show you both around. After all, things have changed a lot in the years since you've been here. But what's the hurry for?"

Castora scooted to the far edge of her chair, leaning back to avoid the spray of food.

"Oh, I don't know if we're in a real hurry per se," replied Zodim. The dark elf continued eating, keeping an eye on Medicus through her peripherals.

"Then forget about leaving before tomorrow. Y'all are welcome to stay for as long as you'd like!"

"No, we wouldn't want to burden you." Zodim shook his head. "In fact, we're on a somewhat urgent mission to Marftaport. But I suppose I ought not put off telling you about it any longer."

Zodim placed his fork down beside his plate, taking a sip of his tea before glancing skyward. He held his left hand over his face, tapping his index finger on his nose.

"It can't be all that serious, can it?" Medicus cleared his throat, putting down his utensils leaning in towards Zodim.

Without the threat of a food shower, Castora leaned forward, trying to eat as quickly as she could.

"I guess the easiest place to start," said Zodim looking directly at Medicus. "Yezurkstal is back."

Medicus winced at the name. He looked down at his plate and picked up his fork, taking a few pokes. "Well, suddenly I don't feel all that hungry," he muttered.

Suddenly, Castora felt like someone was driving a peg into her skull. She gasped, dropping her fork, and clutching the sides of her head as the sharp pain persisted. With eyes shut tight, she pushed away from the table, crying out and falling to her knees beside the table.

With a ringing in her ears, she saw a faint figure forming in her mind. She was horrified to recognize as the figure formed a face -it was her father.

Jet black hair slicked back over his pale white skin. His right eye looked directly at her, the dark black void threatening to consume her whole. The arrow scar on his left eye was left raw and exposed, his weathered face and pointed nose peering directly into her soul.

Her hair stood on end as he spoke, his words like the bite of a viper. "I can feel you are alive my daughter. Why do you not return to your home?"

She could feel him trying to assert himself, attempting to enter her mind. Fighting to keep him out, she screamed, but knew she couldn't maintain it. Just before she fell unconscious, she muttered.

"Help me."

CHAPTER VI

Medicus's Burrow
27 Julla, 1149 MT

Zodim gasped, jerking up from his chair and leaping over the table.

"Is this the medicine?" he asked. He knelt beside Castora and clasped her hand. She felt cold and clammy, like he was grasping a fish to pull up from the stream.

"I can't imagine how!" exclaimed Medicus, standing up from his chair deliberately and stepping over to the unconscious hájje. Lifting her other arm, he placed his index and middle finger on her wrist and closed his eyes.

"Her heart is still going strong." He pulled off his cap and scratched his bald head. "Very odd really."

"How can you tell her heart is strong?" Zodim looked at Medicus with narrowed eyes.

"Not important right now," replied the doctor. He stood back up, looking down at the fallen hájje and humming as he tapped his foot.

"Well, what should we do?" asked Zodim impatiently.

Medicus jumped, stomping on the ground a few times as he shouted: "Wake up!"

Zodim jerked back, his eyes wide.

"Well, you got my heart pounding, but how is that supposed to help her?"

"Let's see," Medicus glanced back at the table. "This should do!" he said, reaching down and grabbing the empty teacup. He looked it over for a moment and shrugged.

Without explaining, he bent over Castora, placing the cup top down on her left breast. He then leaned in and put his ear up against the cup.

"What in Evorath's name are you doing?" Zodim held his arms out to the side, looking down with concern.

"Shh! I'm trying to listen."

Medicus kept his head pressed against the cup for a few seconds. At that point, he took a sharp inhale through his teeth and stood back up. He placed the cup down gently on the table and looked between his burrow and Zodim.

"You stay here and keep trying to rouse her. I must get my listener from inside. If she was a gnome, I'd be worried about her pale skin, but that's how she's looked since you arrived. I imagine her heart works the same as ours though."

"Wait!" objected Zodim, grabbing a hold of Medicus's arm. "What could be wrong with her now?"

Medicus shrugged and pulled away.

"I have no idea yet. Just do as I said, and I'll be back in a minute. I'll figure it out."

Medicus took off with a start, barreling down the hill like a hen fleeing an overzealous rooster.

Zodim considered Castora. She was sprawled out on the hilltop, her face pressed against her right arm. Her stab wound was sitting right on the dirt.

"Well, I better at least move her," muttered the gnome, stepping around. He paused as he placed his hands on the dark elf's side, looking over and reconsidering whether there was enough room. The last thing he needed was to roll her down the hill by accident.

He gave her a nudge, pushing her over to her back. Her left arm swung around, hanging down over the hillside. But she stayed put.

Too nervous to simply wait around, Zodim began pacing back and forth on the hilltop. He hadn't even known this hájje for a full week, and here he was on the verge of panic over her wellbeing. But this couldn't be it.

Plopping down on the chair where Castora had been seated, he steepled his fingers and stared down at her. What would Sora do?

"Tell me to relax and wait for Medicus I imagine."

He shook his head, closed his eyes, and focused on relaxing his breath.

"Like a unicorn!" came Medicus's voice from below. Zodim jumped up, glancing down at the doctor rushing up the hill. His legs were moving like a rabbit, a metallic horn-shaped object held up over his head as he climbed.

"It's not just any doctor, it's Medicus!"

The doctor exclaimed as he bounded to the top. He took a deep breath, holding his knees for a few seconds to regain his composure.

"Perhaps you wouldn't be so winded if you weren't yelling like a fool," suggested Zodim.

"That wouldn't be any fun," replied Medicus between breaths. "Now let's have a listen."

He tapped the metallic horn and walked over to Castora.

"Please, stay perfectly quiet," he instructed. He bent over, placing the wide end of the horn on Castora's chest and putting his ear up to the narrow end.

Zodim waited with anticipation, fiddling his thumbs as he watched. It felt like time dragged on for hours, even though it couldn't have been more than a minute or so. At that point, Medicus sat back up, lowering the horn to his side, and placing his hands on his hips as he looked skyward.

"What could that be about?" he wondered aloud.

"What could what? Is she alright?"

"Oh, yes! From what I can tell, she seems to just be sleeping." Medicus shrugged.

"You saw what I saw! How can she just be sleeping?" Zodim stomped his feet.

"I'm a doctor, not a druid. If I were to guess, whatever is plaguing her is supernatural. Perhaps this will do."

Medicus walked over to the table and picked up the tea kettle. He held it up and stuck his hand inside. After a few seconds, he pulled it out with a nod.

"Yes, this should work if anything will," he murmured.

"What are you?" started Zodim. But before he could complete the sentence, Medicus stepped over to Castora and dumped the kettle on her face.

"By Evorath's grace!" Zodim yanked the kettle out of Medicus's hand, tossing it aside and considering Castora. But the dark elf lay there unmoving.

"Yep, definitely not a medical issue." Said Medicus with a nod. "Maybe you ought to make that journey to Marftaport today after all."

Zodim glared at Medicus, letting out a huff of air.

"You sure there's nothing you can do?"

"Well, I suppose I can try this still." Medicus reached into his left pocket and pulled out a small vial and shaking it a few times. He bent down by Castora's face.

"Wait, what is that?"

"Just some smelling salts. If this doesn't wake her up, nothing will!"

He uncapped the vial, waving it under Castora's nose.

Nothing.

"Alright," he said standing up and shrugging.

"Alright what?" asked Zodim.

"I'd advise embarking on your journey to Marftaport. I can help you grab your bags."

"My bags?" Zodim shouted. "How am I supposed to bring her anywhere myself?"

"Who said anything about going alone?" Medicus considered his listening horn, setting it on the table.

"You just informed me that Death has returned to Erathal. It's my duty as a doctor, a preserver of life, to do what I can. I'll get one of my nurses to prepare a wagon for you. And we can help you get her loaded."

"Are you coming along then?" asked Zodim, tilting his head to the right.

"I'm tempted, but no." Medicus said starting down the hill. "I need to get the word out that Death has returned!"

As his old friend descended the hill, Zodim plopped down beside Castora. She looked so peaceful.

Looking up at the sky and shaking his head, he cried out to the heavens.

"Evorath, why me?"

CHAPTER VII

Marftaport, Jaldor's Farm
28 Julla, 1149 MT

The air before dawn was cool and refreshing, a soft morning breeze blowing across the open pasture. Smells of spring blossoms mixed with heavy humidity suggested rain was imminent. The sun had yet to rise over the horizon, offering only the faint light of dawn to reveal his way.

Jaldor crouched, keeping his right foot planted to brace himself. Samson charged, leaping towards the farmer.

"Oof," Jaldor embraced the near 80-kilo Jyrimoore mastiff. He held on tight, squeezing the dog as he swayed side-to-side. Rocking with his eyes closed, he held on for a few seconds and considered recent events.

"Oh, I still miss her too," whispered Jaldor. As he pulled away, Samson dropped back to all fours, his tail wagging like a hummingbird.

"No time to play today," said Jaldor, patting Samson on the head. "I've got to get the milking done quickly."

He knew Samson couldn't really understand him, but the way the dog begged, it sometimes felt like he did.

"Alright, come on boy," he waved, continuing south towards the barn. Though he was adapting well to his new home in Marftaport, Jaldor was still in disbelief at the beauty and scale of his new barn.

Though the property itself was fully fenced, he had the barn surrounded by an additional fence of its own. Like the main property fence, this one offered a rustic post and beam design to keep predators out and the cows in. The benefits of which were apparent as he approached. Fluffy was already out of the barn, munching on a pile of hay within the fence.

The barn itself was built with a combination of cedar and hemlock. Measuring about ten meters wide by twenty meters long, the front face featured a single large bay entrance with a pair of sliding barn doors. On the long side, there were a half dozen smaller bay entrances with hinged doors, spaced symmetrically to allow for easy access from any point.

The vertical footprint of the barn was massive as well. There was a ladder to the right of the main barn entrance, leading up to an exterior loft entrance. Inside, there were two additional ladders to climb up to the loft. The roof was a simple a-frame design with thatching for rain cover. And there was a gable on the long, south-facing side.

Arriving at the fence, Jaldor unlatched the gate, allowing Samson to trot inside before shutting it. The familiar smell of composting hay greeted him as he proceeded around the side to the nearest bay entrance. Seeing his arrival, Fluffy looked up from her hay and meandered in after him.

Once inside, Jaldor proceeded to the torch just inside the doorway. With only a couple strikes of the flint, he ignited it, the oil-soaked cloth quickly igniting. Reaching into the small pail on the floor, he grabbed a small candle, using it to take light from the torch.

With the happy moos of his herd greeting him as he walked, he made his way around the barn and lit the other needed torches. At this point, he found the cows all congregated in this first section, which meant two torches to the north and south walls and two more in the center posts of the room.

After illuminating the area, he proceeded towards the milking stanchions. Brought from his farm in Paxvilla, these two trusty old stanchions were constructed of solid oak and placed against the northern wall. Individual feeding troughs were placed before each stanchion and covered with a hinged lid. Opening both lids, the cows made the next part easy.

Fluffy, always eager to start the day, walked right into the stanchion on the right, allowing Jaldor to lower the bar and lock her in place. Ruth, who was named for his mother, was next to step up, taking her place in the left stanchion and allowing Jaldor to lock her in. She had a thinner coat than fluffy, but a similar brown fur and pleasant disposition.

Jaldor glanced back at Samson, who was still wagging his tail expectantly. "They'll be joining us soon. Maybe you can have a talk with Mary about her attitude this morning."

With a shrug, Jaldor proceeded to the east wall and grabbed one of the buckets from the stack. Sitting down beside Fluffy, he put the bucket under and began milking. Starting out the day alone was more peaceful than he was used to, but as he filled the bucket with milk, he found himself missing the normal morning banter with Mary and Samantha.

Fortunately, as he finished up with Fluffy and released her from the stand, he heard the unmistakable creak of a bay door. He glanced back, smiling towards his wife and daughter.

Mary's eyes were still red from her morning tantrum and her brown hair was disheveled, but Samantha had at least gotten her to put on her yellow dress and boots. Despite having to deal with an angry child, Samantha appeared as prepared as ever. She wore a simple brown dress and matching boots, and her hair was pulled back into a perfect milking braid.

"Just in time!" Jaldor exclaimed. "I just finished with Fluffy, so the first bucket is ready for you Sam."

He grabbed the full bucket of milk, setting it beside the stanchion. He then proceeded to pat Fluffy on the head, encouraging her to leave the now empty feeder and move along. With a huff, the small cow backed out of the stanchion and meandered towards the large barn door.

While Samantha took the full bucket outside, Jaldor went to retrieve the second bucket.

"You ready to get them their food sweety?" he put the bucket under Ruth, crouching down and patting Mary on the top of her head.

"No, uhm," Mary clasped her hands behind her back, rocking nervously. "Mommy said I should apologize first. Sorry for not being nice."

Jaldor chuckled and shook his head. He knelt down, taking his daughter's hand and smiling at her.

"Thank you for apologizing. I forgive you Mary. Now, let's get this day started off right. The cows are hungry!"

Mary giggled through the gap in her two front teeth and nodded enthusiastically.

"I'll bring the food!" she ran over to the nearby ladder, climbing up to the loft. And so, the milking proceeded as normal.

Jaldor milked a cow. Samantha gathered the milk in a cart outside, and Mary refilled the grain. Though they had perfected this system at their farm in Paxvilla, the larger size of this barn had really helped them streamline the process. And in just under two hours he was finishing up with the final cow.

"Yes, go on inside," came the faint voice of his wife.

Placing down the final bucket and releasing the final cow, Jaldor stepped aside and wiped his hands together, looking expectantly towards the open bay door. George Peterson strode into the barn. Dressed in his usual blue robes and wide-brimmed, pointy hat, he walked with his gnarled staff.

"Good morning, Jaldor!" the wizard exclaimed with a wave. "I hope I'm not too early."

"Good morning, George," the farmer replied, walking over, and shaking the wizard's hand.

"Is everything still working out for you here? You haven't had any more trouble with the cheese cave I hope?"

Jaldor nodded, smiling at his wife as she picked up the last bucket and brought it back outside. He started towards the large barn door, glancing back at George as he walked.

"Yes, I think we're all getting better settled in. In fact, my father has more energy than I've seen him have in years. As for the cheese cave, I think we got the hang of it now. It's amazing how much easier it is to maintain the right environmental conditions using those runestones."

"Hah! You're not kidding! I bet Alset's runestones will be all over Evorath within the next century. Sarah was saying he's experimenting with a stone now to replace woodburning stoves. Can you imagine the possibilities of that?"

As he reached the doors, Jaldor undid the latch and grabbed hold of the right handle.

"I really can't," he admitted, looking back at George. "You mind pulling that one?" he asked, pointing to the other.

"Of course!" The wizard proceeded to tug on the left door, sliding it away. Jaldor pulled his door open as well, allowing the barn to fill with morning light.

"Excuse me," came the soft voice of Mary. Jaldor looked towards the source. She had approached George and was tugging on the base of his robes.

"Yes, Mary?" George smiled at the girl.

"Are you taking my daddy away again?" she asked sheepishly, glancing down, and clasping her hands behind her back as she rocked side-to-side.

George sagged his shoulders, frowning towards Jaldor and lowering into a crouch. "I'm afraid I am. But you know, your daddy and I are doing this to help people, right?"

"I know." She sighed, shrugged her shoulders. "I just miss making cheese with daddy."

Jaldor's heart melted as he stepped over and offered Mary his hand. He looked into her eyes, imagining how the world must have seemed so different to her. George stood up, taking a couple steps away from the two.

"I miss that too bumble bee," said Jaldor softly. "And I won't have to make these trips much longer. But you know how daddy told you about all the people who were hurt last week?"

Mary nodded, a frown on her face.

"Well, they still need daddy's help. And as much as I'd love to be with you, what do we do when there are people in need?"

Mary glanced down, shuffling her feet as if tracing out an image on the ground. After a few seconds of fidgeting, she looked back at Jaldor and sheepishly said, "we help them."

"That's right," Jaldor gave Mary a light pat on the head and looked back to George. "But I think Miss Sarah is bringing Elizabeth and Henry by for you to play later."

George nodded, so Jaldor continued.

"That should be fun, shouldn't it?"

Mary's face lit up, her eyes glistening as she nodded.

"Yes, I like them!"

Jaldor offered a slight nod to George, motioning towards his daughter.

"They like you too," George said assuredly.

"OK, I'll go tell mommy I need to get ready!" Mary took off, dashing south through the bay door.

With a sigh, Jaldor turned back to George.

"I must retrieve the cheese we're bringing. Want to discuss the plan while I do?"

George nodded, starting out through the large barn doors. Jaldor followed behind, his larger stride allowing him to quickly overtake the wizard. Samantha had already opened the paddock gate, leaving just a few cows inside munching on hay.

As they made their way through the gates and started south towards the cheese cave, Jaldor glanced back at George.

"Who all have you already sent?" he asked.

George glanced skyward with pursed lips, rubbing his chin, and bobbing his head side-to-side.

"A lot of the usual suspects. Various members of the Hunters and Mages Guilds. Irontail organized some centaurs again who are helping sort through the wall rubble. Perhaps the most interesting is Tel' Shira. So naturally Vistoro and the barghest brothers went along with her."

Jaldor raised his eyebrows and scratched the back of his head. "I don't mean any disrespect, but what does she intend to do there?"

George shrugged.

"She insisted that she talk with the Paxvilla regent. I can't say what about. Vistoro still has this fanciful notion that they'll get him to step down and turn Paxvilla into a free city. But I don't think Tel' Shira is buying into that. But she seemed quite pensive this morning, even more so than usual."

"You think she had another vision about Paxvilla? I hope the hájje don't go back to finish the job." Jaldor clenched his fists thinking about it.

"Oh Evorath, I sure hope not!" exclaimed George. "But you're probably right about it being vision related."

"Do you still want me playing diplomat?" Jaldor asked.

George chuckled and shook his head.

"Are you playing? I think you've proven yourself to be a fine diplomat. And I think you'll get the chance to exercise those muscles some more today. But like we discussed yesterday, our main goal is just to go back and make sure all the people have food, water, and shelter."

"That's good. I'm much better at that," said Jaldor as they approached the cheese cave.

"I'm just glad I had a nice breakfast. Just seeing that cave of yours is making me hungry," joked George.

With a shake of his head, Jaldor stopped before the door to the cave. After digging out the cavern in the earth, they had used some of the hemlock lumber to frame out a square entryway. Unlatching the door, the farmer stepped inside the brisk, damp air of the cave.

"I always forget how cool it is in here," uttered George, shivering as he stepped in behind Jaldor and shut the door.

"You can wait outside," replied Jaldor.

Not waiting for George's response, he descended into the cave. All three walls were mounted with shelves of three different heights and many of these shelves were already filled up with wheels of cheese.

In the center of the room was the worktable. This long rectangular table had a bottom shelf for holding all the essential materials and the top was where they did the waxing and finishing of the various cheeses.

As per his mother's organization system, the wheels along the left wall were the most mature, with the ones on the top shelf being the youngest and those on the bottom the oldest. However, they had added a secondary table between the main one and the left wall, which they would stock each night with ready cheese.

Proceeding to this table, Jaldor collected the near dozen cheeses and loaded them into a crate beside the table. He crouched down and lifted the crate with a grunt. Pausing to check his balance, he proceeded back outside, where George was waiting for him.

"You ready to go?" the wizard asked with a smile.

"Yes," Jaldor nodded, straining to hold the heavy crate.

"Then, let's not keep them waiting."

George turned south and held up his staff.

"Ixidor!"

The familiar outline of a portal appeared, the blue pulsing energy circling around before the duo.

"After you," George motioned towards the portal.

Jaldor nodded, straining as he stepped through to the other side. While he had gotten a little more accustomed to this sort of travel, the thing that always caused him trouble was the change of smells. Suddenly, as he left his farm and stepped foot back in Paxvilla, the familiar smells of cows was replaced with burning wood and other unpleasant odors left from the battle.

He felt a bit dizzy, perhaps enhanced by the strain of going through the portal. And as George stepped through and the portal closed shut behind, his strain must have been apparent.

"Oh, let me try something I've been practicing!" George lit up and pointed his staff towards the crate of cheese. "Perhaps you should put it down," the wizard hesitated.

Jaldor was more than happy to comply, kneeling down and placing the crate on the grass at his feet. Taking a step back, the farmer stretched his neck and glanced down at the crate.

George held up his staff, pointing it at the crate again.

"Featherize!" he exclaimed.

As far as Jaldor could see, nothing happened, but George stood with a wide smile on his face and nodded towards the crate. "Go on, lift it now. But be careful! It's lighter than it looks."

With an arched eyebrow, Jaldor crouched down again, bracing himself for the heavy weight. But as recommended, he lifted with more care.

"That is amazing!" he exclaimed, able to rise from his squat with almost no resistance. He smiled, holding up the crate higher and examining it on all sides. "I don't know about light as a feather, but this is much lighter. That won't interfere with the cheese, will it?"

"Naw" George waved his hand dismissively. "If it worked right, the cheese is just as heavy as before. It's the crate that's got some magical qualities. But I'm afraid it will only last for an hour, tops."

"Well, perhaps I can hire you to help transport my cheese more often. This could save my back a lot of strain. Thank you."

"You're welcome!" George smiled.

"Well, shall we proceed?" Jaldor asked, glancing north towards Paxvilla and the workers along the wall.

"We shall!" George declared.

And turning to follow the wizard, Jaldor was certain the tides had turned. Today would be a good day.

Chapter VIII

Artimus Jr. leaned back, pushing against the wall and balancing on the back two legs of his chair. He glanced down at his right hand, palm facing away as he inspected his fingernails. With a long sigh, he dropped back to all four, stood up, and stretched out his neck.

Guard duty was never what he would consider fun work, but since the events in Paxvilla he was finding it that much more taxing. He didn't like being alone with his thoughts because they inevitably would lead back to only one place. And despite Mojo's last words, every time he closed his eyes, Artimus Jr. saw the lifeless body of his friend and mentor.

Even thinking of it caused him pain, closing his eyes to try and hold back fresh tears. Covering his face with both hands, the elf moaned and rubbed his eyes. With another sigh, he glanced back down to the runestones lining the tower wall.

Each of the guard towers had recently been outfitted with the latest and greatest from Alset. These runestones were made in pairs, with one being placed in a tree by the road and the corresponding stone sitting in the tower wall. When anyone passed the paired stone on the road, the one in the wall would light up and hum, offering a warning system without requiring the guard on watch to have his or her eyes glued to the road.

Often, this meant Artimus Jr. would bring a book up when he was on guard duty. But he just didn't have the spirit for it since the battle of Paxvilla. Instead, he glanced down at the road, the fleeting idea of jumping a real consideration.

With a loud sigh, the young elf sat back in his seat. As he did, the stone for the main road lit up, emitting a subtle hum.

"Probably just an animal," he muttered to himself. He waited a minute, struggling to muster up the will to stand and look. Eventually, the possibility of it being a real threat motivated him, driving him to stand and gaze down at the main road.

He squinted his eyes towards the tree line, the faint shape of something just coming through.

"Who is that?"

He leaned forward, blinking a few times to try and improve his focus. The whole cart looked a bit too small, but the driver even more so.

"Is that a gnome?" he wondered aloud.

Sure enough, as the cart drew nearer, his elvish eyes were keen enough to make out the coachman. It was a gnome. With a long grey beard and pointed green hat and matching tunic. He looked to be approaching fast, which was alarming enough.

But as Artimus Jr. adjusted his gaze towards the back of the wagon, his eyes almost bulged out of his head.

Without a thought, the elvish guard reached up and pulled the rope. The clang of brass rang out from the watchtower. He squeezed the rope tight, giving it a few more rings.

Not willing to leave anything to chance, he ran back and grabbed his quiver and bow. He placed the quiver down along the wall, notching an arrow and looking back at the hájje in the back of the wagon.

As the wagon drew closer, he realized this wasn't just any hájje. And his heart skipped a beat, his aim faltering as he recognized the beautiful, terrible face of the dark elf lying there.

It was Mojo's killer, the commander of the hájje army.

His knees felt weak. He braced himself against the tower wall, lowering his bow and taking a deep breath. After collecting himself, he squinted back down at the pair.

Was she dead?

Whatever the case, staying up here wouldn't help anything. He slung the bow over his back, strapping on the quiver and grabbing hold of the escape rope tied to the northeast corner. Releasing a loud sigh, he leapt over the edge, sliding down the rope to the base of the tower.

The rope burned his hands, his haste causing him to descend quicker than intended. But he crouched down on landing, shaking out his hands and jogging towards the road.

"What's the bell for?" came an agitated voice from behind.

Glaring back at Luna Freya, he shook his head.

The black-furred felite dashed up beside him, stretching out her arms in stride. As she caught Artimus Jr.'s gaze, her expression softened, her greenish-yellow eyes sagging. She cleared her throat, looking towards the wagon.

"Is that a gnome?" Luna asked.

"I'm more interested in the person lying in the back of the wagon," replied the elf. "It's the hájje commander."

Luna jerked back, looking down at Artimus Jr. with a look of disbelief. She turned back east, cracking her knuckles as she stretched her head side-to-side.

"In that case, you can leave it to me." Luna's eyes narrowed, adopting a severe expression as she assumed a wide stance. She stood like a statue, her fists clenched by her side, chest puffed out and shoulders pulled back.

"I don't think all that's necessary," Artimus Jr. muttered. "The hájje appears to be unconscious."

"Better not to take any chances," she didn't move a centimeter, her eyes trained on the wagon.

The driver of the wagon slowed his approach as he drew near. The creaking of the wheels growing quiet as the dust settled down and he came to a gradual stop about ten meters from Luna Freya's position. Artimus Jr. drew his bow, but kept it by his side as he stepped forward.

"State your business here," he bellowed.

The old gnome stood up, stepping down from the wagon and walking past the horses. He held his hands up beside his head, palms open.

"I look to speak with someone from the mage's guild about an urgent matter," spoke the gnome, his deep voice wizened and gruff.

"And what about your friend in the back?" questioned Luna, pointing towards the wagon.

The gnome glanced back, lowering his hands to chest level. His face twitched as he turned back.

"She is harmless, I assure you."

"Not the last time I encountered her," Artimus Jr. quipped, his voice cracking. He took a sharp inhale through his nose, glancing down as he cleared his throat.

"Oh my," the gnome's voice trailed off, a frown forming on his face as his gaze drifted down. After a moment, he looked up and locked eyes with the elf.

"I'm sure that's true. Please, allow me to start over." The gnome was quite animated, moving his hands as he spoke. "My name is Zodim, gnome artificer and friend to Marftaport. I've brought this hájje because I believe she has invaluable information that concerns us all. And I assure you that in her current state, despite the atrocities she has committed, that she is quite harmless indeed."

He finished wagging his left hand, index finger extended.

Artimus Jr. glanced at Luna, exchanging a look of acknowledgement. Having grown up and trained together for six decades, they had come to understand one another's expressions well enough.

"You say you are a friend to Marftaport, but I do not recall your name. Is there someone here who might vouch for your good will?" Artimus Jr. asked.

"Zodim! By Kelgen's beard is that you?"

Artimus Jr. swung around towards the origins of the gravelly voice. As he guessed, it was none other than the dwarf, Keldor. The master blacksmith's voice was excited, his boisterous energy softening his husky timbre. He wore his usual smithing attire, including the thick black apron. At his waist, he had a belt with various sized hammers and other tools.

Setting down the empty crate, the dwarf tugged at his fiery red and grey beard and rushed to the gnome.

"Keldor!" The gnome smiled and spread his arms wide as Keldor rushed in and lifted him up in a hearty embrace.

Exchanging another glance with Luna, Artimus Jr. shrugged before turning his attention back to the wagon.

"I suspect Keldor can vouch for me," uttered Zodim, his voice strained.

Keldor set the gnome down, glancing up at Artimus Jr. with a wide grin.

"Aye, I can vouch for this little troublemaker," Keldor clapped the gnome on the back. "It's been far too long since I've last seen him though, so maybe we ought to interrogate him to be sure about it."

The duo laughed and Zodim shook his head.

"I hope you're only joking!" he chuckled.

"Of course! But what -by Evorath's majestic braids, what do you have in your wagon?" Keldor gaped, running up alongside the wagon and poking the unconscious hájje.

"Oh, please don't," objected Zodim. He ran behind Keldor and slapped his hand. "She stumbled into my home in Jyrimoore, battered and bleeding. And skipping the journey, there's something wrong with her. I can't wake her up."

"Of course there's something wrong with her. She's a hájje for Evorath's sake! Why would you want to wake her up?" Keldor slapped the side of the wagon.

"Not just any hájje," Artimus Jr. interjected. "She's the hájje who lead the attack on Paxvilla."

Luna Freya yawned loudly, extending her arms out wide and stretching obnoxiously. "Alright then. Artimus, I'm thinking you can handle *The Fairy Princess* and her half-pint grandpas."

She rolled her eyes at Artimus Jr. and marched back towards town, giving a half-hearted wave as she did.

"Hey!" Artimus Jr. called after her. "Fetch mother."

Though Luna made no acknowledgement of the request, the elf expected she would follow through.

"Well, that sounded unkind," muttered Zodim.

"Don't take it personally," replied Keldor.

"Yeah," added Artimus Jr. with a raised eyebrow. "If anything, that means she already likes you."

"I'd hate to hear what she has to say about people she doesn't like. Though, I suppose *The Fairy Princess* comparison isn't too far off." said Zodim.

Artimus Jr. narrowed his eyes and puckered his lips.

"Fairy tales aside," he said. "You mentioned you are looking to meet with a member of the Mage's Guild. Why?"

"I'd like them to wake our princess up."

Artimus Jr. looked at Keldor. Even the dwarf's cheerful demeanor was broken by this statement.

"Zodim, old friend. What could we possibly gain from that? Sounds like we'd all have been better had you left her as you found her." Keldor placed his right hand on Zodim's shoulder, nodding towards the unconscious hájje.

"I'm surprised at that attitude," Zodim carefully removed Keldor's hand from his shoulder. He glanced past the dwarf and addressed Artimus Jr. directly.

"You perhaps, I understand. Were you the one who stabbed her?"

Artimus Jr. nodded.

"Yes, it seemed like the appropriate thing to do after she murdered Mojo."

Zodim gasped, covering his mouth with both hands. "THEE Mojo? The druid and philosopher who co-authored *The Call for Unification*? She mentioned killing a barghest, but that is a tragedy indeed. I'm so sorry."

"She mentioned?" asked Keldor, looking back at Artimus Jr. with wide eyes.

"Yes, she and I travelled much of the way here together. It's a long story, but I assure you, if you help me, she will be a valuable ally."

"A valuable ally?" Artimus Jr. stomped his foot. He squeezed his bow so tight that it hurt.

"I just told you she killed one of the greatest peacemakers of our time and you think she could be an ally? I don't know what rock you've been under, but the hájje just declared war on Erathal. Had the Avatar not joined the fight, they might have wiped out Paxvilla and none of us would be here talking now."

Artimus Jr. nostrils flared. His heart pounded in his chest, his hands shaking with anger. But as he stared into the gnome's steel blue eyes, he could feel that anger melting away.

"I'm sorry," Artimus Jr. said with a sigh. "My anger is not directed at you. But we lost great friends and allies to her army. So, forgive me if I don't see the wisdom in talking with her."

"I must agree with the boy," interjected Keldor. He scrunched his face, scratching at his long beard. "But why don't we start by showing you to the Mage's Guild tower? That couldn't hurt anything, could it Artimus?"

"No, I suppose not. Come on then."

Artimus Jr. spun around, marching west along the stone road. Moving at a snail's pace at first, he waited until he heard the wheels of the wagon turn before increasing his speed.

Glancing back, he saw Keldor had climbed in the wagon with Zodim, and was engaged in conversation. Slinging his bow over his back, the elf turned his attention back ahead.

They passed the inn and after a couple minutes they reached the main road north. Glancing back to make sure they were following, Artimus Jr. started north on the road.

Lost in his thoughts, the elf failed to acknowledge anyone he passed, his eyes locked on the road at his feet. He didn't know how to describe his feelings. It was like bugs were crawling all over his skin and he wanted to cry out for help. But he also wanted to give up, to crawl into a dark hole somewhere and just forget about the world around him.

He was so lost in his thoughts, that by the time they neared the Mage's Guild tower, he almost failed to acknowledge his mother and Ygabb standing just beside the road.

"Junior!" his mother waved her arms.

Coming to an abrupt halt, Artimus Jr. shook his head. He glanced back to see the gnome had brought his wagon to a halt. Keldor hopped off the side of the wagon and helped Zodim climb down after him.

"Well, I'll leave you to discuss it then," said the dwarf, glancing between the mages, Artimus Jr., and Zodim. "Savannah, Ygabb, this is my old friend Zodim. I'd guess Luna Freya already informed you about his passenger."

"She has. Thank you for escorting him this far." Savannah's voice was calm and collected, but Artimus Jr. could tell she was uneasy. The way she tightened her jaw and the focus in her eyes betrayed her unease.

Keldor looked around at the others, offering a nod before retrieving his empty crate from the wagon and starting south on the road.

Zodim stepped up to Savannah and Ygabb, who were standing side-by-side. He offered a slight bow to each in turn.

"Ygabb, Savannah, it is an honor to meet you both. And I understand the passenger I bring is unexpected. But she brings news that you'll want to hear. And I come to offer my help."

"Your help with what?" asked Ygabb.

Though the satyr was usually a firecracker of energy and enthusiasm, Artimus Jr. had noticed her demeanor had hardened since the battle at Paxvilla. If someone like her took things so hard, he couldn't imagine how he'd ever move on.

"I think that's a conversation that should wait until we've revived Castora here. That is her name by the way," said the gnome looking around at the group. His tone sounded almost like he was scolding the others.

"Yes, and we'll discuss that first," replied Savannah. "But before we even consider reviving her, tell us more about how you came to find her."

Zodim held his left hand over his face, tapping his index finger against his nose as he gazed up.

"Well, she found me really. Stumbled into my home a few nights ago on death's doorstep. I patched her up and after she agreed not to kill me, I had the opportunity to talk to her about all manner of things. In fact, she agreed to help me put an end to her people's aggression. But on our way here, she fell into a strange fit. And she has been like this since."

The gnome turned, motioning back towards the hájje in his wagon. Savannah and Ygabb exchanged a glance before the pair proceeded to the wagon. Ygabb climbed into the back, but Savannah was able to look down over the side.

Artimus Jr. watched as his mother and the satyr poked and prodded at the hájje. After a couple minutes, Savannah held her hand over the hájje's forehead, closing her eyes and channeling some green energy.

"I think I can awaken her," she uttered. "But I'm still not convinced I should."

She looked back at Zodim, her eyes narrow and thoughtful. Growing up, Artimus Jr. always considered his mother to be decisive and confident. But right now, seeing her expression waiver, it seemed she was neither.

"I understand your hesitation," replied Zodim. "Because when she first stumbled into my cave, I was tempted to let her die myself. But as a wise woman once wrote, 'Evorath cares not about the terms of your birth or the mistakes of your past. In fact, she often calls on the most unexpected of heroes to do her will.' And if I may say, I believe Miss Castora here is ready to listen to the call of Evorath."

Savannah blushed, her eyes alight from the flattery. Artimus Jr. was pleasantly surprised to hear someone from outside of Marftaport referencing his mother's work.

"I know Keldor vouched for you, but you must know that the safety of Marftaport has to be our top concern," said Savannah after a moment. "So, humor us for a moment if you would. Ygabb, could you?"

The satyr smiled, adjusting her red hat, and rolling up the sleeves on her red robe. She stepped over to Zodim and held out her hands, palms up.

"Please, take my hands," she instructed.

Zodim hesitated for a moment, his hands wavering as he lifted them up to his chest. But with a smile, he reached forward and took Ygabb's hands.

"What do you need me to do?" he asked earnestly.

"Oh, not much," Ygabb smiled. "Just tell me again why you have come here."

"Concisely? I want you to help awaken Castora because I believe she can help us put a stop to the hájje threat. And I wish to help see this threat put to an end once and for all."

"He's telling the truth," Ygabb smirked, pulling her hands away and looking up at Savannah. "Though I think you're leaving something out, aren't you?"

"I am," admitted the gnome immediately. "But it's only because I believe some of the details are best left for Castora to share."

"That's good enough for me," said Savannah.

"So, you're going to help wake her?" asked Artimus Jr., clenching his fists.

"Yes, but before we do, I want to make sure she is secure. "Just in case your truth and hers are different," she finished looking down at Zodim.

"That is wise and fair," Zodim replied.

"Well, I still don't like it!" Artimus Jr. objected. "We should secure her in the dungeon before doing anything."

"You have a dungeon?" Zodim raised his eyebrow and scratched his right ear.

"*We* won't be doing anything," replied Savannah. "But Ygabb and I will bring her down there. Shouldn't you get back to the guard tower Artie?"

"Mother! I don't want to leave you two alone with-"

"First, we can take care of ourselves," interrupted Ygabb. She looked as if she was trying to stand up taller, which made Artimus Jr. smirk.

"And" added Savannah, stepping over and placing a hand on Ygabb's back. "Oogmut is down there interrogating The Albino. So, we have all the backup we'd need should Castora here prove hostile."

Artimus Jr. glanced at Castora in the back of the cart before looking to the other three. He let out a loud sigh and nodded.

"Alright. I should return to the watch tower. But please be careful with her. She's a devious witch."

"We will," his mother replied, offering a reassuring stare.

Taking one last look at the sleeping hájje, Artimus Jr. started back on the road heading south. All he could think about as he walked was how he wished his mother would fail. He wished the hájje would die.

He hated Castora.

CHAPTER IX

Paxvilla
28 Julla, 1149 MT

Zodim followed behind the two mages. He rubbed the tips of his fingers around in a counterclockwise motion, focusing on his footing as he descended the stone staircase. He thought perhaps his excitement was inappropriate for the circumstances, but he couldn't deny the joy of meeting one of his favorite contemporary philosophers.

This nervous excitement was accompanied by an equally strong discomfort. With her writings focused on the sanctity of life and the sovereignty of the individual, it seemed a stark contrast that she would condone -or worse yet participate in- the imprisonment of an individual. Wrestling with this conflict, it occurred to him that perhaps this was the shortcoming of all mortal creatures; no one could live up to their own myth.

Setting aside these ethical considerations, Zodim refocused on the more practical concerns. Savannah and Ygabb had spun together a magical stretcher of sorts, holding Castora up with arcane power. The faint green light of their magic kept the dark elf suspended in the air.

After swearing him to secrecy, the mages had led Zodim down the steps. The stairway was illuminated with small glowing stones, but the steps were just a smidge too deep for his small size. Still, he kept his focus on each step and the mages were moving at a slow enough pace that he could keep up.

As they reached the landing, Zodim glanced around at the cavernous room. There were no decorations about, only more glowing stones lined along the walls. And beyond the landing, past a massive iron door, he saw four distinct jail cells.

"Feels a bit like home down here," he muttered. "Well, aside from the jail cells."

Ygabb chuckled, offering the gnome a friendly smile as they continued through the open iron door. Scurrying to the left of the mages, Zodim tried to get a better view of the inside of the cells. Clearing the iron doorway, he caught sight of Oogmut and pale-skinned human in the back left cell. Aside from these two, the rest of the room was barren as the landing.

Buzzing with anticipation, the gnome resumed rubbing his fingers together. He was struggling to hold his tongue, but he didn't have to wait long.

"I told you I would-" the troll started, his voice deep and slow. He stood for a moment, blinking at the four arrivals. When he got to Zodim, the old gnome smiled a toothy grin.

"Who are you?" the troll asked.

"Zodim, artificer extraordinaire at your service," the gnome blurted in excitement. "And you are Oogmut, co-author of *The Call for Unification*, among other great tomes of course! I'm thrilled to meet you!"

"Oh, is this a social calling now?" the albino man spat, his sniveling voice like charcoal being scrapped together. Oogmut cast a nasty glare at the man before turning back to Savannah and Ygabb.

"What is going on?" he asked. He scratched the top of his head but remained in the cell.

"Hopefully nothing that will interfere with your interrogation," replied Savannah. "But as you can see, we have a couple unexpected guests."

"I'd say," interjected the imprisoned man. "A very special hájje, that one is."

Zodim narrowed his gaze, leaning in to have a closer look at the elf in the cell.

"What do you know of her?" Ygabb asked, stealing the thought from Zodim's own head.

The albino cackled.

"She is your real enemy. A daughter of Yezurkstal himself -one of his generals. You and your idealistic little community will be trampled over and eaten alive by her kind."

"Thank you for that," said Oogmut, patting the man on the top of the head. The albino pulled away, swatting at the troll and revealing his missing hand.

"Don't touch me, wart-infested beast!"

"Well, at least we know now you're not working for the hájje," said Savannah with a shrug. "But do us a favor and be silent please."

"I will do no such-" the pale man collapsed mid-sentence as Oogmut reached down and tossed a handful of white powder over his face.

"I think that's enough of his nonsense for one day," said Oogmut with a shrug. The troll stepped out of the cell, closing and locking the gate behind him.

"Is this really one of Yezurkstal's children?" he asked stepping over and gently cradling the hájje. Savannah and Ygabb ceased channeling their spell, allowing the troll to lower Castora to the stone floor.

"Good question," Savannah placed her hands on her hips, tapping her foot as she looked down at Zodim. "Is she?"

Zodim looked between the three mages. Ygabb had joined the other two in staring at him, but if she was trying to copy the severe look of the others, she was failing. She looked more like she was constipated, or otherwise in a state of discomfort.

"She is," admitted Zodim after a moment's pause. "But that doesn't change anything I've told you!" he stammered. "That was simply one of the details I was going to let her share with you."

The trio of mages all exchanged a glance.

"Alright. I'm still willing to give her a chance," said Savannah. "Oogmut, Ygabb, if you two would stay on your guard. And Zodim, I'd recommend you step back."

Zodim looked at his feet, blinking a couple of times before fully registering.

"Oh, yes. Of course," he mumbled, waddling away from the trio of mages and the unconscious Castora.

"I'll just stand over here."

"That will be fine," replied Savannah. She sighed, folding her hands in front of her and looking down at Castora.

Oogmut and Ygabb took a position to the left and right of Castora, respectively. Standing about a meter away, they looked completely focused, their eyes narrow, and attention fixed on the sleeping dark elf.

Everyone stood perfectly still for nearly a minute. And Zodim was just about ready to interrupt the silence when Savannah knelt, placing her hands on either side of Castora's face, and closing her eyes.

Zodim leaned in, watching the faint glow of green magic forming around Savannah's hands. Again, his anticipation betrayed him as she held this position. And she remained there for another couple of minutes, the magic simply flowing around between her hands.

Suddenly, Savannah jerked her head towards the ceiling and began muttering something under her breath. Zodim scooted a few centimeters closer, but still couldn't make it out. It sounded like incoherent whispers to him. Perhaps it was old elvish?

Zodim pulled away, leaning back as the green energy grew brighter, spreading out from Savannah and coalescing around Castora. Savannah held onto the hájje's head, continuing to pour out magic.

And then it stopped.

The light faded, and Savannah pulled away with a loud gasp. She stood up violently, stepping away from Castora and catching her breath.

Fighting the instinct to run in and help, Zodim clenched his fists and kept his focus on Castora. Oogmut and Ygabb remained in position.

With his unwavering attention on Castora, Zodim could only pray.

Please Evorath, bring her back.

CHAPTER X

Paxvilla, Main Gates
28 Julla, 1149 MT

Dust filled the air, the strained grunts of workers and clanging of hammers echoed throughout the city. Jaldor strained, grasping the stone tightly as he struggled. With exaggerated steps, he stomped over to the debris pile, depositing the damaged section of wall.

Standing up to full height, the farmer stretched his back and wiped his hand across his brow. Taking a moment to catch his breath, he examined his hands, the brown skin cracked and blistered from the morning's work.

But looking back at the crumbled section of wall, he couldn't deny the sense of satisfaction. Dozens of Paxvilla citizens were working to clear away the rubble, accompanied by a couple centaurs and the barghest brothers. In just one morning, they had cleared out the entire section, leaving a large gap in the massive walls.

Walking back towards the gap, Jaldor glanced west to the main gatehouse. They had finished clearing that section out a couple days ago, and dozens more Paxvilla citizens were working with some of the mages to begin the rebuilding process. It was inspiring to see everyone working together.

"Jaldor, you mind grabbing the other end of this one?"

Glancing towards Fredrick, Jaldor offered a nod, walking over and considering the rock in question.

It was oblong in shape -probably twice as large as the last stone he had moved. But with a quick look around, it was also probably the largest stone remaining.

"Alright. On the count of three then?" Jaldor asked.

Fredrick nodded, stretching his neck and back and bobbing side-to-side for a few seconds. With sweat dripping from his hands as he shook them, the blacksmith looked like he had just come from a swim.

"Alright, let's get this thing moved," said Fredrick. "Three, two, one."

Jaldor lowered on three, bending his knees into a deep squat. At the count of two, he wrapped his arms around his end, gripping the stone tight. And with three, he stood up, his legs burning with the weight.

Fredrick's eyes bulged, his face turning red as they scooted sideways towards the pile a few meters away. A stone like this might be salvageable for use in the reconstructed wall, but moving it was not Jaldor's idea of a good time.

Finally, as they reached the salvage pile, the duo locked eyes, halting for a moment and then swinging the rock aside. It tumbled over onto the pile. Jaldor let out a sigh of relief and placed his hands on his knees. He remained bent over for a few seconds until he caught his breath.

"That's going to feel good tomorrow," muttered Fredrick, rubbing his lower back.

Jaldor forced a chuckle to be polite.

"I'm going to grab a drink of water and see how they are doing back at the barracks," said Jaldor, his voice raspy.

He cleared his throat, walking back through the almost cleared part of the wall towards the barracks to the east. A few others waved or nodded his way as he passed. Despite the hard work and attack they had endured, everyone seemed to be maintaining a cheerful demeanor.

But approaching the barracks and the smell of rotting flesh wafting through the air, Jaldor could hear not everyone was keeping such a positive attitude. There were raised voices up ahead and squinting towards them he saw a couple town guards chatting with a bald man in a brown tunic.

As he drew closer, Jaldor recognized the bald man -it was the Avatar. And it seemed he was the one with a raised voice.

"I understand your tradition and I appreciate how difficult this is," despite his loud volume, he was slow and deliberate with his words. "But the longer you leave these bodies unburned, the more you invite danger. Your enemy will employ necromancy and turn all these fallen soldiers against you."

Jaldor continued listening. Approaching the well to draw up water, he could still hear their conversation clearly.

"We're not some pagan monsters! We are civilized. And civilized people don't burn their dead!" argued one of the guards.

"That's right!" added the other, shorter guard "We have friends and family in there. We owe it to them to give them a proper burial with a headstone."

Jaldor glanced over as he poured some water in a cup. The Avatar brought his hand up, covering his face and shaking his head.

"Will you at least start burning the enemies then? And then perhaps you can point me to your commanding officer."

"He's not going to say anything different!" shouted the shorter guard. He puffed out his chest, stepping right up to the Avatar's face.

With cup in hand, Jaldor hurried over to the conflict, taking a swig of water on his way.

"Hey, let's remember we're all working together on this," Jaldor interjected, stepping up next to the shorter guard.

"Shut it traitor!" replied the taller guard. "We're not interested in what you have to say about it -leaving your own people behind while you go live with these strange creatures."

"That's right!" added the shorter guard. He turned and bumped into Jaldor. "Why did you even both coming here to help if you're just going to turn tail and leave after?"

Jaldor closed his eyes and sagged his shoulders. He took a step back and sighed.

"It's a pity," interrupted the Avatar, his tone turning harsh. "That you would choose strife at a time like this. Or do you not believe that Jaldor mourns for the dead?"

The shorter guard took a step back and looked at the taller one. They both frowned. But as the taller one looked at Jaldor and opened his mouth, the color drained from his face.

"Oh God! What is that?" the guard pointed towards the pile of enemy corpses.

Jaldor spun around, the Avatar turning to look at well. A black mist rolled in, as if pouring forth from the dead enemies. But there was something strange about it. Within seconds, Jaldor watched as the mist took on a human form.

"Flee from here," the Avatar muttered.

"FLEE!" he bellowed.

Jaldor jumped back. The Avatar's voice was loud enough to wake the dead. But he couldn't obey. Instead, his curiosity forced him to stand, watching as the mist took form.

It was a hájje.

From bottom up, the hájje took physical form, his black boots, and pants, matching black leather armor, and a large greenish sword with a moonstone in the pummel. The figure reached for his sword, drawing it, and holding it perpendicular overhead.

It was his face that was most chilling. Looking at the pale, sinister face, Jaldor felt so small and insignificant. He wasn't sure if it was the one, void black eye or the scar over the missing left eye, or something else entirely. But what he did know is that he had never been so terrified in his life.

"Yezurkstal," the Avatar muttered. With head held high, the Avatar moved calmly and deliberately, walking towards the hájje with his hands at his side.

The hájje was crazed, his eye wide as he grinned a devious grin.

"I knew I sensed your ilk," Yezurkstal spoke, his words like daggers. Jaldor shuddered, his hair standing on end. It was as if this hájje's very presence oozed discomfort.

As he spoke, he swung his over-sized sword. Jaldor looked on in disbelief, his mouth agape as he watched both piles of dead pulse to life. Moans and crunches echoed from the dead as they crawled, climbed, and clamored.

Screams broke out all around. The volunteers nearest the piles routed, fleeing further into the city. The zombies moved slowly and deliberately, falling into a row formation. Jaldor trembled, his mind unable to process what he was witnessing.

The Avatar walked right up to Yezurkstal, standing less than a meter away from the hájje as he squared off to him. If there was one benefit to his frightened state, it was that Jaldor was able to clearly hear their conversation.

"It's the sword, isn't it?" the Avatar asked. "Is that how you've returned to this realm?"

"I've returned to this realm because my work is not complete. Your feeble mind cannot comprehend how powerful I've become. Even your harlot goddess will bow at my feet when I am done reshaping this world."

"It is not wise to blaspheme your creator," replied the Avatar, clenching his fists. "Nor is it wise to challenge Her right arm. This is not a fight you can win."

"Isn't it?" Yezurkstal sheathed his sword. He lifted his left arm overhead.

The zombie formation turned in unison. They all marched in perfect sync, shambling east towards the town proper.

A bell rang out, shouts echoing from the distance. The loud clanging of brass pulled Jaldor out of his trance. He shook his head and looked down at his trembling hands.

Glancing east, he watched as dozens of town guards took up formation behind him. The other volunteers were grabbing whatever they could, rocks, hammers, picks, and shovels.

Irontail galloped through the Paxvilla lines, followed closely by a half dozen other centaurs. Behind him, the members of the Mage's Guild followed, including George. Not wishing to be stuck in the middle of the battlefield, Jaldor fled towards the mustering defenses.

Intercepting George on his retreat, Jaldor grabbed hold of the wizard's arms and pulled him to the side. He glanced back to confirm Avatar was still conversing with the hájje.

"What is going on?" George looked towards Yezurkstal and the Avatar. "Who is that?"

"The Avatar called him Yezurkstal," replied Jaldor.

"What?" George scrunched his face and leaned back. He looked back at Yezurkstal, extending his staff with eyes closed.

The wizard gasped and stumbled away. His face flushed, turning pale as a ghost. "It's like an endless well," George stared off, his eyes wide and mouth agape.

And then it began.

Jaldor felt pressure pass over his entire body. It sounded like a crash of thunder, and as the farmer turned to behold the struggle, he found himself once again frozen in disbelief.

Yezurkstal and the Avatar grappled one another. The hájje appeared to have the upper hand, stepping forward and forcing the Avatar down to one knee.

But it was the zombies that had the bulk of Jaldor's attention. The horde dashed forth, charging past the two combatants towards the disorganized defenders. Irontail, who had taken a position near the front of the defenses, looked around until he locked eyes on Jaldor and George. He bolted towards them, coming to an abrupt halt just a couple meters away.

"George!" the centaur shouted. "If your skills were ever needed, it's now. Get these people out of here."

George looked with a blank stare, unblinking.

"Snap out of it, George!" screamed Irontail. "Death is upon us!" he shouted loud enough for the whole city to hear. "You must all flee!"

Jaldor had only ever heard stories, but seeing the dread on Irontail's face was enough to know his own fear was warranted. But he wouldn't let that get in the way.

"I've got him," said Jaldor to Irontail. "You do what you can with those…abominations." He pointed towards the approaching zombie army.

"Thank you Jaldor," replied Irontail, turning about.

As the centaur and his troops charged to meet the enemy zombies, Jaldor stepped in front of George and grabbed onto his arms. He looked him in the eyes and shook him.

"Alright!" said George. He shook his head, blowing out a puff of air. He still looked pale and clammy, his hands trembling.

"George, we have to get the non-combatants to safety."

"Yes, of course. Evorath help us," muttered the wizard.

With staff in his right hand, George smacked his left hand over his face and rubbed his eyes. He took a deep breath and as he lowered his left hand, he matched Jaldor's gaze and nodded confidently.

"I'll provide the portal. You get them through."

Jaldor nodded, not waiting a moment to run towards the crowd of gathered civilians. While the soldiers charged into battle behind Irontail and the centaurs, many of the civilians stood with looks of fear and uncertainty. These were the people to start with.

"We must retreat to safety!" yelled Jaldor. "That is the one called Yezurkstal; that is Death."

"But we must defend our home," answered a homely middle-aged man.

"Yes, not all of us can abandon our home so easily," came an unseen feminine voice.

Jaldor looked around at the many faces. His heart broke as they averted his gaze, turning away and murmuring thoughts agreement. Would anyone see reason?

"Fredrick," said Jaldor running up to the blacksmith. "Surely you want to see your family safe. If you stay here, you'll all end up like that!" Jaldor pointed towards the zombies.

It was an opportune moment too, for the group he pointed to was engaged with the front line of Paxvilla defenders. The various guards pushed back with their shields, slashing them away with swords. But as Jaldor watched, a stray zombie broke through, latching onto a forward guard and biting his neck.

And then another broke the line, and other. Within seconds, the zombies were trampling over the Paxvilla defenders. Their cries of pain echoed through the clearing as Jaldor turned back towards the crowd of civilians.

"He's right!" shouted Fredrick. "We're a community. We can rebuild. But we can't replace our lives. And for me, I'm getting my family out of here."

Fredrick turned around. He took off, running north towards the town proper. Murmuring echoed through the crowd, some agreeing with Fredrick.

"Yes, he's right," came another shout. Another man ran back towards town. And then they all seemed to fall in line. Like a landslide, dozens of volunteers fled back towards town.

The homely, middle-aged man stepped forward, and raised his right fist.

"He's right!" the man shouted. "We can't rebuild if we're not alive to do so. What do we do Jaldor?"

"We go through his portal," Jaldor pointed at George.

As if on cue, George pointed his staff towards Jaldor and exclaimed "Ixidor!" A portal opened up just centimeters away from the farmer. The pulsing blue circle expanded, growing large enough to accommodate a row of people.

"I can only keep this open for so long!" shouted George. "So, let's get moving!"

The crowd all hesitated, exchanging nervous glances.

"That means now!" shouted Jaldor. He ran up to the homely man, gently nudging him towards the portal. As they reached the threshold, the man pulled back.

"Is it safe?" he asked sheepishly.

"I sent my whole herd through it. And I've gone through these portals every day since the attack. It's safe."

The man nodded and clenched his fist. He crouched down and ran through.

"Alright, let's follow his lead!" Jaldor yelled.

One after another, groups of people started to pile in. Jaldor stood at the edge of the portal, reassuring them as they passed through. By the time the first group was evacuated, some of the volunteers who'd fled were returning with their whole families. Men, women, and children all piled through the portal, and Jaldor looked back towards George.

"Are you doing alright?"

"For now," the wizard replied curtly. He clenched his jaw, his eyes fixed on the portal. His arms shook as he kept them extended, the quartz on his staff glowing white.

Jaldor continued waving through refugees. But he turned back towards the conflict. The centaurs were amazing.

All seven of them were still at it, working with the Paxvilla guard to contain the zombie threat. They flailed and stomped, pushing through the ranks of undead. Some of the other mages from Marftaport were lined up behind the soldiers, waving their staffs and wands, likely helping in ways Jaldor couldn't possibly realize.

Meanwhile, the Avatar and Yezurkstal had broken apart. They hurled spells at one another. The Avatar cast a bolt of green energy. Yezurkstal drew his sword, using it to absorb the attack. He spun around, countering with a wave of black energy.

The Avatar shielded himself, green energy flashing around him. He charged Yezurkstal, lowering his center of gravity to go in for a tackle. But Yezurkstal was too quick.

"Enough!" the hájje shouted.

Jaldor tensed up and watched in terror as Yezurkstal spun around and planted his blade in the Avatar's chest. The earth quaked and the ground shook. Jaldor couldn't pull his eyes away.

"You love these humans so much," Yezurkstal's voice boomed. "Then join them on their world!"

A column of blue light engulfed the Avatar. And as it faded, he was gone, leaving Yezurkstal standing with his sword extended. The hájje smirked a devious grin, sheathing his sword and spreading his arms wide.

"My dominion is inevitable!"

CHAPTER XI

George couldn't believe it.

He felt Yezurkstal's magic, a portal to another world. It was breathtaking to watch the column of light come down. But then the reality of the spell set in.

The Avatar was gone, sent to some distant world.

George focused on his own spell, his arms shaking with fatigue. He tried to feel for any sign of the Avatar's energy. But there was nothing. It felt as if a tremendous force of magic had been sucked from the world.

Yezurkstal didn't waste much time. He ran towards the rest of the combatants. George thought of Irontail's words -he had to act fast.

"Stand back!" he uttered.

He stepped in front of his portal, preventing anyone else from entering. Proceeding to lower his staff and close the portal, George spun back around, his breathing heavy. Ignoring the cries of confusion and panic from the remaining refugees, he refocused his attention on Yezurkstal.

The hájje continued his advance. He looked almost disinterested, walking casually through the ranks of zombies, and cutting down any defenders who stepped in his path. George had always hoped the stories were exaggerated, but watching Death move so effortlessly through these people made it abundantly clear; the stories didn't adequately express his ruthlessness.

"We don't stand a chance without the Avatar," said George absently. He wasn't speaking to anyone in particular, but it seemed at least Jaldor heeded his words.

"Then what do we do? Can you get us all out of here?" The farmer grabbed George's shoulders and pulled him closer. His eyes trembled, pleading for some solution.

George wanted to scream. He wished Sarah was there to tell him what to do. Or that someone else could take over and save the day. But he knew that couldn't happen. And as he watched Yezurkstal cut through one of the centaurs, he knew his window to act was short.

"I'll try, but I have to do something else first."

George closed his eyes and took a deep breath. He looked up, gazing skyward as far as he could. If he could pull it off, he might just be able to evacuate everyone.

Stepping away from Jaldor, George pointed his staff towards Yezurkstal. He counted the seconds silently, narrowing his eyes and carefully watching the hájje's every movement. He gathered what latent energy he could, focusing it in his staff.

"Ixidor!" he exclaimed.

The portal opened and Yezurkstal stepped through. George snapped the portal shut, falling to one knee and using the staff to hold him upright.

"Where did he go?" asked Jaldor.

George smiled, pointing towards the sky.

"As far as I know, he can't fly."

Jaldor pursed his lips. His mouth dropped open as he looked skyward.

"Will that really work?"

"No time to ask," replied George. "Quickly, everyone through the portal."

George spun around, waving his staff and creating another portal to Marftaport. The people didn't hesitate this time, trampling over one another as they ran through.

"George what is going on here?"

The wizard arched an eyebrow, standing on the tips of his toes and trying to look for the source of the voice. He had forgotten about Vistoro and Tel' Shira!

The pair were pushing through the crowd from the east, flanked by the barghest brothers. Vistoro pressed in tight, pushing Tel' Shira's wheelchair while Morn and Neman created an opening for them to step past the portal.

"We have to retreat," shouted George as they approached. "Yezurkstal is back."

The barghest brothers both wore blank expressions, as if they were struggling to process what they just heard. Neither Tel' Shira nor Vistoro seemed affected by the news, their faces stoic and unmoving as they observed the conflict.

"Where is the Avatar?" asked the elder felite.

"He's gone," replied George, fighting to keep his composure. "I think for good."

Vistoro gasped, locking eyes with Tel' Shira.

"Then it's worse than we thought," he said.

"Indeed," replied Tel' Shira.

"Morn, Neman!" she barked. "Rally the troops for a retreat. We have no hope for victory here today."

The duo didn't wait a moment, barking "urgo" in unison and rushing towards the skirmish.

"Jaldor," Tel' Shira continued. "I need you to come through the portal with Vistoro and me. These people will be scared and confused and we're counting on you to help them understand the situation. Can you do that?"

It took Jaldor a moment to reply. He looked dumbfounded, glancing down at the felite with his mouth agape. But George watched his eyes dart around, and after a few moments, he nodded.

"Yes, ma'am. Let's go."

"George, look at me," said Tel' Shira.

He peered into Tel' Shira's hazel eyes.

"As soon as Death sets down, you must come home. No matter who might still be here, you will leave. Promise me this."

"What do you know?"

"Just promise me!"

"Urgo!" George didn't like this.

A large concentration of Paxvilla citizens were rushing through the portal. But as soon as there was a gap, Vistoro pushed Tel' Shira through and Jaldor followed right behind.

George considered the remaining refugees. Their numbers were dwindling. He really hadn't kept an exact count, but it felt like much of the city had made it through. That just left the remaining guards, centaurs, and members of the Mage's Guild.

Looking back at the wall of zombies, it seemed all their numbers were diminishing. Morn and Neman moved into the fray, picking off some of the zombies on the outskirts. Though he couldn't hear through the bedlam, it looked like they were getting attention. A couple of centaurs near the southern edge of the skirmish galloped away, running through the portal.

But there was little hope for the town guard. The zombie forces were ripping through their ranks. Irontail rushed through with two more centaurs. Funneling through the dozen or so remaining Paxvilla guards, they were able to break free and join the barghest brothers on the outskirts.

"Get out of here. We'll hold them off!" Irontail bellowed.

Morn and Neman, along with the human guards and a couple members of the Mage's Guild all ran for the portal. From what George could tell, that left only Irontail, his two centaur companions, and Bel' Mora to hold the zombies at bay.

And the four of them were doing a better job than George could have imagined. Bel' Mora slid up alongside Irontail and stretched out her arms, casting a wide magic net.

The zombies struggled against the green field of energy, pressing forward. Irontail and the other centaurs kept picking away as enemies slipped through the field. Civilians were still running towards the portal.

And then he felt it.

A surge of dark energy made his stomach drop. He felt the hair on his arms stand on end and a lump form in his throat.

"We must go. NOW!" George screamed, his voice cracking as he yelled the final word.

Then he saw the mist descend, coalescing into solid form only a couple meters away from the others. George trembled, biting his bottom lip, and fighting to hold back tears.

How could Evorath let this happen? He wondered.

Yezurkstal seethed, his eye glowing red as he drew his sword. There was no time.

Yezurkstal stabbed his sword into the ground, a pulse of dark energy pouring out in all directions. George closed his eyes, seeing the faces of Sarah, Elizabeth, and Henry. Opening them back up, he watched Irontail consumed by the black magic, the look of anguish etched in his memory.

George dove through the portal, snapping it shut.

As he landed on the other side, surrounded by all the refugees, he dropped to his knees, clasped his hands over his face and wept.

CHAPTER XII

Marftaport
28 Julla, 1149 MT

Darkness surrounded Castora. Where was she? How had she gotten here?

She was weightless, floating through the abyss like driftwood on the ocean. A numbness overtook her body as she wafted through the void.

What had she even been doing?

There were gnomes.

Or were there?

Yezurkstal.

Yes, that was it. Her master, her god, her meaning for life.

No, there was more to it.

Her father?

A daughter must obey her father.

Yes…

No, that wasn't right.

He is your master.

No, he is a liar!

Her vision blurred, vertigo overtaking her as she tried to listen, to smell, to feel anything beyond the darkness. There was a flash of light, and just as quickly, the darkness returned.

A faint red light slipped through the darkness, cutting through the void like lightning in the sky. But the outline remained. And Castora recognized the form it was taking.

Her father glared down, his giant head floating in the sky. His visage grew clearer by the moment, the pale white of his face contrasting. From the white of his one good eye to the scar where his other had once been, it took form and leered down at Castora.

She tried to move but was frozen in place.

"Why do you resist?"

"You lied to me!" Castora tried to say, but she could not move her mouth. In that moment, she realized she could not hear a thing. Even her father's voice was in her mind.

"I've told you what you needed to know."

"I am the one who decides what I need to know."

"You live to serve me, your father, your master."

"You were my master. But I no longer wish to serve."

"It is not your choice. I am your creator, your god. You will obey me, or you will be punished."

Castora felt a burning pain in the base of her skull. She tried to reach for it, but could not move. Her body tingled, the visage of her father growing larger.

"This is a nightmare," she thought to herself.

"No, this is your destiny. You are my instrument, a weapon to spread the glory of your god and master," her father's voice stung like a bee.

Wake up, Castora! You are in control.

"I am in control?" Castora questioned.

"You are under my control!"

"I can choose my own destiny."

"The choice is not yours!"

"It's not…mine?"

Wake up!

Castora gasped, sitting up and frantically looking around at her surroundings.

"It's alright," said Zodim. The gnome stood at her feet, his face pensive and hands held up, palms forward.

The ground was cold, some sort of rough stone. Castora blinked, looking around at the others in the space. Just to her right was a female elf wearing a green dress and emerald choker. She had porcelain white skin and maintained a cautious posture, her eyes trained on the dark elf.

To her left, she spotted two others. One a lumbering troll, his grey skin ugly and blemished. He wore a sleeveless fur tunic and matching loincloth. About his waist hung a variety of pouches and around his neck a bone necklace. Standing just before him was a small satyr, dressed in red robes and a matching red, wide-brimmed pointy hat. She was equipped with short mythril sword at her side.

"You're in no danger," continued Zodim. "We're in Marftaport, and Savannah here," he motioned towards the elf, "helped awaken you."

"How long was I unconscious?" Castora asked.

"More than a day, less than two," answered Zodim. "Do you remember what happened?"

"Can I stand up?" Castora asked. looking around at the nervous faces.

"Oh, let me help you," said the troll. He stepped forward and extended his hand.

Castora hesitated for a moment, remembering the stories of how unsanitary trolls were. But like most of her upbringing, she reminded herself that was likely exaggerated. So, with a forced smile, she accepted his help.

As she came to her feet, the satyr took a step back, pivoting to a more defensive posture.

"My name is Oogmut," the troll smiled down at Castora. "And this is my little friend Ygabb, and I suppose Zodim already made it clear, that's Savannah!"

Castora tightened her lips and narrowed her eyes as she ran her tongue along the inside of her teeth and glanced around at those gathered. Her instinct and upbringing all screamed for her to fight her way out.

"My name is Castora. Where exactly are we?"

She glanced around, jail cells and dank surroundings providing a safe assumption.

"This is the Mage's Guild dungeon," answered Savannah. Her voice was soft and motherly, the kind of sweet tone that would get a hájje severely beaten for being 'too soft'.

"Am I to be a prisoner in this dungeon?" Castora glanced around, careful to keep her hands down at her side.

"We haven't decided," said the satyr. The small creature's voice was high pitched and cheerful, but the way she glared up at Castora revealed a depth of strength.

"Oh, I'm sure that won't be the decision," interrupted Zodim, stepping between Castora and the Ygabb.

The dark elf considered her options. She could sense the magical prowess of all three of these mages. And the physical strength of any troll was not something she cared to challenge. She had to trust that Zodim was making the right decision, and that these people were less barbaric than she was taught.

"Zodim suggested you might appreciate our assistance," started Castora. She spoke slowly and deliberately, taking time to carefully select each word.

"Yes, so he said," replied Savannah. "And while Zodim might have our trust, we're still not convinced you should earn the same. You weren't willing to talk peace with Paxvilla; why should we trust you want it now?"

Castora squinted, examining Savannah more closely. She thought back to the battle of Paxvilla. It seemed like a lifetime ago. But then it clicked. This was the elf who had tried to open up a dialogue before the fight.

"Oh," the hájje muttered, shifting her gaze to the floor.

"I'm sorry about that," she said more confidently. She looked up and made eye contact with Savannah. "I was operating under a false precept. Thanks to Zodim's kindness, I realize now that I was gravely mistaken."

Savannah glanced at the other two mages. Her lips were pulled tight, and her eyes narrowed. She turned back to Castora with her eyebrows raised.

"Your words are of little comfort to people who have lost so much to your actions. What could Zodim have done to possibly bring about such a drastic change?" asked Savannah.

Castora glanced back at Zodim. She considered the days prior and the stories they had exchanged. She recalled the hesitation she first felt fighting against that handsome elf in Paxvilla and the anguish she witnessed when she had murdered the old barghest. A wave of emotion washed over her as she came to a pivotal realization.

"I don't deserve your forgiveness." She said gravely. "And in truth, I probably don't even deserve to leave this dungeon. But Zodim showed me what I started to suspect during the battle at Paxvilla. That is, he exposed the lies of my father."

"Hold on," interrupted Ygabb. The pipsqueak stepped closer, holding out her hands. "Take my hands and explain. Imagine you're in our position and walk us through how you came to believe Zodim."

The dark elf hesitated for a moment, but with a subtle nod from Zodim, she acquiesced. Taking hold of the satyr's warm and surprisingly smooth hands, she continued.

"I'm not sure if Zodim told you, but I am a daughter of Yezurkstal, a position that I used to take such great pride in. But from what Zodim tells me, my upbringing was not what you would typically expect from royalty. Yes, I was in a position of power and influence, but I was also held to a higher standard.

"You see, as a daughter of Yezurkstal, I had a very clear path set for me. And strength was essential to that path, which meant my childhood was filled with corporal punishment and martial training. It also meant I accepted Hájjeona was the only safe place in Evorath."

Castora paused and cleared her throat. She wondered how detailed she really ought to be. But seeing the expectant faces of those gathered, she continued.

"All hájje children are taught about the violence and savagery of the world. We're raised to believe that hájje are the only civilized people and that we've been chosen to usher in a new era of peace and prosperity. And the way to achieve that is to eliminate all who would sow chaos and disorder. And the first time I ever doubted this was when we first met on that battlefield." Castora nodded towards Savannah.

"You see, I never expected any non-hájje would wave a flag to entreat. I believed we'd be marching into a savage land full of bloodthirsty humans who didn't understand the rules of engagement. But despite your overture to discuss peace before the battle, I was certain of my righteousness."

Oogmut narrowed his eyes. He tilted his head to the right, moving his jaw as if he was chewing on something.

"And during the battle I felt more doubts seeing all the different species fighting together. How could such savage and uncivilized species work together so well? Then there was that elvish archer -I don't know why, but I just couldn't bring myself to kill him."

Savannah's face flushed. She avoided Castora's gaze and twirled her hair in her fingertips. Castora kept her eyes on the elf as she continued.

"But of course I paid for that when he gave me this," the dark elf nodded towards the stab wound in her side.

At this point, Oogmut gasped. He glanced at Savannah, whose face was now red before stomping closer and looking down at Castora intently.

"Were you the commander of the army?" the troll asked, his voice harsh. Castora could feel the warmth of his breath, which reeked of rotting meat.

"Yes, I was." Castora leaned back. Ygabb clasped her hands tighter as she did.

Oogmut's eye began to tremble, growing wider as he looked down and seethed. He glared back at Savannah.

"Did you know?" His words were slow and heavy.

Savannah shook her head.

"I'm sorry," she blurted. "But does it change the situation?" she asked sheepishly.

"It does for me!" Oogmut bellowed and stomped his right foot. He stared daggers at Castora.

The dark elf had to fight an instinct to turn and run. But in the same instant, she knew this was inevitable. She stood her ground, standing up tall and making direct eye contact with Oogmut. She could feel his anger.

"I'm sorry," she said firmly. "I cannot restore the lives I've taken, but you have my word I am no longer your enemy."

Oogmut bent over, leaning in closer. He maintained eye contact, staring straight through Castora. Castora didn't blink, holding onto his gaze.

"You've enough blood on your hands to turn Lake Algarath red. And that barghest you killed right before you were stabbed was not only the greatest peacemaker of our time. He was my best friend." Oogmut's eyes bulged from his head, his lips quivering as he spoke slowly and deliberately.

And as before when she felt sympathy for Zodim, Castora once again felt a discomfort in her stomach. She wished in that moment that she could go back and prevent the attack from ever being launched. She felt pressure behind her eyes, and great shame as she witnessed the pain in Oogmut's face.

"If you wish to kill me when this is over, I won't try to avoid it. I've earned as much." Castora pushed through her discomfort, her voice strong and confident. "But my mission now is to prevent further bloodshed."

"She's telling the truth," Ygabb interjected.

Oogmut snorted and Castora made a sour face.

But the troll withdrew to full height and crossed his arms.

"Tell us what you came for."

Castora glanced down at Zodim. The old gnome had been reserved through most of the conversation, maintaining a stoic disposition and standing with his arms crossed. Catching her gaze, he offered a slight nod in response.

"Well, in my conversations with Zodim, a subject came up that we believed would be important to share with you and the people of Marftaport."

She paused to take a deep breath.

"My father is alive."

Ygabb shrieked. She dropped her hands to her side and stared at Castora unmoving. She appeared to be in shock, her mouth hanging open and eyes blinking.

Savannah's eye grew wide as she brought her hands up over her mouth. The little color she had in her cheeks washed away as she clasped her hands in front of her chest.

Oogmut went through a slew of emotions, his face changing from moment to moment. First, his eyes flared with anger, then his jaw dropped in disbelief. Next, he shook his head and stomped his feet. And then he lurched forward abruptly and grabbed Castora's arms.

"That is not possible! I was there sixty years ago. I watched Death sink into the abyss of Lake Algarath. No one could come back from that." Oogmut shouted, his voice cracking. He shook the dark elf.

But after a moment, he released his hold and stumbled back, falling onto his rear. He left his hands dangling out in front, resting on his knees as he stared past Castora.

Zodim stepped to the side of the troll, slipping between him and Savannah and taking a place by Castora's side. He smiled up at the dark elf before turning back towards the others.

"You should have seen my face when she told me." Zodim muttered. He paused, holding up his left index finger.

"However, this bit of bad news is not all we have. We intend to help put an end to Yezurkstal for good this time."

Oogmut groaned and slapped his knees. With a grumble, he rose back to his feet, shaking his head on the way up.

"I still don't understand," he exclaimed waving his arms wide. Savannah had to duck to the side to avoid getting hit. "How is he alive?"

"I cannot say how, but according to my father, he cannot die. And while Zodim has helped me realize most of what I learned was a lie, I believe him."

The room fell silent, everyone looking around at one another as if afraid to speak. After what felt like a full minute of awkward silence, Ygabb narrowed her eyes and leaned to the right, looking past Castora.

"Does anyone hear that?"

Castora turned around, looking back towards the landing. She heard footfalls echoing along the steps.

A moment later, a woman walked into view. She appeared to be the same height as Castora. She had shoulder-length brown hair, blue eyes, and wore a complementary blue dress. Though she walked with confidence, she wore a blank expression, her gaze distant and distracted.

"Sarah, what are you doing down here?" asked Savannah.

"I," she let the word slip out, staring up towards the ceiling. "The others. They've returned from Paxvilla. It's. I don't know how."

Her face darkened, her eyes filling with dread as she caught Castora's gaze. She stumbled back and narrowed her eyes.

"Who are you?" Sarah asked.

She reached across her body, pulling a small wand out from a hidden pocket in her dress. She pointed the wand at Castora and left her free hand hovering at her hip. This woman had almost as much latent magic as the elf.

"She's a friend!" exclaimed Zodim. The gnome jumped in front of Castora, holding his arms out wide.

Sarah tilted her head to the side and squinted down at the gnome. "I'm sorry, but who are you?"

"It seems they are both here to help," Savannah interjected. She walked over to the newcomer, lowering the woman's wand hand before motioning back towards the dark elf.

"Her name is Castora, and she just shared some troubling news. But I gather you have news of your own."

Sarah looked back at Castora and narrowed her eyes. She pursed her lips and returned the wand to her pocket. After looking around at the others, she lowered her guard.

"Yezurkstal is back," Sarah blurted.

The room again fell silent as everyone exchanged nervous glances. Castora stepped towards Sarah.

"Did you see him?"

Sarah shook her head.

"It was Paxvilla," she said, looking towards the ground, her voice trailing off. "George evacuated as many of them as he could, but it seems that. It seems." She paused and sniffled.

"Paxvilla is gone," she uttered. "We don't know yet the extent of the destruction, but George barely made it out alive. Not everyone was so lucky."

Her voice faltered as she rubbed her eyes.

Castora looked around, taking in the somber faces of the others. Her hands shook and her face burned with anger.

Pulling her shoulders back, she looked towards the ceiling and screamed. She stomped her feet and seethed.

"I will not be his puppet anymore!" she proclaimed.

She stomped over to Sarah and Savannah and turned back to consider the other three, crying out.

"We will defeat my father!"

CHAPTER XIII

Marftaport, Public Gathering Hall
28 Julla, 1149 MT

The room was bursting at the seams, the hall abuzz with frantic conversation. Paxvilla and Marftaport residents alike clamored about, shouting over one another. Artimus Jr. stood at the front of the room along with his mother and father, Luna, Oogmut, Vistoro, Sissera, and the innkeeper, Zachiro.

It was pandemonium.

Artimus Jr. was still not clear on everything that had happened in Paxvilla, so he was eager to begin. All he knew was that George arrived back without some of the aid party and with the addition of nearly a thousand Paxvilla citizens. From there, they prepared the stage in the gathering hall.

The young elf looked around the room, taking in all the scared and desperate faces. Paxvilla residents screamed about wanting to return home, while Marftaport's people shared concerns over food and shelter for the influx of visitors. All the many concerns were difficult to discern, the hum of overlapping thoughts causing Artimus Jr. to go cross-eyed.

But Artimus Jr. was less concerned with the crowd and more concerned with the murderer waiting behind the scenes. He glanced over his shoulder towards the back storage room where Castora, Zodim, Keldor, and Ygabb were waiting. Despite what the others said, he was not ready to trust a hájje, especially not that one.

Members of the Mage's and Hunter's Guilds had been asked to take strategic positions throughout the crowd as well. Though Vistoro and Tel' Shira had rejected the notion of their necessity, at least most of the others agreed to take sensible precautions. Who was to say how these humans might behave?

Artimus Jr. just wished things would get underway. He hated even being in the same vicinity as the hájje woman. And as if on cue, Vistoro stepped up to the podium.

He cleared his throat, the rune stone of the podium amplifying his voice to fill the room.

"Excuse me. I understand everyone is scared and confused. We're all reeling with today's attack in Paxvilla, but if everyone can please be quiet, we'll address these recent events."

There was a clamor as Vistoro began talking. Some visitors continued to try and talk over him at first. But as he spoke, the side conversations died down. And by the time he finished, the room fell into silence.

"Thank you," he continued, glancing around the room.

"Please, allow me to first express my condolences to everyone gathered. I think everyone gathered lost someone dear to them. If not today, then last week when the initial attack took place. And there's nothing any of us can say or do to help with the pain of these losses."

There were some coughs among those gathered, along with faint murmurs. Artimus Jr. couldn't make out anything specific. But after a brief pause, Vistoro continued.

"We still don't know the extent of today's attack and I won't lie; what we do know fills me with a sense of dread. Death, the one named Yezurkstal, has returned."

The room burst into conversation. Competing voices filled the air, creating a garbled jumble of words. Artimus Jr. could only pick out a few stray words, like someone shouting 'lies' and another person screaming about 'the end'. He shifted nervously, looking to the others for guidance as the discordant responses continued.

After a couple minutes of chaotic discussion, the murmurs died down, and Vistoro took the opportunity to reassert himself.

"There's no sense in pretending. This is indeed alarming news. And we'll be discussing plans and strategies over the coming days on how to best counter this returning threat. But in the meantime, know every one of you is welcome here in Marftaport."

"We want to go home!" shouted a man from the middle of the crowd. Artimus Jr. couldn't clearly see who spoke it, but the voice was deep and grizzled.

"Yeah, are we prisoners here?" asked another man.

"Yes, send us back home!" came a feminine voice.

The muttering continued, bubbling into more incoherent chatter as others expressed their concerns.

"Please, let's try to speak one at a time," Vistoro shouted over the noise. "I promise you; everyone is free to leave. But we must not act rashly!"

There was more side chatter, but Vistoro continued.

"Tomorrow, we will send a small scouting party to Paxvilla. But" Vistoro raised his voice, "I urge you all to prepare for the possibility that there won't be a home for you to return to. It's possible Yezurkstal will keep the city occupied by his zombie army. And we're not in a position to fight that battle."

The rabble of the crowd grew louder. Artimus Jr. rested his hand on the mythril sword at his side, glancing around at the others. Some of the crowd were growing unruly.

"SILENCE!" Oogmut stomped his foot, his voice echoing off the walls and ceilings. Everyone turned forward with stunned expressions and fell silent.

"Thank you Oogmut. Please let me finish. If Yezurkstal has left Paxvilla, we will send anyone back who wishes to return. But please understand that we cannot guarantee your safety. Instead, we offer anyone who wishes to stay a place at our local inn or tavern, or space to camp out in the northern fields."

Vistoro paused, glancing around the room. But it seemed Oogmut's shout did a thorough job of silencing any objections, so he continued.

"And if any of you wish to stay in Marftaport permanently, please make that request. Over recent days, I know many of you have asked questions about our lifestyle and shared your confusion about our lack of centralized authority systems. You'll find those of us who call Marftaport home ready to help in anyway we can."

Conversation broke out again among the crowd, but this time it wasn't all directed at Vistoro. Artimus Jr. looked around, watching the various expressions. Judging by their body language, the elf guessed that many of them were considering the offer. Perhaps Tel' Shira was right about humans.

"For now," Vistoro shouted over the crowd, "please feel free to return to your families. If anyone needs food right now, or if you have a family member who needs medical care or special attention, please remain here, and let someone know. Zachiro and Sissera run the inn and tavern in town and will remain behind to help coordinate rooms and food."

Vistoro pointed to the two lizock before continuing.

"You'll find members of our Mage's Guild and our Hunter's Guild throughout the hall as well. They will show people around town as needed, so don't hesitate to ask. And of course, everyone else on stage with me is here to help too."

Artimus Jr. shifted nervously, smiling out towards the crowd as Vistoro continued.

"And finally, any one of you who wishes to volunteer in the fight against Yezurkstal and his army is asked to share that desire. We could use all the help we can get. With all that said, nightfall is fast approaching. So, let's make sure everyone has food and shelter for the night."

Vistoro glanced at the others on stage. He leaned back from the podium and whispered something to Zachiro. The innkeeper nodded in response and whispered something to Sissera before the pair descended from the stage.

Luna leaned over to Artimus Jr., covering her mouth with the back of her hand.

"Have you heard anything about the volunteers?" she asked. She sounded agitated; her eyes narrowed as she looked around the room.

"Not yet," Artimus Jr. replied. "All I know is some of our people were left behind -have you seen George?"

Luna nodded, her whiskers twitching as she glanced at Artimus Jr. "Yeah, he made it back at least. But there's more than a few people still unaccounted for."

She nodded towards the back room, her eyes darting around before looking back at Artimus Jr. "Do you think she really intends to help us?"

Artimus Jr. shook his head and glanced back towards the back room with a grimace.

"I don't know. But even if she does, when this is all said and done, I'll ensure she receives justice. She's killed too many of our friends to go on unpunished."

Luna smirked and nodded along.

"Good luck getting to her before me."

CHAPTER XIV

Marftaport, Vistoro's Manor
29 Julla, 1149 MT

Castora groaned, stepping sideways and glancing back in the mirror. With a sigh, she pulled down on the dress, wiggling side-to-side and forcing it to slide lower. The obnoxious yellow color was bad enough, but the improper fit was maddening.

The dress barely reached her knees, leaving her calves and ankles fully exposed. And while it was too tight around her hips, it felt far too loose around her breasts. She was happy to be out of the smelly, torn armor but she really wished for a better fit. If only she were back home; she could get a fresh set of black leather armor and be on with it.

Squaring up with the mirror, Castora tilted her head to the right and puckered her lips. She pulled her hair back with both hands, fluffing it out as best she could. Still unsatisfied with the results, she glanced back at the small dresser.

Her host had supplied the room with some of the essentials. A small hairbrush, hand mirror, nail file, leatherbound book, and Zodim's old hairpin were laid out on the dresser. Since she wasn't expected for breakfast until sunrise, she wondered for a moment whether she should start reading the book or spend the time brushing her hair.

She glanced back at the mirror, turning left and right, pulling her hair, and letting it fall back down. There were just too many knots to make it work.

So, with a loud sigh, she grabbed the brush and returned to the foot of the bed. She still couldn't believe how soft and comfortable this mattress was; even her bed back home was nowhere near this luxurious. Settling into the soft embrace of the bed, she glanced back at the mirror and began brushing her hair.

While she brushed, she thought back to the events of the past week. She considered her vision of Evorath, still skeptical if it was just a hallucination. But then she thought of her more recent visions of her father and considered the painful reality.

She shuddered remembering the cold, dark despair. That was too palpable to be a dream. And yet, she was terrified to consider the implications of it being real. Her father had violated her very free will. He had invaded her mind. And if Savannah hadn't brought her out of it…

Castora didn't want to accept it, but a tingling in her heart told her she was right. He would have made her a puppet, a mindless thrall to fulfill his wishes.

She closed her eyes and clasped her brush to her heart. With a deep breath, she tried to quell the pressure behind her eyes by focusing on Evorath's promise for fulfillment. But then she felt a new wave of sorrow as her thoughts shifted.

Did any of her people really have free will?

With a sniffle, she wiped away a stray tear. She opened her eyes and resumed brushing. Pushing aside her concerns and fears, she was able to focus on smoothing out the knots until she was satisfied. After about five more minutes of brushing, she stood up and retrieved the hairpin.

Careful to part her hair on the right side, she secured part of her hair with the pin. She tilted her head side to side, puckering her lips and looking in the mirror from a few angles. Happy with the results, she forced a smile and nodded.

"Evorath, if you're really listening, please help me." She whispered, gingerly placing the brush back on the dresser.

Just as she was taking one last look at herself, she was startled by a knock on the door. She turned around and tugged on the dress around her hips.

"Yes?" she called.

The door crept open and Zodim peeked his head inside.

"Good morning!" he exclaimed with a wide smile. "I don't mean to be improper, but would you mind if I come in?"

"Of course not. Please, enter. Oh, and good morning."

"Thank you," replied Zodim waddling inside. He looked towards the bed, the end tables, the dresser, and then considered the mirror before looking back up at the dark elf.

"That dress suits you. It goes well with Sora's hairpin too." He smiled and placed his left hand over his face, tapping his index finger against his nose.

"Thank you," replied Castora, unable to contain a smile of her own. "I," she paused and scratched her forehead. "I want you to know that however things turn out, I am grateful for everything. You saved me from a life I didn't realize I needed saving from and for that, I cannot ever properly repay you."

Zodim waved at the air and shook his head.

"I just did what any decent gnome would do."

"I'm not sure if that's true," replied Castora. "And I appreciate you regardless."

"Well, I'm happy to do what I can." Zodim stood up on his tiptoes, looking towards the exterior window. Like most of the house, even the window was ornately designed with tree branches carved in the trim and along the sill.

"It looks like first light has arrived." Said the gnome. "Shall we join the others in the dining room?"

Castora nodded.

"I'll follow you," she said motioning towards the door.

Turning around, the gnome proceeded out of the room. Castora followed him down the hallway to the grand staircase. She paused for a moment to appreciate the large scenic painting at the top. It was a beautiful mountain vista with a flock of roc flying above the lush forest below. She hadn't the opportunity to really appreciate it the night before, but staring at the brush strokes now she couldn't help but appreciate its beauty.

With ornately carved banisters and a round railing, the dark elf appreciated the regal staircase. The steps themselves had a green carpet runner along the full length, with the oak floor just visible along the sides. Each step she took allowed her to appreciate another artistic detail about the room. From the beautiful, vaulted ceilings, to the crown molding, down to the ornate chandelier that hung in the foyer.

Reaching the base of the steps, she regarded Zodim.

"Do you think they'll be ready for us? Or should we wait in the sitting room?"

Zodim looked at the door on the left. He assumed his thinking stance, his left index finger tapping against his nose.

"I'd say we can go in. And remember," he looked up and caught her gaze. "Though they may be nervous about your help, they need it. I don't envy your part, but we'll get through this together. Understood?"

Castora smiled and offered a subtle nod.

As Zodim pushed the door open to the dining room, she pulled down on her dress one more time and forced a smile. She felt nervous as she walked inside, as if she were a kid again being judged on her Jullari. To make matters worse, there were more people at the table than she expected.

The oval table was larger than any Castora had seen before. Surrounded by twenty chairs, eight on either side and two on either end, the ornately carved table was stained dark. The chairs were carved in a similar fashion to the table, and though most of these seats were empty, the dark elf kept her gaze down, careful to avoid eye contact with anyone.

Sitting furthest from the door at the far end was the elder felite Tel' Shira. Bound to a wheelchair, this white-furred seer seemed the closest to a leader Marftaport had. Everyone showed her reverence and respect and though their interactions were limited, Castora could understand why. There was an impalpable air of authority about her.

Next to her was the host of the manor, Vistoro. The noble-born lizock wore an elegant tunic along with an ornate surcoat. The purple fabric looked soft and silky, with gilding along the sleeves and collar.

Aside from these two, the other two residents of the manor were also in attendance. The black-furred felite, Luna Freya, was seated right in the middle on the northern side. She wore the same leather armor Castora had met her in yesterday, with her vital organs protected while leaving her arms and legs completely open and free.

Across from her was the felite artist, Tor Noga. Castora was glad to see him. His welcoming attitude the night before when settling into her room was both surprising and reassuring. He wore a common tunic, plain surcoat, and a friendly smile.

These four she expected, but she didn't expect to see the others. Standing nearest to the door on this end was an unfamiliar centaur. She was small framed compared to most of the centaur Castora had encountered, with smooth, light brown fur. She wore a long-sleeved green tunic and a simple opal necklace. Her hair was pulled back into a single, long braid.

Next to her was a larger, and likely younger male centaur. Barrel-chested and with arms nearly as big as Castora's waist, the tall centaur wore only a simple leather vest.

The satyr, Ygabb had also joined the breakfast party. She wore the same red robes as yesterday but without the hat. It was strange to see her with her horns uncovered, the white patch of hair on her head drawing Castora's attention.

But it was the guest next to Luna Freya that made Castora grind her teeth. Clothed in a simple tunic and green pants, the handsome archer sat staring down at his plate. Though she had yet to talk with the elf since arriving, Castora felt a lump in her throat as she caught his gaze. She jerked her eyes back down, worried her face might betray her feelings.

Finally, the group was rounded off by Savannah and another elf, who were seated nearest to Vistoro. Savannah had a plain green dress, similar in style to the one Castora wore. She still had on her necklace from before too and was holding hands with the elf next to her. He wore a simple green tunic and pants.

Castora stuck close to Zodim, doing her best to keep her eyes down as she walked around the table. Zodim took a seat next to Tel' Shira, so Castora claimed the one next in line - leaving just one open chair between her and Tor Noga.

She stood behind the chair for a moment and looked towards Vistoro.

"Please, have a seat," the lizock motioned towards her chair. Castora curtsied before taking her seat.

Adjusting her position to get comfortable in the upholstered chair, she kept her gaze down on the table. The place settings were familiar enough, with utensils on either side and a small goblet of water just to her right. With a brief glance around the table, she noticed the others had removed their napkins. She followed suit, unfurling the napkin and placing it on her lap.

"Thank you all for joining us this morning," Tel' Shira said, her voice gentle and welcoming.

"First, I want to offer our deepest condolences to Silkhair and Steelbrow," Tel' Shira lifted her hands, motioning feebly towards the two centaurs. "Irontail was not only a father and husband, but a dear friend to everyone here. All Evorath's free people must mourn the loss of such a hero."

Looking from her peripherals, Castora gazed at the centaurs. Silkhair was stoic, her eyes fixed on Tel' Shira and face drawn taut. Steelbrow was struggling to stay as collected, his soft blue eyes trembling and bottom lip quivering. But he said nothing, keeping his mouth shut tight as he stared ahead.

Glancing around the room, Castora could see everyone was impacted by the news. Savannah's eyes were red and the elf next to her pulled out a handkerchief. Ygabb sniffled, leaning over the table and covering her eyes. But it was Luna Freya that had the most unexpected reaction.

"I don't know why you've all given up on him!" she leapt from her chair and slammed her hands down on the table, drawing everyone's attention.

"Luna, please," the handsome elf stood up and placed his hand on her shoulder. "there's no wa-"

Luna pulled away, slipping her shoulder under the elf's grasp and throwing up her hands in frustration. She growled and shook her head.

"George didn't see him die! He didn't! Irontail couldn't just be gone like that." Her voice cracked, her eyes watering as she stepped towards the wall.

Castora looked down and closed her eyes.

"Please Luna" came a gentle voice from Castora's right. The dark elf looked towards the speaker -it was Silkhair. But despite her stoic appearance earlier, her eyes were heavy, her face stretched thin. Steelbrow balled his fist and clenched his jaw.

"Yes, please compose yourself *zurrurra*." Tel' Shira purred the last word in her native tongue.

Luna Freya clacked her jaws and scowled. With a frustrated snort, she plopped back down.

"I'm just saying, he could be alive," she murmured.

"I'm sorry for your loss," blurted Castora, catching even herself off guard. "My father would not have left any survivors." She stammered, panic setting in. "But I'm sure it was quick and painless!" she lied.

Castora doubled over, covering her mouth with both hands. Why was she so nervous?

"I'm sure that's true," followed Tel' Shira as if on cue.

"Besides," interrupted Savannah, her voice a bit raspy. "The energy George described," She raised her right hand over her eyes and cleared her throat. "That would have killed anyone within a kilometer -at least!"

Castora looked up, happy to have these two take the attention off her. But the air remained tense. The hájje's mind raced, trying to think of something that might relieve the tension.

"Lady Silkhair, if I may" Zodim stood up in his chair. He looked across the table to Silkhair and bowed, extending his arms out on either side in an exaggerated fashion.

"Please accept my condolences as well. I never had the privilege of meeting your husband, but you should know his accomplishments are well-known among my people. In fact, the transformation of Dumner over the decades has helped inspire reform among many of my people. The world is worse without him in it."

Steelbrow's face softened, and Silkhair's mouth curved into a small semblance of a smile.

"Thank you for your kind words," she replied.

Zodim beamed, sitting back down in his chair, and looking around at the others.

"Well, since I'm at it already, let me also say thank you to our host Vistoro. We greatly appreciate your hospitality."

Vistoro smiled and nodded.

"It is a pleasure to have you stay here. And I too appreciate your kind words. The world will indeed be worse without him in it."

Luna Freya growled and crossed her arms. She sunk into her chair, face downcast.

"Now that we're all here," Vistoro continued, "please excuse me while I let the chef know we're ready. In the meantime," he said standing up, "perhaps you can share with the rest of the group what we discussed last night?"

He looked right at Castora. And though she knew he was addressing her, part of her wanted to slink under the table and disappear. Instead, she smiled and nodded.

But as Vistoro walked away, she found herself at a loss for words. She looked around nervously and shifted in her chair.

"Perhaps it would help if I said something first," interjected Zodim, standing back up in his chair.

"More than a week ago now, this young lady stumbled into my home. She was injured, dying in fact. And when I saw her, I'm ashamed to admit that I was tempted to let her die. I've been personally hurt by the actions of her father, yes. But traveling with her for a week has made it clear that I was correct in helping her. So please, hear out my friend Castora. I believe with her help we can put an end to Death for good."

Though she knew Zodim intended to help her, she couldn't help but wish the gnome hadn't said a word. Could she really help deliver on that promise?

As she looked around the table, she could feel everyone's eyes boring into her soul. But after passing over the yellow-green eyes of Luna Freya, she caught the handsome elf's gaze. The elf's eyes looked like a raging storm of blue and green. His stare was like that of a raging river.

"Well, I still wish my strike had been several centimeters higher," the elf's words cut like a knife.

"I don't blame you for feeling so and I don't expect your forgiveness," Castora replied passively.

"Good because you don't deserve it," the elf quipped.

"I can only say for my part that I do regret my actions," Castora continued unperturbed.

"Wish you had killed more," the elf barbed.

Castora swallowed the lump in her throat and continued.

"My father will not stop with Paxvilla. His vision is nothing short of hájje dominion. He wants all life on Evorath praising Him as god and king. And when you grow up knowing nothing but what he teaches you, it's easy to believe the lies."

"Making excuses now," interrupted the handsome elf.

"That's enough junior!" countered the older elf next to Savannah. He stood up, his chair scraped against the floor.

"I just don't know why we're putting up with this witch!" the young elf shouted, spreading out his arms.

"Artimus, please!" Ygabb bleated. She smacked her hands on the table and glared at the young elf. "Do you have no faith in my magic? We told you, her desire to help us is sincere."

Artimus Jr. shrugged before crossing his arms and slinking back into his chair. He glared at Castora.

The dark elf frowned, struggling to keep her composure as she pleaded with the elf.

"I'm sorry for all the pain I've caused you all," she cried holding his gaze. His eyes tore into her soul.

"I know there's no amount of apologizing that will change it. And I'm not asking you to forgive me. But please, let me do what I can to help."

She rubbed her eyes, her breath stuttered as she fought to hold in tears.

The western door creaked back open and Vistoro walked in with another lizock. They both carried large trays of food. Castora breathed a sigh of relief over the interruption, delighted to have people's attention off her.

"Tillura has really done it today!" Vistoro exclaimed as they stepped over to the table. "Scrambled duck eggs, pan-fried ham, and an assortment of fruit, nuts, and vegetables for our centaur guests."

Vistoro walked around to the other side of the table while Tillura walked over just past Castora.

"Please excuse me," the lizock chef said, reached over Castora's right shoulder and putting down the platter of eggs. She shifted the other tray, continuing around to place it down in front of the centaurs. Meanwhile, Vistoro deposited the tray of ham in front of Artimus Jr.

"Would anyone like a beverage besides their water?" asked Tillura looking around the table. "Some fresh-squeezed juice perhaps?"

She lingered there for a few moments, but as no one made a move to respond, she smiled wide and exited back through the western door.

Vistoro reclaimed his seat next to Tel' Shira, placing his napkin on his lap and glancing around the room.

"Savannah, would you say the blessing?"

Everyone else bowed their heads and closed their eyes. Seeing Zodim follow suit, Castora did too.

"Thank you Evorath for this food. Please let us keep our focus on you today and allow us to see past our prejudices as we work to show others your light. Amen."

"Amen," muttered the others, including Castora.

Looking back up, Castora hesitated to make a move. Back home, she was accustomed to being served. But it was clear by the casual manner the chef addressed everyone and by the fact that Vistoro helped her carry in the food that things were done differently here. Was she expected to serve herself?

Luna Freya made the answer easy as she stood up from her seat. She reached over and grabbed the large serving fork, taking a couple thick slices of ham. Turning to Castora, the felite motioned towards the tray of eggs.

"You want to help, you can start by passing the eggs," she remonstrated. Castora fought the urge to retort. As calmly as she could, she stood up and took the tray of eggs. She dished out a spoonful of the scrambled eggs and reached across the table, offering it to Luna Freya.

"Thanks," Luna Freya grumbled.

It took a couple of minutes for everyone to get their food and the ham reached Castora last. But once everyone had served themselves, they began picking away. Not wanting to miss the opportunity to eat, Castora grabbed her fork and knife and started as well. This food was a little milder than the breakfast Medicus had offered, but it was delicious, nonetheless.

As everyone ate, it seemed some of the tension in the room faded. But after a few minutes, Tel' Shira broke the silence.

"Castora, you never finished sharing with everyone. How do you believe you can help with the fight against your father?"

The dark elf finished chewing her food, swallowing the last bite, and dabbing her lips with the napkin. She took a sip of water from her goblet before responding.

"I know his plan, or at least enough of it. And I've learned everything I know about war from him, so I understand the way he fights. With my knowledge, you should be able to mount a successful defense. But truthfully, it's Zodim who has the lynchpin."

She glanced over at the gnome, his cheeks fat like a chipmunk as he chomped away at his food. He mumbled something, his words garbled. And he held up his left hand, gesturing towards Castora.

The hájje raised an eyebrow and tilted her head.

"Do you want me to explain?" she asked.

Zodim nodded, smiling as he continued chewing.

"Ah, well. Zodim has a box of sorts. Well, I suppose it's an old pyxis really. I'm guessing he can show it to you after breakfast?" she paused and narrowed her eyes towards the gnome. Turning back to the others, she continued.

"But from what he explained to me, the pyxis uses an ethereal magic. If we can corner Yezurkstal, we can use it to capture him in the pyxis, imprisoning him for eternity."

Savannah leaned forward. She wiped her mouth with her napkin and stared at Castora.

"Like the Pyxis of Dirkameed?" she asked. "Most scholars believe that is a legend."

Zodim coughed and slapped his chest. He held up his left index finger towards Savannah while he took a swig of his water.

"Aye, Dirkameed was heavily mythologized himself. A lizock mage of tremendous power and acclaim, he was worshiped as a god for centuries. And while many of the legends about his power are exaggerated, I'm happy to say the pyxis isn't one of them. With the right incantation and proper timing, you could imprison anything in there."

"Ha!" Artimus Jr. stood up and shook his head.

"You're telling us that this witch had a change of heart and you, the person who conveniently has the thing we need to imprison her father, are the one who found her? Sounds like a bit too much of a coincidence!"

"It's no coincidence at all," Tel' Shira beamed. "In fact, I now believe I understand some of my recent visions more clearly. But Castora, I'm wondering if you might help me figure out a missing piece."

"I hope so," replied the hájje, she tapped her fingertips together, waiting for Tel' Shira to continue.

"I keep having a recurring vision," Tel' Shira explained. "And in that vision, there are two dead trees on a hilltop, their branches nearly identical. Light trickles down on the first tree, causing it to bloom anew. I believe the first tree is you. However, the now living tree continues to reach out and touch the other dead tree, providing it with the same spark of life. So, I believe you may be the first hájje to be touched by Evorath's light. But you will not be the last. The question I've pondered, is who could this other hájje be?"

"My brother," Castora suggested. "I have a twin brother, Pollux. And though I know not how, I suppose he'd be the most likely person to listen to me. We've always had a-" she paused, reaching over and massaging her left elbow.

"Well, despite our sibling rivalry, we've always maintained a close bond."

"Murdering together tends to build that sort of bond I suppose" Artimus Jr. grumbled.

"Ugh!" Castora shrieked. She jumped to her feet and slammed both hands down on the table. She glared at Artimus Jr.

"I've had enough of your condescension! Zodim insisted you people were different, but your attitude seems like it would fit right in at Hájjeona."

"You're not fooling anyone you snow-skinned harlot!" Artimus Jr.'s face was red. He squeezed the table with both hands, his eyes burning with rage.

"Artimus Atyrmirid Jr. leave this dining room at once!" Vistoro stood up and glared at the elf. His words carried an authoritative tone, conflicting with his passive demeanor.

"I can't believe you're trusting this witch!" the elf stood up and spun around. "I'll be at the archery range when you people come to your senses."

The archer stomped out, grumbling under his breath.

Castora held her hands under the table, trying to keep them from shaking. She felt overwhelmed, a barrage of conflicting emotions washing over her. And the uncomfortable silence that ensued didn't help matters any. But after a few moments of silence and nervous glances, Luna Freya rose from her chair and cleared her throat.

"I'm going too," she proclaimed. "Look, I believe you Ygabb. So, I guess that means I believe her." She pointed at Castora. "But I'm not ready to just sit here and listen to this…to the person who murdered Mojo and so many others."

She turned and matched Castora's gaze for the first time. Her yellow-green eyes looked strained and tired. "A felite's trust is not given so easily. You'll have the chance to earn it in time, so don't let Artimus or I stop you."

With a dramatic flourish, Luna Freya pushed her chair against the table and marched out through the east door. Glancing to her left, Castora caught the embarrassment on Savannah's face, her cheeks red and eyes downcast. Artimus appeared angry more than anything, eyes narrow as he gazed at the east door.

"Well," Vistoro sighed. "I'm sorry about those two. Fortunately, I think we can continue the discussion without them. So, how do you propose use the pyxis on Yezurkstal?"

"I think I can answer that," interjected Zodim.

As he explained, Castora couldn't help but let her thoughts wander to Artimus Jr.

She hated that elf.

CHAPTER XV

"I'm telling you; it just wasn't there!" Zelag shrugged.

Zelag spent so much time studying people's faces that he could tell what George and Sarah were thinking with that glance. George's subtle raise of his eyebrows, Sarah's almost imperceptible twitch in her left eye, and more obvious, the biting of her lower lip. It all relayed some level of skepticism. And though that might bother him in other circumstances, he understood why now.

"You're really telling us that a massive castle just moved?" questioned Sarah after a few moments.

"I don't know what I'm telling you. But the entrance is gone. I put the stone in the tree as before and nothing happened. And I couldn't see any magic at work. That's why I'm telling you, I need to get down and chat with The Albino."

George smacked his hand over his face and rubbed his eyes. Sarah frowned, reaching out with her left hand and rubbing the back of his shoulders.

"Fine, we'll bring you down there," said the wizard after a few moments. His throat sounded a bit raspy.

"Great. This atrium has started to feel a bit cramped, so lead the way," Zelag motioned down the hallway.

George shook his head and strode for the stairwell.

Sarah followed next and Zelag took up the rear. As Zelag had witnessed Oogmut do before, George approached the wall to the left of the staircase. He placed his hand on the stone, traced the symbol, and stepped through the façade. The other two followed behind, descending the steps.

As they started down the circular stairway, Zelag considered the Petersons. Sarah seemed to be dealing with recent events better than her husband, but Zelag didn't have to use his abilities to see they were both hurting. Though he had never been much for comforting others, he felt compelled to say something.

"I'm sorry I wasn't there the other day," Zelag scratched his beard. "I uh. I just want to say that it sounds like you did everything you could."

"Hmph. That's true. It just wasn't strong enough to make a difference," George fumed.

"You know nobody else thinks that" rejoined Sarah. She glared back at Zelag.

Zelag brushed off Sarah's look, shrugging his shoulders.

"I don't know if you remember, but I fought Death sixty years ago," he explained. "And I thought between the arrow Artimus put in his skull, the bones I cracked, and the plunge in Lake Algarath had put an end to his terror. So, I understand what you're going through. I really do."

Zelag clenched his fist as he thought of the battle so many decades before. He took a deep inhale through his nose, narrowing his eyes as he pushed images of Cassandra out of his mind. He wouldn't admit the fear and anger he felt.

"I doubt it," contended George.

"You can doubt all you want," Zelag's voice grew louder. "But that doesn't change how powerful Yezurkstal is. So, hear me when I say, there was *NOTHING* you could do."

Zelag sniffled and wiped a stray tear from his face. Sarah glanced back his way with narrowed eyes. The shapeshifter averted her gaze, shifting his eyes down to the steps.

No one said another word as they descended the rest of the stairs. Even as they reached the landing, Zelag could feel the tension in the air. But George and Sarah proceeded to either end of the wall and performed the ritual.

The massive iron door clicked and rose up into the ceiling, revealing the jail cells within. As with previous visits, it seemed The Albino was waiting for them.

"Ah, is it time for another meal already?" the Albino probed, his words drenched with sarcasm.

"It might be time to let you go," remarked Zelag. "But that's entirely up to you."

"Oh, would you really let me go?" cajoled The Albino. "You hypocrites who claim to be against slavery and imprisonment. And yet here I remain."

"You know he's right though," added Sarah. "We're having a Guild meeting this evening and even just a little cooperation may earn you a reprieve."

"Oh, will it now?" The Albino inquired, his tone betraying him. Zelag smirked, silently praising his luck.

"I'll start with an easy one," said the shapeshifter as he stepped up to The Albino's jail cell. He looked inside, considering the man's appearance.

The prisoner's face was a bit scruffy, his hair was disheveled, and his eyes were outlined with dark bags, which sharply contrasted with his pale skin. Despite his haggard appearance, however, it looked like he had a fresh tunic and pants. Suppressing a smirk as he glanced at the Albino's missing hand, Zelag noted how well the wound had healed.

"I just got back from a visit to your old slave castle out east. The funny thing is, I couldn't find it anymore. Someone like you must be important enough to know. How could that be?"

The Albino blinked. He held Zelag's gaze, his face slowly rolling up into a smile. His smile grew until he let out a chortle. And then he broke into a full maniacal laugh.

Zelag looked over his shoulder back at the two mages. George had his face buried in his hands. He was rubbing his temples. Sarah sighed and shook her head. Was this how every day had gone with The Albino? Zelag wondered.

"Perhaps you're so comfortable down here that you'd like to stay indefinitely," Zelag shouted. It took a few moments for the Albino's laughter to cease.

"If I tell you why that is, will you really push for my release?" The Albino scowled.

"I don't have any say in the matter," replied Zelag. "But I bet it would be a good start. What do you think George? Sarah? Anything else that might help his case?"

"That would be a good start," Sarah grinned. "And I know there's no way you'd show us how to get there, but any other information you regale us with might help your cause. For instance, is there still an entrance we can access? Or perhaps you feel it's time to share why you were interested in Vistoro's pendant. You could be out of here by tomorrow morning."

"I could be out of here by the morning? As if I decided to come here of my own free will?" The Albino chided.

"You should be grateful we're not like your kind!" George fumed. "Maybe we should let Zelag do what he wanted to from the start. What do you say we open the cell and leave Zelag alone with him for a few hours?"

George looked between Sarah and Zelag. With red eyes, a deranged smile, and not even an ounce of sarcasm in his voice, Zelag couldn't help but wonder if he was serious. The way Sarah gaped at her husband all but confirmed the shapeshifter's guess. But she recovered quickly and used the suggestion.

"You might be right George," she remarked. She glanced up, narrowed her eyes, and rubbed her chin.

"Alright, enough!" The Albino shouted. "If I must deal with you sanctimonious heretics for another day, I might kill myself. Look!"

The Albino grabbed hold of the cell bars, leaning up close and staring at Zelag.

"The castle isn't gone. It was never there. The entrance was a portal, much like your wizard here creates. But one of our members has discovered a way to create a permanent gate."

"After you abducted me, they must have decided it was time to move the Erathal entrance." The Albino explained.

"Erathal entrance?" Sarah interrupted.

The Albino chuckled. "Yes, that's the beauty of it really. And I suppose now that the entrance is moved, it won't hurt to share. The people I work with and the cause we serve are bigger than an inconsequential little community like yours. It's bigger than the entire continent of Erathal."

"And what is this cause of yours?" Zelag asked.

"Ha! Why not?" The Albino stepped back from the bars and shrugged. "If you promise to release me by the morning, I'll tell you. I'll even tell you why that dragon pendant you keep asking about is so significant."

Zelag glanced back at the others. Even George seemed to find the prospect enticing, his face contemplative as the trio exchanged glances.

"I think we can promise that. What do you say Sarah? George?"

"If you tell us all that, then I can promise we'll let you out," replied Sarah after a moment's pause.

"But remember," added Zelag. "I can tell if you're lying."

The Albino smirked and slowly nodded.

Zelag focused on expanding his vision, looking at the prisoner's aura. It was exceedingly calm, an unexpected serenity considering the conversation. The dull blue glow remained stable as he began speaking.

"Where shall I begin? Perhaps with the basics. Your town of Marftaport defiles Evorath and your anarchistic views blaspheme Her very name. The Xyvor is quite clear about the way we are meant to live, and you fall short of that standard in every imaginable way.

"Where your people twist the Xyvor to fit your radical chaos, my people seek to institute Evorath's order. We are the true Children of Evorath. And that, in the briefest manner, is the cause we work towards."

The Albino paused. His red eyes bored through Zelag. It was distracting, but his aura remained a steady blue, providing no indications of deception.

"Hold on," Sarah gawked. "Your people are using slave labor, and you claim to represent Evorath?"

"Do you not remember the parable of the troll taskmaster? We provide all our workers with food and shelter. And left to themselves, they'd all be dead by now."

"That troll taskmaster?" Sarah blurted. "That is a lesson on why we *shouldn't* own slaves!"

"Hmph. Knowing you have a satyr high priestess, I suppose I shouldn't expect you to understand. But I won't waste my time trying to ignite your spark."

"As if you could," retorted George. "Just tell us what we want to know so we never have to listen to you prattle on again."

"Oh, does it hurt to think about the fact that your whole community is built on lies?" The Albino mocked.

"Enough!" Zelag leapt towards the cell door, drawing out a dagger as he did. In one smooth motion, he extended his arm through the cell, stopping just a centimeter shy of The Albino's throat. "Talk, or I may take away your opportunity."

The Albino's aura flashed red, but he quickly reeled it back in. With a mad smile, he took a step back and held up his remaining hand.

"Would you take this hand as well? Balance me out while you're at it?"

"That's up to you. The next words out of your mouth should be about the dragon pendant or about where you Children of Evorath call home. Otherwise, giving you a matching nub may be the kindest thing I do to you."

The others might have cared about Evorath, the Xyvor, or many other matters of faith. Zelag just wanted to be done with this interrogation.

"Alright, about where my people are. I never promised to tell you that. And that, of course, is because I don't know. Remember, I am just a small cog in a very large machine. So, I know not where the Children of Evorath call home, but I know it's not anywhere in Erathal.

"And before you ask, no I don't know if they even still have an entrance on this continent. But I keep my word because the Xyvor tells me to. And despite your heretical approach to community, I believe you will keep your word and release me when I reveal the last bit you asked for. You wanted to know about the dragon pendant, correct?"

"Go on." Zelag said flatly. The Albino's aura was still steady, almost too calm considering everything.

"You've continually referred to the pendant as if it belongs to Vistoro. But the truth of that pendant is much older than a former nobleman with delusions of grandeur. Do you not know the full providence of it? I suppose not even your Lord Vistoro knows, does he?"

"Just tell us what you know," insisted Sarah. She sounded even less patient than Zelag.

"Fine, fine." The Albino shrugged.

"The dragon pendant was commissioned by the first lizock king. After the Demon Wars, most of the major powers of Evorath went about forming their respective empires. And the lizock king Zarticann wanted to make sure his line would remain in power. So, he looked for an item of great power that could ensure just that."

George moaned.

"Don't go telling me you believe that fairy tale. Even if dragons really ever existed, can you possibly explain how Zarticann, or anyone else for that matter, managed to slay one?"

The Albino cackled.

"You believe what you wish. But according to the legend, Zarticann not only slayed the dragon. He plucked out both its eyes. And that dragon pendant your Vistoro so casually sold has one of those eyes."

"And why is a dragon's eye so important?" Zelag asked.

The Albino smirked, slinking back against the wall of his cell. "I believe I answered all the questions I agreed to. I expect you to keep your word."

Zelag clenched his fists and glanced back at the others.

George was still distracted. His eyes were heavy and jaw tight. But by his uneven posture and sagging of his shoulders, Zelag knew it was no sense looking for his support.

Sarah, on the other hand, looked a bit more collected. But the frown she wore, coupled with the frizz in her hair told Zelag all he needed to know. Though he wanted to push The Albino further, he knew when to call it quits.

"Alright," Zelag shrugged. "Let's get out of here. I'm sure our albino friend has a lot to think about before his release tomorrow. Without a portal back to his slave master, he's really going to have a hard time finding a place to go. Good luck with that. And hope I never see you again."

Without a glance back at the prisoner, Zelag spun around and waved. He strolled out past the giant iron door and back to the landing. The Petersons' footsteps told him they followed slowly behind. But to ensure he left The Albino as uncomfortable as possible, Zelag didn't stop in the landing. He continued up the first few steps before stopping to stomp in place.

As George and Sarah saw his antics, they exchanged confused glances. Zelag continued stomping, motioning towards the two and pointing at the iron wall. He lowered his hands slowly, still stomping his feet to imitate an ascent up the steps. After a few moments of confusion, Sarah finally got it.

The mages proceeded back to either side and spoke the incantation to close the door. As the iron door closed shut, Zelag ceased his acting and hopped down the steps. Huddling next to the two mages, he held out his arms wide.

"Well, what do you think? Is there any merit to that dragon eye thing?"

"Perhaps," replied Sarah, "but it's odd that none of us sensed that. That pendant would be a more powerful implement than any of our staffs, wands, or amulets."

"Pfft. That's why it must be nonsense," blurted George. "Maybe I'm dense enough to miss that kind of magic, but there's no way Sarah would have missed it. And what about you Zelag? Haven't you been after it for years? Have you noticed a massive amount of arcane energy emanating from it?"

Zelag shook his head.

"No, but I wasn't really looking for it. I don't know if Vistoro shared with you, but he sold that pendant when starting Marftaport to help purchase initial materials and supplies. Anyways, the reason I bring that up is because the gnome he sold it to might know more. He's somewhat of a hermit, but I've done some work for him over the years. So perhaps -"

"His name isn't Zodim by chance, is it?" Sarah asked.

Zelag furled his eyebrows and scratched his beard.

"It is. How did you know that?"

George chuckled and shook his head.

"You missed more than just the return of Yezurkstal."

Sarah placed her hand on George's back.

"Yes, he's right. Perhaps we should start back up to the surface. Maybe it's best we continue this discussion at Vistoro's," suggested Sarah.

George and Sarah started up the steps, leaving Zelag to ponder for a moment.

"Wait!" He called after them, running to catch up. "I've only been gone a few days! Was there really something else big that happened? I thought Yezurkstal returning and killing Irontail was news enough!"

"He didn't just kill Irontail," snapped George. "He killed other centaurs, some of our fellow Mage Guilders, and probably hundreds of other Paxvilla residents." He cleared his throat.

Zelag held his tongue, thinking about George's demeanor as they continued climbing the steps. With the other two remaining silent, the shapeshifter decided he ought to wait until arriving at Vistoro's until he said more.

As they made their way to the top of the steps, he felt a strange guilt overcome him. Yes, he was saddened by the news of Irontail's death. The centaur had proven a valuable ally over the years. And yet, he felt nothing about the loss of some unmet mages and a bunch of humans.

Was he supposed to mourn the death of strangers?

But then he thought a truly dreadful thought. With Death's return, would anyone be safe?

CHAPTER XVI

Marftaport, Northern Development
30 Julla, 1149 MT

Jaldor ran the back of his hand across his forehead. The afternoon sun beat down on his neck as he dished out another ladleful of stew. Passing the bowl down the line to Tor Noga, he accepted another empty bowl from Fredrick to his right and repeated the process.

It was amazing to watch the people of Marftaport giving so much to help the Paxvilla refugees. Glancing to the end of the table, he smiled as a young girl took her tray of food. And with hundreds more refugees ready for lunch, this division of labor was proving to be quite effective.

The northern end of the table started with Fredrick, whose entire job was to hand Jaldor a single bowl. Jaldor then scooped in a couple ladlefuls of stew and passed it on. Tor Noga put the stew on a tray and the process continued. The next person merely added a piece of bread, followed by a fresh piece of fruit, and down the line it continued until the refugee accepted the food on the southern side.

Jaldor was just glad to be included in the planning. Originally, the table was laid out east-to-west, which meant all the volunteers would be staring up at the afternoon sun. But as he passed along another bowl of stew, Jaldor wasn't thinking about the pain and loss from recent events. Instead, he was focused on how happy he was to be providing these people with food.

"I still can't believe they have enough to feed everyone," whispered Fredrick as he handed over the next bowl.

Jaldor glanced at the blacksmith before turning his attention back to pouring.

"I'm still wrapping my head around how everything works here," replied Jaldor. "Mostly it's their magic that makes everything easier. You should have seen how quickly they built our new home. Makes me wonder how things might have been different if the Regent of Paxvilla hadn't banned magic."

"Are you saying they just magically create extra food?" Fredrick gaped.

"Oh, no. At least I don't think so. But a lot of their farmers have been increasing the size of their crops. And apparently, they use magic to deter pests and aid in growth. So, they had an abundance ready to go."

"Well, it all seems extraordinary to me. I'm still flummoxed by how all these different peoples work together in a community like this. I suppose your pops feels vindicated though. He must be thrilled to be living around all these different races."

Jaldor chuckled. The massive stock pot of stew was at its end. So, after dumping the rest of the contents in the next bowl, he walked around Fredrick and deposited the pot on the other side. He then reached under the table and grabbed hold of the next pot. It must have weighed at least thirty kilograms.

Hoisting it up top, he scooped out another ladleful and continued passing bowls down the line before replying.

"Well, you know my father," he said. "You know that one of the elf couples that live here are actually the elves who rescued him and his sister more than sixty years ago."

Fredrick laughed and shook his head.

"I think he's been telling everyone about that!"

"I suppose I expected that," replied Jaldor with a shake of his head. He smiled at Tor Noga as he passed the next bowl.

"How have things been with your parents staying in the house?" Fredrick asked.

"A little crammed," admitted Jaldor. "But we're all happy to help where we can. I'm mostly worried Mary is going to think it's now normal for her to stay in the room with Samantha and me. I know Emma and her kids are happy to have the space though. I hear the inns are a bit overcrowded."

"Not just the inns," remarked Fredrick. "Since I don't have any family, I'm stuck out here in a tent. And it's been a bit difficult. I'm surprised there hasn't been any bloodshed yet."

Tor Noga leaned forward, his whiskers twitching.

"Sorry to interrupt, but do you really fear violent conflict might erupt?" The artist's tone was smooth and friendly.

Fredrick scratched behind his head as he glanced at the felite. "Hopefully not. But everyone's lost someone they knew. And many of them lost close friends or family. I'm probably the only man here who didn't suffer a major loss."

"Ah, I see," remarked Tor Noga. "Perhaps we can arrange some entertainment to help ease tensions."

"What sort of entertainment do you have in mind?" Fredrick asked. He passed another bowl to Jaldor.

Tor Noga shrugged and passed along the next tray.

"What sort of entertainment was most popular in Paxvilla. Perhaps some martial competition would be of interest, or maybe the theater troop can arrange a performance? One of the bards could surely perform as well."

"I don't know," interjected Jaldor. "I think with the sheer number of refugees, anything might be a bit difficult."

"I said back off!" a shrill voice pierced the air.

Jaldor stopped mid-scoop, leaving the stew to drip from the ladle into the bowl. He scanned the clearing for the source of the voice, his eyes stopping as he caught sight of two men standing in the middle of the line. Shaking his head, the farmer finished filling the bowl and passed it to Tor Noga.

"Fredrick, I think you can take over the stew for a few minutes," Jaldor muttered. Hanging the ladle on the edge of the stock pan, he stepped around the serving table. He jogged towards the conflict, considering the participants on the way.

Jaldor didn't recognize either man, but from this distance he could tell he was taller than either of them. The rotund young man had ginger hair and freckled skin. His narrow nose was an odd fit on his round face and his tiny ears were almost invisible under his unkept hair. He wore a simple white tunic and matching brown pants and surcoat. Puffing out his chest, the rotund man glared up at his taller counterpart.

Drawing nearer, Jaldor could see the taller man was at least six centimeters taller than the rotund one, and at least that much shorter than Jaldor. His other features were obfuscated by the large brown cloak draped over his form. He pressed up to the rotund man, pushing him out of line.

"Maybe if you weren't so fat, you won't be running into people!" he shouted. His hostile tone muted by his nasal timbre.

"Hey!" Jaldor hollered. "What's the problem?"

He slowed his approach as both men turned to look his way. With his head held high, Jaldor marched between the two combatants and spread his arms wide, forcing the pair apart.

"This smelly pig keeps bumping into me!" the cloaked man pointed. Jaldor could tell now how old this man was, his weathered and wrinkled skin sagging. His gray eyes were worn and weary, his body thin and tired.

The rotund man snorted; what an inopportune moment. Jaldor had to bite his tongue and close his eyes to avoid laughter.

"You keep bumping into me you old windbag!" The younger man screeched. He tried reaching around Jaldor and swung for the old man.

Jaldor stepped to the side, keeping the younger man off balance. The older man took a step back and shook his fists.

"Knock it off, both of you!" Jaldor shouted. He glared between the two combatants, his eyes aflame.

"Do you think you're the only two here?" he implored. "Everyone has lost enough; we don't need your bickering."

Jaldor ignored the conversations breaking out around him. Murmurs spread throughout the crowd as the line continued to move forward. Those who passed by left a wide birth, glancing nervously as they moved onward.

"What do you know about loss?" the old man trembled. The confidence had left his voice.

"Yeah, get out of my way and let me teach this old man a lesson!" demanded the younger combatant.

Jaldor took a deep breath and stepped out from between the two men. He pretended as if he was going to walk away, which was enough to catch both men off guard. But as they went to close the distance between one another, Jaldor swung back around and grabbed them both by their collars.

With a grunt, the farmer yanked the combatants out of line and pulled them a couple of meters away from the other refugees. Both men reeled, struggling to keep their balance as Jaldor let go.

"If you want to fight, go for it!" he shouted. "But not here! No one needs to hear two grown men going on like crybabies. So, what will it be. Get back in line and shut up, or come with me to get some clubs to bash each other with?"

The two men scowled at each other before glaring up at Jaldor. For a moment, the farmer expected the old man would take a swing at him. But it was the ginger-haired man who made an unexpected move.

He charged, screeching, and flailing his arms. Jaldor stepped to the side, leaving his foot out to trip the young man.

The rotund man whined and fell flat on his face. He lay there unmoving for a few moments. The old man broke into laughter, pointing at his downed adversary. But as Jaldor glared back down at him, he turned his nose skyward and marched back over to rejoin the line.

Rolling over, the red-faced ginger spat and brushed dirt from his face. He pivoted side to side, struggling to get up. His face scrunched up, his eyes watered, and he burst into tears.

Again, he flailed his arms around, rolling over to his right side and shielding his face as he sobbed. Jaldor felt a strange combination of pity and disgust. The duality of these two feelings caused a third sensation: a touch of guilt.

"Come now," Jaldor knelt beside the man. He glanced at the line of people, all of whom were averting their gazes. Was there really no one else in line who would help this poor fellow?

As he pondered this, he watched the older man shuffle back into the line, his eyes fixed on the ground. His shoulders sagged as he hunched over, a frown on his face.

"Tell me, what is your name?" the farmer inquired, looking back at the ginger man.

The man heaved and stuttered.

"My name," he burst back into tears, curling up into a ball and rolling to face away from the crowd.

Jaldor heard some of the crowd mocking the young man. Murmurs floated through the line and a few onlookers even began to laugh.

"What is wrong with you people?" a familiar voice penetrated through the crowd. The gruff feminine timbre of Luna Freya's voice was unmistakable, her words dripping with shock.

The felite pushed through the crowd, hissing at the old man as she shouldered him out of the way. She brushed off the offended arm and considered Jaldor.

Rising to his feet, Jaldor nodded towards the crying man.

"Could you help me get him up?" he asked.

"Yeah, not all of us are heartless nincompoops." Luna Freya sneered.

Synchronizing their movements, Jaldor and Luna Freya knelt beside the man. With a nod of understanding, they rolled him onto his back and grabbed hold of either arm. The man was trembling, his face drenched in tears as he sobbed. Seeing him now, Jaldor felt only pity.

With a grunt, the farmer and the felite lifted the man from the ground. "Come on," Jaldor ordered.

The man offered no resistance as Luna Freya and Jaldor dragged him across the field towards an oak tree. They rested him against the tree and took a step back.

"Alright ginger man," Luna Freya placed her hand on the man's shoulder. "Do yourself a favor and take a deep breath. Lean into that tree, feel the bark on your back, and embrace the serenity of this beautiful day."

Jaldor stared at Luna Freya with his mouth agape. True he hadn't known her long, but he never expected she had a soft side!

The man whimpered. He took a stuttered breath and coughed a couple of times. As his crying softened, he rubbed his eyes and shook his head.

"My name is Gregory," he whined.

Tears continued to roll down his face, but his sobbing gradually became a whimper. He wiped some snot from his face and took another stuttered inhale.

"It's good to meet you Gregory," Luna Freya grabbed his right hand and gave it a shake.

"My name is Luna Freya. I'm one of the warriors who helped fight off the hájje army. And if you've seen me on the battlefield, you might think I couldn't possibly understand what you're feeling. But let me tell you about a dear friend of mine."

Jaldor watched Luna as she spoke. He could see the tension on her face, the heavy weight in her eyes.

"My friend's name was Irontail. When I was just a kitten, no more than a few years old, I was orphaned by Yezurkstal. But I was blessed to be adopted by members of this very community in Marftaport. Though not originally part of this community, Irontail was one of the first people I met. And over the years, I spent time training and sparring with Irontail. He taught me so much about combat. But more important, he taught me how to handle my emotions."

Luna pointed to her heart, tapping her finger against her chest. She maintained a steady tone, only the pain in her face belying the difficulty of her words. Her whiskers twitched as she continued.

"You see, I often felt alone. My mother died in childbirth and my father was killed during the fight against Yezurkstal. And even though my adoptive parents were loving and kind, they were elves! I never felt that they understood me! But Irontail. Sure, he was a centaur. In many ways, even more foreign to me than my adoptive parents."

Gregory had all but stopped crying. He wiped his face, only a few tears continuing to trickle down.

"But you see, Irontail always took the time to listen. And after he listened, he'd say: 'I'm so sorry. Do you want my advice?' And I always loved that, while others would offer unwanted and unsolicited advice, he would always ask whether I wanted it first. Well, when I was a teenager, I had to deal with death again for the first time since my father died."

Luna paused, running her right hand along her eyebrows, and blowing out air through pursed lips.

"And you know what? I have found every time since, I remember that same advice. Gregory, do you want to hear the advice Irontail gave me?"

Gregory looked like a toddler whose parents just refused to give in to his demands. His face was red, his eyes puffy and wet. Mouth quivering, he nodded.

"He told me, 'Evorath can be a tough place and the people we share it with can be cruel. So, when you feel like you can't go on. When Evorath seems to be crumbling around you, remember two things. First, trust your family to help carry you through. And second, never let your enemies see you cry.'"

Luna placed her other hand on Gergory's other shoulder. She looked him right in and eyes and smiled.

"You understand what this means Gregory? It means don't let them see you cry," she nodded her head back towards the crowd. "But more than that, shed your tears and share the pain with those you love."

Jaldor was still in shock. But despite Luna's best efforts, he wasn't so sure it would work. Gregory's bottom lip looked like a dam about to burst; a deluge of tears ready to erupt.

"Now Gregory, remember that second part," encouraged Luna. "And tell me, who is it that you lost?"

Gregory closed his eyes and rubbed the bridge of his nose. With a sniffle, he looked back at Luna Freya.

"My whole family," he cried. "I watched them get slaughtered by the demons. Mum, dad, and my kid sister, Henrietta. So, I've got no family left!" he whimpered.

"Hey!" Luna gave him a shake and leaned in closer. "That's not true. You have a family right here if you want it. In fact, whether you decide to stay in Marftaport or not, I want to ask you. Will you be part of my family?"

Jaldor let out a breath he hadn't realized he was holding. He felt a surge of compassion, the back of his neck tingling at this display of kindness.

"And whether you like it or not," he interjected, "I declare today that you are part of my family. And Gregory, my brother, I am so sorry for your loss."

Luna pivoted to the right, motioning towards Jaldor. The farmer was unsure of her invitation at first, but as he stepped over, she took his hand and guided it to rest on Gregory's other shoulder. With a nod, she looked back down at Gregory.

"So, what do you say Gregory?" Luna asked.

Gregory looked between Jaldor and Luna Freya. His eyes ignited with a sparkle of hope. "Do you really mean it?" he asked, his voice less shrill than before.

"I never joke about family," rejoined Luna. "But be warned, if you say 'yes', you'll have your first family obligation tonight. You and I are grabbing drinks to lament Henrietta and your parents. Think you can manage that?"

"Will you come too?" Gregory glanced back at Jaldor, the look in his eyes reminiscent of a dog begging for scraps.

Jaldor hesitated for a moment, thinking about his obligations to Samantha and Mary at home. But of course, what example would he be setting for Mary if he refused?

"Of course! I wouldn't miss it," exclaimed Jaldor.

"Then it's settled!" proposed Luna. "My brothers Gregory and Jaldor, I'll see you at Sissera's at dusk."

She reached back out, grabbing Gregory's left hand and Jaldor's right. She nudged Jaldor, who followed suit and took Gregory's right hand. And Luna declared.

"Let Evorath know, no one will harm my brothers unless they wish to face my wrath."

CHAPTER XVII

Marftaport, Archery Range
1 Zerrum, 1149 MT

The air was humid, the sky overcast from the morning rain. With more dark clouds hanging ominously over the horizon, Artimus Jr. wondered how long he'd even have to train.

He picked up his right foot, shaking his leg to dislodge some of the caked-on mud. The entire training grounds was riddled with puddles after the heavy rain. Of course, the young elf considered the gilded edge of the weather; he had the archery range all to himself. Still, as he trudged to the ten-meter mark, he wished that it wasn't quite so dreary.

Artimus turned to face the targets. He considered the ten circle targets. Staggered unevenly behind the target line, his plan was to run across the field and plant an arrow in each target. Thanks to the haphazard, uneven placement, most of the targets were more than ten meters out. And more importantly, the uneven spacing between each target would mean he'd have to be flexible in his targeting.

After taking a few breaths to focus and calm his mind, the elf took off with a start. He reached over his shoulder, pulling out the first arrow and notching it in his bow. As he pulled back on the arrow, he started walking east and squinted towards the first target. Releasing on exhale, he picked up his pace.

He notched another arrow, refocusing on his next target and letting it loose. Then another, and another. Picking up the pace, he let the next two arrows loose in a jog, and the one after that he reached a full run.

"Damn it!" Artimus Jr. cursed, fumbling with an arrow as he stepped right into a puddle. His boot sunk past the top vamp, causing him to lose his balance and stumble. He let loose his arrow, the projectile sinking into nearby mud as he struggled to regain his balance.

The elf moaned, shaking his foot off before stomping towards the targets. He cast his bow aside in frustration, shaking his head and mumbling profanities under his breath. It was bad enough that they were sheltering a hájje in Marftaport, he thought. Couldn't the weather at least cooperate?

He continued to pout as he reached the seventh target. "Second ring," he murmured as he pulled the arrow from the target. "Not good enough."

Shaking his head, he went along to each of the targets to retrieve his arrows. The sixth was closer to the center, but the fifth was in the outer ring. The fourth was better at least, resting just a few centimeters outside the bullseye. The third and second targets had arrows on opposite sides, but both were similarly close to the bullseye.

"At least I got one," he mumbled as he arrived at the first target. The arrow was planted just a hair off dead center.

Replacing his final arrow in his quiver, Artimus shook his head and trudged towards the western wall. He considered calling it quits. But as he looked towards the wooden gates, his frustration was instantly replaced with rage.

The doors creaked open, and walking through beside Zelag was the pale devil, Castora.

As the pair stepped through the gate, Castora stopped dead in her tracks, her hands hanging by her side as she stared towards the elf. Zelag stopped mid-stride, turning to look at Artimus and smiling.

"Oh, Little A! I didn't expect anyone else to be out here," the shapeshifter spouted.

"And I didn't expect to see you consorting with the enemy," Artimus Jr. chided. He ground his teeth, glaring at Castora with contempt.

"The enemy? You mean Castora?" Zelag raised an eyebrow. He scratched at his beard and looked between Artimus and the hájje.

"Yes, I can't say how, but she's tricked the others into believing she's here to help. I didn't think you'd fall for the snow-skinned harlot's spell." Artimus Jr. scorned. He approached Zelag with fists balled.

"Alright, we need to settle this!" Castora snarled. Her cheeks were red with anger as she stomped towards Zelag.

"OK, this can't be right," Zelag stepped into Artimus's line of sight. He looked back and forth between the two.

"I'm not going to play mediator here!"

"I don't need a mediator," seethed Artimus. "Just get out of my way and I'll take care of this murderess."

"You want a fight?" Castora rebuffed. "Then I hope you're ready to finish what we started in Paxvilla."

"No one is finishing anything they started in Paxvilla!" Zelag's eyes were wide as he glanced between the two.

Unwilling to debate the matter, Artimus Jr. took a sharp right turn. He plodded towards the weapon racks. They were just a few meters away, right outside a small storage shed. There were two separate racks, each of them a full two meters tall and filled with practice weapons of all variety.

"I'll beat the truth out of you!" Artimus shouted. He grabbed a pair of swords and spun around.

Castora had changed trajectory as well. She stomped towards the elf, her black eyes pulsing with anger. He threw the first sword towards the hájje, simultaneously tossing the second into his sword hand. Clasping the wooden practice sword, he assumed a defensive posture.

The hájje was unphased, catching the sword midstride. If looks could kill, Artimus would have dropped dead that very instant. Her fierce determination seeped from every pore. And in that moment, just as he did back in Paxvilla, the young elf felt an inkling of hesitation as he considered her person.

How could such a wicked person look so beautiful? He wondered. But he wouldn't let his base qualities impact this most important work.

"I went easy on you before," Castora spat. "But this time I'll teach you how a competent fighter handles a sword. Too bad it's not the real thing!"

"Too bad indeed!" Artimus shouted and charged with his sword held overhead.

Castora cried out, running to intercept him.

Reaching the hájje, Artimus Jr. clenched the sword with both hands and swung wildly. Castora blocked at ninety degrees, pushing the elf off balance with a surprising show of strength.

Going with his momentum, Artimus rolled over backward, springing back to his feet. He side-stepped to the right, adjusting his grip to wield the sword in his right hand. But Castora didn't let up.

She screamed, arching her weapon at a forty-five-degree angle towards Artimus's left shoulder. The elf grinned, spinning away from the attack and swinging his sword in a wide arch. With a clunk, he struck the back of Castora's sword, driving it into the mud at her feet.

Without pause, Artimus jerked back, elbowing Castora in the face. The dark elf growled. She let go of her sword and hooked her arms up, grabbing hold of Artimus's sword arm. Before the elf could react, she wrenched his arm around, forcing him to drop his sword.

Artimus clenched his jaw, struggling to slip out of the hold. But Castora pushed harder, driving his right arm up towards the back of his neck.

"Let. Me. Go!" Artimus squatted low and dug his heels in. With a forceful exhale, he kicked off the ground, flinging himself backward. His heavier weight did the trick, allowing him to topple over backwards on Castora.

The impact loosened her grip and he scurried free. As he crawled away through the mud, he reached for his sword. But Castora yanked on his leg, pulling him back.

"Give it up witch!" he kicked towards her.

"Only when you admit I could have killed you!"

Again, the hájje demonstrated surprising strength as she yanked Artimus Jr. towards her. With felite-like agility, she rolled back and sprung to her feet. Artimus reacted on instinct, kicking his right foot in front of Castora, and planting his left behind her. With a hard jerk around, he wrenched her off her feet. She yelped as her back hit the ground.

Heart pounding in his chest, Artimus pushed back up to his feet and dove on top of the dark elf. She flailed, trying to push him away and he grabbed her wrists and pinned her in the mud. She snarled and barred her teeth, blood tricking from her nose.

"Why didn't you kill me?" Artimus fumed.

Castora kept pushing in vain, but she slowed her squirming and looked up at Artimus, her eyes ablaze.

"I wish I had!" she cried. And suddenly, just for a moment, her anger lifted. Artimus could see her brokenness.

But as Artimus loosened his hold for just a moment, Castora took advantage of his lapse. She jabbed her left arm up and grabbed Artimus's tunic. While pulling down with her left, she pushed up with her right hand and bucked her hips to the left. Before the elf realized it, he was flung over on his back.

And in a flash, Castora sprung on top.

Artimus covered his face instinctually. Castora jabbed him in the ribs, knocking the wind from his lungs. She swung again, but after a momentary struggle the elf grabbed with his right and seized hold of her left wrist.

Castora slapped him with her free hand.

"You fight like a child," Artimus spat.

"I guess you lose to a lot of children," Castora barbed.

Suddenly, Artimus's right hand felt hot, like he was clasping a burning coal. Releasing his hold, he planted the hand in the mud to cool it down. The hájje took the opportunity, clutching his throat with both hands.

"I could crush your windpipe and end it now," Castora threatened. "But I told you, I'm no longer your enemy."

Her eyes wavered, oscillating back and forth as she looked down and pleaded with Artimus.

"You killed so many. You killed Mojo!" Artimus Jr.'s voice was hoarse. He ground his teeth to squelch his tears.

"How many times do you want to hear that I'm sorry! I'm sorry, I'm sorry, I'm sorry!" Castora shrieked.

Artimus felt a surge of adrenaline, his heart ready to fly out of his chest. He shoved his hands between Castora's, spreading them apart and leaving her to fall towards him. Using the shock of the moment, he rolled over, forcing her onto her side. But he wasn't strong enough to complete the move, leaving the pair to lay sideways facing one another.

And for a moment, neither made a move.

Artimus watched his opponent, blood still dripping from her nose, her body stained in mud, breathing heavily from the struggle. She had such fire and determination in her eyes, but he saw beyond that. He saw the pain in her eyes, the agony from a lifetime of fear and abuse. Suddenly, he believed what the others had already accepted.

She was not his enemy.

And seeing her again in this light, he looked at her with a fresh set of eyes. He thought back to their parlay prior to the battle of Paxvilla and the initial sparks he felt. Just like that, he felt it again. Even with mud-caked in her hair and blood tricking from her nose, this dark elf was stunning.

As this realization came into focus, Castora rolled back over, pushing him onto his back and pinning him down. Her eyes burned with the same desire he felt as she gave him a squeeze, leaned in, and kissed him.

Pulling away from the embrace, the dark elf regarded Artimus Jr., her mouth folding up into a smile. The elf wished he could capture her expression and keep it for eternity.

But the moment was broken when Zelag stepped into sight and cleared his throat.

"Should I leave you two alone?"

Chapter XVIII

Marftaport, Archery Range
1 Zerrum, 1149 MT

Castora couldn't believe herself. She considered Artimus Jr. laying beneath her. The allure of his hazel eyes, his smooth jawline, and strong arms. Even covered in mud, the dark elf couldn't deny her attraction to him.

But what possessed her to kiss him, she couldn't say.

"Should I leave you two alone?"

She blinked and remained unmoving for a second. Blushing, she pushed herself into a kneeling position. After taking a moment to glance around with her peripherals, she stood up, shaking the mud from her hands.

Artimus remained prostrate before her; his head tilted to the left as he blinked at her. Castora felt like she spent hours deliberating her next move. Should she run away? Perhaps a slow turn and casual stroll would be better? Or maybe she should resume the fight.

Instead, she extended her hand. She kept her expression blank, her muscles tense as she awaited the elf's response.

The elf smirked and accepted. He grasped her wrist, and she grabbed hold of his, leaning back and pulling him to his feet.

He averted Castora's gaze, shifting back and forth on his feet. "Uhm, thank you." He uttered.

"You're welcome," she muttered back.

Zelag cleared his throat.

Castora spun around, withdrawing her hands behind her back and grasping her left wrist in her right hand. With a toothy grin, she looked up and shrugged.

"Well, it's at least safe to say you aren't going to try and kill each other. That is safe to say, right?"

The dark elf glanced down to her feet, but before she could reply, Artimus Jr. stepped next to her and spoke.

"I. We. I mean." The elf glanced at Castora, but as soon as she caught his gaze, he turned away and rubbed the back of his head.

"I promise I won't be killing anyone here," vowed Castora.

"Yes, same!" echoed the elf.

"In that case, I think I'll leave you two at it. As I was saying Castora, this is the archery range, but I'm sure Little A can give you a more interesting tour." Zelag smirked and waved.

Artimus winced at the use of 'Little A', blushing and averting his eyes from Castora. Without another word, Zelag spun around and strode for the gates.

Castora sniffled, touching her nostrils with her left hand, and inspecting the blood. Her face throbbed, the base of her nose tender to the touch. But with only a bloody nose and some dirty clothes, she considered this interaction a success.

"I don't suppose you have a handkerchief," she pondered.

"Oh, of course!" Artimus reached into his surcoat breast pocket and pulled out an unsoiled, white cloth. With a nervous smile, he offered it to Castora.

"Thank you," she returned his smile and accepted the handkerchief. Only as she blotted the blood from her nose did she look up to realize the sun had finally come out.

The cloud coverage from earlier had cleared away, leaving only a few stray forms floating through the sky. And as she considered the warmth of the sun on her skin, she couldn't help but giggle. It was as if the kiss she shared with Artimus had put an end to the dreary day. There was renewed hope.

"What's so funny?" Artimus leaned forward, arching an eyebrow as he examined Castora's face.

"Oh, nothing. The day no longer feels so dreary, does it?"

Artimus pursed his lips, nodding as he glanced skyward.

"Would you look at that," he clasped his hands behind his back and rocked back and forth.

Castora folded the handkerchief over and pressed it back against her nose, holding it there as she tilted her head back. She reached around with her right hand to tease her hair. Grimacing, she pulled out a lump of mud and flung it to the side.

"I um. I hope you'll accept my apology," Artimus Jr. mumbled, his voice sheepish.

Castora looked directly at the elf, taking the cloth from her nose, folding it again and blotting. Seeing it free of any new blood, she tossed it to the elf.

"Thanks," she smiled. Artimus fumbled with the handkerchief, grinning nervously as he replaced it in his surcoat.

"But I think we need to spar a bit more before I'm willing to forgive you. Think you're up for that pretty boy?"

"I, uh." Artimus blushed. He bobbed his hands around, as if struggling to grab something from the air. "Are you sure you're up for it?"

"Hmph. Not if you keep acting like a timid sheep," teased Castora. "But if you can show me the same fire you had last time, then absolutely."

Castora reached back and ran her fingertips through her hair again, sifting through some more mud and tossing it aside. She stared at Artimus expectantly.

Artimus returned her stare. Looking into his deep, thoughtful eyes, she watched the spark reignite. She felt butterflies in her stomach and couldn't help but let her lips curl up into a wide grin. She bit her bottom lip and narrowed her eyes.

"Then let's begin," she muttered. Artimus returned the smile and turned around as if to go retrieve the swords.

"I meant now," clarified Castora. As the last syllable slipped past her lips, she crouched and darted towards the elf.

Artimus was too slow to respond, only just turning back towards her as she reached his position. His eyes looked like they might burst out of his head. Castora kept low, sweeping Artimus's legs out as she ran past. As the elf went down with a thud, the hájje ran for the swords.

"Now you're asking it!" Artimus shouted after her. She smirked, running past the first sword to retrieve the further one. With a quick flourish of the weapon, she turned back around. Artimus was but a few meters from the other sword.

But she wasn't going to make things easy. She took off again, taking the sword in her left hand and sliding to retrieve the other in her right. Artimus dove for the sword too late, flying just over Castora and rolling away.

As Castora came back to her feet, Artimus followed suit.

"Take one if you can," Castora taunted.

She adopted a wide stance, her feet squared up against her opponent. With a sword in either hand, she simply stood her ground, waiting to see what technique the elf would try.

Gazing into his eyes, she could see the elf working through the situation. He stood unguarded, his hands hanging by his side as if inviting her to attack. At least he wasn't dim.

After a few seconds, Castora began to worry if he'd ever make a move. But then he did.

He darted towards her in a flash.

Pivoting her right foot back, Castora shifted her weight, leaving her left foot pointed towards Artimus while leaning back on her angled right foot. She held out the sword in her left hand perpendicular and angled the one in her right to point towards the elf. She sunk into her squat and kept her eyes forward.

As he drew near, Artimus flung his hands forward, spraying Castora with mud.

The dark elf recoiled. She winced, relaxing the grip on her leading sword, and swatting at the flying mud. Artimus used this distraction to charge in and grab hold of her left arm.

Castora stabbed with her right sword, but in a surprising display of dexterity, the elf wrenched her left arm and used it to deflect her own attack. Pivoting her left foot back, she pulled the elf towards her and attempted to slip from his grasp.

Instead, Artimus used the momentum of her maneuver and swung himself in the same direction. Without any resistance, Castora jerked around, her lower back objecting as she twisted. She closed her eyes and gritted her teeth, but her footing was too unstable in the mud, causing her to stumble backwards.

As she fell, Artimus released her left arm and continued his own momentum, spinning around to her other side in a whirlwind.

Castora released her left sword, slapping the ground with her arm to cushion her fall. Meanwhile, she flourished her primary sword, hoping to keep Artimus at bay.

But the elf was too smart, diving to the left and grabbing the other sword as he rolled to his feet. Castora didn't delay, rolling away to her right and springing upright. She jumped into a defensive stance and squared up against Artimus.

"You fight better without a weapon, don't you?" Castora grinned.

"You're welcome to believe that if you want to lose," replied Artimus with a smirk.

Castora glared at the elf. He assumed a balanced stance, his feet and sword both pointed right at her. But the angle of his blade was just a bit too low, and his feet just a couple centimeters too far apart.

"I'll take my chance," Castora retorted, lunging towards the elf.

Artimus's eyes widened as he parried her first attack. He took a step back and kept his guard up, a wide smile still plastered on his face.

"I like to see the confidence at least," Castora winked and lunged in again.

Castora gained ground, pushing her opponent back with each exchange of blows. Artimus's footwork was a bit sloppy, but it seemed the mud was offsetting that advantage. But after pushing him back at least three meters, the dark elf finally spotted her opening.

She feigned an attack, shifting her weight to the right just enough to bait Artimus into a preemptive move. And as he brought his sword left to deflect the strike, she arched her sword around the other way and hooked it behind the elf's legs. Pulling the weapon towards her, she swept his feet out.

As he tumbled onto his back, spreading his arms to cushion his fall, Castora stepped her boot onto his sword arm and held the tip of her sword against his throat.

"Maybe I do fight better without a weapon," joked Artimus, blinking towards the sword in his face.

"You just need to tighten up your form and narrow your focus. I noticed you react to every little movement I make before I even commit to it. You're lucky you're handsome."

Artimus gasped, his eyes bulging from his head.

"What's that?" he barked.

Castora turned her head, her senses catching up with her too late. She felt the wood of Artimus's sword strike her calf and yelped as she fell backwards.

But she refused to let him get away with such a dirty trick. She reached inward and tapped into her arcane power, forming a thin layer of dark magic to cushion herself. Meanwhile, she returned her gaze to Artimus.

As she landed, she repositioned her sword to block his approach. And he walked right into her sword, jabbing himself in the stomach before backpedaling.

Castora rolled back and kicked her legs up, jumping back to her feet. She crouched and tackled Artimus, pinning him on his back and grasping his throat.

Glaring down at the elf, she leaned in closer, so their noses were only millimeters apart.

"Do you yield?" she whispered.

Seeing the shocked look on Artimus's face, she leaned in and sealed her victory with a kiss.

CHAPTER XIX

Marftaport/Paxvilla
2 Zerrum, 1149 MT

"If that's the plan, shouldn't I just peak my head through the portal?" Zelag scratched the back of his head.

"I wouldn't recommend it," replied George.

Zelag and the others all looked to the wizard as if expecting him to elaborate. But after realizing he wasn't going to, the shapeshifter continued.

"Alright. Why not?"

"I don't know," George shrugged. "And that's the problem. What happens when you split yourself between two locations and hang out there? Are you in the ether? Are you on Evorath? Are you in both locations? If you want to risk it, be my guest. But I don't know enough about the ether to know what it might do, especially to someone like you."

Zelag squinted towards the wizard, tightening his lips. A brown aura of sadness surrounded him. But Zelag really hoped this trip would give George some closure. He just hadn't been himself since Yezurkstal returned.

Of course, whatever apprehension George had about the portal, Zelag had that much more about Yezurkstal. He wouldn't admit to anyone else, but he was terrified. In fact, as the group stood discussing the plan, he did his best to ignore the circumstances of his mission.

This was just routine recon. Look in, get out fast.

"I suggest we avoid any risks," interjected Savannah. "You should go all the way through and take a quick glance around. Then come back."

"So, we're thinking ten seconds or less?" Zelag asked, glancing around at the others.

He considered all their auras. Both Artimus and Savannah were alight with a nervous yellow energy. Jaldor, and the other two humans whose names Zelag hadn't bothered to listen to, were even more nervous, a subtle orange glow surrounding the trio. Then there was George, and next to him Sarah, whose peculiar aura looked like a wash of brown, green, and yellow. And finally, both Silkhair and Steelbrow rounded out the group with brown and yellow competing with just a hint of excited blue energy bouncing around.

They still had hope for Irontail's survival, a realization that nearly caused Zelag to lose his composure.

"Or less, yes." Stressed Artimus. It had been years since Zelag had heard that tone from the former ranger. The confidence and authority in his voice contradicted his nervous energy.

"I still don't like this," interrupted Sarah. "I know I never faced him, but from everything we've heard, Yezurkstal is too powerful to miss a portal like this. If he's still there, what will stop him from getting through?"

"Me." Replied Zelag with a confident façade. "If I see any signs of dark magic, I'll come right back through."

"That's right," added Savannah. "And Zelag is not only immune to magic, but he has the added benefit of his unique sight. While it might take us a second or two to sense around for magic, he'll see it right away."

"Exactly," Zelag threw his hands up and shrugged.

He noticed Artimus looking a bit too intently at him. Was his fear showing through the surface? He wondered.

"Sounds like we have it all figured out then," George fumed. "Should we get it over with then?"

"I'm ready." Zelag nodded.

He glanced back down at his waist, adjusting his belt and taking a deep breath. Looking back up, he turned to face the east wall, staring at the cold stone in anticipation.

George outlined a circle along the wall and pointed his staff. Zelag watched from the corner of his eye as the arcane energy flowed through the staff and shot out against the wall. The portal opened in an instant.

Clenching his fists, Zelag stepped through. Pulsing rainbow lights assaulted him the moment he breached the portal, disorienting him as he stepped through the other side. Shaking his head to fight the vertigo, he looked around the empty field.

He wondered if his focusing on arcane energy caused the disorientation, but as he opened his eyes, he was dumbfounded.

Ash and dust surrounded him for as far as he could see. The smell of smoldering wood and ash filled the air. Yezurkstal had destroyed everything.

But that wasn't what surprised Zelag the most. Instead, as he looked around, trying to see into the arcane world and detect any signs of magic, he found nothing. He rubbed his temples, squinting around for any signs of arcane energy. There was nothing, not even a faint glow.

Yezurkstal hadn't just obliterated Paxvilla. He took the very magic from the land.

Zelag's legs trembled, his knees buckling and giving way. The shapeshifter fell to one knee, his jaw clenched as he pressed his face into the palm of his hands.

He screamed, folding forward, and leaning into his knees. With the Avatar gone, how could they possibly hope to defeat such a powerful enemy?

But Zelag couldn't think about that now.

He breathed deep in through his nose, running his hands down his face, he tugged on his beard as he pulled down. Sitting back, he placed his hands on his knees, blew the air from his mouth, and stood back up.

Refocusing his vision to just rely on his human sight, he stepped back through the portal. The lack of light this time confirmed his suspicion, but as he came out the other side, he was greeted by the hopeful and apprehensive faces of his allies.

Zelag looked around, stopping to lock eyes with Artimus last. The elf sighed, dropping his gaze, and shaking his head.

"Well, what did you see?" Steelbrow gaped.

"I'm sorry," Zelag looked down at the centaur's hooves.

Silkhair snorted, stomping her front hooves. Zelag looked up and watched her face melt into despair. Her eyes swelled up, her mouth trembling, and she burst into tears. Steelbrow choked up and embraced his mother, pulling her in close.

Sarah and Savannah rushed to comfort the centaurs. They came up alongside Silkhair, placing their hands on her side.

"What does that mean?" George chided. "You're sorry for what? What did you see?"

"There's nothing left," Zelag mumbled.

"What do you mean, nothing?" asked Artimus, his eyebrow arched, head tilted to the right.

"I mean Yezurkstal obliterated Paxvilla and razed it to the ground. There is no sign of life, no sign of habitable shelter, and" Zelag trailed off, scratching his beard as he pondered the best way to explain the rest.

"And what?" begged George.

"I don't know how, but it seems he's depleted the entire city of magic. I couldn't see any signs of magic left."

"Pfft. That's impossible," George scowled, tapping his staff on the floor. He shook his head and turned to Jaldor and the other humans.

"You want to see for yourselves?" he asked.

"Aye. I must see this with me own eyes to believe," uttered the shortest of the humans. He was a flabby young fellow with blue eyes, black hair, and only a few days' growth of a beard on his face.

"We still must exercise caution," interrupted Artimus. He stepped up beside George, placing his hand on the wizard's shoulder. George immediately shirked away, shaking off his robes. He glared back at Artimus.

"Then come along and exercise whatever caution you must. But we've waited too long already."

George turned back to the east wall and opened another portal. The two unfamiliar humans stepped forth immediately, not even hesitating to walk through the portal. Jaldor followed close behind, but paused to glance back at the others. His gazed stopped on Artimus, who offered a nod in reply.

Returning the nod, Jaldor stepped through next.

"Alright, last call for anyone wanting to go," George was sounding more impatient every time he spoke.

"Zelag, let's go too," suggested Artimus.

"I planned on it," replied Zelag. He looked back to the centaurs, who were still bawling in the western part of the room.

With a sigh, the shapeshifter stepped back through the portal. As he came out on the other side, he saw the humans were taking it just as he had. The flabby fellow stood dumbfounded, glancing around, his mouth wide open. The other man, with pale skin, amber hair, and brown eyes, looked nauseous. He stood staring north with one hand on his hip and the other over his face.

Jaldor maintained his composure, looking all around him. But with a closer look, Zelag could see his aura had darkened, the bleakness of the situation weighing on the farmer.

Artimus stepped through the portal next. He shook his head once as he stepped through and immediately surveyed the area. "This is unbelievable," he uttered.

Sarah emerged from the portal next, followed almost immediately by her husband, the portal snapping shut just behind.

Zelag considered them all, standing amidst the dust and ash of the once prosperous city. It was all so eerie.

"I can't believe this," George muttered.

The wizard looked pale, his eyes shaking in disbelief as he looked back towards the shambles of the city wall. He stumbled backward, but Sarah stayed by his side. Running up beside her husband, she reached out and offered him support. But dread filled her face as well, her aura turning a dark brown.

"What sort of monster could do something like this?" she questioned.

"The worst kind," answered Artimus. With a frown plastered on his face, the elf approached the mages.

"At best, Yezurkstal thinks of us as insects to be squashed. But worse than that, he looks at some of us as tools to advance his cause. As with all tyrants, he feels justified to use any means necessary to achieve his goal."

"And what is that goal?" Jaldor asked.

"To reshape the world in his image," the elf replied.

Zelag looked around, watching the collective mood damper even further. If the ashy air wasn't eerie enough, seeing so many dark auras left Zelag's skin crawling.

"What about the castle?" Jaldor asked, his face lighting up and aura softening. "I mean, look!" he pointed towards the southern walls.

"Those walls are all salvageable. Even if Yezurkstal destroyed the whole of Paxvilla, I doubt he took the time to demolish the castle. There may still be hope of rebuilding."

"Aye, I bet you're right! Hell, there may even be survivors hiding out there" agreed the flabby fellow. "What do you think William?" He nudged the other man.

William shook his head, his eyes still downcast.

"Sure, maybe. How do we even find where the castle is? I mean, what about the roads? I can't even see them."

"Just look north," interjected Jaldor. He walked a few steps in that direction and leaned forward, holding his right hand just over his eyes.

"Yeah, there it is," the farmer pointed.

"Where?" asked the flabby fellow.

William stepped up beside Jaldor and squinted.

"I still don't see it," he complained.

"That's fine," interrupted Artimus. "There's still a lot of ash and smoke in the air clouding our sight. But before we go marching in that direction, let's all get on the same page. The odds are there are no survivors. And there's a chance Yezurkstal has made camp in the castle or left some of his undead minions behind in case anyone returned."

"So, here's how we proceed," Artimus continued, pausing for just a moment, and making sure everyone had eyes on him.

"Zelag, you and I will take up the rear. Keep your eyes wide and look for any signs of magic. I want to know how far this devastation extends. George and Sarah, you take up the front. Make sure to keep your senses alert. Any indication of magic at work, and you raise the alarm for the rest of us. Jaldor, William, and Charles, you three remain in the middle. And everyone, stay close and stay alert. Everyone clear?"

The elf looked around. His aura had lightened, turning a confident shade of blue. Everyone in the group gave some affirmation, ranging from nods to an "urgo" from Sarah.

Zelag smiled. He had forgotten how much he appreciated Artimus's ability to keep a clear head amidst situations like these.

Sarah leaned over and whispered something to her husband. Whatever it was seemed to give George some needed motivation, his aura growing lighter as he walked to the front of the group. Once there, he held up his staff.

"Alright, everyone stay close," he announced.

Without awaiting a response, he lowered his staff and started forward. Walking alongside him on the left, Sarah took her husband's hand and the couple proceeded north.

Jaldor, Charles, and William followed just a couple meters behind the mages, in that order. And Artimus and Zelag moved into line at the rear.

"I should stay at the back," suggested Zelag.

"Agreed," Artimus replied with a nod. With his bow drawn and ready, the elf stepped forward and Zelag kept close behind, slowly shifting his gaze left and right as they walked.

For the first few minutes, no one said a word. And Zelag didn't blame them, especially the Paxvilla men. He understood better than anyone how it felt to see one's home so completely obliterated. Of course, the shapeshifter didn't want to dwell on such thoughts.

"Did you bring us in at the barracks?" Zelag shouted ahead to George.

The wizard glanced back, but continued forward.

"Yes, the same spot we evacuated from a few days ago." His voice was laced with despair.

"Ah, of course," Zelag replied, likely too quietly for the mage to hear him.

"Wait, that was the barracks?" questioned Charles, his voice labored by heavy breathing. "Maybe we should teleport to the castle. That's at least. What? Five kilometers away?"

"No teleporting until we need to," shouted George, his eyes glued forward.

"Why not?" Charles whined.

"Didn't you hear what Zelag said?" Sarah turned and shouted back. "The magic is all but gone from this area. George has his staff, hat, and robes to draw magic from, along with his latent energy. It would be foolish to waste limited magic when we could just as easily walk there."

"Well, it's not so easy for all of us," Charles pouted. He crossed his arms but kept up his pace.

"Limits of magic aside," interrupted Artimus, "it would be foolish to teleport to the castle. If Yezurkstal is there, or left behind any of his minions, the last thing we need to do is stumble right into them."

"You can't argue with that," added Jaldor.

"Well, does anyone see any signs of life? Or of magic?" William asked.

"We'll announce the moment we do," assured Sarah.

No one else had anything to add, so the party continued forward. Zelag kept glancing side-to-side, looking out for anything beyond the ash and smoke. But everywhere he looked was more of the same. It was like the very essence of magic had been stripped from every corner of the land.

It was truly terrifying how thoroughly Yezurkstal had decimated the city. Everywhere he looked, Zelag saw piles of ash and dust. Entire buildings were erased, leaving nothing but their stone foundations.

As they passed by what used to be the blacksmith's forge, Zelag finally spotted some topography. The forge itself was still standing -or at least part of it. The only reason he could tell was the large anvil sitting in the center, surrounded by various hunks of stone and metal.

Zelag focused on the anvil, hoping the iron would have some residual magic. But as with everything else, he saw nothing but the black of the iron. How had Yezurkstal so completely drained the magic from everywhere? This question weighed on Zelag as they continued trekking through the ash and dust.

No one said another word for some time. The lack of wind created an eerie silence, which was broken only by the occasional party member's cough. And as they walked, Zelag watched the group's mood dampen even further, the extended trek through such destruction weighing on them all.

Over the next hour, without any signs of life or magic, George and Sarah had gained some ground on the others. But as they drew near the castle, the couple stopped, allowing the rest of the party to catch up.

Zelag considered the castle just up ahead. Though he tended to steer clear of it when visiting, he always found the building a bit ugly, the asymmetrical layout of the fortress a bother. But there was no questioning its sturdiness, especially seeing it now amidst the ruins.

Of course, as he looked over the exterior walls, he realized it was not free from damage. Both eastern towers appeared damaged, and the roof of the gatehouse was collapsed in, which would make entry a bit trickier. Moreover, some of the corbels on the keep had collapsed.

As the other humans reached their position, George pointed just to the east. "What was that?"

Zelag followed George's gaze, squinting towards the pile of rubble. Like everything else, it was devoid of magic and covered in ash. While the rest of the party seemed hesitant to proceed past the mages, Zelag took the initiative to continue towards the rubble.

Crunch.

He stopped in his tracks, looking down with mouth agape. Extending his gaze along the path, he realized he was stepping on glass. And then he realized: it was the marble fountain. He could still remember it from his last visit, the grand white stone standing overhead, the calming sound of flowing water, and the sandy ground beneath his feet. It took Zelag a moment to accept this was really the same place.

"It's the fountain," he called back. "The ground has been turned to glass."

"To glass?" Charles squeaked.

"Astonishing," uttered Artimus. Walking just a few paces away from Zelag, he bent down and looked more closely at the ground. He picked up a small shard of the glass, carefully observing it before tossing it aside.

Wiping his hands off, the elf stood back up.

"I'm still not feeling any magic," said Sarah. She stepped through the glass, wincing with every crunch. "Do you see anything Zelag?"

"Nothing that you don't. Tell me, do either of you have any idea how he so thoroughly stripped this place of magic?"

"I won't even speculate," George replied, stomping through some of the glass and taking position next to his wife.

"Yeah, I've no idea either," admitted Sarah. "This will undoubtedly be a subject of debate at the Mage's Guild for some time to come."

"Alright," interrupted Artimus. The elf took another couple steps towards the castle, centering himself ahead of the group and turning to address the others.

"Since it seems there's nothing here, we'll proceed with caution into the castle. It looks to still be in one piece. But there's no guarantee that the halls will be free of danger. So, we'll stick together in there. Charles, William, if there were survivors hiding out, where would they be?"

The pair exchanged a look of understanding. With a nod from Charles, William shrugged and addressed Artimus.

"There are secret passages throughout the castle, including one that leads to an escape tunnel in the mountains. If anyone survived, they'd hopefully know to flee there."

The party looked around at one another nervously.

"We'll make for the most direct route to the escape tunnel then," declared Artimus. "Going forward, we stay close together. Charles, William, do you want to volunteer to join George and Sarah at the front? We'll need one of you to show us the way."

William raised his hand and stepped forward. "I'll do it."

"Excellent. As before, let's stay on guard. If you see anything, speak up."

And with that, the party proceeded towards the castle.

CHAPTER XX

Paxvilla Castle
2 Zerrum, 1149 MT

George groaned. He ducked under the final rafter, staying low as he crouched through the rubble. As he stood up on the other side, he removed his hat and shook off the dust. Light trickled in through the collapsed ceiling illuminating the foyer just enough to see the aftermath of Yezurkstal's brutality.

Everywhere he looked there was destruction. From the broken furniture to the torn tapestries, the fallen chandelier, and even the blood stains on the wall, the place was in shambles. And yet, there was not a body in sight. Come to think of it, he realized they hadn't seen a body anywhere in town.

As the others made their way through the mayhem at the entrance, George considered the extent of it all. It still hurt to think back to Yezurkstal's arrival. But seeing the destruction left in his wake, he knew that Tel' Shira was right. He made the only choice he could.

And yet accepting this made him feel even guiltier. It was beyond his ability to comprehend. The sheer power it must have taken for Yezurkstal to pull off such complete and total destruction was beyond anything the wizard had imagined. George was simply too weak to stand a chance. If he had just been stronger…

This thought ignited a fire in George, one unlike any he'd felt before. He was furious.

"Care to share those burdens?" Sarah touched the outside of his hand gingerly and captured his gaze.

George responded with a half-hearted smile, taking his wife's hand, and giving it a squeeze.

"Perhaps, yes. But not in present company." He glanced back towards the others. Jaldor and William were attempting to help Charles squeeze through the narrowest part of the passage.

"I understand," Sarah reached up and touched his cheek, gently redirecting him to look back at her. "Just tell me seeing all this that you believe you made the right choice," she whispered. "Because Henry and Elizabeth still need you. And so do I for that matter."

"I do," George choked. He peered into Sarah's deep blue eyes. For the first time in days, he felt like there might be some hope left in the world. Wiping back some stray strands of hair from her face, he smiled.

Sarah beamed. She fell into his arms and embraced him, pulling him down and whispering in his ears, "I love you."

"I love you too," he whispered back.

Sniffling, he squeezed his wife and rocked a couple of times. But the moment couldn't last long.

"Just push me through!" Charles cried.

George and Sarah broke their embrace. They both turned back and watched. Artimus leaned into Charles's back, shoving him into the foyer. William and Jaldor braced themselves on either side, stabilizing Charles as he came through.

Artimus slipped through next, and Zelag followed just behind. Neither of them seemed to have too much difficulty.

"Alright, as discussed, William will lead us from here. George and Sarah will be by your side William, and Zelag, Charles, Jaldor and I will be right behind. Any concerns before we proceed further?"

"It looks dark ahead," Charles panted.

"I can handle that," Sarah promised. She reached into her hidden pocket and pulled out her wand. Crafted from a branch of the same Erath tree as George's staff, the wood curved to the right at a gentle angle about eight centimeters up the handle. A small peridot was set in the base and an inlay of mythril encircled the handle. The wand tapered up from there to its full length of about 21 centimeters. For such a small magical focus, the inlays afforded it an impressive level of magical stores.

With a flick of her wrist, the wand glowed a soft, warm light. She glanced back at the others and smiled.

"Are we all ready to proceed?" she inquired.

"You two sure you'll sense any threat, right?" William scratched behind his neck and bit the top of his lip. He looked between George and Sarah nervously.

"If I don't, you can trust she will," replied George.

"And worst case," interjected Zelag, "you won't have to worry about it for long if they don't."

"Zelag!" Artimus glared at the shapeshifter.

Zelag shrugged.

"Let's face it," said the shapeshifter. "If Yezurkstal does surprise us, I'm the only one who will be alive long enough to have to really worry about it. Just saying."

"Well, let's just stay on our guard and not worry about that," sassed Sarah. "How does that sound?"

"Urgo!" quipped Zelag. After tossing the shapeshifter a look of disapproval, George shook his head and reoriented towards the castle interior. William started forward. He kept his hands planted in his pockets as he crept further into the foyer.

Sarah walked just beside William and, taking his wife's hand, George walked in line next to her. They proceeded at a snail's crawl for the first few minutes, creeping through the foyer. There were more signs of struggle in here, chunks of stone spread along the path and streaks of blood stained along the walls.

After stepping right into another hall, George glanced back to make sure the others were following. Though not far behind, he noticed they had already begun to stagger. Jaldor and Artimus were no more than a meter behind, but Charles had fallen further back, and Zelag was trailing at least another meter behind him.

George kept his eyes open, and his senses extended. Each new turn they took or hall they entered, he sent out a wave of energy, looking to feel anything in response. But as with the rest of the city, there seemed little point to it.

It took them about ten minutes to arrive at what appeared to be a library. And upon arrival, William stopped and looked back to the others in the group.

"Are we still clear of danger?" he asked sheepishly.

"Still no signs of anything other than us," assured Sarah.

George glanced around. By the light of Sarah's wand, the room was bright enough to see the bookshelves lining the walls. But unlike the rooms they'd visited so far, this one looked suspiciously undamaged.

Aside from some books strewn about the room, it was in surprisingly good shape. Sure, it was small and unimpressive, at least compared to the one back at the Mage's Guild tower. But with bookshelves lining the walls from ceiling to floor and two additional shelves spanning the length of the room, the room was still in surprisingly good condition.

"If nothing else, we have to come back here and save some of these books," observed Sarah, running her fingers along the spine of a large tome.

"I hope we can save more than a few books," commented Jaldor. He knelt and picked up a small book from the floor, placing it back on the shelf.

"Well, I don't know the range of that magic of yours," replied William. "But if we don't come across anyone soon, we may not find anyone at all."

He walked over to the eastern wall, holding his hand up towards the ceiling. Starting on the southern end of the wall, he walked a few paces, keeping his eye on his hand. Just about halfway down the line, he stopped and reached for a thick black book. But as he pulled on the book, George heard a clicking sound from behind the shelf.

George stared in wonder as William pushed on the bookcase, the entire shelf shifting to reveal a passage.

"That's one way to hide a passage," remarked Zelag, stepping over and gazing down the hall. "So, is this the escape tunnel then?" he asked turning back to the others.

"No," William shook his head. "This leads to various other hidden passages in the castle. But if you know where you're going, one of those passages leads to the escape tunnel."

"Well, let's not delay then," suggested Sarah. She looked over at George with a frown, casting her gaze towards Zelag.

"Right, let's keep moving then," agreed George. "William, perhaps if it's easier, you can stay back and let Sarah and I walk up front -it doesn't appear we can move through this corridor three at a time."

"Oh, please be my guest," William replied. He stepped aside and motioned towards the passage.

Staying between his wife and the shapeshifter, George escorted Sarah to the mouth of the entrance. They paused for a moment, and he considered the passage. Now illuminated by Sarah's wand, he could see it wasn't the most welcoming of spaces. The walls were coated in a layer of dust and cobwebs lined the ceilings.

But as they started down the path, even George was able to see others had passed through recently.

"You see that?" Artimus asked from behind. "Let's keep our guard up. Someone has been here recently."

George smiled, squeezing his wife's hand.

"What is it?" she whispered.

"Just happy to hear Mr. Observant back there echoing my thoughts about this passage," he admitted.

"I heard that!" quipped Artimus. "And if you don't think you need me to observe, tell me what else you see."

"Pfft." George swung his right arm back dismissively and shook his head. "Go on Mr. I Need to Impress Everyone with My Observational Skills."

Sarah giggled. "That one's a mouthful."

"I'll let you have that one George," replied Artimus. "I just thought in this case everyone would like to know that the layer of dust on the ground makes it easier to see footsteps. And by my estimates, there's been a sizable amount of activity in this tunnel recently. William, is it safe to say by the level of dust that this passage isn't commonly traveled?"

"Aye, that's a safe statement," William replied, his voice carrying a bit more optimism than before. "Every servant in the castle is taught about these passages for emergencies, but we're not supposed to use them. Do you really think some survivors fled through here then?"

"Let's not assume anything," interrupted Zelag. "I'm not so sure about these footprints Artimus."

Sarah cleared her throat. "Let's hold that debate. There's a crossroads ahead. Should we go left, or right?"

"Take a right," William replied.

George kept his eyes focused ahead, trying to ignore how narrow the passage was at this point. He hadn't noticed it at first, but the more they walked, the more he had to push up against his wife. Not that he minded the proximity to her, but the walls just made him feel a bit claustrophobic.

Fortunately, as they turned the corner, George realized they weren't just entering another corridor. Instead, it appeared a convergence of sorts, an open room at least half as large as the library they started in. And including the tunnel from the library, he counted twelve different passages to choose from.

Making room for everyone else to file into the space, George looked around, sensing for magic.

Still nothing.

"So, what are you saying about the footprints Zelag?" asked Artimus as the shapeshifter stepped into the room.

"They look too uniform," he replied. "Like they were walking through slowly and patiently. People running from Death would be much more chaotic."

Artimus scratched his right cheek and arched an eyebrow. He glanced back towards the corridor and tapped his right foot.

"Perhaps they heard the alarm bell toll and evacuated before Yezurkstal even made his way here." suggested Artimus.

"Or perhaps we're following a bunch of zombies and are about to walk into an ambush," countered Zelag.

"Either way, it does us no good speculating!" scoffed Sarah. "So, let's stay on guard and proceed, shall we?"

George grinned. He adored Sarah's tenacity.

"Yes, let's keep moving," agreed Jaldor. "Which of these passages leads to the escape tunnel?"

"This one," William walked over towards the middle passage on the left of the room. Or at least left of where they had entered. George had lost track of which direction they were traveling along the passage.

Charles stepped over next to William, holding out his hands and bracing himself against the wall. He appeared distressed, his face red and breath heavy.

"Can we take a short breather here?" he asked.

"Why don't I scout ahead while you all take a beat?" Zelag suggested. He stepped up to the right side of the doorway.

"How far to the next crossroad and which direction do we go from there?" he asked after a brief silence.

"Another hundred meters at least," breathed William. "And it's just a left from there. Once you reach the end, there's a shelter with provisions and sundries. They should still be waiting there, hoping for news of victory."

"Perfect," Zelag clapped his hands. He stepped into the next passageway. "I'll be back in a few minutes."

As Zelag crept away down the corridor, George stepped back over beside his wife. He appreciated having a few minutes to breathe and collect his thoughts.

"Can he see in the dark now?" Sarah questioned.

"Oh, I hadn't thought of that," George rubbed his chin, glancing down the corridor. Zelag had already slipped out of sight into the darkness ahead. "Perhaps something with his native vision allows him to?"

"I've known him longer than either of you two have been alive and I still don't understand how his abilities work," interrupted Artimus. The elf brushed some dust off his sleeves.

"I've been hesitant to ask, but what exactly is he?" Jaldor asked nervously.

"A Preajin," explained Artimus. "Like I said, I still don't know how, but from what my wife has explained, they are creatures of pure magic. And they have the unique ability to imitate any form, living or not."

"So, could he turn into something to see in the dark?" pondered Jaldor.

"Sure, but it's not an instant thing. And it's very painful because when he changes it involves physical morphing from one solid form to another. You'll be fortunate if you never see it. But you should understand Zelag himself is probably the one that can relate to you all the best." Artimus motioned towards William and Charles.

"Why do you say that?" Jaldor scratched behind the back of his head.

"Because he's the last living Preajin. His entire species was wiped out by Yezurkstal." Artimus explained.

Jaldor sighed and shook his head.

"Damn. I guess that explains why he seems so closed off," the farmer observed.

"I'm not sure anything can fully explain him," Sarah muttered.

"No, perhaps not," agreed Artimus. "But let's talk next steps from here. William, Charles, would you both agree that, based on the state of things here, there's no sense in coming back to Paxvilla? At least not until the dust settles a bit more."

William rubbed his eyes and nodded gently.

"I wish I didn't, but yes," he sighed.

Charles looked between William and Jaldor, and glanced over at George and Sarah, his eyes fluttering and mouth trembling.

"I just hope we find some survivors," he choked. With a sniffle, he rubbed his nose and shook his head. "I can't believe this is all happening." He held his shaking hands out in front of his face and shook his head.

"We had beaten them!" Charles cried. "How did one man come back and do all of this? What are we to do in a world with magic and zombies? This whole world is cursed!"

He slid down the wall, pulling his knees into his body as he sat down on the floor.

George considered his wife. He could see her heart breaking with pity as she looked down at the sad man. And he himself felt a sort of strange shame.

Were they all being too insensitive about the situation?

"Come on Charles," exclaimed Jaldor. He walked over, leaned against the wall, and slid down to sit next to Charles. Leaning back, Jaldor placed his arm on Charles's shoulder. William glanced down at the duo but took a step back from them.

"Don't lose hope on us now. Zelag could be walking back now with good news."

"Oh, I definitely have some news," Zelag's voice came from just beyond the darkness.

The next moment, the shapeshifter strolled down the corridor wearing a wide smile. Charles's eyes widened and the dread washed from his face as he scrambled to stand back up. Jaldor held out his hand and Charles accepted, leaning on the farmer to rise to his feet. Jaldor didn't waste time pushing against the wall and standing up himself.

Everyone circled up before the tunnel entrance.

"What did you find?" Sarah asked.

"Let's talk along the way," Zelag suggested. He turned around and waved for the others to follow.

Sarah narrowed her eyes, looking back at George with a frown. Both Charles and William started after Zelag. Jaldor shrugged and filed in after them. Artimus stopped to catch George's gaze. He shook his head and followed behind.

"Let's just follow," George whispered.

With a sigh, Sarah stomped after the others. George took off just behind her.

"Notice how the slope increases here. It gets steeper as we go, but don't move too quickly. There are survivors down there, but I didn't reveal myself. So, we probably don't want to go charging in there and scare them all to death."

"How many survivors?" Charles begged.

"A few dozen at least. I got close enough to confirm they're not zombies. And as I'm sure George and Sarah are feeling by now, there's magic up ahead as well. It seems there was some limit to whatever Yezurkstal did."

George glanced over at Sarah. She nodded, so he redirected his attention forward. There it was! It felt faint at first, but after a few more steps, he could feel the familiar call ahead.

"Did you get a good look at any of them?" Charles asked, his voice labored. His pace grew more rapid with each step.

"No. Since you and William work at the castle, perhaps you two should take the lead and," Zelag paused midsentence.

Charles was breathing loudly, his pace increasing with each step he took. He appeared to be in pain, his face red and sweaty as he jogged past Zelag.

"Charles, you alright there?" William called ahead. He pumped his arms, running to catch up to Charles.

"I must," Charles breathed. "I have to know if she made it!" he cried.

The rest of the group picked up their pace. George could feel his legs starting to burn. He tried extending his stride to avoid having to outright run.

"What happened to going slowly?" Artimus threw up his arms in objection. But it was too late. The group reached the end of the path, the barren stone wall just up ahead marking their destination. And leading the charge, Charles turned left and shouted down the corridor.

"Molly! Are you down there, Molly?" his desperate, whiney tone echoed through the tunnel.

William followed right behind him, and Jaldor turned the corner as well. But Zelag stopped at the crossroads and turned back to the others.

"So much for going in slowly," he muttered.

"Let's just try to ensure no one gets hurt," Artimus uttered as he slipped past, following the other humans. Sarah kept on without delay too, so George followed right behind her, leaving Zelag to take up the rear as they all descended the final passage.

As he turned the corner, George could already see light coming from the doorway up ahead. Charles dashed through into the light, tumbling onto his knees as he arrived. George hurried after, leaning on his staff to help expedite his pace.

A pair of Paxvilla guards stepped just in front of Charles. Gaping at the oncoming group, they placed their hands on their swords, but kept a relaxed position.

"Charles what happened?" asked the guard on the left.

"William!" exclaimed the one on the right, relaxing his stance and holding his arms out wide. William slowed his approach, running in to hug this second guard.

George glanced at Sarah on his left as they both slowed their approach. She wore a content smile on her face, her eyes hopeful as she beheld the reunion. As they approached the light of the shelter, she flourished her wand, extinguishing the light. And she replaced it in her pocket.

Even George felt like a weight was lifted as they stepped into the light. Looking around the room, he took in the many surprised faces of those hiding out. Everyone looked overjoyed to see others arriving, their faces all alight as they considered the new arrivals.

The room itself was quite spacious. By the looks of it, they had tunneled into an existing cave system, the expensive, rocky ceiling much higher than George expected. The raw mountain walls were adorned with torches and featured various shelving units spread throughout the circular space.

More interested in the people than the accommodations, George focused his attention on getting a headcount. There were more than a dozen children, all of them huddled together up some steps on the left side of the room. A few of the women stood behind these children, looking down in anticipation. And all the other small groups spread throughout the space had refocused their attention on the new arrivals.

Most of the men were gathering right at the base of the entrance, behind the soldiers. With a final tally, George figured there were at least forty-seven survivors hiding down here, maybe more. And as he and Sarah meandered into the room, he could feel the fear and tension of all the onlookers.

"Charles, William, what news do you bring?" asked the guard on the left.

"Is Molly down here?" Charles panted.

"Charles! Oh Charles! I'm here!"

Looking towards the light and airy voice, George spotted a plump young woman, around the same age and dimensions as Charles by the looks of things. She had similarly black hair and dark green eyes and wore a simple white dress. She bobbed up and down in the crowd, waving her arms.

"Oh Molly!" Charles cried out. He pushed through the crowd towards the woman.

And as the duo reunited, George felt a tingling in the back of his head. He realized he was smiling from ear-to-ear, and looking about the room he could see the tension and fear leaving everyone's faces.

This was the reason he had to fight.

And this was the reason he knew they would win.

CHAPTER XXI

Castora sipped on her tea, gazing at the fireplace as she listened to Zodim's story.

"And Sora, well Keldor can tell you, she was always strong-willed. I don't know if I ever saw her so angry. Her face turned as red as a turnip, and I could practically see steam pouring out of her ears. She just looked right up at the satyr with a stare that could make the sun blink."

Keldor laughed and slapped his knee. Vistoro leaned forward in his chair, staring intently at Zodim. Artimus Jr., who stood just a few meters away by the fireplace, also seemed intent on hearing the story's end, his eyes fixed on the gnome. But Tel' Shira, parked just beside Vistoro, merely stared off. It was hard to tell if she was even listening.

"But I bet no one can guess what happened next," Zodim tossed his hands up before continuing. "You see, the satyr tried to hold her gaze! Hand to Evorath, they stood there for at least ten minutes, neither of them blinking. I could feel the air between them thickening and was convinced I'd have to drag Sora out of there. But just as I was ready to try my hand at deescalating the situation, the satyr finally relented!"

"And bam!"

Zodim jumped from his seat and clapped his hands, startling Castora and nearly causing her to spill her tea.

"Just like that, the satyr started to laugh. It was like looking at a different person. His face softened and his jaw loosened, and he just shook his head. Not only did he stick to his original agreement, but he even threw in a barrel of red wine!"

"Oh, there was never any winning against Sora!" Keldor chuckled and shook his head.

"It certainly sounds like it," agreed Vistoro. "I sincerely regret I never had the opportunity to meet her."

"I reckon she would have loved what you've created here," replied Zodim. He smirked, glancing down at his teacup and swirling it around. "But I'm sure no one needs to listen to an old man go on about his adventures. Are we here to discuss more of our plans around the pyxis?"

"Ah, but you've started off our tea time as any should; with a good story, and some hearty laughter," suggested Vistoro. "But alas, you are correct that wasn't the reason for the invitation. In fact, I think you'll be delighted to see what I have to show you."

Vistoro leaned over, reaching into a small leather pouch beside his chair. He withdrew a sparkling amulet from within, the large silver piece filling the palm of his right hand. As he let it drop down and dangle by the chain, Castora leaned in to get a better look.

The silver construction of the pendant glimmered in the light, the hand-carved dragon reminding Castora of the legend of Zarticann, and the dragon he slayed. With two shimmering rubies for eyes and a large diamond for a mouth, the amulet had to be worth a small fortune. Glancing over at Zodim, she recognized his enthusiasm for the piece.

His eyes lit up. He leaned forward and steepled his hands, gazing at the pendant in awe.

"How did you?" he gasped. "I never thought I'd see that again. I considered it lost when I heard rumors that The Collector had added it to his collection."

"He had," replied Vistoro flatly. "But with the help of one of our mutual acquaintances, we've been able to get it back. And since I sold it to you all those decades ago, I see it as only fair that I return it to you."

Vistoro held out the pendant. With a smile, Zodim walked over and accepted the amulet. He held it up overhead, running his thumb over the carved dragon.

"There is one thing I'd like to request though," added Vistoro. "You see, we've heard a strange claim from the thief known as 'The Collector'. He insists that Zarticann encased a dragon's eye within this amulet."

"A dragon's eye?" Zodim chuckled. "Oh, don't tell me you believe that legend. I certainly won't give you any grief for believing in dragons -I do! But to think a lizock could have slain one himself; that reeks of a tall tale."

Castora took another sip of her tea, glancing at Artimus Jr. as she did. The elf smiled, but quickly averted her gaze.

"I know my father believed the legend," Castora offered. "If it's true, I should be able to sense such powerful magic."

Vistoro leaned back, tilting his head to the side. His tongue darted between his lips as he stared intently at the dark elf. "What do you sense?" he asked.

Castora sighed. Rising from her seat, she set down her teacup on the round table to her side. She stepped over to Zodim and extended her hand. The gnome was looking over the amulet intently. But after only a few seconds' delay, he handed it over with a smile.

"Thank you," Castora whispered.

She brought the amulet up close to her face and carefully inspected the surface. If there was something inside, it was well hidden. There was no visible seam anywhere on the amulet, or any indication it might be possible to open. But as promised, she probed the amulet, funneling some arcane energy to feel for any latent magic.

As suspected, the diamond hummed with arcane power. It wasn't at full capacity, but by the large stores of magic held within, it must not have been drawn from in some time. The rubies felt much fuller, an impressive amount of red energy emanating from such relatively small stones. And the white gold (not silver, she realized) itself held some latent magic, but like other precious metals, not enough to warrant suspicion.

Castora closed her eyes, gently blowing out some air as she attempted to delve deeper into the amulet. She looked past the bright glow of the diamond and the fiery blaze of the rubies to see the gentle sheen of the gold beneath. But as far as she could feel, there was nothing more beneath the surface.

"I'm afraid I don't feel any indication of a greater magic within. I'm sorry."

She shook her head and handed the amulet back to Zodim. The gnome chuckled as he took hold and skipped back over to the sofa. Sitting down just in front of it, he placed the amulet between his legs. Reaching into the green leather pouch along his back, he pulled out a small red cloth.

"Perhaps The Collector was lying," Artimus Jr. suggested. Castora smirked and nodded in agreement.

"Or he already removed the eye," Tel' Shira proposed.

"Either one seems plausible," Zodim remarked. "But if there is something in here, there ought to be a way to open it up."

He unrolled the cloth, revealing an assortment of tiny little tools. Having no knowledge of jewelry making, Castora couldn't really tell what any of the tools were used for. But as the gnome picked up a couple of small metallic objects, he focused first on the diamond.

"I hate to do this to such an old piece," he murmured. He leaned in, squinting down at the pendant as he wedged one of his tools around the diamond. He stayed perfectly focused, circling the diamond completely with the small tool. And after running around the edge, he held the piece up closer to his eyes.

With a subtle nod, he lowered it back down and used the second tool, which looked to provide a pincer grip of sorts. His hands were perfectly steady as he used the pincers to take hold of the diamond. Closing his eyes, Zodim pulled on the gem.

Castora could see him clenching his jaw, his hands shaking as he tugged.

Pop.

Zodim grunted, opening his eyes, and examining the diamond. "I'm sorry about that," he whispered, as if talking to the amulet. He placed the diamond down on his tool roll and regarded the amulet again.

"Just as I suspected. See this?" He lifted the amulet, moving it around for everyone to see. The dragon's mouth was empty, a cavity where the diamond had been. But she couldn't see whatever Zodim was pointing out, and she wasn't alone.

"What are we supposed to notice?" Vistoro asked.

"Alright, let me show you," Zodim withdrew the amulet. He picked up the small tool he used earlier to loosen the diamond and carefully maneuvered it towards the cavity. As he wiggled it around, Castora heard a faint click.

"That's better!" he exclaimed. "Now we just need to give it a twist. Let's see."

Zodim held up the amulet, carefully positioning his right hand under it and placing his left on top. He hunched over and grunted, twisting on it. "There it is," he moaned. But as he separated his hands, splitting the pendant in two, his eyes sagged, and he frowned.

"Well, whatever was in here is gone now," he held up the two halves, revealing the hallow space within.

"That sniveling weasel!" Keldor groaned.

"You think The Collector already removed it?" Zodim arched his eyebrows.

"The scales fit the dragon," Artimus Jr. observed. "Zelag failed to steal the pendant from him in the past. And he might have known the hájje were after it too. Perhaps knowing this threat, he decided to stash it elsewhere."

"Wait, what do you mean 'the hájje were after it'?" Castora asked. She narrowed her eyes and considered the elf.

He caught her gaze and looked away. With a nervous, toothy smile, he scratched behind his head.

"I uh. It's kind of a long story, but there's a lizock that has a sizable bounty on Zelag. And we were going to trade the pendant to ensure that bounty was forgiven. But when we went there, she was meeting with a hájje. Zelag was pretty confident that hájje had plans for the pendant."

"What did this hájje look like?" Castora clenched her fist.

"Square jaw, pointed nose, and generally sharp features. He had long hair pulled back into a ponytail. And he was tall, perhaps even a bit over two meters. Muscular too; and he was definitely wearing custom-fitted armor!"

Castora's nostrils flared. She clenched her fists so tight that it hurt as she looked around at the others.

"Do you know who it is?" Zodim asked disarmingly.

"Ezerbane." Castora seethed.

"I take it you're not too fond of him," observed Keldor. He took a swig from his mug.

Castora face felt hot as she considered the statement. She must have looked angry enough to explode, for Artimus Jr. stepped over beside her. She averted his gaze, but the elf didn't give up so easily. He reached down and took her hand.

After an internal debate on how to respond, Castora decided to go with it. As Artimus clasped both her hands, she looked up and matched his gaze. His beautiful eyes seemed to cut through her soul, relieving some of the anger she was feeling.

"Remember you're among friends," the elf whispered. "What can you tell us about Ezerbane?"

Castora's eyes twitched, but with a loud sigh she nodded. Pulling away from Artimus, she looked around at the others. Tel' Shira looked right back, as if she was trying to see through the dark elf.

"Ezerbane is the son of Yezurkstal and Queen Valkyrie. Their first son, he is first in line for succession of the throne. And whatever ideas you have about how brutal and unforgiving my people may be, Ezerbane is so much worse."

She looked down, her hands shaking as she thought back to some of the memories she had of Ezerbane. It made her nauseous even thinking about it.

"Do you think it's possible he had other motivations in his visit to Lizock City than just obtaining the amulet?" asked Tel' Shira. She wore a peculiar expression, as if she were chewing on something but still unsure about its taste.

"I really don't know," the dark elf admitted. "I don't think so, but I didn't know he was after the amulet."

"Let's forget about the amulet for now," replied Tel' Shira. "I'd like to know more about this brother of yo-"

"Cousin!" Castora corrected.

"Wait a moment," interrupted Keldor. The dwarf's eyes darted side-to-side as he scratched at his beard. "Didn't you say he was Yezurkstal's son. And you're Yezurkstal's daughter. That would make him your half-brother."

"What?" Castora scowled, hunching down and holding her hands out to the side. "That's not how hájje do it. Yes, we have a common father, but there is no 'half-sibling' in hájje society. You're considered a cousin if you just share one."

"Fascinating," remarked Tel' Shira. "And how many direct descendants did Yezurkstal have?"

"Well, I have twenty-five cousins. So, including my twin brother Pollux, my older brother Felabor, and me, that makes twenty-eight children of Yezurkstal. Though, I'm fairly certain a few of them fell in the battle at Paxvilla."

She relaxed her shoulders, only just considering her own words. It was under her leadership that her people had died. That blood was on her hands. The realization made her light-headed.

"Do you think your brothers will listen to you about your father now?" Tel' Shira asked.

Castora shook her head. She closed her eyes and rubbed her temples as she considered the question.

"I don't know. I've always been closest to my brother Pollux. So perhaps him, but I doubt Felabor would listen."

"And your cousin Ezerbane," Tel' Shira continued. "Was he involved in the attack on Paxvilla?"

"Not directly, no." Castora glanced back at the sofa. Still feeling a bit uneasy, she sat back down and reached for her teacup. After taking a sip, she looked back to Tel' Shira.

"Please, go on," instructed the felite.

"I was responsible for planning and executing the attack. I received my orders directly from my father. But Ezerbane is the Supreme General, so he assigned the contingents."

"Hmm. I see," Tel' Shira glanced at Vistoro. They looked to exchange a glance of understanding, the lizock giving a subtle nod as their eyes met.

"And you were a general yourself," Tel' Shira clarified. "But you weren't involved in any plans beyond the attack on Paxvilla, correct?"

Castora nodded, placing her now empty teacup back on the side table.

"Yes, like I explained before, I was supposed to secure the city and await further instructions from there."

Tel' Shira's ears twitched. A moment later, Castora could hear footsteps from just outside the door.

Knock. Knock. Knock.

"Please, enter," instructed Vistoro.

The door creaked open, and Savannah stepped inside. With a glance around the room, she walked over to Tel' Shira.

"They've returned from Paxvilla with some more survivors," she explained. "Artimus and the others are working to get them settled and to reunite some families."

"Any word about Irontail or the others?" Artimus Jr.'s face lit up, a glimmer of hope in his eyes.

Savannah's face said it all.

"I'm afraid they're gone." She sniffed. "Which is something I wanted to ask our new ally about." She glanced at Castora. "Any idea how your father would have stripped the entire city of magic?"

"Stripped? I'm not sure what you mean."

"I wasn't sure at first either," admitted Savannah. "But after they returned with survivors, Sarah explained that all the magic was gone -from everything! I had to see for myself. But there's not a whisp of magic left in Paxvilla."

Castora glanced down, grinding her teeth as she considered it. She twiddled her thumbs for a few moments before looking back at Savannah.

"I'm sorry, I don't know how he did it."

"You don't seem surprised though," countered Savannah.

The dark elf shook her head.

"He's talked about the idea before -removing magic from the hands of 'inferior species' as he says. His vision of the world would leave him in complete and total control of all magic. If he's found a way to do as you said, it could mean he's getting close to realizing that vision."

"Well, that sounds wonderful." Zodim interrupted, his words dripping with sarcasm. "Perhaps we should focus on how we can use the pyxis to imprison him before he figures out how to fully realize that vision."

Savannah looked down. With pursed lips and narrowed eyes, she reached up and started twirling her necklace between her fingertips. She stood like this for a few seconds, allowing an awkward silence to fill the room.

"I'm calling an emergency Guild meeting tonight. Castora, Zodim, would you two both be willing to attend?" She looked at Castora, her emerald eyes begging.

"Count me in!" Zodim exclaimed with a smile.

"I'll help any way I can," promised Castora.

"Good. I'll come by later to escort you. Please be ready just after dinner."

She stood there twirling her hair for a few more seconds. With a sigh, she turned around and left the sitting room.

"That is alarming news indeed," whispered Tel' Shira after a few moments. "Vistoro, would you please wheel me to the shrine outside? Now is a time to pray."

"Urgo," Vistoro smiled, coming to his feet. He didn't waste a moment, grabbing hold of the handles and pivoting Tel' Shira around.

"Wait," Tel' Shira ordered as they neared the door. "Castora, would you care to join us?"

"I don't really know how," admitted Castora.

She blushed, looking away nervously as she scratched the back of her neck.

"I will show you. That is, if you wish to learn."

Castora glanced to Zodim, who gave her a reassuring nod. She then shifted her gaze to Artimus Jr. The handsome elf grinned and nodded towards the door.

"Then I accept. Thank you." Castora rose to her feet.

Vistoro smiled, turned back around, and wheeled Tel' Shira out of the sitting room. Castora followed right behind. They proceeded through the foyer towards the front door. Wanting to make a good impression, the dark elf picked up her pace and strode past the duo. Reaching the doors first, she twisted the brass handle and pushed it open.

Castora squinted, holding up her left hand to cover her face as the blinding afternoon sun washed over her. She didn't mind the heat, but like most of her kind, she was quite sensitive to the bright light. Still, she held the door open, allowing Vistoro to wheel the felite elder through.

"Thank you," the lizock smiled as he walked past.

Returning the smile, Castora offered a slight bow and followed behind. It took a couple of minutes for her eyes to adjust to the light, by which point they had reached the hedged pathway heading west. Of everything she had learned since arriving in Marftaport, it was gardening that filled her with the most enthusiasm. The idea of growing plants simply for aesthetic purposes was unheard of back home. But she found the blend of colors and smells to be delightful.

With the sounds of chirping birds and the gentle spring breeze, it created a truly unique experience. And walking in silence to the shrine allowed Castora to really soak it all in. She thought about how if she survived the inevitable battle against her father, she'd build a garden of her own to celebrate.

The shrine was another beautiful exercise in aesthetics. It featured four marble columns measuring about five meters tall and nearly half a meter thick. Beyond the veining of the marble, jasmine vines grew halfway up the columns, allowing it to blend in with the landscape. With a smooth surface area underneath, it offered enough space for a handful of people to congregate within and admire the sculpture.

And the sculpture was quite impressive. Carved from marble, it was crafted into the feminine form of the goddess Evorath. Castora thought back to the night she arrived here and first saw the statue -it so closely resembled the figure of light from her vision just a couple weeks before. As if Zodim's stories and the actions of these people wasn't enough to convince her, seeing this statue felt like a final confirmation that she was doing the right thing for once in her life.

In truth, she was hoping to have an excuse to come back and look at it again. But not just for the statue. Instead, as she looked up, she once again felt her heart flutter. The mural was breathtaking. It was unlike anything she had seen before, the abstract style and heavy brush strokes evoking strong emotions. She had been told it was an artistic rendition of Evorath's creation story from the Xyvor. But before she lost herself in the painting, she shifted her focus to the others for guidance.

Afraid to say something wrong, she kept her lips shut tight as she glanced between the others. Vistoro wheeled Tel' Shira just beneath the shrine before he stepped around to her left. Castora stood a couple meters away, waiting for some direction. But as Vistoro knelt beside Tel' Shira's chair, she wondered if she should do the same.

With but a moment's hesitation, she stepped over to the right of Tel' Shira and took a knee. She glanced to Vistoro for more guidance and attempted to mimic his position. He was on both knees, so she went to both knees. And as he brought his hands together, his fingers pointing up and palms touching, she regarded her hands and did the same.

Vistoro leaned forward and closed his eyes. Castora hesitated to follow this, glancing up at Tel' Shira. But seeing the felite had also closed her eyes, the dark elf followed along.

But what now?

She knelt there for what must have been the longest minute of her life. But in that silence, with the chirping of the birds and the sweet smell of jasmine, she felt a slight tingling along the back of her neck. Exhaling a heavy breath, she felt tension leave her neck and shoulders.

And then she felt a rush of emotions. She considered everything that had happened in the past couple of weeks and the new friends she had made. As she reflected, it was almost as if someone else was there with her, whispering reassurances in her ear. All Castora could think was *"thank you."*

“Vistoro,” Tel’ Shira interrupted her thoughts. “Will you please leave Castora and I here alone? I’m sure she can wheel me back inside when we’re done here, right Castora?”

Just barely cracking her eyes open, Castora glanced up at the felite. Catching the felite’s gaze, she opened her eyes the rest of the way and offered a sheepish nod.

Tel’ Shira smiled, and Vistoro rose to his feet.

“Yes, ma’am. I think I could use a longer stroll myself. I’ll meet you back in the sitting room when I’m done?” he asked.

“Yes, thank you Vistoro.” Tel’ Shira glanced back at the dark elf. “Please Castora, would you come to your feet?”

As Vistoro left, walking around east, and heading north towards the trees, Castora stood up and looked down at her elder. The white-furred felite shifted her gaze back towards the statue of Evorath.

“You recognize this likeness of Evorath, don’t you?” the felite inquired.

“I think I do, yes. When Zodim found me, while I was resting and recovering, I had a vision of a woman like this. She appeared as a bright light.”

Tel’ Shira smiled a toothy grin.

“Remember that light will always be with you. It lives within the hearts of all who believe in Evorath and can grant you great strength. Tell me,” Tel’ Shira narrowed her gaze, staring intently at the dark elf. “What do you know about the magic that you so regularly rely on?”

Castora scratched her scalp, averting the felite's gaze.

"I don't really know. Growing up, I was taught that my father wrestled the power of magic from the gods. But I've seen enough in these past couple weeks to know that isn't true."

"Fascinating," observed Tel' Shira. She rapped her fingers on her wheelchair. "It might surprise you to learn that most mages don't even know the truth about magic. And that truth is why mages like Sarah, Savannah, and Ygabb are so prodigiously powerful compared to the average magic user."

Castora leaned forward, unconsciously tugging on some of her hair in anticipation.

"You see, Evorath didn't just fill this world with magic. The magic that you and every other mage taps into is The Spirit of Evorath herself. It's her very essence that she shares freely with her creations. But while anyone can access Her Spirit with the right training and discipline, those who understand the truth of magic can accomplish truly extraordinary feats."

Castora titled her head to the right. She starred at Tel' Shira trying to assess the felite's assertion. If magic was part of Evorath's spirit, why would She let people misuse it? Surely, if it was Her spirit, She could prevent Castora's father from wielding it to such devastation.

"I understand your doubt, Castora. And of all who will play a part in the events that are soon to unfold, I fear your role is the hardest," the felite warned. Her voice was still soft and gentle, like a loving mother, or at least like Castora imagined a loving mother would sound.

"But when the time comes, I hope you'll remember and accept the source of magic. Because even if you doubt it now, I know with absolute certainty that you're so much more powerful than you realize."

Seeing Tel' Shira's eyes rest on her so intently made the dark elf nervous. She felt a tingling sensation go down her spine. She snorted, looking back at the statue of Evorath.

"Yes, let us do what we came here for," said Tel' Shira.

Castora raised her right hand as if to object, hesitating for a moment and second guessing herself.

"Weren't you going to show me the proper way?" Castora started, but Tel' Shira beamed at her, shaking her head.

"There is no trick to prayer. Standing, sitting, kneeling. Out here by the shrine, under a tree, inside your bedroom. Eyes closed, hands clasped, arms spread wide. The real secret to the prodigious power of prayer is in its simplicity." Tel' Shira's tone was almost hypnotic, her voice tranquil and serene.

"But what do I say?" Castora asked.

"That's the neat part," replied Tel' Shira with a grin. "It's not dependent on you. Simply raise your voice to Evorath and listen for her response."

With a sigh of frustration, Castora knelt before the statue, closed her eyes, clasped her hands, and prayed.

Evorath, help me to understand.

CHAPTER XXII

Marftaport,
2 Zerrum, 1149 MT

Castora shifted in her chair, pulling down on her borrowed yellow dress. As if the short length wasn't annoying enough, the rigid wooden chairs made matters even worse. She wondered if part of Mage Guild membership required masochistic tendencies, because the straight backs and flat seats on these little wooden chairs made for the most uncomfortable sitting experience ever.

In fact, they were so uncomfortable that she would have preferred the gaudy chairs back at Vistoro's manor. And yet, as she glanced around the meeting hall, she didn't notice anyone else having such a difficult time.

She did her best to avoid eye contact with the audience as she looked around. There had to be around fifty people gathered in the hall. And it felt like every pair of eyes was focused on her. But as she glanced around at the stage, she tried to reign in her anxiety. Zodim sat just to her right. The gnome's eyes were glued on Savannah as the druid spoke.

And across the stage, she saw George and Sarah both seemed calm as well. George slouched in his seat, a blank stare on his face as he looked out at the crowd. Despite his poor posture, however, the wizard in the blue robes looked mildly content, a far cry from the cloud of dread that was hanging over him since Castora had first met him just days before.

Sarah looked as calm and collected as ever. Her hair was pulled back into a single, thick braid. And though her mouth rested in a neutral expression, her blue eyes glimmered with hope. She wore a simple blue dress, remarkably similar in design to the one Castora had borrowed.

Turning her attention back to the crowd, the dark elf considered all the unfamiliar faces. Lizock, lamia, satyr, elf, felite, barghest, and the troll Oogmut standing in the back of the room. This was like a nightmare. But she thought back her to conversation with Tel' Shira that afternoon, reminding herself that even if the journey would not be easy, it was worthwhile.

"But, like I said, I only got a glimpse of the devastation," Savannah expounded. "So, without further ado, I'd like to invite George and Sarah to share more of what they found."

Sarah smiled and stood up to the mention of her name. Clasping her hands just above her stomach, she offered a shallow bow and proceeded forward. George took a few moments to follow, waiting until his wife had passed before bracing his hands on his knees and slowly standing up. He sighed and walked over to stand beside his wife.

Savannah smiled at the couple, offering a curtsy before returning to sit in the empty chair on Castora's left. She passed the hájje a grin as she adjusted her green dress and looked back towards George and Sarah.

"Thank you, Savannah," Sarah began.

"As Savannah explained, George and I returned this morning to Paxvilla to confirm whether Yezurkstal had remained and to find any survivors. After using a portal to return to the Paxvilla barracks, we found the entire city razed to the ground. We traveled by foot to the castle there and one of the Paxvilla servants from the castle led us down an escape tunnel to rescue a few dozen survivors."

Murmurs echoed through the room. Sarah paused for just a moment before continuing.

"While the complete and total devastation of Paxvilla was alarming, the real mystery was in the state of magic there. Or more properly said, the lack of magic. George and I couldn't find even the subtlest whisp of arcane energy anywhere in the city. It wasn't until we made it all the way down to the escape tunnel in the Jyrimoore mountains that we could sense its return."

Voices in the crowd grew louder as side conversations erupted. Castora leaned forward, narrowing her eyes and trying to distinguish anything of substance. From the bits she could pick out, it didn't sound like there was much agreement. With so many discordant voices and opinions, she wondered how they got anything accomplished.

Sarah took a step back from the podium, allowing George to take center stage.

"From what we can tell," he shouted, quieting his voice as the side conversations diminished "there was no sign of remaining enemy presence."

George glanced back at Sarah. He closed his eyes as the final murmurs died down among the crowd.

"We've already asked Castora whether she had any insight into how this was done. But it seems she was as stumped as the rest of us. So, unless someone here has a plausible explanation, I recommend we take this as an opportunity for study. We must determine what Yezurkstal did and how he did it. Starting tomorrow, I will therefore offer to transport anyone who wishes to study the ruins."

There were a few stray murmurs, but to Castora's surprise, the audience quieted down quickly. George stepped back from the podium, allowing Sarah to step up again.

"Before we open the floor to questions and discussion, we wanted to also take this meeting as an opportunity to formally introduce the two visitors we have on stage. You've all heard about them by now, but I know few have had the chance to meet them. We want to make it abundantly clear that these two are our allies in the inevitable battle against Yezurkstal. So please, treat them as such."

Sarah placed special emphasis on her last sentence. She paused and looked around the room, as if confirming everyone was on the same page.

"Zodim, Castora, would you please come to the podium?" Sarah tilted her head to the right and pursed her lips.

"Perhaps you can bring his chair to stand on," she suggested, pointing towards it.

Castora paused, glancing down at the gnome.

With a shrug, she grabbed his chair and walked it over to the podium. Zodim waddled alongside her. While George and

Sarah returned to their seats, Castora placed Zodim's chair just behind the podium, watching as he climbed to stand on top of it.

Zodim cleared his throat and scratched his beard. He looked around the room, which was silent in anticipation.

"Good evening and thank you for the warm welcome. As the esteemed Miss Peterson already expressed, my name is Zodim. I'm afraid at my age, my vision isn't what it used to, but I know there are those here who've been in Marftaport since the beginnings. For you, perhaps we've met along the way, so I look forward to seeing you again. And for those who I've never met before, I am equally excited to make your acquaintance."

The gnome paused, glancing up and bringing his hand over his mouth, tapping his index finger on his nose in thought.

"You may have heard stories of the eccentric gnome who bought Vistoro's pendant. Or the perhaps you've heard Keldor talk about his friend, the old hermit of Jyrimoore. And I'm humble enough to realize many of you haven't heard of me at all." Zodim shrugged.

"Regardless, please don't hesitate to introduce yourselves. If you are planning to aid in the fight against Yezurkstal, I look forward to the planning sessions and getting to hear about your unique talents and arcane gifts."

"But" Zodim held up his left hand, finger pointing towards the ceiling. "Let me introduce an even more valuable ally in our upcoming fight. My friend, Castora."

Castora took a deep breath, closing her eyes as she blew the air from pursed lips. Zodim stepped down from the chair and stepped over beside the dark elf. He offered a wink and nodded towards the podium.

After moving Zodim's chair back next to her own, Castora stepped up. She took a moment to look around the room. Her mouth felt like it was packed with cotton and her hands were clammy. Even back home, she loathed public speaking.

"Good evening," she whispered. Her raspy voice echoed through the room. Pausing to clear her throat, she continued, smiling to hear her usual, clear tone.

"As you all know, my name is Castora. And I'm sure some of you would prefer I not be standing here now -you'd be completely justified to feel that way. I am a daughter of Yezurkstal, and until my encounter with Zodim, I was fully devoted to his teachings."

"I formally protest this witch!" a shrill voice rang out from the crowd. Castora felt her heart tight in her chest as she looked towards the speaker.

It was a middle-aged elf with an average build, wearing a rather unattractive sackcloth dress. The dress was originally dyed yellow by the looks of things, but now looked more mustard brown. But as Castora looked up at the elf's face, she thought perhaps the ugly dress was a smart move.

Her entire face seemed to reject the very notion of symmetry. One eye drooped a full centimeter lower than the other. Her hair was frizzy. Her nose was crooked and blemished with the most hideous mole!

In that moment, the only thing that kept the dark elf from responding in force was her trying to decide whether the dress or the woman was uglier. But the thought caused her pause, that soft voice in the back of her mind itching to know what merit one ought to assign aesthetics. Perhaps it warranted further thought - but now was not the proper time.

"Aye! I'll not suffer to listen to this murderer!" called a weaselly looking elf from the other side of the room. His clothes were even worse than the first elf's, tattered and stained in what looked like bird droppings.

It seemed somewhat fitting considering his weasel-like features; with a receding hairline, tiny eyes, an oversized nose, and the largest overbite Castora had ever observed. But as she thought this, murmurs broke out among the crowd, some cries of condemnation, others of forgiveness, and a smattering of sentiments all along the spectrum.

With eyes wide, she held her hands loosely by her side. Her skin felt hot with the anger of the crowd. And she gathered her arcane power to the ready, her hands buzzing with anticipation. Perhaps a lifetime of experience made this response inevitable, or perhaps she just struggled to shake old prejudice. Whichever the case, she once again found some hope, but this time from an external force.

"Alright, that's enough of this nonsense talk!" Ygabb bleated. She charged to the foot of the stage.

"You're the ones acting like witches, imps, devils, and demons!" the pipsqueak satyr cried and stomped her hooves.

"Castora has confessed her sins. She seeks to make amends for those mistakes and to help us put an end to Death's terror, once and for all!"

"Yes, this objection is noted, but irrelevant." Castora felt her eyes widen as she looked towards the thundering voice. It was Oogmut, the burly troll standing at full height, shoulders pulled back and eyes aflame.

The clamor came to an abrupt halt as the troll stomped towards the stage, his eyes still on fire. And for a moment, looking into those eyes, Castora feared for her life.

But the flames smoldered, the troll's face folding into an unnerving smile. He extended his hand, the gnarled lump of flesh hanging out before the dark elf's face.

Castora blinked, finding the odd turn of events difficult to process. With a nervous grin, she extended her own hand, grabbing hold of one of the troll's fingers and offering a firm shake. The troll nodded, turning around to address the room.

"I can forgive this hájje. This hájje who killed my best friend, Mojo, during an unholy siege. If I can make peace with her, all of you can put aside your sanctimonious pride. Remember, judgment is fit only for Evorath to dispense."

The silence that followed for the next few seconds seemed to suggest everyone else agreed. But Castora sighed as the weaselly elf stood up and held his skinny arm up high, shaking as he spoke.

"But it's not about judgment!" the elf stammered.

"Feotidus, please," Savannah pleaded.

"No!" The weaselly elf stomped his foot. "We must be certain we can trust her! How do we know she's not just here to spy on us! What if she's feeding intelligence back to Yezurkstal and planning an attack on Marftaport?"

A buzz erupted, spreading through the room like wildfire. Castora couldn't make out a single word, the voices growing louder and more garbled. The dark elf glanced around. George and Sarah were whispering something to each other. Zodim simply smiled up at her, but his shoulders were tense, betraying an uneasiness.

Savannah stood up from her seat and shook her head. She hurried to the podium and Castora stepped aside to give her space. As the elf stepped up, she cleared her throat, the sound lost amidst the chatter.

"I feel like I'm back in the Erathal senate chambers!" Savannah yelled, the magical amplification making her voice boom through the hall. Her initial words were enough to cause the chatter to diminish, but murmurs still floated about.

"Consider it official record that I, Savannah Sylvanas Atyrmirid pledge support and trust for our guest Castora." She paused, glancing back at Sarah and George. They offered a nod. "And Sarah and George Peterson add their support."

"Don't leave me out!" Ygabb leapt onto the stage. "Remember one of my disciplines is in discerning such matters as these. We can trust Castora."

By this point, the crowd had quieted down enough that Castora imagined everyone could hear Ygabb's boisterous voice, despite it being unamplified.

Oogmut stood his ground for a few more seconds, looking around the room as if to confirm there would be no further objections. Leaning to the side, Castora watched Feotidus slowly lower back into his seat. And as the crowd noise died to a faint murmur, Savannah passed the dark elf a grin.

"Now, if we could exercise some common courtesy and allow Castora to introduce herself, that would be great." Castora smirked and gave Savannah a slight bow as she stepped back to the podium. Her chest felt tight, and her hands were shaking, but just like removing the shaft of an arrow, she figured it would be less painful to just go for it.

"Thank you all for your support. I understand the trepidation many of you have. And I hope you'll offer me the opportunity to put your concerns to rest. Regardless, my new friend Zodim has woken me up to the reality of my father. And the most recent events in Paxvilla have made it abundantly clear that I was on the wrong side of things."

She paused as Oogmut stomped over to the right side of the stage, allowing her a clearer view of the audience. It felt like every eye in the room was on her now. With a deep breath, she continued.

"With my knowledge of hájje battle tactics, I hope to ensure we can take the fight to my father. And with all your help, I believe we can put an end to his reign once and for all."

"So, thank you all for the opportunity to do good for once in my life," Castora stepped back from the podium, eyes stuck to the floor as she shuffled back to her chair.

She tried to ignore the murmurs of the crowd that followed, catching a glimpse of Zodim's smile as she sat down.

"You did just fine," the gnome whispered.

Castora said nothing. She slowly raised her head, looking back out at the crowd as Savannah returned to the podium.

"I believe that concludes our meeting for this evening. Rather than keep everyone hung up here, I'd ask that anyone who wishes to discuss the matter of Paxvilla's disappearing magic remain. And as a reminder, tomorrow is our first planning lunch for our battle strategy with Castora. If you haven't signed up to help with this and wish to join the campaign, please add your name to the list posted on the bulletin board."

As expected, there was some chatter from the crowd. But to Castora's delight, no one screamed, shouted, or otherwise yelled for her removal. Perhaps these people were more accepting than she gave them credit.

"Excellent," Savannah exclaimed. Castora jerked back to attention, looking towards the druid.

"This formally concludes our meeting on the second day of Zerrum, the 1149th year of the current age. Thank you all for attending and may Evorath bless us all."

As Savannah stepped away from the podium, the soft mutters of the crowd bubbled into a full uproar.

Castora looked around, seeing Sarah and George had already risen from their seats. They moved quickly, George placing his hand on the small of Sarah's back and walking down the steps to the side to make a hasty retreat.

Savannah, on the other hand, walked over to Castora and offered a smile. Forcing a smile of her own, Castora stood up and clasped her hands together.

"Thank you," the dark elf lowered her gaze.

"You can thank me by proving me right," Savannah chuckled and brushed back her hair. "But if you want to earn some other people's trust, I'd start by sticking around and chatting. I could introduce you to some of the mages who signed up to help with the fight."

Castora glanced back at Zodim. The gnome beamed with enthusiasm and nodded his head.

"Yes," agreed Castora. "I would appreciate that."

And as she followed Savannah from the stage, she said a silent prayer.

"Please give me patience to deal with these people."

Chapter XXIII

Marftaport, Mage's Guild
3 Zerrum, 1149 MT

George glanced to his left, lips pursed and eyes narrow as he tried to gauge Sarah's reaction. Aside from the sounds of mastication and the clang of silverware, the room had gone silent. Seeing his wife's wide eyes and open mouth, he suspected her sentiment was shared by most in the room. And George couldn't blame them. It was a sobering thought.

As he looked around, he could see everyone processing the news. Savannah twirled her hair in her fingertips, her stern gaze cast down. Ygabb simply stared across the table at Castora, as if looking at some massive, unbelievable sight in the distance. Even Oogmut appeared uncertain, his gaze skyward; he looked to be chewing on something in the corner of his mouth, which George recognized as a state of deep contemplation for the troll.

Looking around the rest of the room, George could tell the rest of the group was just as surprised. Some simply chewed along with blank stares. Others stared at their plates, mouths hanging open in disbelief. Even Zodim, who had always seemed so cheerful, and eccentric wore a somber look.

"So, to be clear," Castora continued after a momentary pause, "I don't even know how many he keeps down there. But I suspect when he does unleash the horde, they will make the army I led against Paxvilla look like an inconsequential force by comparison."

"And your father would expose you to this, even as a small child?" The deep and deliberate tone of Oogmut was unmistakable. But the inflection he placed on the words told George even the troll had doubts.

"It was just another part of life." She reached behind her head, rubbing the base of her skull.

"If anyone died, enemy or ally, he'd reanimate them and put them down in the dungeon. When I was young, my brother and I would even play games down there, testing to see if we could get one of them to react to us."

She brought her hands down to her side. "It wasn't until I was older that I realized my father was in full control of them. It was forbidden for anyone but his children to roam the castle, so I should have known better," she sniffled and closed her eyes.

"What happened?" asked Sarah.

"I brought one of my friends down there," she shook her head and frowned. "My only friend really. And well, let's just say I never went down there again after that. I should have learned better than to defy my father's edicts."

She reached back with her right hand, massaging the base of her skull again.

"Did he teach you necromancy?" Katas interrupted, looking around the room. The brown-skinned lizock spoke quicker than usual. He hadn't touched any of his food since the start of lunch.

"I, not really," Castora frowned, glancing down. "He doesn't share that magic very openly. So, I'm afraid I can't truly answer your question either Savannah," she looked to the druid, but averted her gaze.

"That's alright," Savannah assured the hájje. "But if you can tell us anything about how it works, it may be helpful. Does he actively control them?"

"Yes," interjected Allesandra from the other end of the table. "Knowing how his necromancy works may allow us to devise a way to break the control he has." The lamia's tone was soft and gentle, reminiscent of how Sarah often talked to one of the children when trying to explain a difficult concept.

"Like I said, I never learned how," Castora reiterated. "But when I say full control, I mean he senses everything they do and has complete control over each one individually. My older brother, Felabor, had some training in the art."

"You mentioned him earlier," George turned towards the masculine voice, uncertain who was speaking at first. It was Keldrin, the red-bearded dwarf's tone uneasy. "Do you think you could convince him to join our cause?" he asked.

"I don't think so," Castora shook her head. "He and I were closer when we were young, but as we grew older, more recent years in particular, we hardly ever talk. My brother Pollux may be more easily convinced. He and I were always competing for my father's attention, which kept us closer, but I hate to say he never really excelled at magic."

"Hold on," the sweet sound of Sarah's voice brought a smile to George's face. He glanced over at his wife, her beautiful eyes shimmering with hope.

"I know we've been talking thus far as if we're going to mount a defense against his next attack, but what if we're thinking about this the wrong way?" Sarah held her hands out to the side, pausing to look around the table.

"If he has such a large force of zombies, on top of a substantial army of hájje and demons at his disposal, wouldn't we have a better chance with the element of surprise? You said he was a creature of habit, didn't you Castora? What if we use his habits to our advantage?"

"I don't think I like what you're suggesting," interjected Oogmut, scratching his head.

Side conversations broke out all about the table, the room falling into an intelligible mess of fractured discussions. George looked around, trying in vain to distinguish anything of meaning. The general sentiment, from the words he could discern, was not positive. He could feel his chest tighten, his skin turning hot.

"I think it's a brilliant idea!" George slapped the table and jumped to his feet.

"We won't need as big of an attack group this way, so we'll be risking less of us. Castora can give me the location to teleport to, and I can drop us right where we need to go. Then we just need Zodim to use the pyxis and we can put an end to Yezurkstal once and for all."

"Me? Ha! I don't think so," Zodim objected. The gnome shook his head, holding his hands up, palms forward. "I'll teach you guys how to use it, but the stakes are too high to leave it in my shriveled old hands."

George stared unblinking at the gnome. Judging by the stark silence in the room, the gnome's objection took everyone by surprise.

"I should do it," Castora muttered. "I must do it," she proclaimed more confidently. George considered the hájje with her thousand-kilometer stare.

She was stoic.

"Perhaps we should learn about the spell before we decide who should cast it," Katas suggested sheepishly.

"No, I think the princess is right," Zodim shook his head. "I reckon she's the perfect person. And I'd say it'd be unfair of us to deny her the chance at redemption."

"But when the time comes, will you be able to follow through?" Allesandra asked, glaring at Castora.

"If she says she can do it, I trust her," Zodim declared.

"As do we!" Sarah agreed. George smiled, happy to know his wife was on the same page, as usual.

"Yeah, I trust you too," added Ygabb.

"It's a valid concern," Oogmut interjected. The wizened old troll sighed, shifting in his massive chair.

"He's right," Savannah agreed begrudgingly. "It's really not as simple as whether we trust you or not Castora," she addressed the dark elf directly. "Do you really feel you can condemn your father to such an imprisonment?"

"I'm still not clear on that," Katas interrupted, clicking his tongue. "How does the pyrex work?"

"Pyxis," corrected Zodim. "And it traps you in a pocket dimension devoid of magic. The jar is sealed with a powerful spell, preventing whatever's inside from escaping."

"Hmph. Are we even sure that will work on Yezurkstal?" Keldrin asked. He leaned forward, eyes wide as scratched at his bushy red beard.

"It'll work," Castora quipped. She bit her bottom lip, eyes narrow as she gazed past the dwarf. "It has to work."

"Need aside," Zodim added on, "the pyxis isn't just devoid of magic. It completely drains the magic from its captive. Trust me. It's a tight fit in there. The only way out is if someone releases him, either intentionally or by destroying the pyxis."

"Wait." Katas leaned forward, his tongue darting between his teeth as he looked at Zodim. "If it can be destroyed, what will stop a hájje from one day getting a hold of it and unleashing him again on the world?" He paused, glancing around the table. "Wha-"

"That brings up an important point," Oogmut declared, his loud voice cutting off Katas. The lizock hesitated for a moment before sitting back in his chair.

"Sorry, Katas. But you're right. If it can be destroyed, we need to carefully guard the pyxis. I suggest those of us gathered here consider it part of our responsibility. As members of the Mage's Guild, we not only seek to safely and peacefully explore Evorath's magic. We must also safeguard items like this that can cause such grave harm."

"So, what are you suggesting?" Alessandra asked.

"After this is done, we must take all measures to protect the pyxis. And we must do so secretly, careful not to share the information with anyone who doesn't need to know it." Oogmut's booming voice always demanded attention, but George had never heard his tone so severe.

"That is a wise approach," replied Savannah. She leaned back in her chair, eyes gazing towards the ceiling as she twirled her hair between her fingertips. "But perhaps we should table that discussion until after we have executed the first step. And while I agree with Sarah's recommendation of a surprise, small-scale attack against Yezurkstal, I don't think that is the first step. We need to ask a more basic question. Should we involve others?"

"If Zelag is still willing, we should include him," Ygabb suggested sheepishly. "His resilience to magic makes him a unique and powerful ally against such a force."

"Agreed," said Oogmut.

George glanced at his wife. She frowned, prodding her fork at the remaining bits of chicken on her plate.

"Should we involve any other non-magic users?" Keldrin asked.

"No," George blurted, surprising even himself. He looked around the table, blushing as he caught all eyes on him.

"That is, I don't think it'll do us any good. If you had seen him the other day, I think you'd all agree. Even with the pyxis. I." He looked down, his voice fading as he struggled to articulate his thoughts.

His chest was tight, his shoulders tense. He could feel a pit in his stomach. With clenched fists, he shook his head.

"That last spell he cast in Paxvilla. All of us at this table combined couldn't tame such a massive amount of arcane energy. The fewer people we involve, the better."

Feeling Sarah's hand on his left shoulder, he glanced over from the corner of his eyes. She smiled, her eyes lighting up and filling him with reassurance.

"You fear we can't win, even with the pyxis." Ygabb observed. Her empathic senses were always impressive.

George nodded but kept his gaze down.

"Well, that's a perfect transition to the next step," Savannah interjected. "We need practical preparation for this battle. We need to plan every detail of our infiltration. And then we need to practice that plan. I believe we can convince Zelag to be our stand-in for Yezurkstal."

"Yes, I suspect we'll need to schedule daily drills," agreed Oogmut.

"But we mustn't wait too long," interjected Allesandra. She fiddled with her ruby choker, her eyes heavy as she looked around at the others. "After all, the longer we wait, the more opportunity Yezurkstal has to launch another assault."

"I should try to have another look down there," suggested Katas, holding up his hand. "George, perhaps you can send me to Lake Algarath in the morning, and I can send a messenger falcon back to share any new intelligence I gather."

"Wait, what?" Castora sat up in her chair, the wood scrapping on the stone floor. "Are you saying you want to try and infiltrate Hájjeona? That would be suicide."

"Katas is an expert at staying unseen," Ygabb bragged. "His reconnaissance is how we prepared our defense of Paxvilla so well."

"So, you're saying you've been to Hájjeona before? And you weren't caught?" Castora questioned. She stared at Katas, her head cocked to the side and right eyebrow arched.

"Well, never inside the walls, no," Katas looked away and fiddled his thumbs. "But I have my ways. At the very least, I can keep an eye on troop movement."

"Well, that's excellent!" exclaimed Zodim, holding his arms up overhead, palms open. "That solves one of our immediate concerns anyways. Katas can keep a vigil down there, make sure to mind any activity. Then when it comes time for our infiltration, we can join him prior to the attack and make sure we have our gears aligned."

"Gears aligned?" Allesandra asked, wrinkling her nose.

"Oh," Zodim held his left hand over his mouth, tapping his index finger on his nose. "Uh, we must make sure we cover every detail."

"Ah," Allesandra nodded. George was just happy she asked, so he didn't have to.

"I think we're leaving out one important consideration," Elorius remarked from across the table. The wizened old elf in the green robes hadn't said a word during the entire lunch. As usual, he just observed, looking from person to person as they spoke and occasionally nodding in agreement.

"What's that?" George asked after a few seconds of silence. He always found the old man a bit pedantic.

"As you yourself said, Yezurkstal's magical prowess far exceeds us all. Don't you think we ought to consider defenses against his magic? Castora, perhaps you can share some of his secrets." He was always so smug.

"I'll share anything I can," Castora sighed.

"Perhaps we can make that part of our planning and preparation," Sarah suggested.

"Indeed," Elorius agreed with sly smirk. "It would be wise to include such an agenda item. Which brings up another point. It would behoove us to create an itinerary for the training and preparation we'll require. Has Tel' Shira had a vision that would suggest an imminent attack?"

Elorius glanced around the table. With steepled hands, he looked around, but as usual, with his nose pointed to the ceiling, he failed to make any eye contact with the others.

George gritted his teeth and shook his head.

"Tel' Shira will share when she has a vision relevant to our planning," Savannah replied. "I think this luncheon has gone long enough, however. Perhaps you can prepare a suggested itinerary and we can reconvene on it tomorrow?"

"Hmph," Elorius crossed his arms and sat up straight in his chair. "Perhaps we should take a vote."

"Good idea," George rejoined. "Who else motions to conclude the meeting for today?"

Nearly everyone at the table raised their arm.

"Well. It seems it's decided then," Elorius conceded.

"Excellent!" George exclaimed. He hopped to his feet, slapping his hands softly on the table. "Sarah and I will be home with the kids if anyone needs us."

Without giving anyone time to object, the wizard offered a hand to his wife. And the two strode from the hall, eager to return to their home.

CHAPTER XXIV

Marftaport
3 Zerrum, 1149 MT

Artimus Jr. wiped some stray fuzz off his left shoulder. He looked back at his reflection in the mirror, taking a deep breath as he considered his appearance.

His surcoat was at least without blemish now, the well-fitted green fabric offering a good match for his eyes. The tunic was a bit itchy however, but it was a small price to pay to ensure he looked his best this evening. With his hair pulled back into a small bun, he pivoted right and left; he lifted his arms, and lowered them, trying to get a good look from every angle.

He felt a strange fluttering in his stomach, a nervous excitement like he used to get in anticipation of the annual Gratitude Festival when he was a child. But this time it felt even more intense. Even in the moment as he saw his own face grinning back from the mirror, he wondered if he was getting in over his head this time.

Yes, Castora was beautiful. But she had murdered so many. With her upbringing, who could blame her? The Xyvor taught infinite forgiveness and talked of a new life when accepting Evorath. Why shouldn't that apply to Castora, or any other hájje for that matter?

Artimus Jr. blew out a long breath, closing his eyes and centering his thoughts. This was no big deal after all, or so he told himself. It was just a date.

With a smile, the young elf looked back at his reflection. He nodded and turned around.

Walking from his bedchambers to the front door of his tiny little cottage was only a matter of steps. But as he reached the front door, he hesitated for a moment, glancing towards his bow and quiver. He also considered his sword belt, hanging just beside the bow.

He smirked, considering whether he ought to bring one or both along. But after some silent deliberation, he shook his head and stepped through the front door. Closing the door behind him, he waited a moment to take in the evening sky.

The sun was setting to the west, hues of orange and yellow stretching across the partly cloudy sky. Glancing to the southeast, he considered his mother's Yggdril tree. Its magical branches stretched up higher than most trees in town. With shimmering silver-green leaves shaped like teardrops, the tree was the last left in Erathal.

Its tender golden fruit was just barely visible through the thick foliage. Artimus Jr. could still see some white flowers ready to blossom as well -it would be ready for the annual harvest in just a few weeks' time. Looking upon the tree always brought him fond memories. Whether it was harvesting the annual yield of fruit, or just learning about the intricate maintenance requirements, he always felt blessed to be involved.

As he walked northeast through the field towards Vistoro's Manor, his thoughts shifted back to the evening plans. He wanted to show Castora just how much the town offered.

A cool breeze blew, carrying the mixed smells of compost from the nearby farm and subtle hints of jasmine from the courtyard garden. Arriving at the gated entrance, Artimus Jr. took a moment to compose himself. He looked at the wrought iron bars and the gate latch. With a deep breath, he unlatched the gate and stepped on through.

His boots clacked on the stone as he proceeded towards the fountain. Taking one more deep breath to calm his nerves, he glanced towards the well to the northeast. Just as planned, he spotted his date standing there. She looked gorgeous.

Walking east around the garden beds, he kept his gaze ahead towards the well. As he approached, Castora turned towards him, a smile forming on her face. She quickly looked away, glancing down at her feet.

She stood there swaying in the evening breeze, arms behind her back. It looked like she had her right arm clasped in her left hand, rocking side-to-side and still averting his gaze. As he drew near, Artimus Jr. took in every detail of her appearance from head to toe.

Her black hair was pulled back into a hairstyle unlike any he'd seen before. A small silver hairpin served to keep a part in the left side of her hair, Evorath's tree of light reflecting the last bits of sunlight. The hair to the left of this pin was pulled back behind her ear. Her bangs hung down to the right, the rest of her hair on this side brushed over to the side and braided together.

And she wore makeup, eyelids colored a subtle shade of lavender and featuring dark accents around her eyes. Her lips were a deep red, and as he took those final steps towards her, she bit her bottom lip and looked back to meet her gaze.

Her beautiful black eyes seemed to sparkle, causing Artimus Jr. to falter for a moment, his heart skipping a beat. Dressed in a flowing black dress that reached all the way to her ankles, Castora had even found herself a pair of dress heels, black leather adorned with a floral design.

Stopping his approach about a meter from the dark elf, Artimus Jr. smiled nervously. As their eyes met, he could see a hint of pink on Castora's cheeks. And before he said a word, she greeted him with a low curtsy, once again averting her eyes.

"You look." Artimus Jr. paused, struggling to pick the best word. "You're breathtaking!" he blurted.

She smiled, her cheeks growing redder.

"You don't look too bad yourself," she remarked.

"Well, when you're courting the very image of beauty, it's prudent to look your best." Artimus Jr. smiled at his own comment and silently thanked Evorath for the thought.

Castora shook her head, and clasped her hands just above her stomach. She narrowed her eyes, tilting her head to the right.

"Is that truly how you would describe me, or just cheap flattery intended to woo me?" she questioned.

"Oh, it's certainly intended to woo you. But that doesn't make the sentiment any less true." The elf held up his right hand and placed his left over his heart, looking right into Castora's eyes and locking her gaze before continuing.

"Hand to Evorath, you are the most gorgeous person I've ever met." He maintained eye content as he spoke.

Castora broke his gaze, blushing even more than before.

"Well, my smooth-talking courter, what wonders are you going to show me tonight?" She looked back at the elf, her eyes ready to light a fire.

With a smirk, Artimus Jr. spun around and started back towards the path south. He waved for Castora to follow and waited for the sound of her footsteps following before continuing.

"I thought about this quite a bit. Perhaps even lost a couple hours of sleep last night trying to decide. And I have an adventure planned for us that you'll remember for the rest of your life. But here's the best part. How we start that adventure is up to you." He held up his right index finger and glanced back at Castora as he walked.

"How do you feel about visiting barghest district, or the Barghest Block as we call it? They have a nightly tradition just after sunset that I think you'll find fascinating. But if that's too exotic for you, there's always a table at Sissera's. I don't believe you've eaten there yet, have you?"

"I'll follow you wherever you lead," Castora replied. Artimus Jr. wasn't nearly as talented as his father at interpreting body language and tone of voice. But the uneven timbre and half smile both suggested discomfort.

"The Barghest Block it is. Don't worry, you'll love it. Would you feel better if I told you about what we're in for?"

"If it's something I might need to be prepared for, yes." said Castora. "But as long as we're getting food there, I don't mind a pleasant surprise."

She came up alongside Artimus Jr., matching his pace and offering a smile before turning her attention back ahead.

Artimus Jr. grinned and nodded. The roads were mostly empty at this time of day, people having already settled in for the evening meal. But as they walked south, he spotted a few people hanging outside the public gathering hall. He offered a smile and wave as they passed by, and glancing towards the hall door, he realized why. They were using the space to serve more meals to the human refugees.

As they proceeded west from the gathering hall, Artimus Jr. motioned to the road ahead. "We'll turn left from there and continue west until we get to the end of the road. Then it's a straight shot to Barghest Block."

Castora nodded. She walked with her hands held loosely by her sides, eyes drifting around to take in her surroundings. Judging by the tenseness in her shoulders, Artimus Jr. put the pieces of the puzzle together.

"You're safe here," he promised. "I understand why you're uneasy, so if you feel the need for a change of scenery at any point tonight, just let me know."

The dark elf stopped mid-stride, clasping her hands in front of her stomach. She glanced over at Artimus Jr., tilting her head to the right as if studying his face. After a few moments, she shook her head.

"I don't." she paused, biting her bottom lip as she shuffled her feet. "Are you sure the barghest of all people will be alright with my being there?"

Artimus Jr. turned around and squared up with Castora. He looked straight into her eyes and extended his hands. She hesitated for a moment but accepted his invitation by clasping his hands. Meeting her gaze, he nodded.

"I want to ensure you feel safe. How about we go to Sissera's Tavern instead?" He smiled gingerly, keeping his breath calm, and maintaining eye contact as he spoke.

Castora averted his gaze at first, eyes darting around as she bit her bottom lip. But as she matched Artimus Jr.'s gaze, her lips curled into a smile. Her eyes danced in her head, as if thrilled at receiving good news.

"Yes, I think I would prefer that."

"Ergolicious!" Artimus Jr. exclaimed, gesturing to the west with his left hand. "In that case, we can just continue west on this road."

As Artimus Jr. marched that way, Castora cast him a sideways glance. Her eyes were narrow, and lips pursed. After a moment, she trotted after him, catching up to walk by his side.

"What does 'ergolicious' mean?" the dark elf asked.

Artimus Jr. chuckled.

"I guess the new trendy words don't make their way down to Hájjeona. Basically, just means that it's a fantastic choice and I'm fully supportive of it."

"Hmm. Interesting," Castora scratched behind her head, casting her eyes towards the sky as they meandered on.

Artimus Jr. glanced up as well, considering the clear night sky. The faint orange glow of the day's last light was quickly fading, the waxing gibbous moon was already visible in the eastern sky. As most of the nights recently, it was a touch too humid, but the cool southern breeze more than compensated.

For the next few minutes, the pair simply walk along in silence. As usual, foot traffic was virtually nonexistent. This set a nice ambiance for a quiet walk, with nothing but the sounds of their footsteps on the cobblestone road and the occasional crow of a rooster in the distance.

"I suppose I should ask," remarked Artimus Jr. as they walked under one of the oaks. "Do you have a favorite food? Or a favorite kind of cuisine?"

"Hmm." Castora sighed and glanced at the branches overhead. "I'm sure I already told you, the cuisine here is much tastier than anything I had back home. I'm still adjusting to this custom you have of social eating. Eating is not a social event for the hájje."

"I suppose that makes sense," Artimus Jr. thought. "With what I've heard, your father doesn't sound like he cares much for the culinary arts -or socializing for that matter."

"Or any art really," added Castora, her gaze drifting towards the cherry blossom tree ahead. "So, I suppose I don't really have a favorite food. I've enjoyed everything I've eaten here so far. Is it strange if I want to try something new?"

Artimus Jr. smirked and shook his head.

"Absolutely not. I imagine anyone with an upbringing like yours would want to try as many new foods as possible."

Glancing back at Castora, he watched her eyes sink and mouth fold into a frown. She looked down towards the road, slowing her pace as she continued forward.

"Maybe," she muttered, keeping her eyes cast down on the road ahead. "I guess I never really questioned it; it was all I knew." Her pace grew slower as she spoke, ending her sentence and looking Artimus Jr. square in the eyes.

Seeing the uncertainty in her eyes, the elf stopped his progress, turning towards her. He opened his mouth, ready to reply. But a slight tingle on the back of his neck told him to wait.

"Why are we even doing this?" the dark elf implored. "Someone of my upbringing. What do I have to offer you? You grew up in this amazing community, surrounded by people who love and care for one another. How can you even stand to be around someone with my upbringing?"

Castora's hands were shaking. Her voice shot up in pitch as she spoke, her eyes trembling as she leaned in.

"I don't even deserve your kindness!" she cried.

She turned away. Her hair whipped around and nearly hit Artimus Jr. in the face. He hesitated for a moment, as he heard Castora sniffling, he stepped around to face the dark elf. She looked away and closed her eyes. And as she shook her head, Artimus Jr. decided to speak from his heart.

"I'm so sorry," he pleaded. "Look, whatever sins you committed in the past are just that -they're past! But when I hear about your upbringing, and considering the spell you were under when you arrived here, I simply don't believe you're the same hájje you were then."

"What do you mean not the same?" Castora shrieked. She grabbed Artimus Jr.'s hands and pulled closer to him. "You feel those hands? They were the ones that slew your mentor and friend. They're the same ones that killed dozens of humans in the same battle, and the ones that have inflicted pain upon countless other creatures over the decades. So, tell me, how am I not the same hájje I used to be?"

With wide eyes, Artimus Jr. wrestled with his next move. Castora's intensity scared him. The way her eyes bore into his soul made him uneasy, but as she squeezed his hands and pleaded with him for an explanation, he could hear a gentle, reassuring voice in the back of his mind. Clinging to that voice, he responded as best he could.

"Look, I'm just a simple elf. I don't have all the answers. But looking at you now, seeing the regret in your eyes and hearing the pain in your voice, I can tell your heart has changed. Yes, you may have the same physical body. But tell me: if you were asked to invade Paxvilla again. If you had the choice to do it over, would you lead the attack?"

"No!" Castora pulled away, shaking her head violently. "I wouldn't want anything to do with it."

"Then you answered your own question!"

Artimus Jr. swung his arms out wide.

"Because what's out here is not you," he said motioning back towards his body. "What's in here," he tapped his fist over his heart, "And up here," he pointed to his forehead. "That is what I'm concerned about. So, while you may be the same person in the literal sense, I know by your own words that you've changed. Don't let the sins of your past prevent you from pursuing your future."

He glared into Castora's raging black eyes. It only took a moment for her gaze to soften, her lips curling up into a smile. She pulled away, stomped her right foot, and shook her head. The next moment, she locked back in on Artimus Jr.'s gaze.

"Thank you," she curtsied before abruptly turning and resuming the trot westward. "Though I know I still owe a great debt, I am grateful for your forgiveness. It is more than I deserve. But what makes you so interested in me as I am now? Is it my heart you are after, or my mind?" She glanced back and winked.

Artimus Jr. stood dumbfounded for a moment, but as Castora winked his way, he smiled and followed behind. As he caught back up to her side, he considered the question. With an exaggerated motion, he reached up and rubbed his chin, glancing at the sky as they walked west.

"Hmm. I mean, let's not underestimate your beauty," he smirked, hoping she picked up on the intended sarcasm. "Truly though, I think it's a bit of both. You're clearly intelligent, which is a quality I appreciate. And I suppose I don't fully know your heart yet, but that's what we're here for."

“Oh, is this a test then?” Castora smirked.

Artimus Jr. chuckled.

“Yes, let’s say it is. And that’s another reason I like you - that motivates you, doesn’t it? I sense you’re always up for a challenge, always ready to pass a test.”

Castora flared her eyebrows. She rubbed her hands together, grinning from ear to ear.

“I won’t lie. I’m excited to pass your tests, yes. But I hope you’re up for the challenge of passing mine.” Her ominous tone and the way her eyes lit up as she spoke the word ‘excited’ sent a chill down the elf’s spine. He couldn’t decide whether he should be worried or excited.

As he deliberated this, he noticed they were nearing the end of the road and turned his attention to the north. Unlike the rest of the walk here, there was some traffic along the road leading to Sissera’s. A couple of centaurs were approaching from the north, along with a few groupings of elves and lizock. Squinting towards the tavern, he saw a couple of other parties, both walking north towards the tavern.

“That’s our destination for tonight,” Artimus Jr. pointed north and nodded towards the tavern.

Castora followed his gaze. She glanced towards the tavern, slowing her gait.

“It appears to be a popular destination,” the hájje observed, her tone falling flat. With squinted eyes, the elf looked back upon her and saw the muscles in her face tense.

"But the only two people who matter tonight are the two of us." Artimus Jr. quipped.

"Do all your people truly share your forgiving nature?" Castora arched her right eyebrow, tilting her head up to the right as she looked the elf over.

"It's the will of Evorath," he said, forgetting for a moment that a hájje may not comprehend his meaning.

"That is," he scratched behind his head, coming to a stop, and stepping to the side of the road. He passed a nervous nod to the passing centaur couple, flashing an awkwardly toothy grin.

"Remember, the whole purpose of Marftaport was to create a community where no one person is to be elevated above another. A place where we are all free to create art, tend our fields, and care for our families. By our belief in Evorath, we never believe there's a valid reason to initiate force."

He looked around nervously, his shoulders tense as he lowered his arms, holding them out to drift down by his side. With a forced smile, he stared at Castora, watching her face soften and tension melt from her eyes.

"I suppose if you feel confident to bring me here, I should trust that you thought it through," the dark elf conceded.

She jerked her head, nodding towards the tavern. "Let's get some food already! I'm getting hungry," she skipped off towards Sissera's. Her playful tone brought a smile to Artimus Jr.'s face as he jogged to catch up yet again.

"You think about what you might want to eat?" he asked.

"Is my selection a test? I think it's only fair to know." Castora glared back at the elf.

"Of course not! There'd be no purpose to such a test that I can imagine. You eat what you wish to; it does me no harm. I was simply curious, and it seemed an easy way to restart the conversation," Artimus Jr. chuckled nervously.

"Oh, I'm sorry," Castora offered a subtle bow, but didn't break stride, marching towards the tavern. "In that case, I would love if you'd pick something out. Perhaps something unique or special to Marftaport. Think you're up for that challenge?"

"I think I've got just the dish in mind. I just hope it's available," Artimus Jr. wagged his index finger.

"Available? Is it a rationed delicacy?"

"Oh, no!" Artimus Jr. shook his head. "It's just they need to catch them fresh, and they do tend to be popular."

"Now I'm just curious to find out what this special food is!" Castora's face lit up as she strode forward.

Artimus Jr. chuckled and shook his head. This was sure to be an interesting evening.

CHAPTER XXV

Marftaport
3 Zerrum, 1149 MT

Artimus Jr. glanced back at the road ahead. They approached the next group leaving the tavern, a trio of lizock.

"Good evening, Artimus!" the shortest of the bunch waved, his tongue darting between his teeth as he smiled.

Artimus Jr. considered the short lizock, his yellow scales and simple brown surcoat. He recognized all three of them; they were fishermen, but in that moment, he couldn't recall their names. So, with a forced smile, he nodded towards the group and returned the wave.

"Good evening!" Artimus Jr. kept his eyes trained on the trio as they passed. The tallest of their group, an older, grey-scaled lizock with deep blue eyes, stared at Castora with narrow eyes as they passed. Fortunately, it appeared Castora's gaze was glued on the tavern. Though, Artimus Jr. himself had to fight the impulse to call out the lizock's rude behavior.

As they arrived at the door to the tavern, the elf picked up his pace, walking ahead of his date to grab the brass door handle. With a twist, he pulled the door open and motioned for Castora to walk through. The dark elf flashed him a smile and stepped through the doorway.

Artimus Jr. followed immediately behind, pulling the door closed as he took in the familiar surroundings. His ears were flooded with the sounds of laughter and merry making as he scanned the crowd. He looked first to the stage in the back left corner of the tavern, where he spotted the dwarven quartet.

They were a group of brothers, Benji, Kenji, Tenji, and Zenji. They were nephews of Keldor -or was it cousins? Artimus Jr. couldn't quite recall. Either way, he was happy to see they were the ones on stage tonight. Their unique a cappella style of harmonizing was always a hit. And since, to the elf's knowledge, the brothers had invented the style, it meant Castora would not have heard any such music.

By the looks of it, they were just taking the stage for the night. Artimus Jr. often got the four of them confused, but he was pretty sure it was Kenji and Zenji who were moving the harpsichord to the back wall of the tavern. The other two brothers were rummaging through their satchels.

Continuing his survey of the room, the elf noted the large circular tables nearest the stage were packed full. Dwarves, elves, lizock, and a couple of unfamiliar satyrs all packed into the tables, exchanging words, raising glasses, and enjoying their evening feast.

The bar was mostly filled up as well, only a few stray stools left open. The rest was covered with all manner of people, including a couple of trolls at the far-right corner, who appeared to be engaged in courtship. Glancing to the right side of the tavern, Artimus spotted two open tables, but the rest were occupied by various parties, including a few families.

Bobbing his head back and forth to see past the trolls, Artimus praised his luck. The sofa was open.

"Let's go this way," Artimus Jr. placed his hand on the small of Castora's back, directing her to the right and pointing towards the back corner.

Castora's eyes were wide as she looked around the room, but she walked along without objection, passing Artimus Jr. a receptive smile as they approached the bar and veered right. The pair made their way around the crowd, but the elf noticed a few odd looks from some of the patrons along the way.

Ignoring these outliers, they made it to the back corner, the rune stones a bit dimmer in this spot. As they approached the small table, Artimus Jr. held out his hands towards the sofa.

"I'm guessing you wouldn't mind a more private setting?"

Castora licked her lips and nodded. "Yes, this is perfect," she beamed.

"Excellent," Artimus Jr. grinned and walked around to the sofa. He extended his right hand, nodding towards the seat. With a shallow curtsy, Castora accepted his hand and sat down on the left side of the sofa. The elf waited for her to get comfortable in the seat, watching for a few moments before sitting beside her.

"This might be a dumb question," Castora whispered, lips pursed as she glanced around, "but how do we order any food sitting in this dimly lit corner?"

Artimus Jr. chuckled and nodded towards the bar.

"Sissera is known for her hospitality. It's pretty common to see people travel from the Satyr Island or as far east as the Felite Confederacy just to enjoy a meal here."

As if on cue, Arnona walked out from the kitchen. She looked towards the couple, beaming with enthusiasm as she danced across the room. Reaching the end of the bar, she brushed her hair aside and lifted the counter hatch.

"Good evening!" the free-spirited elf exclaimed, twiddling her blonde locks between her fingertips. "You both look absolutely lovely this evening. Can I get you started with drinks?" Her honeyed words flowed at a steady tempo, her eyes listing around as she spoke.

Castora cast Artimus Jr. a quizzical glance, her lips pursed, and right eyebrow arched.

"Yes," Artimus Jr. smiled. "We'll take two goblets and a bottle of Allebasi red. Do you still have some of the 1147 vintage?"

Arnona closed her eyes and nodded, her lips folding up into a broad smile. "Yes, an excellent choice!"

"Perfect," Artimus Jr. glanced back at Castora with a grin. "And I hope our timing is right. Can we get a plate of moryota to start as well?"

"Oh, you're in luck!" Arnona squealed, hopping in place. "The foragers just brought back a couple of baskets. I'll have them run out right away so they're fresh, and I'll be back with your wine. Is there anything else you'll want to start?"

"No, thank you." Artimus Jr. nodded.

"Ergolicious! I'll be right back."

As Arnona skipped off to the kitchen, the band started singing their first song. Artimus Jr. could hear the low timbre of two brothers harmonizing. It was the soft start to a moving melody the elf had come to appreciate more with age. But he focused his attention back on his date. Castora watched their server skip away, her eyes wide and mouth agape.

"Is there something wrong with her?" she asked after a few moments.

Artimus Jr. chuckled.

"I think she just enjoys the pipe weed a bit too much. But she's new to town, so I don't know her too well."

"What is pipe weed?" Castora asked incredulously.

Artimus Jr. leaned back, bobbing his head side-to-side as he considered the question.

"I'm not sure about the exact qualities, but it's a medicinal herb that some of the citizens grow. When smoked, it produces various effects, some of which you've already seen."

Artimus Jr. paused and held his tongue. He almost mentioned Mojo's fondness for the herb, but squelching the sting of that memory, he held his lips tight.

"I just figured she had a sandy foundation. Is there some long-term benefit to it?"

Artimus Jr. shrugged and shook his head. "I'm not sure. I've never tried it myself."

"Your people really treasure comfort, don't they?" Castora pondered.

"Pfft," Artimus puffed his lips. "I never really thought of it that way. I mean, some do, yes. But generally, we just let everyone live their lives as they see fit. I think the only common sentiment you'll find among everyone in Marftaport is that we desire to live peacefully with one another, as Evorath intended."

"But for people who claim to love peace, you sure train a lot for violence," Castora observed. "After all, my people train our whole lives for warfare. And it was your people who really won the day at Marftaport."

"Well, I'm not so sure we would've pulled it off without the Avatar. And I hope in time you'll consider that, for us, that wasn't a victory at all. A victory would have been convincing you to talk prior to the battle."

Artimus Jr. averted Castora's gaze, immediately regretting that comment as he looked down at the wood floor.

"I'm sorry," Castora sighed.

Artimus Jr. shook his head.

"Let's focus on the present," he suggested. He reached out and took Castora's hands, holding them up and smiling. As she met his gaze, her lips curled up into a smile.

"I think that's a good idea," she nodded. "So, tell me about these moryota we're about to eat."

"Well, you won't have to wait long," the elf nodded towards the bar. Arnona stepped through, leaving the counter hatch open and walking over with the plate of moryota.

Artimus Jr. could smell them as soon as Arnona reached the edge of the bar, the pungent odor wafting across the room. The freshest batches were always the smelliest, with three distinct odors. Despite the moldy cheese odor and the even more offensive damp cloth smell, there was a sweet third scent, reminiscent of honey suckle that somehow made the whole thing work. Even Castora, who at first looked offended by the odor, smiled as Arnona placed the plate on the table.

"Here you are," the whimsical server breathed. She stood up and placed down the two wine goblets on either side. "Your bottle should be right out."

"Thank you," Artimus Jr. nodded.

"My pleasure!" Arnona beamed. She turned and looked right at Castora. "You're in for a real treat! I recommend trying one now, and then again when you have the wine. The pairing is absolutely divine."

Without awaiting a response, Arnona curtsied, spun around, and skipped back towards the bar.

Artimus Jr. looked back down at the plate and took a quick count. He smiled, thirteen of the moryota set about on the plate. They looked perfectly fresh, the bulbous flesh on their backs still as white as snow. With six legs and long stemlike tails, these ones couldn't have been harvested more than a few minutes ago. In his experience, that meant they had about ten minutes before they began to yellow. And once they darkened further, the now magical blend of flavor would quickly turn sour. He had no intention of letting that happen.

"What exactly are they? Do we eat them with our hands?" Castora asked, looking down at the plate quizzically.

"To answer your second question," Artimus Jr. reached down and grabbed the nearest moryota in his index finger and thumb. Bringing it up to his mouth, he took a shallow breath through his nose and plopped it in. Biting down on the soft shell, he savored the release of flavors as he chewed, the sweet savory mixture like a portabella mushroom stuffed with blue cheese and topped with a honey glaze.

He kept his eyes on Castora, delighted to see her follow his lead. She reached over, grabbed a moryota and paused with it just outside her mouth. With a flare of her nostrils, she took the first bite, the uncertainty melting away from her face. Smiling as she chewed, she nodded her head, her eyes widening in delight.

"Alright, now you really must tell me. What are these?" she gushed.

"That's a bit of a story," Artimus Jr. smirked.

He nodded back over Castora's shoulder. Arnona stepped up to the table, holding out the bottle of wine.

"I beg forgiveness for my interruption," she bowed. "But would you like me to pour your first cup?"

"Yes, please." Artimus Jr. motioned towards the goblets. Castora glanced over her shoulder at Arnona, offering a subtle nod and grinning from ear-to-ear.

"Oh, I see you've tried your first moryota. Just wait until you have a sip of this wine to go with it. You'll wish you could eat them all the time."

She poured as she spoke, somehow maintaining eye contact with Castora while still offering perfectly level pours. As she filled Artimus Jr.'s goblet and placed it back on the table, she took a step away from the pair.

"Would you two like dinner tonight, or are you just here for the wine and moryota?"

"Yes, what is the chef's special tonight?" Artimus Jr. asked as Castora picked up another moryota and plopped it in her mouth.

"Oh, I think the special is just what you need with your wine choice. It's a seared, lemon-pepper tuna steak with seasonal greens and roasted potato. If you're thinking of leaving room for dessert, perhaps you two would like to share it on a platter. We have a delicious fruit, nut, and cheese plate tonight. Sissera got her hands on some aged cheddar from that new human family that just moved here, and it's been a big hit tonight."

"That all sounds perfect!" Artimus Jr. affirmed. Castora seemed too enthralled with her moryota, her eyes skyward and shoulders relaxed as she swallowed her second one.

"Ergolicious! If you need anything while you wait, I'll be around," Arnona nodded.

With a low bow, she danced back to the bar, her hips swaying to the rhythm of the upbeat music.

"I see you're still enjoying the moryota. You ready to try it with the wine?" Artimus Jr. lifted his goblet.

Castora nodded, grinning ear-to-ear.

"Yes, but first I must hear this story. What are these and how do I get more of them?"

Artimus Jr. chuckled, placing his goblet back on the table.

"Alright, so there's this member of the Mage's Guild named Feotidus. He has some unconventional ideas -well, the reasoning isn't important. What's important is he's developed his own branch of magic that's all about culinary creations. And these moryota are the result of one of his experiments. It's an insect that, by magic, grows from mushroom spores that 'hatch' around sunset each day."

"An unnatural amalgam?" Castora gasped.

The dark elf leaned back, holding her hands over her mouth. With wide eyes, she stared off.

"What's wrong? They're perfectly safe. At least no one here has ever gotten sick from them." Artimus Jr. leaned in, his voice full of concern.

Castora shook her head. She took a deep breath, closed her eyes and nodded.

"I'll be fine," she whispered unconvincingly. "I'm sorry," she opened her eyes and peered straight through Artimus Jr. "I know I'll be alright. It's just this sort of creation is taboo to the hájje. It's considered a frivolous waste of magic to use it for such things as creating something to eat."

"Really?" Artimus Jr. leaned back, his eyes widening as he struggled to temper his reaction. What sort of tyrant tried to tell people what they could or couldn't eat?

"I know it shouldn't bother me now. I'll be alright." Castora sighed. She smiled, her eyes shaking. "They are delicious after all!"

It took Artimus Jr. a moment to center his thoughts, but after a brief pause, he shook his head. "It's perfectly understandable that it bothers you. I'm sorry I didn't warn you before. That was thoughtless of me."

Castora shook her head and lifted her wine goblet.

"You've no need to apologize," she winked. "Let's see how it pairs with this wine."

"Alright," Artimus Jr. smirked and raised his glass. "Here's how to get the best experience. I mean, the wine 'experts' might disagree, but I've found this really delivers the perfect flavor."

He leaned in and picked up a moryota, offering it to Castora. The dark elf took it with her free hand, matching Artimus Jr.'s gaze and leaning in closer. The elf took one of the moryota for himself.

"Now, just follow my lead. You'll want to have a sniff of the wine. Really take in the floral notes and the sweet undertone. Then as you sip your wine, hold it in your mouth and have a sniff of the moryota. Swallow and toss that scrumptious moryota in your mouth. And as you chew, follow up with another sip of wine."

"That's quite a ritual!" Castora giggled. "But I'll follow your lead!"

"Good," Artimus Jr. nodded, smiling as he took a sniff of the wine. As the signature smell of the 1147 vintage filled his nostrils, he leaned back and took a sip of wine, just enough to cover his tongue. Sniffing the moryota he could already taste the transformation in his mouth, the flagrant odor bringing out the sweet notes of the wine in his mouth.

And only a moment after swallowing, he threw the moryota in next, the soft spongy texture melting in his mouth. Mid-chew, he took the next sip of wine, completing the ritual and releasing the full impact of the flavor. His tongue tingled, the explosion of taste filling him with comfort and warmth.

As he finished, he turned his full attention to Castora. The dark elf closed her eyes, sinking into her seat. The tension melted away from her face, smiling and letting out a low moan.

"That is the most delicious thing I've ever eaten," she breathed, locking eyes with her date.

And peering back into her deep, dark eyes, Artimus Jr. knew this would be an evening to remember.

CHAPTER XXVI

Marſtaport
4 Zerrum, 1149 MT

Zelag leaned back. He closed his eyes, breathing in the soothing scent of the hemp pages. When he agreed to take Artimus Jr.'s guard shift this morning, he had expected to find a more interesting book to pass the time.

But alas, Vistoro insisted he check out this massive volume on comparative political systems. The book was heavy and thick, and though he'd trudged through only one hundred pages so far, it felt like he'd been reading all day.

The shapeshifter had always found Vistoro's writing to be dry. But this one had to take the prize for the most disinteresting piece of literature to date.

Groaning, Zelag sat up straight.

"Alright Vistoro. There's got to be something interesting in here," he flipped through to the next chapter. "Hmm. 'The Myth of Divine Authority'. Perhaps this is something."

As he read through this next chapter, unsurprisingly finding it just as boring as the rest of the book, he wondered what sort of people truly enjoyed this type of book. No personal stories, no added drama, and not even a parable to hammer home the point. Just cold hard information, written in such plain language that a child could read. It was worse than listening to one of the Avatar's sermons, a thought that caused him to feel a touch of guilt.

Finishing this chapter, he took a pause and considered. He would gladly sit through another one of those sermons if it meant having the Avatar for the upcoming battle against Yezurkstal.

But the hum of a runestone caught his attention.

Zelag stood up, tossing the book onto his chair, and walking up to the ledge of the watchtower. He leaned forward on the railing, focusing on the figure in the distance.

His eyes tingled as he squinted, his vision growing sharper. He was still wary of exercising such abilities, the potential for injury always top of his mind as he flexed his shapeshifting muscles. But over the years, he'd found ways to augment this human form using attributes of other creatures in Evorath. In this case, he simply replaced his human eyes with elvish ones, which offered considerably better distance vision.

And as the figure came into focus, Zelag let out an audible gasp. Riding on horseback was a familiar but wholly unexpected visitor. It was Zeidrich, the General of the Erathal Republic.

Shifting his gaze past the general, Zelag scanned the surrounding area for any signs of others. He let his innate vision take over, the auras of life filling his sight with various colors. Though he spotted various small critters, there was nothing of consequence beyond Zeidrich. It seemed the general was alone, which really piqued the shapeshifter's curiosity.

"I wonder if he'll recognize me," Zelag mumbled. He paused, considering whether to climb down the ladder or take the rope. He never was much for the slow approach.

Without a second thought, he grabbed hold of the escape rope and vaulted over the tower ledge. Sliding down the rope, he considered his options. And as he reached the bottom of the tower, he shook out his hands, his ascent a touch too rapid.

Considering how far away Zeidrich still was, Zelag decided the best course was to get a head start on notifying the parties that might be of interest. He dashed west towards the inn. At this part of the day, at the edge of town, there wasn't much activity, but there were smattering of people spread out among the front of the inn.

And as luck had it, Zachiro was among the crowd. He appeared to be entertaining some elvish children, puffing out his cheeks and making silly hand gestures. The kids giggled at his antics as Zelag slowed to a stop just behind them.

"I'm sorry to interrupt children," Zelag offered with clasped hands. "Zachiro, you might want to send word to Vistoro, and perhaps Artimus and Savannah. Zeidrich, the Erathal general, is approaching town."

"What?" Zachiro's face flushed, his shrill tone revealing his concern.

"He's alone," Zelag said reassuringly. "So, no need to sound the alarm. But I doubt he's here to ask for a cookie recipe."

"It's probably about Arnona. I knew he'd be here eventually," Zachiro shook his head. "Children, why don't you play out here for a minute. I'll be right back."

"Wait, why would Zeidrich care about Arnona?" Zelag called after the innkeeper.

Zachiro glanced back and shrugged. "Well, she is his daughter," he answered before proceeding towards the inn.

As the innkeeper walked back up the steps, Zelag felt his throat constrict. He felt embarrassed he hadn't known that before becoming intimate with Arnona. Struggling to repress his disappointment with himself, he strode east towards the town entrance, determined to maintain a calm demeanor.

Fiddling with his sword belt as he walked, he kept his gaze east. Zeidrich approached at a slow trot, which left Zelag to meander at a relaxed pace. As he strolled outside of town, the young shapeshifter stepped over to a nearby oak tree and leaned against it. He kept his gaze east.

After a few minutes, as the general drew closer, Zelag stepped away from the tree and waved his right hand.

"Welcome to Marftaport General," he called out.

Zeidrich shook his head, his eyes narrowed as he looked around. It took him a moment, but when he caught Zelag's gaze he returned the wave.

"I'm afraid you have me at a disadvantage," the general called out, his voice a bit softer than Zelag had remembered. He maintained a steady approach, his tan destrier's hoofs clacking on the cobblestone road as he drew near.

"Oh, I didn't think an accomplished general like you would forget such a handsome face." quipped Zelag with a grin.

Zeidrich chuckled, a forced laugh by the looks of his yellow aura. He was nervous.

"No one here will hurt you General," Zelag volunteered, lowering his voice as Zeidrich drew closer. "That is, assuming you're not here to hurt anyone. Remember, you're entering a free town now. So, I'd recommend leaving your title at the door."

As he approached, Zeidrich pulled back on the reins and squinted down at Zelag. He came to a stop, staring at the shapeshifter for a few moments. And then his face lit up, his eyes widening in recognition.

"You're that shapeshifter, Zelag! You know, if I -never mind." He shook his head.

"I appreciate the welcome, even if I question its sincerity," he muttered, his familiar, gruff tone coming out.

"Oh, you should know I'm always sincere," Zelag joked. "But let's not waste our time with repartee. What brings you to this peaceful little town?"

"I'm looking for a missing person," Zeidrich glared.

"Missing person?" Zelag scratched his beard, gazing skyward as he tapped his foot. "I don't think you'll find any of those here. Everyone here comes and goes of their own free choice; unlike that Republic you work for."

Zeidrich squeezed his right fist, his aura flaring red for a moment before he smiled through his teeth.

"Let me rephrase. I'm looking for a young elf who came this way not too long ago. Perhaps I can inquire at the town inn?"

Zelag nodded. "Sure, sure. That seems like a reasonable place to start. Follow me."

Without waiting, Zelag turned around and started west. He intentionally took his time, walking at a snail's pace and flagging for Zeidrich to follow.

"You must be really running short on lapdogs if you're coming out yourself to investigate this person. Is no one left in the Republic capable of tracking someone down?"

"I have a personal stake in this," Zeidrich scoffed.

"Personal stake?" Zelag feigned ignorance. "Did your wife run away with a satyr? I hear they can be quite charming."

Zeidrich didn't respond immediately, a few seconds slipping by with nothing but the clack of his horse's hooves on the road and the chirping of birds in the air. But just as Zelag was about to follow up, the general barked.

"Just mind your business, vagabond!"

"Oh, I guess the marriage really is on the rocks then," the shapeshifter murmured, failing to stifle a smirk. "But enough about that," he picked up his pace and shook his right hand in the air. "Maybe I can help. Who are you looking for?"

Zeidrich mumbled something under his breath.

"What was that? You'd be a fool not to accept my offer?" Zelag chided, glancing back at the general. "Yes, I agree."

"Why would I accept help from a lowlife like you?"

"A lowlife? Now you're just being hurtful," Zelag shook his head. "But I'll forgive you since I know it's tough right now at home."

Zeidrich growled, a sound that made Zelag grin from ear-to-ear. The children outside the inn dispersed as the pair drew near, and Zelag spotted Zachiro walking back down the steps and out towards the road. The old lizock innkeeper waved as they drew into earshot.

Taking that as an offer to help, Zelag called out.

"Ah, Zachiro! The General here is apparently looking for someone. He hasn't seen it fit to reveal to me who, but perhaps your silver tongue can do the trick."

"Perhaps you can at least remove this imp from my presence," Zeidrich quipped, a hint of sarcasm in his voice.

Zachiro shook his head. Lizock had a natural advantage in matters of deception, their scaly features making it difficult to discern emotions from their expressions. However, Zelag could see the nervous energy around the innkeeper.

"I know who you're here for," Zachiro admitted. "But perhaps you would like to bring that horse of yours around to the stable and come inside for a cup of tea, on the house."

Zelag considered the elvish general. He appeared to be considering the offer, his face pensive as he pulled on the reigns and loosening his legs around his horse. As the young destrier slowed its trot, Zeidrich nodded towards Zelag.

"If you make it a mead and this one takes my horse to the stable, then I accept your terms," Zeidrich softened his tone like before, but his red aura revealed an underlying aggression.

"That sounds like a swell idea!" Zelag agreed.

"Then it's settled," Zachiro smiled.

The old innkeeper placed his hands on his hips, his tail swinging as he watched. Zelag stepped over, grabbing hold of the reins with his right hand and offering his left to Zeidrich.

"Hmph," Zeidrich shook his head. He swung his left leg around and hopped off his horse.

"I expect he'll be put in his own stall," Zeidrich commanded. "I don't know what poor conditions you let your horses get in without anyone overseeing their health."

Zelag shook his head. He clicked his tongue and led the horse around the side of the inn. As he did, he heard Zachiro's shaky voice reply.

"Oh, I assure you our stablemaster maintains the highest standards. Our horses are all quite healthy and happy and your destrier will have a fine stall and some fresh hay to snack on while it waits for you."

The silence that followed tempted Zelag to turn back and see Zeidrich's expression. He was disappointed the cantankerous old soldier didn't offer some retort.

But as he walked around the side of the inn, the shapeshifter picked up his pace. Taking wide strides, he hurried towards the stables, eager to return and hear whatever unpleasant discussion was sure to ensue. With any luck, he'd beat Vistoro and Artimus there.

Trekking towards the stables, he considered how Zeidrich would react when Arnona inevitably refused to leave.

The General might have been arrogant enough to try and force his way if it were just Zelag around, but with Artimus and Savannah, there was no way he'd be that stupid, or so the shapeshifter thought. As he considered this, he caught sight of a stableboy just ahead.

The boy was elvish, no more than a couple of decades old at most. Clothed in a brown tunic and slacks, the skinny young elf was working some hay with a pitchfork. With light blonde hair, hazel eyes, and unremarkable features, Zelag couldn't recall if he had met the boy before.

"Good morning!" Zelag called to the boy.

Mid-scoop, the stableboy finished shaking the hay from his fork before turning towards the shapeshifter.

"Good morning. Uh, Mr, Zelag, isn't it?" the boy's voice was hoarse, his shrill tone catching Zelag off guard.

"Yes, just Zelag though, please. And you are?" Zelag maintained his approach, pulling Zeidrich's destrier behind.

"Oh, it's Elias," the boy shrieked, offering out his hand.

Still a few meters to go, Zelag watched Elias's blank stare as he approached. Reaching out, he gave the boy's hand a quick shake. At least his grasp was firm.

Pulling away, Zelag nodded towards the destrier. "We have a visitor from down south. Can you store this guy in a stall? Preferably one that will leave him nice and smelly."

The stableboy glanced back towards the stables and scratched behind his head.

"Uh, I just finished cleaning the stalls before this, so I don't think we have any smelly ones. Is it alright if I just put him in any available stall?"

Zelag chuckled. "Yeah, that will be fine."

Letting go of the reins, Zelag watched as the stableboy stepped up to the horse. The destrier snorted and sniffed at the boy's hand. But with a shushing noise, the stableboy reached up and patted the horse on its side.

"Let's get you some hay to munch on," said the boy, leading the horse north towards the stables.

Zelag waited for only a moment, watching as the boy led the horse onward. Satisfied that he had things handled, the shapeshifter turned around and jogged back along the field. He kept his focus ahead, eager to get back.

As he turned the corner to the inn, he spotted Artimus and Savannah. The couple moved at a brisk pace, wearing concerned looks as they rushed towards the inn.

"Artimus, Savannah," Zelag waved, jogging to intercept the couple.

The elves slowed their pace, turning to consider the shapeshifter. Savannah squinted towards Zelag and Artimus shook his head.

"How angry is he?" Artimus asked as Zelag stepped alongside them. The trio continued their walk towards the inn.

"I don't think he'll take it easy, but I doubt he's dumb enough to do anything rash."

"And you left him alone with Zachiro?" Savannah questioned. "You sure that was a good idea?"

"He was behaving well enough," Zelag shrugged.

Savannah sighed, twirling her hair between her fingertips as she hurried towards the inn. As they approached the door, Artimus leapt ahead, grabbing hold of the weathered iron handle and pulling the right door open.

With a nod to her husband, Savannah proceeded inside. Zelag paused, motioning for Artimus to follow. As the elf slipped inside, Zelag followed immediately behind. He pulled the door shut behind him.

The inn was laid out differently than any others Zelag had encountered in his travels, a quality he found endearing. In fact, the entire place was designed for the sole purpose of lodging, as opposed to most taverns he visited. Entering in the front door, they passed through a small, square foyer, decorated on either side with paintings and lit with a simple gold chandelier illuminated by six runestones placed symmetrically in a hexagonal shape.

Walking along the purple carpet of the foyer, they entered the main hall, which stretched the entire length of the building. The space before them had wood plank floors, an open area of at least a hundred square meters to welcome guests. This square reception area was designed symmetrically, with arched hallways leading in all four directions.

Beside the left and right hallways were mismatched steps, the ones on the left shallow to accommodate centaur guests.

Zelag smiled towards the young receptionist, whom he'd seen only once before. She had unusually short, light brown hair and her yellow-green eyes sparkled with a thrill for life. Sitting behind the natural mahogany desk, she returned a toothy grin.

"Good morning Mr. Artimus, Mrs. Savannah," she bubbled. "Zachiro is in his office with the caller from Erathal. He's asked you proceed right on through," her voice was sweet and innocent.

"Thank you Relixia," Savannah nodded, sweeping past the desk. Artimus simply nodded towards Relixia, following closely behind his wife.

But as Zelag started around after them, Relixia stood up and cleared her throat. She maintained a wide smile, her eyes like small slits in her face as she addressed Zelag.

"Mr. Zelag, Zachiro has requested you go to retrieve Ms. Arnona. I believe she is working at Sissera's this morning."

Zelag stopped midstride, his eyes narrow as he considered whether to acquiesce the request. Figuring the most interesting part would involve Arnona, it took him only a moment to agree.

"Huh, alright. That sounds like an excellent idea," he exaggerated his enthusiasm. "I'll go fetch her then!"

With a dramatic spin, Zelag turned around and stomped back through the foyer and out the front door. He paused once outside and shook his head.

"Kids here just don't realize how fortunate they are," he mumbled as he trotted down the steps.

Starting on the main road, Zelag took off at a brisk jog, quickly making his way past the blacksmith and archery range. But as he passed by the public gathering hall, noticing a host of humans hanging around outside and mingling with some of the locals, he reconsidered his pace. He slowed to a slow walk, a smile forming on his face. Just because he was fetching Arnona as requested, didn't mean he needed to be quick.

Strolling by, he greeted anyone who paid him mind. Nodding to a woman and her child on the right, waving to a man on his left, and exchanging a few "good mornings," along the way. He made it past the windmill, the smell of fresh bread wafting from the bakery to the north as he continued forward.

And for the rest of the walk, he kept his attention wide and his pace slow and steady. It took a full fifteen minutes before he made it through to the dockside, the briny smell of the ocean filling his nostrils as considered all the homes around here. Even in the past week, they had started constructing another half dozen houses out this way, and the streets were busier than usual too.

Making his way to the end of the road, he waved towards an elvish mother and her two children playing just outside one of those newer homes. Turning north, he meandered up the curved road, his eyes set on Sissera's up ahead.

Like most days at this time, the road leading to the tavern was empty; it was too late for the breakfast crowd and too early for lunch. So, as he pulled open the large door, he wasn't surprised to find most of the tables empty. In fact, there were only five patrons, including a group of four barghest sitting at a table in the southwest corner of the tavern.

Zelag didn't pay them any mind but took note of the busboy wiping down tables in the northwest part of the room. He also spotted Sissera tidying up around the stage in the northeast corner. And finally, he considered the one other patron, a slim, auburn-haired elf with hair so long it almost touched the floor. She sat at the bar, giggling.

"So, I told him that," Arnona looked up and smiled. "Zelag!" she squealed. "Evorath must really be smiling upon me this morning. Have you met my friend Laurena?" she motioned towards the skinny elf.

Zelag shook his head and offered a courteous smile. Judging by the stench of pipe weed and the redness in her eyes, Laurena was even more fond of the herb than Arnona. And by the stains all over her white dress and the absence of shoes upon her feet, she wasn't someone the shapeshifter cared to become better acquainted with.

"You should hear my news before you assume my presence is a blessing," Zelag interjected, speaking before Laurena had a chance to do so.

"Oh, and what news is that?" Arnona inquired, wearing her usual wide smile and gazing off towards the ceiling.

"Your father just rode into town. He's looking for you."

It took a moment for her to react, but Zelag could see her face processing the news. Her eyes wavered, drifting down to meet Zelag's gaze. Her mouth folded flat, the muscles in her cheek tensing. And her nose twitched, a subtle but definite indication of discomfort.

"I don't know why he'd be looking for me. The General never seemed to care if I was around when I lived in Erathal. Why should he care to visit me here?" Arnona's tone was much crisper than usual, her voice laced with uncertainty.

"I really don't know," Zelag shrugged. "But I don't think he's leaving until he sees you."

"He's going to try and make me leave," Arnona pouted. "And since I'm not leaving, it sounds like a waste of my time."

"Preach sister!" Laurena held up her right hand, palm open as she shook her head.

Zelag scratched the back of his neck. He really hated this sort of job. "Like I said, I don't think he'll leave town until he sees you. Perhaps you could explain to him how you've found a home here. Artimus and Savannah are talking with him now, so I'm sure they're buttering him up for you."

"If he really wants to see me, he can come have a meal here. But I've got nothing to say to him," Arnona crossed her arms and turned around to face the back wall.

"Yes!" Laurena clapped her hands slowly.

"Alright, I'll relay that message then."

Zelag shook his head and started back towards the door, wondering how he'd turn this around. As he pushed the door open and stepped outside, he considered his next move. And suddenly, he realized he no longer felt any pleasure at the thought of annoying the General any further. He closed his eyes, stifling a tear as he considered the situation.

Zelag would have given anything to see his progenitor again. How bad could Zeidrich have been to Arnona that she would be so cold?

With clenched fists, Zelag took off in a sprint, running southeast through the fields. And as he ran, he did what he learned best in this human form: he suppressed those feelings of love and loss.

By the time he made it back to the main street, he found himself slowing from a run to a jog. And as he passed the windmill, he eased back into a brisk walk. But he kept his focus ahead, ignoring anyone he passed along the way to the inn.

His heart ached as he stepped inside and wiped the sweat from his brow. With a forced smile and an air of confidence, he walked past the reception desk, ignoring Relixia as she held up her index finger and opened her mouth to speak.

And with the smuggest smile he could muster, he steeled his heart and stepped into Zachiro's office.

CHAPTER XXVII

In her sixty years on Evorath, Castora had never much seen use for laughter. Sure, on occasion she had laughed at the expense of her brothers, or one of her cousins. But aside from those moments of humiliation, nothing really seemed funny.

"Stop it!" she chortled. "You're making my face hurt."

She reached up and gently massaged her cheeks, closing her eyes as she leaned back against the towering oak. As she opened them back up, she took a moment to appreciate the beautiful form of her date, Artimus Jr. His lean body, tanned skin, and luscious brown hair. And the way the light hit his eyes, sometimes showing off tones of green and other times flashing blue like the sea made her heart flutter.

Of course, as she had found quite often over the past few days, as soon as she felt such strong positive feelings, a deep apprehension took hold. She felt her muscles tensing, her face forming into a frown.

"Is something the matter?" Artimus Jr. inquired with a frown. "I can cut back on the jokes."

"No, it's not that," Castora glanced down, watching the grass blow in the gentle evening breeze. The moonlight trickled through the branches overhead, providing a beautiful spectacle of light for her night-time eyes. She wondered if Artimus Jr.'s inferior night vision afforded him the same splendor.

"Is it something you want to talk about?" the elf pried. "If not, that's fine. I just hope you feel safe sharing your thoughts."

"I do!" Castora looked back up, locking the elf's gaze. His eyes glowed a hopeful blue in the moonlight. But she could see the concern behind his gaze.

"It's just sort of difficult to talk about," the dark elf brushed her bangs aside. With a long sigh, she rose to her feet.

"How about we walk? You mentioned the shoreline was a sight to behold at night. Can we head that way?" she asked.

"As you wish!" Artimus Jr. exclaimed. He jumped to his feet and adjusted his belt before holding out his hand.

Castora smiled, accepting his hand and walking northwest towards the shore. She could already hear the waves lapping against the shoreline. And as they made their way through the tree line and into the open field, she could see the light reflecting off the ocean in the distance. They continued silently for a solid ten minutes, the dark elf perfectly content to just feel the warmth of Artimus Jr.'s hand in her own.

As they drew closer to the sea, the briny smell of the oceans filling her nostrils, she glanced over at the elf and smiled.

"Alright, there's something I feel you should know. Because especially since we've been spending so much time together these last couple of days I" she paused, her throat constricting as she tried to find the words.

"Well, I really like you. And from what I've gathered since being here, your people tend to have more drawn-out courtships than mine. Before we go too far into that process, I want you to…" She felt a lump in her throat. Closing her eyes, she cleared her throat and took a deep breath.

As she exhaled, she stopped and turned to face Artimus Jr. "I need you to know that I was married before," she blurted.

Artimus Jr.'s eyes dilated. He blinked a couple of times. And in that moment of uncertainty, Castora felt like her heart might explode from the anxiety. But that fear melted away as her amazing courter reached out and took her other hand. Gingerly grasping both hands, he nodded.

"I suspected that was a possibility," the elf admitted.

Castora leaned back, arching her right eyebrow. She squinted at the elf, unable to discern if his statement was one of disappointment, or if, by some miracle, of acceptance.

"How would you have suspected that?" she pleaded.

"Oh, it's alright," Artimus Jr. breathed. "Remember last night you spent a solid hour telling me about hájje society. I didn't want to pry, but I did pick up on the fact that all your cousins have multiple spouses and children. And if you're not ready to tell me more than you've already said, you can rest easy knowing it's alright, whatever it is."

Castora bit her bottom lip. Her eyes fluttered and she felt an overwhelming pressure in her chest. With a sniffle, she shook her head.

"No, I think I have to tell you this now," she choked.

"Take your time." Artimus Jr. let go of her left hand. He reached up and placed his hand gently on her shoulder.

She looked back up and matched his gaze, his sweet, friendly eyes filling her with warmth.

"Alright," she shut her eyes tight and nodded, remembering what Tel' Shira said about prayer.

After uttering a silent prayer for strength, she opened her eyes and once again met her courter's gaze.

"Well, there's a reason I'm no longer married. And perhaps more pointed, a reason I was only married once." She cleared her throat.

"I'm sorry, this is difficult to say," her voice went up a full octave. She could feel her eyes tearing up.

"I'm barren," she cried.

She threw up her hands and covered her eyes before bursting into tears. But what happened next was quite unexpected. In one moment, she felt Artimus Jr's hand on her arm, and next she felt him wrap his arms around in a warm embrace. He rubbed her back and clung to her tight.

"It's alright," he breathed, giving her a squeeze. "I'm so sorry, but it will be alright."

"What do you mean?" she sobbed. "How can it be alright? I can never bear a child!" she sucked in too much air and coughed out mucous.

"I mean, 'if Evorath wills it, so it shall be.' I trust Evorath to guide us, and if we can't have children, then so be it. But" the elf reached up and took her hand. "you'll learn soon enough that living here we don't believe anything is beyond hope. Perhaps your change of heart brought about other changes."

"But how can you possibly just accept it?" Her mind raced, struggling to process her courter's response. "Can you really betroth yourself to someone who cannot bare you a son?"

She pulled away but held fast to his hand. Her bottom lip quivered, that gentle voice in her head coaxing her to consider the possibility that Artimus Jr. was right. What if, through some miracle, she really could have a child? But if she could, was it right to try with a foul blooded creature?

No!

Castora shook her head and instinctually pulled away. But regaining control of her response, she flung herself at Artimus Jr. She wrapped her arms around him and squeezed him tight, sniffling in an attempt to regain her composure.

"I really can, that much I am sure," the elf promised.

He tightened his embrace, letting loose a long sigh as they swayed side-to-side.

Castora took a deep, stuttered breath, and chuckled upon release. She pulled away, wiping her nose and shaking her head.

"I'm so embarrassed," she slipped.

"And I admire your courage," Artimus Jr. countered. Was that sarcasm in his voice?

No!

She knew it wasn't.

It was becoming easier for her to recognize the voice of her father. He was a voice she no longer trusted, for she realized his motives did not account for her well-being. She was but a tool for him to use, but no longer! This was an opportunity to declare her independence, to embrace her own strength. And perhaps, to embrace something even greater.

"Thank you. It feels almost like an impossible dream. Like some sort of fabricated reality concocted in childhood-"

"Like a fairy-tale?" Artimus Jr. interjected.

"Yes, everyone seems so fond of that term, fairy-tale. I suppose like that, yes." Castora nodded.

Artimus Jr. leaned in and pecked her on the cheek.

"I feel we may be living our own fairy-tale." The elf quipped, his cheeks growing rosy.

With a wide grin, Castora spun around, pulling her courter along behind. She marched northwest, heading towards the reflection of the moon in the ocean ahead.

The elf followed in stride. Seeing his wide grin, she couldn't help but smile.

"I have an idea," Artimus Jr. picked up his pace and pointed to a large cylindrical structure ahead. "You see that lighthouse there? I think you might like to meet its keeper. What do you think of that?"

Castora considered the large building. The large white tower was at least as tall as the defensive turrets back home, and aptly named. For at the top she could see a large fire burning, the flickering light reflecting out to the ocean.

"Why do you think I'd like to meet the tower's keeper?" Castora arched her eyebrows and pursed her lips as she considered it.

"Well," Artimus Jr. rubbed his chin with his right hand and glanced up towards the moon. "If you want to really know what Marftaport is about, he paints a compelling picture."

"Oh, is he an artist too?" Castora gaped.

"No," the elf shook his head. "I mean he'll tell you a story that'll help you better understand the mission of Marftaport."

"Oh," Castora blushed, glancing down at her feet. "Alright. If you think he won't mind the unannounced visit, I don't mind either."

"No way, Argos is always happy to receive visitors."

They walked for the next couple of minutes in silence, enjoying the cool ocean breeze and the soft sound of waves lapping against the shore. Castora wore a wide smile as they did, glancing over at her date every few seconds to admire his face in the moonlight.

"Well, here we are," said Artimus Jr. as they reached the door to the tower. The raw cedar of the door contrasted against the whitewash of the stone tower, a crescent moon carved towards the top quadrant, right in the center.

A large iron knocker was set in the center of the door, along with a matching handle to the side. Artimus Jr. stepped up to the door and pulled back on the knocker. With a couple raps of the iron, he took a step away and smiled at Castora.

"We shouldn't have to wait long," he whispered.

And before Castora had a chance to reply, she heard footsteps coming from within, followed by a deep rumbling voice. There was a clear joviality in his tone.

"Just a moment," the voice called.

Combing back her hair with her left hand, Castora smiled at Artimus Jr. and squeezed his hand. The elf returned the gesture, nodding towards the door.

With a click, the door swung inward, revealing an elderly lizock standing just within. But as Castora assessed the keeper's appearance, she found herself staring in disbelief.

The wizened lizock's brown scales had faded with age, a dull gray overtaking much of his body. He wore a simple white tunic and faded brown slacks, his tail hanging limp and dragging behind the rest of his form. And while the crest at the top of his head was somewhat unique, topping his head almost like a fern, it was his eyes that took the dark elf by surprise.

For looking into those white voids of eyes, Castora could immediately tell Argos was blind.

"Artimus Jr." the lizock smiled, his tongue darting between his yellow teeth. "And you've brought someone with you. I'm sorry, have we met before miss?"

Argos offered out his right hand to Castora. The dark elf hesitated for a moment, but seeing a reassuring nod from Artimus

Jr., she accepted the handshake. The lighthouse keeper's face lit up as he grasped her hand.

"Ah, you must be the hájje everyone is talking about," Argos smirked. "Not this truly is an unexpected treat. Please why don't you both come in. I have a kettle of tea on, one of your mother's blends," Argos nodded towards Artimus Jr. before turning around and retreating inside.

Castora glanced at Artimus Jr. with narrow eyes.

"I may be blind," Argos called back as if hearing Castora's thoughts, "but, I've learned ways to 'see' the world that don't require sight."

Artimus Jr. grinned and gestured for Castora to proceed. Still a bit uneasy, she followed behind the lighthouse keeper, keeping her eyes wide to observe the way.

It was a cramped space, the low ceiling no more than two and a half meters tall. The walls were almost completely bare, the raw stone reminiscent of Castora's own upbringing in Hájjeona. Her eyes were drawn to the small port window though, positioned just a few meters into the main room and featuring multicolored stained glass. With its eastward position, she imagined it created quite the spectacle at sunrise.

As one might expect in a blind lizock's home, the room was sparely furnished as well, featuring a sofa underneath that stained glass window with a pair of chairs on the opposite side. And at the north end of the room, she spotted the stove.

The modest iron stove sat just beside the wall, the exhaust pipe running directly out through the northern wall. Resting atop the stove, she spotted a copper kettle, whisps of steam rising from the spout. And hanging just to the right of the stove, on a custom wooden rack, she spotted about half a dozen teacups.

On the right side of the room, she spotted a small round table with four chairs. The table was bare, save a small copper jar in the center with a handle sticking out. Proceeding around the table, Argos pulled out the eastern chair and motioned towards it.

"Please, have a seat," he instructed. "And Arty, you can sit here," he stepped over and pulled out the northern chair.

Castora gave pause, glancing back at her courter and waiting for his nod of approval before proceeding to take her seat. As she scooted up to the table, she did one more sweep of the room. She noticed the stairwell on the western side of the room, two large buckets set at the base of the steps.

That explained the peculiar smell. It had to be some kind of oil, likely used to keep the flame above burning bright.

While Artimus Jr. took his seat, Argos stepped over to the stove and pulled down three teacups. Castora adjusted her dress, taking one final sweep around the room. The rattling of the tea kettle drew her eyes back to the stove, watching as the steam poured from the spout. Meanwhile, Argos returned and placed the three teacups down, putting the third one on the western side of the table.

"I couldn't have planned the timing better myself," Argos muttered, stepping back over to the kettle.

He grabbed a thick towel from beside the stove and picked up the kettle. The steam diminished as he walked back over, first dying to a small mist and dissipating to the occasional whisp by the time Argos reached Castora.

"Here you are dear," Argos whispered as he poured out the perfect amount of tea to fill her cup, leaving just a couple centimeters empty at the top. "And you can help yourself to sugar if you'd like," he nodded towards the copper jar.

"And Arty, here is yours," he pivoted around, filling up Artimus Jr.'s cup. From Castora's perspective, it appeared he poured out an identical amount of tea.

Without another word, the old lizock circled back around to his cup and filled it up. Finally, he placed the kettle down in the center of the table and took a seat himself.

Artimus Jr. reached out a took the lid off the sugar jar, pulled out a spoonful of sugar, and dumped it in his tea. Castora considered her own cup, inspecting the dark yellow liquid and giving a sniff. She could pick up some hints of chamomile and a subtle note of citrus, but it mostly just smelled grassy to her. With that consideration, she opted to follow Artimus Jr.'s lead and poured a spoonful into her cup.

Argos simply smiled as they did and held his cup up to his nose. He sniffed, his nostrils flaring and tongue darting out.

"I find it interesting that my lizock guests always take this one without sugar, but you elves pour in that spoonful of sugar without fail. I wonder, does your mother usually take this tea with sugar as well Arty?"

Artimus Jr. leaned back, holding his tea a few centimeters from his face and blowing gently on it before responding.

"I'm not sure. I think sometimes, but she often says sugar distracts from the natural flavors of tea. You know how particular she is about her blends."

Argos nodded and took a sip. He smiled, settling into his chair and placing the cup back down.

"Well, don't let me hold you up!" he beamed.

Castora considered the tea one more time, the cloudy liquid still a bit unappealing. But not wanting to cause trouble, she took a sip. She didn't let it rest on her tongue for even a moment. Her eyes widened as she swallowed, the sugar overpowering the earthy flavor and providing for a crisp, refreshing taste. The gentle warmth she felt forced her to smile, the unexpectedly mild taste almost pleasant.

"I'm sure you didn't come here for tea though. So, what brings you two youths to my door at this late hour?"

Artimus Jr. glanced at Castora and smiled.

"Well," he said turning back towards Argos and holding up his teacup. "I've been showing Castora here around town and trying to find ways to explain what makes Marftaport so unique. And, well, if it wouldn't be too much trouble, I'd love if you'd share the story of how you came here with Castora."

Argos nodded, a slow and deliberate move. He took another sip of his tea, letting out a soft sigh as he placed it down. Artimus Jr. kept a wide smile, taking another drink from his cup.

"Where should I begin?" Argos started. He placed his teacup back on the table and with narrowed eyes he scratched his chin with his index finger.

Castora shifted in her seat, and nervously sipped on her tea. No one said a word for at least twenty seconds. But just as the dark elf was ready to break the uncomfortable silence, the lighthouse keeper began his story.

"I won't burden you with the details of my early life," the lizock decided. "But I'll say a lot of poor life decisions landed me on the streets of Lizock City. A blind beggar is lucky to last a week in the slums of the city, and to say I was lucky would be an understatement. I lived a couple years there, not knowing if I'd eat, whether I'd have shelter for the night, or even survive until the next morning.

"But one fateful day, Evorath smiled upon me. It just so happened that the street corner I was begging at was right around the corner from a home Zachiro was visiting. You see, in the early days of Marftaport, many of the original founders would sneak back into town to help others escape the city and find refuge here. I had heard rumors about it, but truth be told I didn't really believe any of them."

Argos took another sip of tea. He held the cup up to his lips a few moments past, smiling and taking another sniff before putting the cup down.

"I mean, imagine it! The young prince Vistoro really left his castle and built a community where everyone had a say in how their life unfolded. It sounded like a fairy tale."

"But that day, when Zachiro walked by, there was this soft voice in the back of my mind that told me to follow him. And though I'm not proud of it, I slunk up next to the home he was visiting and listened as best I could. Unfortunately, the family he was chatting with decided not to come along -I still sometimes wonder how they are doing today. But I digress!

"You see, when Zachiro stepped out of that home, I took my chance. I told him in no uncertain terms that I would do anything to come live in that community he described. I got down on my hands and knees and begged him. No, I didn't know what I could contribute, but yes, I needed a chance to turn my life around. Even as I tugged at his robe, begging him to take me along, I figured it was just a fool's hope.

"But alas! I believe Evorath worked a miracle that day. Zachiro welcomed me to come along with him, assuring me that if my intent was true, I would find safety and security in Marftaport. And boy, was he right!"

"Wait a minute," Castora interrupted. "You're telling me the innkeeper in this town used to sneak into Lizock City and smuggle people out to help populate the town? And he was alright just, on the spot, taking you with him? There must be more to that story."

"Hmph," Argos shook his head. "You'll have to ask Zachiro for his side of events, but that's how it unfolded. I like to think it was all part of Evorath's design, just like our meeting here tonight. But I suspect the next part of my story might interest you more."

"Yes, please continue Argos," Artimus Jr. interjected.

Castora squinted towards the elf. She wasn't too impressed with the old lizock's storytelling, but she decided it was best to keep listening in silence.

"So, when I got to Marftaport, I was overwhelmed by the reception I received. Mind you, there were only a couple hundred people living here at the time, and I met every one of them! They were all so kind, especially Artimus Jr.'s mother.

"You see, she was as fervent as Vistoro -or perhaps even more so- about building an Evorath-centered community. She and a handful of other mages had only just started to form what is now the Mage's Guild, but after many months of trying to find a cure for my blindness, all while taking care of little infant Arty here, it was Savannah who had the idea.

"What if they taught me to harness my inner magic? And so, they made me this necklace," he reached into his tunic and pulled out a simple silver chain with a small, pale-blue stone affixed at the end.

"It was with the help of this necklace and the dutiful training of Savannah and the other mages that they completely changed my life. They taught me to use the magic that's all around us, to channel it through this necklace and give me a sort of sight."

Castora leaned back and took a gulp of her tea, which had cooled down to a more pleasant temperature.

"So, even though you are blind, you can see us?" she asked incredulously.

Argos shook his head.

"No, it's not so clear as that. When I say a 'sort of sight' I'm afraid it's because that's the closest way I can describe it. But I don't 'see' anything per se. I sense it all. You know they say merfolk, and some other sea creatures too, they say they rely on a sort of sound-based system to better navigate underwater. I think it's like that. The magic sends echoes that inform me of my surroundings. And with it, I'm able to tend this lighthouse and offer something of value to the community."

"But how did you know I was a dark elf?" Castora leaned in, squinting at the lizock, her lips shut tight as she observed.

Argos took another sip of his tea before replying.

"That involved a bit of common sense. Everyone's echo is a bit different and yours was unfamiliar. And I'm sure by now the whole town has heard that Arty here has been *showing you around*," he added an exaggerated emphasis to those last three words. Perhaps this magical sense of his was even more keen than he let off.

Castora pursed her lips and nodded. She took her final swig of tea and deposited the cup on the table. Tilting her head to the side, she looked back at Artimus Jr. and wondered aloud.

"And do you think of me like a blind beggar, needing Marftaport to save me from my father?"

Artimus Jr. looked like a deer staring down a hunter with her bow drawn and ready to loose her arrow.

"I uh," he blinked and looked back and forth between Castora and Argos.

Argos chuckled and took another sip of tea. "I suspect you're far better looking than this old beggar at least," he joked.

"I really wasn't trying to compare your situation to Argos's," Artimus Jr. stammered. "I was hoping his story would put the town into perspective though. Argos, would you say you're a rarity in Marftaport?"

The lizock shook his head.

"Not at all. This community is more like the old stories of the Xyvor. When the dryads first created the forests and all its people lived together in peace. Few who call Marftaport home came here with anything to contribute beyond the desire to live peaceful and productive lives. If I may be so bold, I think the real meaning young Arty is trying to share with you is this: we don't care about your past here."

Castora nodded, rubbing her chin as she considered the old man's words. There was that soft voice again, poking at the back of her mind and telling her to take it at face value. But her own experiences left her wary, her mind still struggling to process how a community built on such compassion could really exist in such a cruel world as this.

"Well, I think I've given you some things to ponder," Argos observed. He pushed away from the table, standing up and smiling at Castora. "If I may suggest Ms. Castora: have Arty here show you his old spot by the docks. I know the tide may leave you a bit wet, but I've heard the view there is magnificent."

“Hey, don’t spoil my plans now Argos!” Artimus Jr. quipped. He gritted his teeth and glared at the old lizock.

Not wanting to overstay her welcome, Castora stood up and smiled towards Artimus. She gently placed her hand on his left shoulder and offered a reassuring nod before looking back at Argos and curtsying.

“Thank you, Argos. You’ve certainly given me some things to ponder. Perhaps after Arty,” she smirked, “shows me that spot of his, we’ll spend some time discussing it more.”

“It fills me with joy to know even as an old fool I can still have some impact. Please, my door is always open if you wish to talk. Arty, it was a pleasure to see you as always.”

Walking back over to the stove, Argos picked up the poker and opened the stove door. He poked at the logs, embers sparking as the wood crumbled.

“I’ve some tidying up to do around here,” he muttered, glancing back towards Artimus Jr. and Castora. “Please feel free to show yourselves out.”

Artimus Jr. walked around and offered his hand. Castora hesitated for a moment before accepting. And as they walked together out of the lighthouse, she couldn’t pull her attention away from an uncomfortable thought.

Could someone with her background ever really hope to fit into such a perfect community?

CHAPTER XXVIII

Jaldor blinked. He stared with mouth agape, the news still not fully sinking in. But as he replayed his wife's words, he felt his lips curl up into a smile, a tingling sensation running down his back as he reached out and embraced Samantha.

Rocking back and forth, he rubbed her back, unable to hold in his enthusiasm.

"Are you sure?" he gushed. He pulled away and peered into her beautiful green eyes.

She nodded, her eyes sparkling and teeth glistening in the morning light. Brushing back her brown hair, she danced in place. "I must admit, that's the real reason I didn't help this morning. I had your mother watch Mary so I could pay a visit to Savannah. She said in a couple more weeks we can even tell if it's a boy or a girl!"

Jaldor's jaw dropped, and his eyes widened. He moved in and squeezed Samantha again.

"Be gentle," she gasped.

"Oh, I'm just so excited! Mary is going to be thrilled to be a big sister!" he exclaimed.

"Yes," Samantha nodded and pulled away. She placed her right hand on Jaldor's cheek and smiled up at him. "I figure we can tell her when you get back this afternoon."

"I don't know how I'm going to contain my excitement!" Jaldor shook his head.

"I hope it's alright that I told you now. I just couldn't wait myself," Samantha admitted. "And, as I was walking home, I figured this good news might help you get through the morning."

"Just promise you won't tell Mary until I return." The farmer looked down at his wife and held her gaze.

"I promise," she nodded. "But I shouldn't hold you up any longer. The others are supposed to be departing soon. You'll have to hurry to get down to the inn."

"Right," Jaldor nodded, his smile wavering as he considered his destination.

"Well, you stay safe and think of me while you're making up the cheese. I love you!"

Jaldor moved in and gave his wife another hug, holding on for a few moments. With a final squeeze and a quick kiss, he turned around and started his march south, glancing back to give one final wave.

"I'll see you this afternoon. Love you too!" Samantha waved goodbye.

With a pep in his step, Jaldor made haste. His heart overflowed with joy, his mind racing to consider the possibilities.

In fact, Jaldor was so deep in thought that he lost track of where he was going. Before he knew it, he looked up and beheld Savannah's enormous Yggdril tree, its leaves glistening in the morning sun.

"She must have told you the news," a feminine voice beamed. It took Jaldor a moment to refocus, looking around to see the smiling faces of Artimus and Savannah just outside their front porch.

Grinning from ear-to-ear, the farmer approached the elves with a wave.

"Congratulations," Artimus smirked.

"Thank you!" Jaldor replied, his cheeks hurting from smiling so wide.

"It's really blessed timing," Savannah suggested. She held Artimus's hand, stepping down from the porch and walking out to intercept Jaldor.

"We really should be meeting the others at the inn," Artimus cupped his right hand over his eyes, looking up towards the sky. "George won't wait forever, and the memorial starts within the hour by the look of things."

"Of course," Jaldor glanced down, pulling his lips tight to temper his smile.

"Irontail would have been delighted to see you and Samantha doing so well here already," Savannah blurted. She bit her top lip, twirling her hair and looking down at her feet. "So, I guess just don't let today bring you down," she sniffled.

As the couple walked south, Artimus draped his arm over his wife's shoulders. "She's right," he said glancing back at Jaldor, who followed just a couple meters behind.

Jaldor scratched behind his ears nervously.

"I wish I had the opportunity to know him better. He was such a polite and helpful guest when he was staying to guard the farm. I was mortified when Mary asked to ride on his back that first morning, but he didn't mind one bit. I never expected a centaur could be so…human."

The farmer considered his own words, thinking about how strange it all was. He hadn't even known the centaur a full month, but throughout the entire ordeal with Paxvilla, there had been no one who worked as hard to ensure everyone was taken care of. It must have been difficult for those who had known him so much longer.

"I am really sorry for your loss," Jaldor added after another moment of consideration.

"Thank you," Artimus uttered, his voice hoarse. He cleared his throat and continued forward in silence for the next couple minutes.

As the group turned the corner and continued east. Jaldor could already see a crowd of people up ahead, all gathered in front of the inn. There had to be a hundred people at least, a humbling sight for the young farmer. Irontail hadn't even lived in Marftaport, but all these diverse people were coming together to pay their respects.

"You're welcome to stick with us," Savannah offered, slowing her pace and glancing back at Jaldor.

Jaldor nodded and followed behind the elves. Most of the familiar faces were gathered at the front of the crowd, just before George, Sarah, and their kids.

"Alright, we'll be dropping in just outside the memorial site," George shouted, his voice booming. "Please file through the portal one at a time and remember to keep moving when you pass through. Granitefoot and Marblechest will go through first to help keep the line moving."

Jaldor surveyed the crowd, considering all those who gathered. Yes, there were a fair many centaurs spread throughout, but seeing all the lizock, elves, satyr, trolls, barghest, and even a couple lamia was astounding. Growing up among humans, Jaldor had always thought other species were just as homogenous as they were. But this turnout really demonstrated just how connected the different people of Marftaport were.

He wasn't sure if it was just the news he received this morning, but as he considered this astounding show of community support, Jaldor felt a strange sense of calm overcome him. Whatever danger the world might hold, whatever threats he might face, his family had found a home worth fighting for. And as the crowd started through the portal to Dumner, he knew Mary and his other child would have a tremendous life.

Zelag kept his gaze low, doing his best to avoid any conversation. He couldn't help but glance at the obelisk as he passed, quickly averting his gaze. The temptation to stop and read through the inscription was strong, and to read the names of all the victims was even stronger. But especially considering the reason for his visit, he wanted nothing to do with the ugly stone monstrosity.

And as he passed by, he involuntarily closed his eyes, taking a quick breath and holding it for a moment before blowing out through pursed lips. Refocusing ahead, he maneuvered through some of the trees and stuck close to the western side of the memorial site. He refused to even turn his gaze east.

Though he made it a habit of avoiding these sorts of memorials, even Zelag couldn't ignore the obligation he felt to make an exception. The shapeshifter smirked, the memory of his first meeting with Irontail creeping to the forefront of his thoughts. He really didn't think much of the warrior centaur back then. But over the decades, Zelag could count on one hand the number of people he trusted like Irontail.

He shook his head, a more recent memory slipping back into his head. Irontail had always encouraged him to return to Marftaport and make amends. And as he recalled the incident, he remembered Irontail's words that day.

"Look Zelag," Irontail had said. "The longer you wait, the more it will fester. George and Sarah are both faithful servants of Evorath. You can return to Marftaport any time -it's your pride that holds you back."

Perhaps the centaur really was sager than Zelag ever gave him credit. But one thing was for sure, Irontail was popular.

The Memorial Site was crawling with hundreds of Marftaport residents, or so Zelag presumed. Along with, it seemed, the entire village of Dumner. It was so much more crowded than the day this site had first been designated, the trees serving as a morbid reminder of that occasion.

Zelag glanced at his hands, his heart skipping a beat as he jerked away. For a moment, he could see the pool of blood at his feet, his hands crimson. But then it was gone.

He cursed and clenched his fists. This place always brought back the worst memories.

"Zelag, perhaps you would accompany me," the garbled old voice, deep and throaty, could only belong to one person.

"Oogmut!" Zelag pivoted right, holding his arms wide, palms open. "I was planning to take a spot near the back, so perhaps you should."

Without using his unique vision, Zelag could already see Oogmut's pain. Beside the lack of enthusiasm in his voice, his hunched shoulders, pinkish hinge in his cheeks, and drooping of his left eye could only mean one thing.

"Perhaps you wouldn't mind sticking a bit further from the crowd?" Zelag altered his intended barb. "Or wherever you'd prefer," he conceded without thinking.

"Oh, that is kind of you. We've lost another bastion of Evorath in Irontail. I feel my old heart can't handle any more of this." Oogmut sighed.

"I'm sorry," Zelag offered. He scratched his beard, glancing around the crowd. "I for one am looking forward to our revenge. I can't imagine being locked up in that pyxis will be a pleasant fate for Death."

Oogmut snorted and gently shook his head. "I imagine not. I do wish Mojo and Irontail were still here to execute that plan though," he glanced down at his shaking hands, his voice wavering and eyes watering.

"Let's go have a seat," Zelag motioned towards a willow.

He didn't wait for the troll, starting off towards the long stone bench beneath the willow. While some of the trees were adorned only with stone markers, many included sitting features like this. Whether a collection of wooden chairs, stone benches, or even old tree stumps, this gave grieving visitors a chance to sit and mourn their lost loved ones.

Arriving at the bench, Zelag looked up at Oogmut with a forced smile. He waited a moment before taking his seat, motioning for the troll to sit down beside him.

"I think this gives us a great view, don't you?" he asked, glancing up towards the stage.

The small wooden stage had been erected just a couple meters before the obelisk. Two centaurs were already standing on stage and Silkhair and Steelbrow stood just to the right at the base of the steps, talking with Vistoro and the high priestess Dioney.

Oogmut glanced around, walking over to the bench and inspecting the inscription on the side.

"Thank you Nor Leon, for your sacrifice," the troll whispered, resting his hand along the inscription. He stood bent over for a moment more, his eyes shut, presumably in reflection. Zelag clasped his hands together and fiddled his thumbs.

Oogmut turned around and plopped onto the bench, the entire seat shaking from his weight.

"This is a good vantage point, yes." The troll agreed.

Zelag smirked as he regarded the lumbering old troll. Oogmut really had a lot in common with Irontail. Both were big and ugly, physically intimidating and wise beyond their years. And both were as pious as clergy and loyal as a Jyrimoore mastiff. Whatever the future might hold, Zelag vowed in that moment to savor the time he had with Oogmut.

"Perhaps once we've dealt with Yezurkstal, I can come with you to visit your turtle friend," Zelag offered.

Oogmut's left eye widened, his mouth wavering as he glanced down at the shapeshifter.

"She would be happy to meet you," he smiled. "And I would be happy to have a traveling companion."

"Good," Zelag nodded.

He still had his doubts about the existence of this giant turtle friend, but with all things considered, he figured it couldn't hurt to play along.

"Good morning, everyone," a deep voice boomed across the field. Zelag squinted towards the stage, where the smaller of the two centaurs had taken position behind the podium. It was hard to make out his features, but from his average build to his simian face, he appeared quite ordinary, save for his bright white ears; they were notably too large for his head.

"Welcome people of Dumner and our esteemed guests. I am Cottonear, and I'll be serving as acolyte for today's service."

Zelag smirked, shaking his head at the centaur's name.

"Though we gather today for a somber occasion, it is my privilege to invite Dioney to the stage to open today's memorial in prayer. Please, if you haven't already settled in, find yourself a seat and we can begin. If you wish to give a testimony, you can start the line behind Silkhair and Steelbrow to the right of the stage."

Cottenear paused and glanced away from the podium to cough into his fist. He cleared his throat and leaned back up towards the podium, allowing the runestone to amplify his voice.

"Silkhair, I know I speak for everyone when I say the loss of your husband is a blow to us all. And Steelbrow, though your father is no longer with us, his legacy lives on through you. As long as you rest your hope in Evorath, you will find peace."

Cottenear paused yet again, this time simply bowing his head for a few seconds.

"Now, without further ado, I welcome the High Priestess Dioney from Marftaport Cathedral."

As Cottenear turned around and rejoined the other, much older centaur at the rear of the stage, Dioney skipped up the steps. She wore a ceremonial robe, the green fabric flowing loosely in the wind as she proceeded to the podium. Her hair was tied back, woven through her large horns with blue, violet, white, and yellow flowers for adornment. She was tall for a satyr, about 1.6 meters by Zelag's estimate and her long, thin goatee was held together in a braid, hanging down to her chest.

Stepping up to the podium, Dioney looked around the field and stroked her goatee.

"May Evorath's blessings descend upon us this day," Dioney cried out, her soothing voice echoing through the field. She held her hands up overhead, palms facing the sky. She tilted her head towards the sky, holding the pose as she prayed.

"Please Evorath, welcome our brother Irontail into the heavens. We look forward to the day when this world is restored to your image, and we may reunite with him and so many other loved ones in the afterlife. In life, Irontail was one of your staunchest defenders. May we remember him as such in death, and always remember that good will triumph over evil."

Zelag glanced around during the prayer. He noticed Oogmut had his head bowed, hands clasped, and eyes closed. He spotted Artimus and Savannah up towards the front, sitting just behind Tel' Shira, Morn and Neman. A dozen or so other mage guild members were also positioned around this bunch, including the annoying Ygabb.

Glancing towards the east, he saw Artimus Jr. had brought the hájje along. The dark elf appeared nervous, her shoulders tense and fists clenched as she glanced around. Zodim stood on the right side of Castora, his hat held in hand and gaze fixed on the ground.

"Before we begin hearing testimonies," Dioney continued, drawing Zelag's attention forward. "I know many of you have shared concerns about Irontail's remains. There is no easy way to say it: Death left nothing behind to burn. So, in light of planting a tree to honor the fallen chieftain, warrior, poet, and friend, the people of Dumner have agreed to construct a statue of Evorath in this spot to commemorate Irontail's life."

"Now I invite Dumner's most revered elder, Stonehair, to share Irontail's final wishes and to make an important announcement about the future of Dumner."

Dioney glanced over her shoulder and exchanged a nod with the old centaur. She stepped away from the podium and proceeded down the steps to the right. Zelag kept his eyes on her, watching her exchange words with Silkhair. But as Stonehair spoke, Zelag shifted his gaze to the podium.

"Thank you Dioney and thank you everyone who graces this holy site with your presence. As the eldest member of Dumner, it is my duty to present to you the final wishes of our great Chieftain Irontail. And upon prayer and reflection, I've decided it is best for me to share this with my own testimony and considerations."

The elder reached down and pulled a folded piece of parchment from his satchel.

"I didn't think much of Irontail when he assumed the role of Chieftain. I, like many others, was trapped in the old dogma of our people. But over the decades, as Irontail shared his vision with our people and worked hand-in-hand with the free peoples of Marftaport, he opened my mind and my heart to his ways. And I know now that he was a true servant of Evorath, the greatest chieftain Dumner has ever seen."

Stonehair glanced down and unfolded the parchment. He cleared his throat.

"But whatever sadness we feel today, I trust Irontail's wisdom about the future of our village."

"Hereby I declare Stonehair, acting Chieftain of Dumner, as of 5 Zerrum, 1149 MT, that from this day forth, upon the final wishes of our great Chieftain Irontail, that this village will be devoted wholly and completely to the service of Evorath and her mission. The Official Tribal Charter, established in 547 MT by our first Chieftain Silverleg is hereby nullified. Signed and approved by all the elder counsel of Dumner."

Stonehair held up the parchment, pivoting around as if to show it to the crowd. Zelag rolled his eyes. The scales fit the dragon, but he had no patience for this sort of pageantry.

"This means, upon voluntary agreement of all tribe members, that every centaur of Dumner is now considered a free resident of Evorath and is thereby free to pursue any interest they see fit. All public land belonging to the former tribe of Dumner is hereby designated to serve as a place of learning, education, and peacemaking in the name of Evorath."

Zelag listened intently as murmurs spread through the crowd. Some cries of concern, but mostly gasps of excitement and anticipation. Irontail had already whittled that archaic Charter down to but a few laws, but knowing the centaur didn't live to see this day made Zelag's heart sink. The freedom of Evorath's people was his obsession.

"The sacred mound, located at the center of Dumner, will serve as the primary grounds upon which this will be facilitated. All the people of Dumner are welcome to continue living as they have, to relocate to Marftaport, or to establish new residence anywhere in all Evorath. Now, I invite Silkhair to the stage to read a letter from her late husband."

Silkhair started up the steps to the stage before Stonehair finished speaking. They exchanged a nod of understanding as Stonehair retreated to the rear of the stage and Silkhair took her place at the podium. Her fist was clasped, and she too unfolded a piece of parchment, placing it on the podium. She looked around at the crowd, smiling through her teeth.

"My brothers and sisters, if you are hearing these words, it means that I have met my end," Silkhair's voice was unexpectedly strong, her tone soft and eyes resolute as she looked around the crowd. "However, I met my end, rest easy knowing that I am with our creator, Evorath." She smiled.

"I wrestled with the idea of writing a comprehensive speech, but when I considered Silkhair having to read this, I decided to keep the message brief. So, as I pass into the next world, I want to leave you with this." Silkhair closed her eyes and let out a long sigh before continuing.

"Evorath loves each one of you, and through my relationship with our creator, I hope I shared that love, every day. Some of you may remember me as a warrior, others as your chieftain, and still others as a philosopher and peacemaker. Whatever you might choose to focus on, I hope first and foremost you remember me as a friend."

Silkhair bowed her head. She sniffled and lowered the parchment down to the podium. And as Zelag watched her aura dampen, he felt his heart sink in his chest.

A world without Irontail was sure to be darker.

CHAPTER XXIX

Marftaport,
6 Zerrum, 1149 MT

Castora felt sick. She frowned, looking up at the massive double oak doors. The gilded handles of the cathedral were extravagant, long curved handholds and separate round knobs. The tree of life was etched within the wood, forming a complete picture with both doors closed.

She struggled to focus, her skin crawling as she considered stepping inside. Everything inside her told her to run and forget about the whole thing. That is, everything except that soft, gentle voice. Closing her eyes, Castora relaxed her shoulders and said a silent prayer for peace.

"It's going to be alright. I'm in this with you," Zodim provided comforting reassurance. She looked down at the gnome, his dark, wrinkled face folded into a supportive smile.

With a faint smile and nod, Castora pulled on the handles, the heavy doors resisting for a moment, the cold iron handles sending a chill down her arm. Pulling it just ajar enough to slip inside, she motioned for Zodim to proceed. And as the gnome waddled in, she followed immediately behind, letting the door close behind her.

Though Artimus Jr. had shown her around the grounds, this was her first time inside. And as she glanced around at the ribbed vaults, the massive, stained glass windows, and the rows of wooden pews, she felt so small and insignificant.

It was massive, yes. But more than the scale of the place was the beauty of it all. It was breathtaking, seeing the light trickle through the multi-colored glass and spill throughout the massive hall. She considered the carved columns, so delicately crafted that they looked to have actual vines growing upon them, complete with colorful flowers. Even the pews, constructed of oak and darkly stained, were intricately carved, arm rests formed to resemble the trees they were crafted from.

Castora felt powerless to move, her feet stuck to the hardwood floor as she took it all in. As her eyes ran to the front of the room, she beheld the grand statue of Evorath, a monumental carving that put the small one at Vistoro's shrine to shame. It was magnificent, at least three meters tall. Even from this distance, the dark elf could make out the detail of the statue, the perfectly carved features of the Creator goddess.

Castora stood with mouth agape as she glanced up from there, the domed ceiling revealing yet another surprise. She gaped at the mural. It appeared to depict a host of feminine figures emerging from various trees. And at the center of these figures was an abstract, bright light, sending a cacophony of color out among those trees. And circling around the dome was painted flora, vibrant growth exploding from the trees.

After an uncertain amount of time spent admiring the statue and painted ceiling, her eyes drifted back along the sides of the room. She gasped, realizing there was even more to see. There must have been some rooms beyond this grand sanctuary, for placed on the right and left of the cathedral, towards the front quarter of the room, there were two lofted areas.

These lofts were just as intricately carved as the rest of the building and by the looks of it could accommodate no less than a few dozen other visitors. In total, considering the scale of the building, Castora guessed this cathedral could accommodate at least a thousand people at once.

She closed her eyes, imaging what this place must have looked like while full. The clamor of all those people coming together for a single cause. Her heart trembled.

"It's amazing what a community of artisans can accomplish, isn't it?" Zodim asked, his gruff voice bringing Castora back to the moment.

"I never could have even imagined people building something like this," she marveled.

She stood in awe, glancing around to soak in the experience. Her appreciation of the space was interrupted by the clacking of hooves from off to the right. Turning her attention towards the noise, she caught sight of one of those doorways to another room on the right. It blended in perfectly with the wall, only becoming visible as it swung open.

And out stepped a satyr, clothed in a plain white robe with her hair braided around her rounded horns. It took Castora a moment to realize it was Dioney, the high priestess from Irontail's funeral. But with her relatively tall height, cream and brown colored fur, and long, braided goatee, there was no mistaking her.

"Oh, so today is the day!" Dioney beamed, her voice a bit shrill as she skipped towards the dark elf and the gnome.

Castora arched her eyebrow. Scratching the back of her head, she considered the satyr's enthusiasm.

"Oh, were you anticipating our arrival?" Zodim questioned as the high priestess drew near. That was much nicer than the way Castora was about to ask it.

Dioney touched clasped her hands together and took a slight bow.

"Not quite, no. But I have anticipated the chance to meet you both." She smiled and glanced between Castora and Zodim. "How may I be a blessing to you today?"

Castora squinted down at the satyr. Her bubbly voice and enthusiasm were off-putting, but something about the way she smiled put the dark elf at ease. She couldn't say why, but staring into Dioney's deep blue eyes, Castora felt safe.

"I would just like to look around the cathedral," Zodim replied after a short pause. "But I believe our friend Castora would like to have a talk with you, perhaps somewhere private."

Dioney looked between the two with an unwavering smile. After a few moments, she pulled her hands apart and held them out to her sides, palm up.

"Please feel free to explore at your leisure. This is a house of Evorath and open to all her children," she explained, nodding towards Zodim. She then adjusted her gaze, locking eyes with Castora before continuing.

"And you, my dear Castora. Please, accompany me back through the vestibule."

She held the dark elf's gaze for a few moments. Castora felt a certain magnetism, unable to break her gaze. Dioney spun around abruptly, skipping back through the open door.

Castora hesitated for a moment, waiting for a nod from Zodim before following. She stepped through into the vestibule, keeping her eyes wide to take in the setting. This hallway was just as ornate as the rest of the cathedral. There were small stained glass windows depicting satyr, elves, and centaur. The vibrant colors of the hall were enchanting, with green crown molding shaped to look like vines and bright white base boards.

They proceeded further into the cathedral, Dioney skipping along and Castora following cautiously behind. It took no more than twenty seconds before they reached a doorway on the right. This was a rather simple door compared to the rest of the scenery. Featuring a rounded archway and a plain oak construction, Dioney twisted the handle and pushed the door inward. She stood to the side, motioning for Castora to proceed.

The dark elf paused at the doorway. Despite the welcome, she couldn't put aside her innate cynicism. But with a quick survey, she recognized the room was safe.

Stepping inside, she was surprised at how small and simple this room was. The walls were flat, featuring raw wooden boards and a small, circular stained-glass image, which appeared too abstract for Castora to discern what it depicted. To the right side of the room was a single, small painting. The painting depicted many different races of Evorath including some Castora had never seen. They all stood in a circle, holding hands around a large, ritual fire.

Aside from the usual suspects, an elf, felite, centaur, satyr, and others, Castora was intrigued by the other creatures. There was a bovine beast, a bipedal frog creature of some sort, a four-armed, blue skinned creature, another strange biped that appeared almost squirrel-like, and even a dryad. Or at least that's what Castora assumed based on the bare, green skin and mossy hair.

"It's a fascinating piece, isn't it?" Dioney asked. She stepped into the room behind Castora, closing the door and stepping around to the chair behind the desk. She pulled the chair back and motioned towards the painting.

"It was drawn by the satyr prophet Paneer many centuries ago and is meant to depict the many children of Evorath, all united together. It's called la'miro com'pure, or 'The Perfect Love' in common tongue.

"I don't recognize many of these races," Castora muttered, still trying to take it all in.

"I wouldn't expect you to," Dioney smirked. "It's easy for us to forget that Erathal is but one small continent floating on the world of Evorath. But please, take a seat," the satyr motioned towards the two chairs in front of the desk.

Castora took another moment to appreciate the painting before taking a seat. With a smile, Dioney plopped down in her chair and leaned forward, resting her elbows on the desk.

"Castora. How are you this beautiful morning?"

The dark elf shifted in her chair, glancing around the room uncomfortably as she pondered the question. People in this town were friendly, but Dioney was on another level.

"I um. I suppose I'm well," she scratched behind her head and bit her bottom lip, avoiding direct eye contact with Dioney. But as she sat there for a few moments in silence, she felt compelled to continue.

"If I am to be honest, I am nervous," she admitted.

"Nervous?" Dioney sat up straight and twirled her hands out to the side. "What are you nervous about?"

Castora leaned back, bringing her hands together. She tilted her head to the side, trying to decipher Dioney's expression. It was easy enough to know what her cousins were thinking by their facial expressions and body language, but these satyrs were so unfamiliar that they felt impossible to read.

"I uh. Well, I just don't know how I'm supposed to do this," she glanced away, her eyes drawn back to the painting.

"To do about what?" Dioney asked without pause.

The dark elf frowned at Dioney.

"Well, Artimus said you could help me. It's just. Well, it's my past. I don't know. Repentance?" Castora squirmed, her hands feeling clammy as she fiddled with her thumbs.

"Oh, I see!" Dioney's eyes widened. She leaned back in her chair, smiling from ear-to-ear. "Do you think you need to seek repentance from me?"

Castora blinked, wondering if this was some sort of test.

"Well, I. It's. I've hurt a lot of people. I know I can never make up for the harm I've done, but I want to do the right thing in the eyes of Evorath."

Was that the right way, she wondered?

"And you believe to do that, you need to seek counsel from a priestess, is that right?" Dioney grinned.

Castora's chest felt tight. She was screaming inside, afraid of saying the wrong thing.

"It's just. Artimus said. I don't…" she stammered, her face feeling hot as she struggled to find the words.

Slow and gingerly, Dioney reached across the desk and laid her hands on Castora's.

"Artimus Jr. suggested you should seek forgiveness by coming to me and confessing your sins. Is that right?" Dioney whispered, her voice calm. Castora could feel the tension in her chest lighten as she looked into the priestess's eyes.

"Yes. I have done so much harm to Evorath," she sniffled.

Dioney smiled and pulled her hand back. She sat up straight, maintaining eye contact with the dark elf.

"Do you believe you must confess to me for Evorath to forgive your sins?" she asked.

"Don't I?" Castora retorted defensively. "I killed one of Marftaport's elders. I can never repay that debt." She lowered her gaze, looking down at the floor to her right.

"Do you regret that act?" Dioney inquired.

"Of course I do!" Castora's voice went up a full octave as she looked back up, her eyes pleading for mercy. She grasped the arms of her chair to keep her hands from shaking.

"And have you prayed to Evorath expressing that remorse? Have you asked for her forgiveness?" Dioney maintained a soft tone, her mouth forming a confident, but subtle smile as she stared at Castora.

"I. Yes. But how do I know I'm doing it right? How do I know Evorath hears me?" Castora whined. She could tell her composure was crumbling, but she no longer cared.

Castora stared, her eyes pleading and bottom lip quivering. But Dioney didn't respond right away, leaving the dark elf in agony as she awaited the response. After what seemed like an eternity, the high priestess pulled open a drawer on the right of her desk and pulled out a leatherbound book.

She slid it across the table and nodded towards it. Castora considered the book, the same tree of life embossed in the leather cover. It was thick and well-worn, the brown leather peeling off around the edges.

"This book was assembled by the dryads of Evorath many centuries ago. This one is written in the common tongue."

"What am I supposed to get from this?" Castora interrupted. She clenched her fist, considering the old book.

"You'll get as much out of it as you put in," Dioney replied without hesitation. "But if I may help you with what you came for, let me say this. Evorath has forgiven you. Not because I say so, but because I know Evorath's heart is off forgiveness. You'll find this wisdom within the pages of this holy Xyvor. And when you learn to trust Evorath's voice, you'll find you it becomes that much clearer in your mind."

Castora considered the book, glaring down at the unassuming tome. Could it really contain such great wisdom? In truth, Castora had never found much use for books. But as she beheld the weathered Xyvor on the desk, that soft, gentle voice in her head seemed to call out.

Listen.

And then it all felt so clear. A fleeting, surreal high swept over her as she recognized the truth.

She could hear Evorath's voice, if only she listened. That hesitation she felt before the attack on Paxvilla -it was that same soft, gentle voice.

Unable to hold in her revelation, she clasped her hands over her mouth, failing to hold in a gasp. Her skin tingled with excitement, and she felt tears welling up in her eyes.

Dioney stood up from her chair, her radiant smile lighting up the room as she watched Castora's gaze.

"Cling to that voice," Dioney sang. "The voice of love and all that is good!"

Castora sniffled and wiped the tears from her eyes. She stood up, glancing down at the priestess with a new sense of purpose and confidence. The weight of her past felt somehow lighter, as if someone else helped carry the burden.

"Thank you, Dioney." Castora smiled.

"It is my pleasure," the satyr rejoined. "Remember, whenever you stumble, turn to Evorath with a repentant heart and you will be forgiven."

"I will, thank you," Castora grabbed hold of the Xyvor, clutching it close to her chest.

"And if I may offer one piece of wisdom," Dioney added, holding up her right index finger. "Remember to never stop listening to that voice. Even as you read the Xyvor, a great source of wisdom and tradition, remember the key to understanding is within you. You'll always find Her voice to steer true."

Castora nodded. "I will always listen."

"Excellent!" Dioney clapped her hands. "While you are here, is there anything else you wish to talk about?"

The dark elf pondered this for a moment, but she couldn't think of anything besides the excitement she felt. After a brief pause, she shook her head.

"No, thank you, uh…Dioney?" Castora tilted her head to the side, just realizing she was uncertain of the proper way to address the high priestess.

"Yes, Dioney is fine. Unlike some practices of old, we recognize that Evorath doesn't require us to stand on ceremony or worry about titles. We are all Evorath's children."

Castora smiled and nodded.

"Well, if that's all you had," Dioney motioned towards the door, "what do you say to rejoining Zodim? I can give you both a more complete tour of the cathedral if you'd like."

"Yes, that would be wonderful," Castora agreed. She opened the door and stepped through, standing to the side to allow Dioney to pass by first.

Passing her a smile in response, Dioney proceeded down the vestibule and Castora followed closely behind. They entered the sanctuary through the same door as before. Scanning the area, it took Castora a moment to catch sight of Zodim, the gnome's pointed hat just barely poking up over the pews.

Seeing Dioney still squinting around the room, Castora placed her hand on the priestess's left shoulder and pointed towards Zodim.

"He's over by that window," she indicated.

"Oh, thank you," Dioney skipped left through the pews and Castora followed.

"That one has quite a fascinating story," Dioney called ahead. Zodim shook his head and glanced towards the sound. With a smile and nod of recognition, he looked back at the window, holding his hand over his mouth and tapping his left index finger against his nose.

Approaching the gnome, Castora considered the window for herself. Whatever story it told, it wasn't apparent to her. The various shades of green, blue, and yellow created a spectacle of light but lacked a definite form. The different colors were all assembled in uneven and discordant shapes, a chaotic and discordant clash of colors.

"It's an abstract interpretation," Dioney explained as she stepped alongside Zodim. "It was donated by one of my brethren on Satyr Island. What do you suppose she sees in this glass?" Dioney glanced between Castora and Zodim.

Castora shrugged.

"It feels reminiscent of Innap's descriptions of creation," Zodim volunteered after a moment. "The seemingly disconnected colors all come together to form a stunningly beautiful window. From chaos, springs beauty."

Dioney smiled, offering a singular nod.

"That's right," she confirmed.

Castora tilted her head to the side, trying to consider the stained glass more closely. But the sound of hoofs from the entrance disrupted her focus, drawing her gaze back around.

Ygabb clacked down the aisle towards the trio. Adorned in her usual red robes and matching wide-brim hat, Castora noted the absence of her sword. But she had her usual jovial demeanor, a smile plastered across her face as she skipped across the pews towards the window.

"So, it was true," Ygabb bubbled. "I'm happy to see you exploring Marftaport's biggest work of art."

"Good morning Ygabb," Dioney nodded towards her fellow satyr, eyes closed.

"Good morning!" the exuberant mage exclaimed. "I've come with a somewhat urgent request. Tel' Shira would like Castora and Zodim to join us in Vistoro's study."

"Oh, that's a pity," Dioney shook her head. "I was just about to show them around the rest of the cathedral. Perhaps it can wait until we've finished the tour?"

Ygabb shrugged.

"I don't know if we want to keep her waiting."

"She's right," Zodim interjected. "It could have something to do with The Enemy."

"Yes," Castora agreed. "If this vision involves my father, it's best that we not delay."

"Well, please know you are welcome to come back for a tour anytime," Dioney conceded with a frown.

"Thank you," Castora curtsied. "I will certainly accept your offer when I get the next chance."

"And I as well," Zodim nodded.

"Then please, do not let me keep you," Dioney smiled and extended her right hand towards the sanctuary doors.

"Great!" Ygabb exclaimed. She jumped, spinning around in the air to reorient towards the entrance. As she skipped towards the door, Castora glanced back at Zodim, motioning for him to go first. With a nod of understanding, the gnome waddled after the satyr and the dark elf followed just behind.

And as Castora stepped back outside, shielding her eyes as they adjusted to the morning light, she thought back on the journey travelled thus far. These past weeks had felt like a blind journey through the ether, but as she considered her new friends and this peaceful town they built, she found herself hopeful for the future.

In fact, as she watched Ygabb reach into a barrel outside the cathedral and pulled out her sword belt, Castora realized this was the most peaceful she'd ever felt. The voice in her head tugged at her heart, and she considered the satyr mage.

"Zodim, would you go on ahead?" she asked. "I'd like to ask Ygabb something privately if you don't mind."

The dark elf and the gnome locked eyes and exchanged a look of understanding.

"Of course!" Zodim held up his left hand, index finger pointing towards the sky. "I will see you both at Vistoro's."

Zodim walked off towards the gates as Ygabb secured her sword around her waist.

"What would you like to ask?" Ygabb smiled up at the dark elf.

"Well," Castora scratched behind her head, struggling to find the words. "I guess first, I just want to say thank you. The other night at the mage's guild, you stepped in when I most needed support." The dark elf paused, shuffling her feet nervously. "So, uh, I just wondered…why?"

Ygabb grinned. She adjusted her belt, positioning her sword at her left side before addressing Castora.

"I thought about how I might have felt in your shoes, and I knew someone needed to step in. The others were relentless, cruel even. And I knew you were ready to fight. But!" Ygabb held up her right hand, palm open. "I could also see the great potential within you. It was like seeing a little seedling placed out in the field and getting too much sun. If I left you there, you'd whither from the heat, never having enough time to establish your roots. So, I stepped in to provide some shade. I hope after we take care of this ugly business with Death, err, with your father, that I'll get to see you blossom."

Castora tilted her head and considered the eccentric satyr.

"Thank you," she breathed, her lips curling into a smile. "And I hope so too."

Ygabb nodded, still wearing a wide grin.

"Well, we best not keep the others waiting!"

And as the satyr clad in red skipped off towards Vistoro's manor, Castora stood and watched for a moment, still struck by the creature's kindness. After savoring the moment, the dark elf followed close behind, her hands tingling with anticipation for whatever news Tel' Shira had to share.

With allies like this, perhaps they really had a chance.

Will this vision hold the key to defeating Yezurkstal? Stay tuned for Book 3 of the Legends of Evorath, *The Secret of Dumner*, releasing July 2025.

The Dark Elf and the Gnome is the second book in the Legends of Evorath trilogy. <u>Visit us online</u> for free access to additional stories, and to sign up for notifications about future releases.

If you enjoyed this book, please help other readers find that same enjoyment by returning to where you purchased it and leaving a positive review. Your voice matters.

<u>www.evorath.com</u>

Explore the Legacy of Evorath

The Evorath Trilogy

Over sixty years before the events of this story, see how Artimus, Savannah, Irontail, Tel' Shira, and the other heroes of Evorath formed unbreakable bonds of friendship. As they all find their world shaken, they must set aside their own ambitions and focus on a way to defeat this terrifying new evil.

Read Book 1 of the Evorath Trilogy Now

The Evorath Calendar

A small planet with five distinct continents, Evorath has a total of 356 days spread over 12 months. The Evorath calendar begins in Spring, with the New Year commencing on 1 Pertga.

Appendices II

Glossary of Selected Terms

◆ Barghest - A broad-shouldered and wide-chested species of bipedal canines. Nearly all living barghest in Erathal make their home in the town of Marftaport.

◆ Bulwark - A rare creature native to the Runeturk Mountains. Believed to have developed in volcanic activity and is known to have skin as hard as diamonds. They have two pairs of arms, one large and muscular, the other smaller.

◆ Centaur - Half-horse and half-man, the centaurs of Evorath make their home in the village of Dumner.

◆ Dryad - Guardians of the forest, there is one dryad for each type of tree on Evorath. They have untold powers over the forest and work to maintain balance.

◆ Dwarf - A short and hardy species that is known for having thick, full beards. Though primarily living in the Runeturk Mountains, there is a growing dwarven population among the forest of Erathal, specifically within the town of Marftaport.

◆ Elf - Similar in stature to the humans of Earth, Elves are the most abundant sentient species in Evorath. They have pointy ears and almost exclusively have light features.

◆ Erathal - Name of the continent this story is set in. Also, the name of the major Elvish City.

◆ Ergolicious - A contemporary slang term to express happiness or satisfaction with a choice.

- Ether - The space between different worlds. Reaching through the ether requires great magical abilities and allows a mage to summon creatures from one of these other worlds.

- Feklar - An expletive often used to express anger, fear, or similar unpleasant responses.

- Felite - One of the most populous species on the continent of Erathal, felite are a bipedal feline species that resemble their four-legged cousins.

- Hájje - Elvish word for a dark elf. It comes from the elvish word Haijja, which means 'dark', or 'evil'.

- Imp About - A common colloquialism that indicates one is fooling around or otherwise being reckless in their behavior.

- Lamia - A sentient race with the lower half resembling a snake and their upper half is that of an elf. With dwindling numbers, many fear the once powerful and noble species is nearing extinction.

- Lizock - One of the most populous sentient species on the continent of Erathal, lizock are a bipedal reptilian race that resembles the common lizard. Though they can vary in size, shape, and color, the race is most well-known for its warriors and merchants.

- Marftaport - A free society without any formal rulers or authorities. Established by Vistoro and a group of Lizock who grew disgruntled with their government, it serves as the first truly free community in Erathal.

- Rocpiss - A profanity that suggests something is untrue or otherwise fabricated.

- Runeturk Mountains - Major mountain range bordering Erathal forest to the north. This range is populated by thousands of dwarves, some gnomes, and less civilized creatures like ogres, orcs, goblins, and wild animals.

- Sandy foundation - A common colloquialism used when someone is behaving erratically, or irrationally. Often meant to imply the person in question is mentally unstable.

- Satyr - A sentient species of Evorath once known for great works of art and music, they are now known more for their proclivity towards alcoholism. These bipedal creatures are half-elf, half-goat, with their upper half being the former and their lower half resembling the latter.

- The scales fit the dragon - A saying that indicates something fits as expected. In contemporary earth terms, "par for the course." roc

- Troll - A sentient species of Evorath. Nomadic in nature, trolls are both tall and menacing in their physical features.

- Urgo - An elvish word of affirmation. Essentially equivalent to saying "yes, sir" or "understood."

- Xyvor - A compilation of stories written by the ancient prophets of Evorath. Details stories of the world's creation, its early history, commands from Evorath herself.

Appendices III

Assorted City Maps

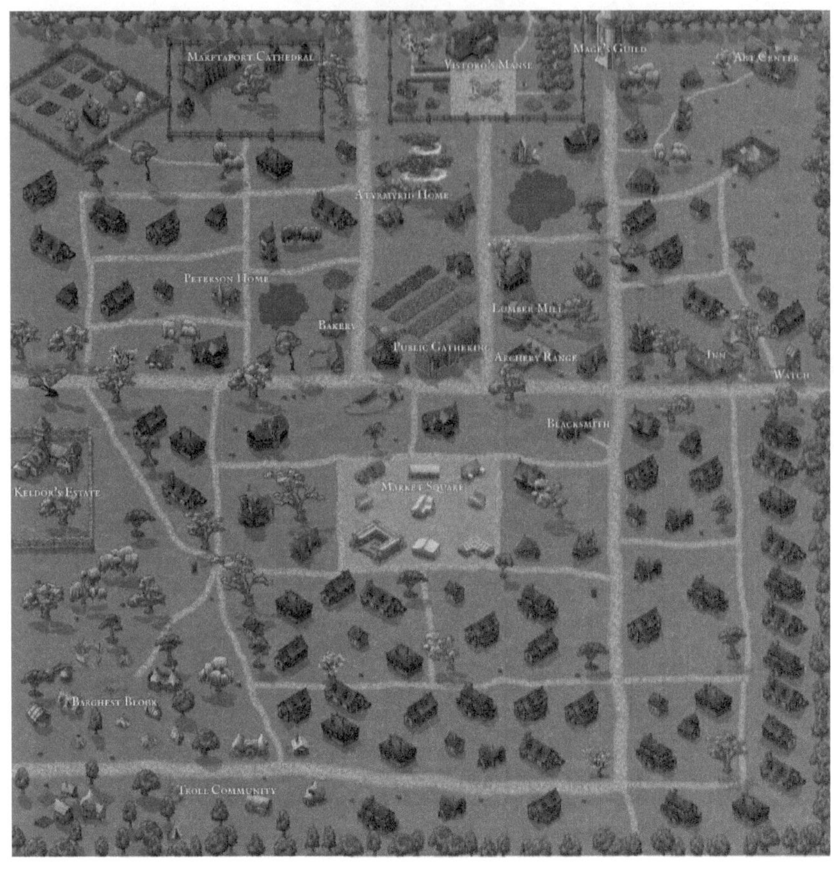

Marftaport, Town Proper

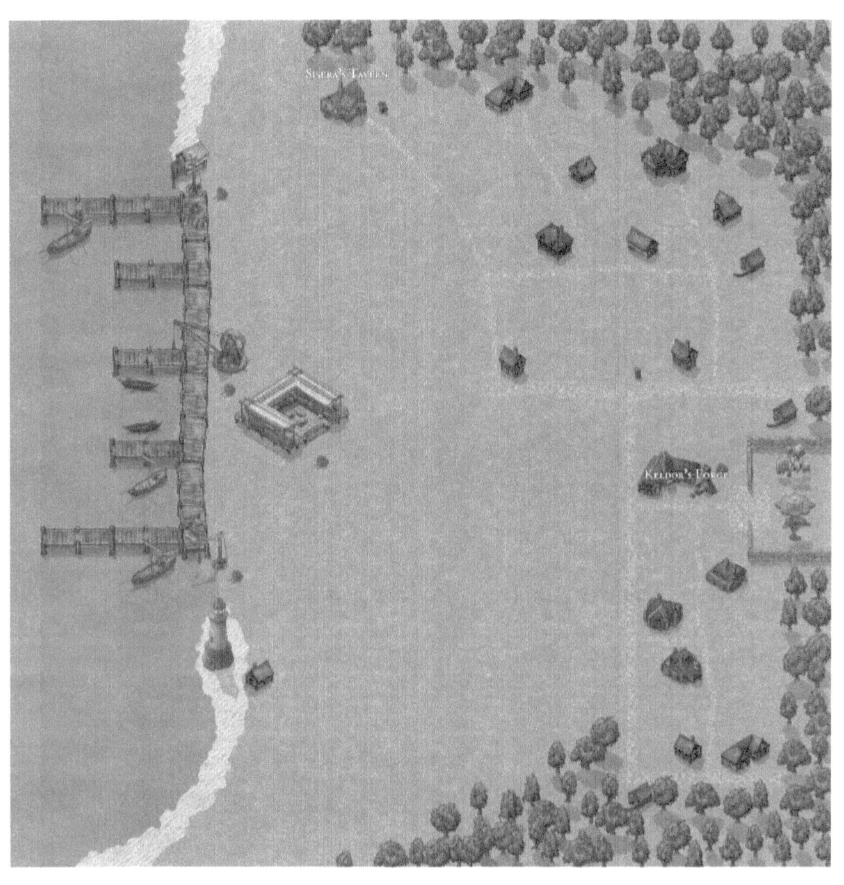

Marftaport, Docks